Hidden Mythics

# Quaking Soul

A Novel

Jennifer M. Zeiger

Published by Jennifer M Zeiger of Zeiger Adventure Publishing

Printed by IngramSpark

First Paperback Edition: March 15, 2021

Edited by: Felicia Sanzari Chernesky

Cover Design: Justin Allen

Illustrated by: Esther Rohman

ISBN- 978-1-7351226-1-8

jenniferzeiger.com
jennifer.m.zeiger@gmail.com

To Leslie

For all the times you've brainstormed with me, read for me, and enthusiastically encouraged me.

Get rid of all bitterness, rage and anger, brawling and slander, along with every form of malice. Be kind and compassionate to one another, forgiving each other, just as in Christ God forgave you.

—Ephesians 4:31–32 (NIV)

No one else had arrived for the meeting yet.

*Perfect.* Na'rina came early, chancing more time in the human city precisely because she wanted to find a place to hide. Something was harming dryads—one had even been driven insane—and this gathering promised information, but she also had no idea who called the meeting. It could be a trap.

*Where to hide?* The concrete plaza offered few options for a tree nymph. *Come on, Na'rina, Mamma's counting on you.*

She eyed the two sickly trees sprouting from squares cut into the concrete. They drooped despite the spring rains. A night breeze howled through the plaza, swaying the elms' branches while Na'rina tried to convince herself to meld with one of them.

Although the plaza stood empty, which was surprising in a city this large, Na'rina knew it'd soon be occupied. Just not by humans. She eyed the trees again and cringed. The larger elm might work, although it was small for melding. Still, once inside, she'd only be a bulge in the trunk.

*No time, Na'rina, just do it.*

Footsteps scuffed on concrete and Na'rina ducked, her heart jumping into her throat. The hand she braced against one of the stone benches surrounding the plaza shook. After a moment the footsteps faded, and she released the breath she held. It was just a human passing through the park. Even if he saw her, she'd appear human unless he got close enough to examine her lithe figure.

Disgusted with herself, she stood up and shuddered. The bench beneath her hand emanated the sense of weight and a disturbing lack of life. Na'rina craved her forest home, where everything flowed with *zoi aima*—the forest's swirling lifeblood. Another shudder shook her before she rubbed her palm against her pant leg to remove the dust from the bench. It didn't budge, instead sticking to her sappy sweat like dirt on pitch.

*Gah! I shouldn't be sweating.* But no amount of training could dull her anxiety at being surrounded by the cold architecture of the humans. Without thinking, Na'rina touched the golden leaf nestled in the hollow of her throat for comfort. It warmed and a wisp of zoi aima, sweet-tasting like the life from her *Rina*, her grove, misted into her. Na'rina longed to sense her aspens back in Colorado, but, since she'd reached Tennessee the previous day, she felt nothing. The mental reach was just too far for her grove and it left her hollow. She sighed.

*I can handle one meeting. Mamma finally thinks I'm ready. Now hide, Na'rina.*

She scanned the plaza one last time. It didn't match her idea of a park. Other than the two droopy elms, it was treeless and in place of deer trails, there were concrete sidewalks. At random spots, fissures designed by the humans made it look like an earthquake had torn those sidewalks apart. Water ran through the cracks, perhaps for children to play in, but the concrete edges were sharp and hard.

*Who would call a meeting of mythics here, of all places?* Mythics—nymphs, dwarves, Sedessans, elves, and a number of other species regarded as lore by the humans—avoided the predominant species as a general rule.

Na'rina hoped a nymph arranged this meeting, but it was unlikely. A nymph would never send a Sedessan messenger. She suppressed another shudder but the droopy elms quivered in reaction anyway. Her mother taught her Sedessans blended seamlessly into any culture—adapting speech patterns, habits, even the gaits of those they walked beside—although Na'rina had never seen one until the Sedessan woman arrived in their groves a week ago, to pass along the call to this meeting.

Na'rina had mistaken her for a dryad, with her long chestnut hair, bare feet, and slender figure swathed in a light dress. It wasn't until the Sedessan offered her mother the message that Na'rina realized she wasn't a nymph. Her mother

3

had hesitated.

By all accounts, the Mother Drydanda, queen to the dryads, should have been more intimidating in her psychic abilities. Yet Mona'rina hesitated.

Only then did Na'rina look close enough to see the faint facial markings on the tiny woman standing before her mother. When Mona'rina finally accepted the message, the Sedessan boldly laid her palms against Mona'rina's temples and slid her fingers into the taller woman's ashy brown hair. Although she appeared delicate, she did not waver.

Afterwards, her mother likened the experience to looking into a glassy pond in the dark of night. Faint images rose to swirl across the surface, but Na'rina knew that pond could force you deeper, submersing you in your fears until you drowned. Sedessans were a twisted species. Perfect messengers for someone with darker intents.

Na'rina shook herself. *I need to hide.* Striding across the plaza, she chose the larger of the two trees.

With her back to the elm, she gripped the trunk behind her hips. As she connected, she felt the moisture in the chill air seeping into the bark and the flutter of the elm's flower buds in the breeze as the sensations became her own. It was a Princeton American Elm. She waited as the tree's consciousness stirred for some hardy comment — "Duck up, Drydanda, you're shaking worse than my leaves."

Her smile faded and she almost jerked away when what she mistook as consciousness did not sharpen into thought. This elm had never held a Ptelea dryad of his own. He was a clone. The flutter she'd misread told her this copy had been grafted from a natural tree. Na'rina stifled a sob. What pain the dryad must have endured when his home was cut apart.

Unnerved, she started to let go, when movement caught her eye. She cringed. It was too late now to hide elsewhere. Na'rina sank her zoi aima into the tree's core and her hands melded into the bark. The elm's lifeblood mixed with her own, swirling and itching along her skin as it pulled her into the trunk. Moments later, two figures sauntered into the plaza.

"We're early," the shorter of the newcomers muttered in a husky drawl. His companion grunted, and they sat on one of the benches in the plaza.

"Off my coat," one dwarf grumbled, swatting his companion's shoulder.

The other scooted toward the end of the bench with a muttered apology.

*Perhaps these two called the meeting.* Na'rina watched them, fascinated. Remnants of the dwarven race lived in the Pyrgos Mountains, the Rockies as the humans called them, near Na'rina's home. These two were darker than those she knew, their olive skin reflecting the Appalachian dwarves, but their gruff conversation and heavy shoulders were just like the dwarves she called friends back home. Considering she was standing smack in the middle of Chattanooga, encountering Appalachian dwarves was not a surprise, and it might explain the meeting's location.

Another figure crept closer while the dwarves grumbled. He skirted the light from an overhead lamp, but there wasn't enough darkness in the plaza to avoid the glow completely. Sneakers covered his feet but they thudded softly with each step in a way Na'rina recognized. He lacked toes to keep the soles from flopping. Her heart jumped. *A faun.* She hadn't seen a faun since dancing with them as a child. A thriving black market for their hooves had all but made them extinct. This one wore baggy cargo khakis to accommodate his furred hips and legs. He sported a black t-shirt under an unzipped windbreaker and a bulging ball cap to hide his ears. Those bulges twitched, but the clothing obscured his inhuman features. With it, he could pass for a slim, if wide-hipped, man.

Na'rina negated him as the one who called this meeting—fauns would never willingly approach a Sedessan—but the elm quivered as she suppressed the urge to run and embrace him.

The dwarves rose when they spotted the faun but he shied back.

"Obek-Ak-Lea of the Omichlodis Mountains—Obek for short." The stouter dwarf thumped forward with an outstretched hand.

The faun stared at the thick fingers, a frown pulling at his brows. Na'rina guessed he wanted to correct Obek. No one used the ancient names anymore, but perhaps the dwarf clung to the formal Omichlodis over Appalachian as a matter of pride. Finally, the faun's brow cleared as he gulped and bowed instead of taking Obek's proffered hand. "Afre son of Oba-Afren."

Obek hesitated with his hand still out, then dropped it to bow. "Oba-Afren's son?" he mused. "It gladdens the heart to hear he's still alive. Are his people well?"

Afre's face tightened. "We survive."

"Good, good." Obek ran a hand down his face, clutching his beard as he searched for words. The other dwarf, who had not approached, cleared his throat. "Ah, yes. Do you know what this is about?"

Afre shook his head.

Covering disappointment with a shrug, Obek gestured at the benches. "Guess we're early then."

Na'rina swallowed her own disappointment as she watched them sit down. It would have been reassuring if the dwarves had called this meeting.

Afre sat on the bench opposite the dwarves. Bouncing his legs up and down, he clutched his windbreaker closed across his chest as his sneakered hooves clopped on the sidewalk.

*Obek-Ak-Lea and Afre son of Oba-Afren.* Na'rina trembled

and the elm's leaves rustled. She didn't have to know them to recognize their importance. Their names announced them as princes of their respective peoples and just like herself, the Daughter Drydanda of the Dryads, they would someday lead. And here they gathered, called by someone unknown who summoned them via a Sedessan. Her one advantage lay in that whoever called the meeting was expecting the Mother Drydanda, which indicated he or she might not know of Na'rina's existence. Not many beyond the nymph world did. Even still, Na'rina couldn't shake the dread building within her.

She almost closed her eyes as the next attendees of the meeting arrived, but she couldn't keep from staring. The nymphs flitted from behind a fountain, disappeared around the squat restroom building, and reappeared in a streak of motion that vanished as they ducked behind the statue of a horse. The nymphs relied on their light feet instead of blending in to protect themselves, and their arrival didn't bring the relief Na'rina had hoped for. Instead, a stone of dread settled into her belly. She sank farther into the elm, hoping by some luck the others didn't spot her. An auloniad, a naiad, followed by an oread entered the plaza. They stopped to scan its occupants.

The auloniad's reed-thin body swayed like the wheat in which she resided. Wild hair and golden eyes shifted. Before arriving, Na'rina had changed her skin from her natural light green to an ashy white that resembled her aspen's bark. It helped her blend into human society. The auloniad had not taken that precaution and her skin glowed a deep gold. She was moderately safe at a glance during the night, but close scrutiny would reveal the too-even tone, the almost perfect texture of her skin.

The naiad bounced on the balls of her feet beside the auloniad, the silvery mass of her hair shimmering in waves from the top of her head to her heels. No amount of camouflage would make the brook naiad look human.

Standing near but apart from the naiad, the oread occupied her own space with a calm reserve. Broad shoulders and dark tight curls accentuated her large eyes as she took in the gathering with deep patience. As a mountain nymph, she was probably older than any dryad alive. She reached out and placed a heavy hand on the naiad's shoulder, stopping the other's bouncing. As soon as she dropped the restraint, however, the naiad began again, her hair swaying.

Somehow, none of the three noticed Na'rina. The tree's camouflage worked well with creatures who lived on a physical plane, but the other nymphs should have spotted the collection of zoi aima melding Na'rina with the elm.

Those gathered were peace-loving species and the presence of the other nymphs heightened Na'rina's agitation. Few nymphs could travel far from their elements because the distance stressed their psychic bond, eventually killing the nymph. Either these three were like the dwarves and faun in terms of status among their people—leaders strong enough to handle distance—or they were close to home. Somehow, Na'rina doubted the latter.

Nothing announced their arrival. No leaf fluttered, no breath of wind carried an unusual scent, no scuff of footsteps on the cold concrete gave warning. Na'rina stared at those gathered as they spoke among themselves, and then her breath froze.

*Fire.*

Even though they carried nothing in their hands, Na'rina could only see red-tongued flames eating away at aspens and feel the lick of flames against her Rina's bark.

*They always bring fire.*

The dryads' *Collective Wisdom*, a genetic history, burned images through her mind. The memories were not her own, but she felt them as though she'd experienced the ashes and smoke.

With effort, Na'rina tamped them down until the memories sat in the back of her mind as a terrifying warning. Usually the Collective Wisdom informed her of the dryads' history, but in instances like this, the power of the emotion behind the memory made it spring forth with a vengeance.

To the dryads, the wer-im would forever be associated with fire.

The naiad turned to run, but a creature stood in her way.

Even as she shifted right and left to dart around, more figures materialized from the darkness, surrounding those gathered. The naiad spun back toward the middle of the plaza—to find a wer-im standing there eyeing her.

He lifted his chin and took a long sniff.

Na'rina's heart went out to her fellow nymph. With her scent, the creature could track her anywhere. The naiad's hair hung limp as she stilled.

Na'rina shushed the elm when he shook with the thick fear coating the air, forgetting there was no consciousness to quiet. It was her own quaking that caused the leaves to shudder.

The wer-im gave the naiad a predatory flash of teeth and stalked to the center of the plaza. His pride formed an indistinct perimeter as he took in those present with an air just this side of contempt. *Do wer-im run in prides?* Na'rina couldn't remember ever hearing of such a thing. The Collective Wisdom spoke of their banishment, not their social structure.

The creature pivoted, eyeing each member of the meeting in turn. His head tilted to the side as his eyes left the naiad to take in the unwavering stare of the oread. Na'rina could not say which was more indomitable. The mountain nymph regarded the wer-im with broad shoulders back and lips tight. He met her gaze like it pleased him to see her defiance. He tilted his chin to her before moving on to the dwarves.

As his gaze swept toward the elm, Na'rina cringed. *Don't*

*see me.* It wasn't an unreasonable hope. Wer-im were physical beings. They did not view zoi aima alongside the tangible world.

*I'm not here. You don't see me.*

His hazel eyes settled on her. The air heated like he breathed against her face and a thrill sank through her middle as the spicy scent of him reached her nose. It was a predator's lure, she knew, a scent intended to hypnotize until he reached his prey.

Desperate, Na'rina shot her consciousness down the elm, into his roots and out to anything she could grasp. She'd never mixed with more than one zoi aima at once and her nerve endings burned as she connected with azalea bushes, lilacs, dandelions, even the grass that forced its way up through the concrete. The heat on her skin, however, vanished.

Those compelling hazel eyes blinked and the wer-im looked—pleased? His gaze moved on and Na'rina's breath escaped in an exhale that quivered the leaves of the elm.

"My friends." He smiled, acknowledging the irony of his greeting. His low voice hovered, a vibration that reached out to touch each one present. It carried a husky edge brushed smooth but raw, like molten gold. Compared to Obek's rock-dusted vocal cords, this wer-im's purr invited one to lean in with a desire to hear.

Na'rina shuddered. Her mother said a wer-im's passions ran hot. The truth in that seemed clear by the way this one commanded the plaza. "You failed," he said. "You're dead." His teeth flashed. "Only one of you survived my test. Can you guess who?"

The six gathered glanced around, anger, confusion, shock, but mostly fear in their expressions. Wer-im didn't toy with their prey.

The wer-im leader sauntered past each member of the gathering. Moonlight slid across his human-like profile and he lifted his chin like he tasted their conflicting emotions. Faint black lines ran from the corners of his eyes out into the hair above his slanted ears.

Na'rina's gaze stalled on the wer-im's ear. A small, feathery tuft of hair topped it into a point but it was the jagged, white puckering of skin around the cartilage at the back of the ear that made her pause. Due to their ability to heal rapidly, mythics rarely scarred. For him to bear such a scar meant he'd been in a serious fight.

*Is he a lynx?* Na'rina forced herself to look away from the scar. His face was narrow, the bridge of his nose accentuating the feline quality of his eyes. Na'rina tightened her muscles to suppress a shudder as she noticed the line of his lips failed to hide the points of his top canines.

*Mamma, they've broken the banishment!*

Na'rina's silent cry fell on deaf ears. Without contact with her Rina, the message would never be heard. Human lore named this creature a were-cat, but he was not a shape-shifter. When the moon highlighted his face, he could be taken for a human man, although a passerby might question what nationality gave his features such sharp angles. Na'rina, however, knew he belonged to a species of mythics banned for their violence almost two hundred years ago. Wer-im made the Sedessans look like children. Why were they here now when they hadn't been seen since the 1820s?

The wer-im stopped meandering to face the elm. "Show yourself."

Na'rina hesitated. *Those teeth can't reach me.* The thought was stupid, though. He might not be able to attack her directly but he could burn the tree or tear it down or—*Anything he does to the tree will be done to me.* Na'rina released the zoi aima holding her. Legs wobbling, she leaned against the elm until she could step onto the concrete without stumbling. *Don't show weakness.*

Obek grunted but it was the oread's *hum* Na'rina felt through the ground into the soles of her feet. The mountain nymph studied her with the same shrewdness she'd shown the wer-im and Na'rina wanted to shrink from that ancient, piercing gaze. Instead, she focused on the wer-im.

"What are you doing?" Na'rina's voice quivered despite her resolve. "The dryads are still strong enough to banish you again."

Several wer-im hissed. A breeze carried the scent of wet

concrete and human trash from the restroom, but beneath those odors, Na'rina picked up the smell of angry wer-im. Its sharp tang sang in her unsteady nerves.

Afre stared at her with huge eyes—eyes not filled with fear, as expected, but with curiosity. *Don't look at him. Don't draw attention to him.*

Na'rina met the hazel eyes of the lead wer-im instead, and veered her gaze away from his grin to gesture at the perimeter. Her long fingers glowed chalky white in the moonlight. Even afraid, she didn't return to her natural green, but sticky sweat coated her palms.

"We remember the strength of the dryads." His husky voice stayed soft.

"Why this?" She gestured again, chancing another look at him.

The wer-im's grin widened further, crinkling the corners of his eyes and accentuating his feline features. "We survive because we're a myth to the humans." He released her from his gaze. "That survival is threatened."

"I've known other Wer-Kadises and they cared for nothing but their own. Why would you care for us?" the oread challenged, bits of broken concrete bouncing with the vibration of her voice.

A wer-im standing behind her spit, but the leader just sauntered over to study the mountain nymph. Instead of answering, he said, "Humans have been capturing mythics."

Shock rippled through the group.

"They've captured dryads, dwarves, fauns, oceanids," he continued, gesturing at each respective species, indicating the brook naiad in place of oceanids. The naiad whimpered at his brief attention and stepped behind her auloniad cousin.

*Can that be true?* Na'rina wondered. *Why would the wer-im care?*

"Your knowledge of this means you've been on our land," Na'rina pointed out, surprised to hear her own voice. All eyes swung to her. The urge to sink back into the elm made her sway, but now that the words were out, she couldn't leave them alone. "You've steered clear for generations. I doubt you broke the boundary without cause." Her brain hit the logical conclusion a second before her mouth, and the little bit of color in her face drained away. "They attacked the wer-im, too."

Na'rina knew from the stories of their banishment just how dangerous—and difficult—such an attack would be.

"They captured some of you," she whispered.

"Ah," the oread rumbled. "How does telling us help you?"

The wer-im did not respond, confirming Na'rina's guess. An irrational part of her wanted to touch his shoulder in sympathy. She swayed. *Stop!*

The silence stretched taught. Finally, the leader threw

his head up, breaking the stillness. "We've been watching the humans," he said, ignoring the oread's question again. "They sent a Sedessan to the Rocky Mountain dwarves last month, calling them to a meeting like this one. Those dwarves haven't been seen since."

Na'rina shuddered. Afre still watched her and she flashed a timid smile while the wer-im leader was turned away.

"Why should we trust you?" Obek argued scathingly, gesturing at the wer-im.

"You don't know about these missing dwarves?" the oread asked.

Obek shook his heavy head. "Our kin keep to themselves."

"Dryad." The wer-im fixed Na'rina in place as he stalked toward her.

She swayed, reaching a steadying hand toward the elm. *Don't run.*

"Where is the Drydanda we called for?" He stood so close the temperature of his skin radiated against her.

For a dryad, Na'rina stood at medium height but under this wer-im's gaze she felt tiny. More disturbing, he knew she was not her mother, which meant he knew what Mona'rina looked like.

"She had more important business," Na'rina squeaked.

"Explain."

"There—" She swallowed and restarted. "Reports reached us saying the pine dryads north of Pikes Peak in Colorado had not been seen for a while. We didn't question it until a pine dryad showed up raving about the silence. The Mother Drydanda went to investigate."

"The silence?" Obek asked. "I don't follow."

The oread closed her eyes in pained comprehension, but shook her head as if to deny what she heard. The other nymphs clutched each other.

"My Rina, my aspen grove," Na'rina clarified, "is not close to the visitor's, Obek-Ak-Lea. To travel so far from his tree can only mean two things: he was either a Drydanda or he was insane, and a Drydanda he was not. Insanity in a nymph is rare unless violence occurs. We fear something severed him from his tree."

"Hence the tree had been silenced or killed?" the wer-im pressed.

Na'rina only nodded. Her stomach rolled at the thought of her Rina being made dumb as a human's wooden doll. Such vibrant zoi aima pulsed through a dryad's tree. To have that life stilled would be a living nightmare.

"Disturbing," the oread rumbled.

"I thought only one Drydanda lived," the wer-im murmured.

Na'rina swayed. She'd revealed more than she should

18

have, but, unlike her mother, she had little experience in dealing with other mythics. *You believed me ready, Mamma. I'm afraid you made a mistake. I won't even make it home to tell you why.* She almost touched her necklace for comfort. Her mother hadn't had a choice, unless she wanted to ignore one of two possible dangers. *Na—she debated which potential threat was the most serious, and sent me to the lesser of the two.* The insane dryad verified *something* had gone wrong in the Pikes Peak pine forest. The Sedessan only hinted at danger.

The others did not seem to catch the wer-im's words. Obek and his companion kept muttering together, their low voices creating a deep hum. Afre continued to watch Na'rina and the wer-im from the corner of his eye, however, a deep furrow creased his forehead.

Na'rina cleared her throat, silencing the dwarves. "What do you propose we do?"

The wer-im smiled, displaying his canines as he backed away. "The humans have attacked on both the East and West Coasts. With their operation spread across the States, we need to find their central location."

The scuff of approaching footsteps caught everyone's attention.

"We've stayed too long," Na'rina breathed.

"Indeed," the wer-im agreed. He gave the group a meaningful look. "Remember what's at stake and the danger we're in. We'll meet again this coming evening on Lookout Mountain." He pointed to the southwest. "You have my word we won't harm you if you attend."

Na'rina blinked. She felt the shift in the air this time, but even knowing they were moving, she did not see the wer-im perimeter vanish. "You should be there," their leader whispered to her before disappearing with them.

Blood pounded in Na'rina's ears. *He didn't kill us.*

Several humans appeared down the sidewalk, teasing each other in their oblivious way as they neared the plaza. Their voices buzzed in her head and Na'rina swayed, blinking against the wer-im's lingering spicy scent.

"Dryad," Afre said, slipping his arm through hers as the other mythics dispersed. "Let's sing and dance."

"*What?*"

"We've had a wonderful evening drinking," Afre whispered covertly, pulling her toward a path opposite the approaching humans. "Now we're wandering home." He raised his voice in a slurred song and began to dance. After a moment, Na'rina joined him in the ruse.

Na'rina stared at the city below, wrestling with what to do next. The human shoes she'd donned for her trip sat beside her on the ground, but they were the only part of the disguise she'd shed. Human dwellings dotted the forest between her vantage point on Lookout Mountain and Chattanooga like mole hills across the slope. From their style, she guessed this area housed the more privileged humans. She'd skirted fences and pools to get to this secluded spot, glad for the time of year since the bushes and trees sprouted fresh growth in which to hide. She was loath to put the shoes back on. They pressed against her long toes and muffled her sense of the zoi aima within the ground, but the clothing—the t-shirt, jeans, *and* the shoes— helped her escape human notice.

Everything her mother taught her said she should return home. The wer-im's presence threatened their safety and the sooner her mother knew about them, the sooner they could be forced back onto the southern continent. *Except—what if they're right?* Na'rina wasn't sure the dryads could deal with a human attack on their own.

Na'rina stretched her toes against the ground, scratching ten divots in the dirt as she savored the life pulsing beneath her soles. After enduring concrete sidewalks, she felt every root vibrate through her senses. Right now, she registered the sweet tones of the maple she leaned against. *Honey, do you see my new leaves? Don't I look like a ball of green fire? In the fall, I'll—*

"I'm depressed just looking at your expression, and for a faun, that's terrible." Afre lowered himself beside her, crossing his hooves beneath his knees. Like her human shoes, he'd shucked his ball cap as soon as he felt safe enough to expose his ears, and now his curly hair stuck out at odd angles.

"I miss home," Na'rina stated, fingering her necklace, which warmed beneath her touch. Her mother had gifted the golden leaf to her so that when she traveled beyond her Rina's touch she could sate her craving for her grove's life. It was small solace, but holding the leaf left a sweet taste similar to her grove's touch on Na'rina's tongue, and she thanked her mother for her foresight.

Afre rested his fingers on her free hand. His fingers were stubby but sported enough calluses to attest to his work ethic. From almost any other creature such familiarity would seem odd, but not from a faun. Fauns were friendly as twin does with anyone they accepted.

"Tell me of your Rina." He smiled and leaned back to listen.

Excitement zinged through Na'rina as she thought of the smell of sun-warmed aspen bark and the soft shushing her leaves made when they fluttered in the breeze, giving the trees their name: quaking aspens. "My Rina's beautiful. Right now the leaves are budding and there's that clean smell as the snow melts into the ground."

Afre's smiled faded and his face turned tense. Na'rina stopped talking and gave him a curious look.

Afre ducked his head. "Sorry. I wanted a distraction from the wer-im. They make my insides watery." He shivered at the admission. "I hoped to make you smile. You look so much like your mother with your dark ashy hair and green eyes. Mona'rina's always amazingly, comfortingly sure of herself." He paused and then nudged her. "You know, in the city, all you needed to do was smile at the humans and they'd just stare and let you go on your way."

Na'rina snorted. Dryads looked similar enough to humans that they could mingle some—the myths of nymphs enticing men came from somewhere—but mingling slowly ended as human technology grew. Humans liked to study and test things, and it was safer to remain hidden because eventually a human would want to know why a nymph didn't seem to age.

Afre blurted, "You almost look True Born." Then,

seeing the stricken look on her face, he bleated, "I'm sorry. I didn't—"

Na'rina threw an arm around his lean shoulders. "I am my mother's spitting image... supposedly." She didn't explain that while she looked almost exactly like her mother, she didn't seem to have her mother's abilities, despite being True Born. Then another thought hit her. "The wer-im leader knew I wasn't Mona'rina."

Afre flinched as she brought the conversation back to the wer-im. Na'rina tucked an unruly lock behind his ear. He slumped into her embrace. It was easy to sit beside him while his ears twitched in thought.

"I can't believe you're considering going to the second meeting," he said. "That wer-im shouldn't be able to tell you apart from Mona'rina, not unless he's seen her up close."

Afre's obvious unease mimicked the roiling inside Na'rina's stomach. She hated not returning home, the idea of being near the wer-im again, but—

"I'm terrified," Na'rina breathed, almost unable to give the words air for sound, "but the humans might pose a real threat, and he gave his word not to harm us."

"Na'rina, please don't go." Afre clutched her hand to his chest. "Word or no word, they'll destroy you. Doesn't the Collective Wisdom tell you that?"

Images hit Na'rina. Aspens turning black, peeling into

ash as flames raged from branch to branch. Heat burned in her nose, laced with the acrid scent of wet *live* wood burning. She shuddered and there was no way to hide it from the faun. Na'rina pushed the images down with an effort that brought sticky sweat to her palms.

"I'm terrified," she repeated, her hand shaking in his grasp. Now it was Afre's turn to throw an arm around her, and he held her palm against his chest, seemingly unaware of the sappy sweat clinging to his fingers. "I know why we banished them," she whispered. "I feel the pain from the burning trees despite not being alive then. You know our Collective Wisdom shares actual experiences, but Afre, what if the wer-im are telling the truth?"

His ears drooped. "What if they aren't? The wer-im were straightforward killers, but it's been generations since anyone's interacted with them. What if they've changed and are playing us for fools?"

"They could have killed us at the meeting if they wished," Na'rina argued. She'd been considering the possibility of what Afre suggested, but one perplexing thought kept resurfacing. "What better way to pay back Mona'rina than to kill her daughter? My mother was the linchpin to their banishment. This was the perfect opportunity to hurt her, and the wer-im didn't take it."

Afre drummed his fingers against the back of her hand

while he considered. "I can't go with you," he whispered, dropping his eyes.

"You have to report to your father," Na'rina said. "I don't have contact with my grove or I'd speak with my mother before going."

Afre's face tightened. "Right." His voice hitched and he cleared his throat with a soft bray.

"Were you there during the banishment?" Na'rina asked.

He bit his lip, then shook his head.

"The dryads are strong," Na'rina mused, "but we don't interact much with the outside world, much less with humans. Our isolation makes us vulnerable."

"What if you reach out to the other mythics? See if they know anything. It'd keep you clear of the wer-im."

Afre's earnest advice made sense if Na'rina were only concerned with herself. If she went to the meeting, she'd be at the mercy of the wer-im—but, if what the wer-im said was true, the dryads might need the expertise of a more warrior-like species. As a Drydanda, it was her responsibility to make decisions for the dryads if their existence was threatened.

"My mother trusted me to be here," Na'rina said. "I must consider all the dryads, not just myself." She paused and then pressed on. "I think the wer-im's telling the truth, Afre. I think he's seen what he says he has."

Afre sat back with a huff. The maple grumbled at the

thud against his trunk and Na'rina suppressed a smile. Some characteristics ran true for each mythic species. Dryads wanted seclusion, dwarves lived inside mountains, and oceanids had short tempers. As for fauns, they loved truth. They listened for what rang like a bell to them and had an uncanny ability to decipher what was true from what was not. Judging from Afre's reactions during the meeting, Na'rina suspected a great deal of his agitation came from how unexpectedly honest the lead wer-im had been. He may not have shared everything he knew, but what he did say was forthright.

As though reading her thoughts, Afre asked, "Have you considered the wer-im leader?"

Na'rina shrugged.

"He found you when your sisters did not," Afre pressed.

"He also knew he'd called a Drydanda to the meeting. It was logical to guess my hiding place. It's not like there were a plethora of trees to choose from."

"But he did not guess," Afre insisted. "He saw *you*, not the elm. You don't find that disturbing?"

"What am I supposed to do? I can't ignore this and I can't contact my mother."

"There's something not right about him," Afre grumbled, but he didn't press further. Na'rina wanted to cry. She'd forgotten how much fauns cared. Perhaps that's why they were so easily hunted. They tended to put themselves in precarious situations because they put others before themselves. *I don't want Afre to do that for me.*

"Let it go," she said. "Go warn your father, Afre. Perhaps he can hide your people. I cannot move my grove or my people's trees but you can. Protect your people."

"Be careful, Drydanda." Afre gave her shoulders a squeeze and then withdrew to hug his arms tight around his middle. "Dryads are rare enough anymore. Don't let them lose their queens."

Tears threatened. Na'rina touched her fingertips to Afre's cheek, then leaned against the maple. As she sank into the trunk, she watched his brown eyes blink away his own tears. *Is this also Afre's first assignment on his own?* She couldn't help but feel she was letting the faun down, although she couldn't think of a better way to respond.

The maple flooded her with his joy over the spring warmth and his budding leaves and Na'rina let his joy crowd out her worries for a time.

When she emerged, Afre was gone. Beside her shoes sat a jar of honeyed wine that glowed golden in the sunlight and Afre's black ball cap. Na'rina touched the rim of the jar with a thoughtful finger. She already missed Afre's easy company. She tucked the wine and the ball cap into the bottom of her pack before glaring at the white shoes on the ground. With a resigned sigh, Na'rina shoved her feet into the hateful contraptions.

The sun marked the time at a little past noon, still early for the meeting, but a study of the area before being trapped in close quarters with the wer-im might grant her a comfort she craved. Na'rina stood and extended her toes in an effort to stretch the fabric of the shoes. She huffed when it didn't do much good.

*Stop stalling.* Resolved, she took off for Lookout Mountain, touching each tree she passed. This made her flit from place to place at a pace faster than a human's run but she yearned for the forest's touch. The soft call of various trees fluttered in her ears.

*Drydanda, you should be your natural self,* a cedar said. *Why the white skin?*

*There's darkness covering the sun,* a maple complained. *I need the rays to show off my leaves.*

*It'll rain soon,* an oak said. *Moisture coats my bark in unseen beads of promise. We'll all get to drink our fill.* For an oak, that was saying something. Even before the rain, Na'rina could sense the gallons of water the tree held within its being.

Their zoi aima invigorated her. The feel of this forest differed from her Rina like maple syrup differed from honey. Both forests left a sweet taste on her tongue along with the residue of their thoughts, but the actual flavor could not be called the same.

Na'rina hummed, taking in colors and smells, the depth of the living wood and the strength in each tree. This forest's strength was a hard thing compared to the resilient, bendable strength of her home, but it boasted its own grace, allowing the wind to play in waves through the branches.

*A Drydanda!* An oak exclaimed.

*Are you sure?* Another asked.

*Nobody could mistake it. Can't you feel her?*

Na'rina cried out as she almost collided with a wer-im who stepped out to block her path. She skidded to a stop and swayed in place, taking in this new creature while her focus adjusted to his sudden appearance. *Why didn't the forest alert me about him?*

He barely reached her shoulder as he tilted his head back to regard her with a furious stare. Na'rina stared right back despite the rudeness of it. This wer-im's hair was orange. Not red or auburn but orange-striped and his eyes glinted the same green as aspen leaves just after they opened. She smiled.

He blinked, then smirked. "You're early."

"I could say the same for you," she bantered, for some reason without the wariness she felt at yesterday's meeting. This wer-im did not carry the same air as his leader.

"*Na*, we are waiting."

Na'rina cocked her head. So much for looking over the

area without the wer-im present. "Have others arrived?"

"*Na*," he sneered.

"Guess we'll wait for them." She held out an arm just as she would have with Afre, but he ignored the gesture and turned to lead her forward.

"The Wer-Kadis will be surprised," he muttered.

Na'rina glanced at him, but she didn't ask.

She followed the wer-im along a deer path to a small clearing. With their position on the hillside, Na'rina could see houses below and the highway leading into Chattanooga right alongside the Tennessee River. There were no houses nearby, even though the farther they went the more groomed the area appeared. She winced at the occasional stump of a tree that had been cleared to make way for a human trail.

They came upon three wer-im, each much larger than her escort, in a small glade. All of her former uneasiness hit Na'rina like a gust of wind.

One creature leaned over a tiny fire roasting strips of meat. Na'rina gulped at the smell of fire and dripping fat. Then the small flames brought on the Collective Wisdom with a vengeance and she gasped. Her stomach churned. Although the wood they burned came from deadfall branches, she couldn't ignore the image of burning trees.

The cook caught Na'rina's repugnance before she contained it. "We must eat," he said, misunderstanding her reaction. True, the roasting meat would have turned her stomach, but it was nothing compared to the fierce pain she associated with the flames. She stared at him in horror until he shrugged his heavy shoulders and went back to tending the meat where it sat on a heated rock.

The other two paid no attention. One was sleeping, while the other scanned the area with the hyperawareness of a feline on guard. He must have already dismissed her as a threat.

Na'rina glanced at the sleeping wer-im. Even in rest, he sent a warning through her nerves like pricks of ice. His chest rose and fell with a slow rhythm.

"Return to your post," the cook ordered her escort. Na'rina had forgotten he stood beside her. The orange-haired wer-im hissed but left.

From their coloring and manner, she likened the three wer-im in the clearing to wild cats. Lynxes, perhaps, or bobcats. The cook's stalky build and broad face reminded her of the later. Even his gray beard, with its down-turned black stripes like mutton chops, spoke of a bobcat's bushy appearance. Her escort, on the other hand, resembled a tabby. The contempt for him she noticed in the cook's eyes seemed to confirm a hierarchy. Perhaps the contempt rolled down hill, because the cook was smaller in stature than the other two.

The guard also resembled a bobcat but he was both bigger and older than the cook. If their hierarchy indeed ran according to size or age, that would explain his complete disregard for the cook and the escort.

Her escort gone, Na'rina found herself at a loss. She watched the cook with her hands limp at her sides, until the rise and fall of the sleeping wer-im's chest caught her attention again. An urge struck her.

*Bad idea.*

Tingles ran through her hands as she contemplated the situation. She might never again see the Wer-Kadis in a relaxed state and every insight into him could be helpful.

*Bad idea*, her better judgment repeated.

Na'rina swayed. The cook's yellow eyes fixed on her, taking in the motion of her body and the direction of her gaze.

"I wouldn't," he warned, but there was a mischievous glint in his expression.

Na'rina swallowed. She took a hesitant step, ignoring the cook's hiss. She took another step. The pad of her feet, even in shoes, made no sound. A third and fourth step brought her almost close enough to see the Wer-Kadis' sleeping face, which was turned away from the clearing.

She was mid-step when the guard swung around with a growl that revealed his long canines. He looked much like the cook, but without the mischief and with an angry scar running through his bushy black beard alongside the gray.

Na'rina gulped.

The leader's eyes snapped open. An instant before the guard pounced, Na'rina bolted. Clasping the trunk of the closest tree, she disappeared with a *pop* into the ash just as the guard's claws raked across the bark.

The ash's sensations flooded through Na'rina, bringing simmering pain. She flushed with shock, and on its heels a heat similar to the slow burn of a severe sunburn tightened her muscles. Zoi aima rushed to her until she felt full to bursting. The ash shuddered under the sudden change.

The guard lashed at the bark again. *Say now,* the ash complained sleepily, but then pain flushed through her and her words choked off.

Na'rina waited for the guard to step over a thick root, and then she flooded the ash with zoi aima. Living wood turned fluid, snaking around his ankles and hardening into wooden shackles. As he fell, she released more zoi aima into the ash's roots to capture his wrists and neck, pinning him to the ground. Once the roots settled back to a normal state, the deep rumble from the wer-im's chest vibrated into the tree.

*Girlie,* the ash complained, *I'm bleeding. I feel strange. These old roots don't grow like they used to.*

Na'rina's anger melted into cold awareness of what she'd done. Not only had she gotten the Meliai hurt, but she'd forced her to move in ways she was never meant to move. The strange feeling the tree complained of was an ache Na'rina

34

recognized from times when her Rina bowed under the weight of snow, almost to the point of damaging a limb.

*What is that?* The vibration coming from the wer-im's chest confused the ash.

*What do I do now?* Na'rina had stopped his attack but she hadn't thought beyond that.

Uproarious laughter from the cook echoed through the clearing, accompanied by a much fainter sound. A whisper, barely audible beneath the cook's chortling, it may as well have shouted: the Wer-Kadis *snicked* the lighter open again as she met his gaze. He let the flame burn for a moment. Afre's words—*he saw you*—echoed in her ears.

The faun had been right. Those shrewd eyes studied her indecision as he snapped the lighter shut.

*Why does he have to use fire?*

Na'rina almost cried out as arms encircled her from behind. The zoi aima now touching her skin felt similar to the ash tree, but lighter.

*Hello Drydanda-Sister,* a lilting voice spoke.

*I am sorry, La'meliai,* Na'rina said to the other dryad. She knew without looking who held her and it was both comforting and guilt-inducing.

She'd intruded on another dryad—taking over her ash, her Meliai as the dryads would call her, with impudence and getting her hurt in the process. So few of her sisters still existed that Na'rina hadn't even considered the possibility this ash's dryad lived separately from her.

As La'meliai held Na'rina, the Wer-Kadis blinked and tilted his dark head.

*I thought curiosity killed the cat,* La'meliai commented wryly. *Although I don't condone your method of waking me, Drydanda,* she continued, *I appreciate you pulling me from dissolving into my Meliai.*

*It's refreshing to feel* alive *again.*

The Wer-Kadis studied the tree, pacing around it while La'meliai spoke. He ignored his guard, still trapped, when he stepped over the roots.

Ignoring the wry comment, Na'rina asked, *He cannot see me?*

*I blurred your lifeblood to match my Meliai.*

*Your Meliai's pain—* The scratches seethed as the ash bled sap over them. She whimpered but did not complain again.

*Heal her when you leave,* the other dryad requested.

*Of course, La'meliai.*

"Drydanda, you can't stay in there forever," the Wer-Kadis said, unaware of the dryad's conversation. "Come out. No harm's been done."

*He's wrong,* La'meliai said. *This one has harmed my ash. I will not let him go until an agreement has been set in reparation for the pain.*

*I will heal your Meliai—*

La'meliai made a negative sound. *He must make some reparation, too.*

Na'rina didn't argue. Had it been her Rina, she would have demanded the same. She just wasn't sure how the Wer-Kadis would respond.

*I'll present your case,* she said.

*Farewell, Drydanda-Sister,* La'meliai said, releasing her.

Na'rina suppressed a shudder at the change in zoi aima

against her skin. She emerged more slowly from the ash than she'd entered, her body puckering with gooseflesh despite the warm spring wind that carried the smell of dogwood flowers. With the wer-im watching, she resisted hugging herself.

"Better," the Wer-Kadis said. His gaze made her palms sticky. She couldn't tell if he was angry or pleased.

Na'rina's jaw tightened. "Fire? *Really?*"

He grimaced. "Perhaps that was a poor choice." He gestured toward his captured companion. "My guard?"

"It is not for me to release him." Na'rina raised her chin, but her heart raced. *Can he hear it?* If the Wer-Kadis intended to trap her, as Afre feared, he was playing his hand well.

The guard snarled in protest.

"You are not helping yourself," Na'rina commented.

The guard sneered.

Na'rina shrugged, feigning nonchalance as she wished she'd waited to make sure other mythics came to the meeting before interacting with the wer-im. Besides La'meliai, she stood alone at the moment. Steeling her resolve, she turned back to the Wer-Kadis.

"Release him," he demanded.

Na'rina shook her head. "La'meliai fears his anger. Until he calms, the roots stay."

Dryad names always reflected their trees but not everyone knew that. Somehow the Wer-Kadis understood who

38

she spoke of without her explaining. He grimaced. "That will take some time."

"Good." Na'rina gave a fleeting smile, but her expression hid the thrill she felt at her own audacity.

His eyes narrowed.

Na'rina took a breath and continued, "La'meliai also demands reparation for the harm done to her Meliai."

The Wer-Kadis' eyes narrowed to glittering slits.

This was the delicate part. Na'rina's mother taught her to appear nonthreatening during negotiations. *Aggression begets aggression, but there's a fine balance between being nonthreatening and looking weak.*

She watched the guard renew his struggle to free himself as the roots holding him bowed under the strain. Na'rina cringed, remembering the ache she'd already caused the ash. *I started this. I need to fix it, hopefully without more violence.*

The Wer-Kadis stepped toward her until she had to look up. "You are half responsible. The reparation should come from you."

*How would Mamma handle this? Forget that. Mamma wouldn't have gotten into this situation.*

"I've agreed to heal him, but for La'meliai to release him, your guard must agree to something, too."

"He will provide the zoi aima for the healing."

Na'rina rocked back on her heels. Her mother had that

ability but few knew about it. *How does he know?* She shook her head.

The Wer-Kadis hissed. "*Na?*"

"It's not possible."

"You lie." He leaned close, almost touching her, his heat radiating like a warning that, push too far, he'd boil over. "I've seen a Drydanda pull zoi aima from animals."

Na'rina froze. Seen it? *Impossible.* Even seeing Mona'rina perform such a feat didn't mean a person understood what she was doing. Even nymphs, physical and psychic beings, didn't comprehend the totality of the Mother Drydanda's skills—and this creature, this physical being, claimed to have *seen* and *understood?*

"Not all Drydanda are equal," she whispered, her heart pounding. *Can he hear it?* "You called for Mona'rina. She sent me instead. I do not have the same abilities." A pang hit her at the admission.

The Wer-Kadis captured her wrists. Fear zinged through her and for a moment her skull felt too tight. Then, his intention struck her. Na'rina curled her fingers into fists to keep him from placing her open palms against his skin. She couldn't draw on an animal's zoi aima, but she could feel it the way one could feel the pulse of blood beneath another's skin. But it would burn when she tried, and leave her raw like she'd been sunburned.

"Relax," he ordered. The pressure of his fingers ached in her bones.

"This isn't right." She curled her fingers tighter.

The Wer-Kadis pried Na'rina's index finger open. Against her efforts, he forced the next finger open. As he moved to the next the guard uttered a strangled cry. The Wer-Kadis touched Na'rina's ring finger and watched the root around the guard's neck constrict further.

"I see." He released her hand, and the root eased up. "What price would be acceptable?"

"Perhaps a similar wound?" Na'rina suggested.

The Wer-Kadis scoffed. "That would not be equal. You cannot heal him."

Na'rina relaxed as he turned away. She watched the taut muscles across his shoulders as he moved. *Without a doubt, he would have overcome me if La'meliai hadn't intervened.*

Ears twitching, the Wer-Kadis paced, his long legs carrying him from one side of the clearing to the other in less than five steps each way. He moved with an easy grace but it was different from a dryad's. He exhibited the sinuous edge of a feline.

"The human's activities have spread to this region," he mused. He gestured toward the guard. "Tarn will stay here to protect this Meliai and her dryad. Agreeable?"

Stay with La'meliai? Na'rina wasn't sure if that would

lessen the danger to the dryad and her tree, or heighten it.

*I'm agreeable,* La'meliai spoke, her lilting voice sure.

*Why? It's a wer-im, for wind's sake!*

La'meliai shared the brief flash of images Na'rina's mind pulled from the Collective Wisdom.

*Drydanda,* the other dryad sighed, *trust is hard to rebuild, but I am willing to try. Are you?*

The Wer-Kadis tilted his head, waiting for her answer, but she was stuck on La'meliai's question. Her mother would have answered with an emphatic *Na,* but the ash dryad sounded so sure that such a response felt childish.

She shook off her consternation. "For how long?"

"For as long as it's needed."

*Needed by your estimation or mine?*

"Is this agreeable?" she asked Tarn.

Tarn frowned at his Kadis, confused. "I stand beside you?"

"Do this and I view it the same," the Wer-Kadis answered.

"It's not the same."

"I know."

Tarn's jaw remained tense as he considered. "Let me see her," he said to Na'rina.

"You will agree?" Na'rina pressed.

"*Sa,*" Tarn growled.

"If you break this faith, I will bury you alive." Her stomach churned as she uttered the words—*to suffocate another being*—but Tarn's face went pale, indicating he believed her. *It might afford La'meliai a little protection from the wer-im.* It was the best she could offer given the circumstances.

The Kadis' lips lifted in a half-smile, approving. Na'rina wanted to throw up.

"Let me see her," Tarn repeated, still gruff but subdued.

La'meliai emerged one thin limb at a time. Bones protruded at her wrists and ankles, proof of her extended dormancy.

Na'rina's eyes widened. Her intrusion might have been the only way to wake La'meliai. Over the years many dryads chose to ignore the outside world as it encroached, letting humans overtake their homes without any hint of what lay inside the trees. Once a dryad stayed in the tree long enough, she became a part of him or her, unable to walk the earth again.

La'meliai stretched her arms and her joints creaked with an audible grinding. Satisfied, she floated on the balls of her feet to stand over Tarn. The wer-im's eyes darted between her and Na'rina.

"You're so—different."

La'meliai let out a slow silvery laugh. "We are from different lines."

Na'rina savored the sound. In the past, she'd mistaken

the speech of ash dryads for a dull intellect, but she'd learned better. The dryad was unhurried in the same way her ash was in no rush to grow.

"I accept the agreement," La'meliai said.

Na'rina could not understand the peace on her face. Even now Tarn looked ready to gnash his teeth at her. The ash dryad crouched, popping more joints, to lay her slender fingers against the root system. It receded and Tarn scrambled to his feet, rolling his shoulders in relief.

"Sister." La'meliai approached to lay her fingertips on Na'rina's cheek. "I'm sorry to ask this of you, but I cannot heal her like you can."

Na'rina returned the gesture, drinking in the earthy feel La'meliai radiated. Despite her long dormancy, the other dryad was beautiful. Her hollow cheeks flushed a soft rose and her silvery eyes sparkled, reflecting the vitality Na'rina felt in her psychic presence. The golden leaf against her throat warmed as she shared a brief understanding with the ash dryad.

"I will do what I can," Na'rina promised before turning to the tree. Her fingers settled into the deep ridges of the bark.

*Never in my day,* the Meliai muttered, *would a Drydanda have acted so rashly.*

Na'rina grimaced.

*Meliai,* La'meliai chided, *she needed protection. Would you have denied her that?*

The Meliai harrumphed.

Na'rina proceeded as the Wer-Kadis watched. His *I've seen a Drydanda pull zoi aima from animals* caused her to shudder. *Can he really understand what I'm doing?* Na'rina jumped when the Wer-Kadis' breath brushed the back of her neck, his spicy scent hitting her nose.

"Observing," he said, his words warm against her ear.

The Wer-Kadis' warmth radiated against her back. In a way, it reminded her of the sun on her Rina. Just as she cooled and warmed with the sun on her trees, her back began to warm. Something occurred to her.

"They captured some of you?"

The Wer-Kadis grunted, surprised.

"Your heightened metabolisms didn't burn off their tranquilizer?"

He sighed, exasperated. "Heal the tree, Drydanda."

"You'll see little," she said, hoping it was true.

Her forehead sank against the ash's bark, which opened her fully to the pain seething along each long gash. It would take a lot of zoi aima to repair the damage. For once, Na'rina wished she could tap into an animal's zoi aima like her mother. With the wer-im's metabolism, their zoi aima must be amazing. No wonder the Wer-Kadis had suggested it. Na'rina shuddered and negated her previous thought. She'd tried tapping into an animal before and she didn't wish to experience that burn again.

A stray thought struck her. She wondered how the wer-im's claws worked. The Wer-Kadis' were not visible but Tarn's clearly left their mark. Na'rina paused to steal another peek and noticed a white line on the Kadis' hand in the web between his thumb and forefinger. *Ouch. Another scar?*

*Focus, Na'rina,* she told herself. Her mother would scold her for her lack of attention. *Stop stalling.*

"Hush, Meliai," she whispered to the ash, who harrumphed again.

The world faded to a peripheral blur as she gathered zoi aima around the first set of scratches. To use the tree's slow lifeblood to heal would harm it. The healing would thicken the area until no nutrients could flow in or out, killing the spot. But a dryad healed faster. Her hands melded into the bark over the dripping sap and, for a time, she became part of the tree, healing it with the wounding and healing of her own body.

Great gashes opened along her back. They wept sappy blood, which trickled down her spine until her body's healing closed them into scabs and then new flesh. Her hands emerged from the new bark and she moved on to the next set. Meld with the tree's wounds, become part of them, heal and retreat. *Meld, heal, and retreat.* Na'rina stepped over a root to finish on the last set.

The bark snagged her toes, still in the human shoes, and she stumbled, bracing against the ash to keep from hitting her knees. A hand caught her elbow and helped her reach for the last area of weeping sap. Na'rina didn't question the hands holding her own against the bark because it took all her strength to pull together enough zoi aima to meld one last time. The control slipped through her grasp like water. She tried again, wavered, and with a surge of effort, sank her hands into the bark. Blood soaked her shirt as the wound closed sluggishly. Finally, the ash pushed her away because she lacked the strength to sever their connection.

Na'rina sagged as her vision faded, and someone caught her before she hit the ground.

"Lay her there," a lilting voice instructed.

She was placed against the tree and warmth rushed into her skin from the ash's root.

"Her control's impressive," the lilting voice commented.

"How so?" asked the Wer-Kadis. His smooth words coursed through her like they were psychic instead of spoken. *Too close*, Na'rina's instincts insisted, but she had nothing left to move away.

"Most dryads return to their natural color under such strain."

Na'rina wanted to check but her eyes refused. A feathery touch drifted through her mind like a memory half-recalled, bringing with it a swell of loneliness.

*My Rina?*

The faint touch warmed. It had been days since she'd felt her grove and now, having passed through dozens of root systems, her Rina could only manage a misty touch. When Na'rina left home, she hadn't been sure if the distance would be too great for this type of communication. She should have known it would only delay her Rina as she pieced together a path to follow. Na'rina flushed with pride. Even her mother's grove shied away from extending messages such a distance.

*I am well*, she reassured. She felt the touch again, misting zoi aima into her before withdrawing. A sweet flavor that spoke of sunshine and rain, of mountain wind and cool night air, coated Na'rina's tongue with the essence of home.

As Na'rina became aware of the world again, her body reported every ache pulsing from her neck all the way down to her legs.

"The meeting starts soon. Should we wake her?"

She recognized the voice of the cook but remained still with her eyes closed. A part of her desperately wanted to take stock of her aching body before facing the wer-im again.

"Who came?" the Wer-Kadis asked.

"The dwarves and the oread," the cook answered with an inarticulate dwa-f-s around something in his mouth. After a short pause, there came a sharp crunch and more chewing.

"Wake, Drydanda." The Wer-Kadis gently shook her shoulder.

Na'rina flinched. His voice moments ago had been farther away. As she peeked an eye open, her sight came to rest on the cook grinning at her from the other side of the clearing with that mischievous light in his eyes as he chomped down on

49

what looked like a rabbit leg.

Na'rina recoiled and turned away to heave.

A bone. He was chewing on a *bone.*

She felt the Wer-Kadis touch her hair and she shied away, warnings coursing through her. The hand disappeared but the crunching continued. Her stomach heaved again despite there being nothing left to lose.

"Enough, Felis," the Wer-Kadis ordered.

Felis spit and the bone plinked against a nearby tree.

"Just finishing dinner," he grumbled.

"Come, Drydanda."

Na'rina glared through her hair at the Wer-Kadis but he missed the look, or chose to ignore it, as he stood up.

A leaf dropped on her head. Tarn stared down at her from where he perched in the branches of the ash. His nostrils flared as she met his eyes. La'meliai's thin face appeared out of the bark. She flicked his ear and retreated back into the ash before he could respond.

Felis snorted, trying to hold in his mirth. In the wer-im hierarchy, Felis clearly ranked lower than Tarn or he'd have guffawed aloud. Even still, his saving grace was Tarn's distraction at having his ear stung by a nymph.

La'meliai mused to Na'rina on a psychic level, *This Tarn is a stubborn one, but I'll see what I can do about his disposition. Thank you, Drydanda-Sister, for your healing.*

Na'rina pushed away from the ash to stand. The dried blood on her back itched and her vision swam. She swayed and braced herself. *Don't show weakness!* It was too late for that, but she'd be burned if she allowed these wer-im to see much more.

"I'll follow," she told the Wer-Kadis.

His black brows drew together, which drew the markings on his temples tight on his narrow face. Na'rina gulped. If that simmering anger ever escaped the Wer-Kadis' control, she'd be at serious risk. She tilted her head down, hoping the curtain of her hair hid her terror. When she glanced up again, the Wer-Kadis and Felis were gone.

She said goodbye to the ash and stepped away, stumbling. She should be used to the lack of sensation in her feet through the human shoes, but it still caught her off guard. With a stutter step, she managed not to hit her knees but the scabs on her back cracked. *I'm a mess!* Her human clothes had held up remarkably well thus far, but her t-shirt stuck to her back where she'd bled. Pinching it at the shoulders, she pulled and the material tore free of her skin.

Na'rina scowled. The jittery feeling made her hands shake but her Rina was too far away to settle her. Instead, she closed her eyes. Even through the shoes, the flow of trees, shrubs, and flowers breathed calm vigor through the earth. Na'rina wished for the warmth of the sun but it was hiding behind heavy clouds. With a sigh, she moved to follow the wer-im when an itch at the base of her neck drew her attention back to the small clearing.

Tarn dropped from the ash, landing with a soft thud. "I don't like you."

Na'rina froze. "Likewise."

His toothy grin said he knew how fast her heart was racing but the smile melted as quickly as it appeared. "I don't like you, but you pushed the Kadis to make his own choice. Silas would be furious."

"Excuse me?"

Tarn just shook his gray head with a sneer and jumped back into the tree.

Na'rina hesitated but she didn't have time to press Tarn to explain. *Will I ever deal confidently with these creatures?* She left the clearing with a new sense of unease.

The meeting spot was not far away and she entered it to find Obek, his companion, and the oread already there. With relief, Na'rina saw Afre was not among the group. Thankfully, this open space was larger than the clearing near La'meliai's ash. Otherwise, it would have turned crowded with all the dwarves, wer-im, and nymphs present. As it was, the dwarves occupied their own section on the south side by the trees, as far away from the Wer-Kadis as they could get. As before, the wer-im formed a perimeter with their leader in the center.

The dwarves spoke together, ignoring everyone else for

the time being. Dressed in cargo pants and plaid jackets, they could pass for lumbermen among the humans.

A subtle vibration rolled through the earth and up Na'rina's legs as the oread joined her. She wore a welcoming but solemn smile.

Now that Na'rina was not distracted by the shock of the wer-im, she received flashes from the Collective Wisdom regarding the oread. Love and respect, layered with regret and grief, washed through the genetic memory. Surprisingly, no visual images accompanied the feelings but Na'rina knew by the zany mental fabric that it came from her grandmother, Ver'rina. It wasn't unheard of for a memory to be pure emotion, but usually something strong enough to create multiple emotions was accompanied by images.

Na'rina lamented that the Wisdom didn't give her the history associated with those emotions but then she shrugged it off. *Be glad there's another nymph present, Na'rina. You don't need the world.*

"Tense," the oread's low voice rumbled.

Na'rina scoffed, startled at the understatement, and shared a look with her. The oread's curly hair touched the branches of the maple they stood beneath, owning the space just as a cliff would own the land on which it cast its shadow.

"I don't care for this," the oread whispered. "Let us nymphs stick together. We may need each other's support before the wer-im are done."

The words reached out their olive branch and Na'rina accepted with a shallow bow of her head.

The oread could almost pass for a human woman with her dark brown, lightweight pants and loose-fitting v-neck shirt, but if her enormous stature didn't cause a raised brow, her enviably bare feet would. Large calluses bulged out around her toes and heels, attesting to hours spent walking over rocky ground. Perhaps the oread figured blending in was not an option, so why try? Na'rina wondered what mountain she called home. If it was secluded enough, she might not have to worry about encountering humans often.

"You were saying the humans have attacked both coasts. What proof do you have?" Obek's question pulled Na'rina's attention back to the gathering.

The Wer-Kadis didn't respond, but continued reading a piece of paper he held.

"Patience," a wer-im with a broad nose spat from up in a tree behind Obek.

Obek shot him a scowl over his shoulder and opened his mouth.

The Wer-Kadis' hand shot up. Obek's lips snapped shut and the wer-im hesitated from jumping out of his tree. Na'rina couldn't say if the staying hand was for the dwarf or the wer-im but both obeyed without seeming to realize they'd deferred. In

Obek's case, that was telling. As the Ak-Lea's son, being forced to wait, which was highly rude to someone of his rank, was more likely to set him off than to make him hold his tongue. Was he as uncomfortable in this situation as she?

Within moments, the Wer-Kadis finished reading. He flipped the page over for more, but there was nothing on the back.

Na'rina almost squeaked when the cook appeared at her side. *Ugh, Na'rina, you can do better than this!* The wer-im shouldn't be able to surprise her, and yet again one of them had moved up on her unawares.

*Honey,* a nearby maple murmured, *they are comfortable here. We barely notice their footsteps.*

Na'rina didn't respond, disturbed at the maple's use of the collective "we" to indicate the entire forest.

Felis flashed a knowing grin and pointed at her golden necklace. "Pretty."

She scowled and looked away from the mirth in his yellow eyes.

"We've rescued two wer-im," the Wer-Kadis said, breaking the silence. He crumpled the paper in a fist and pitched it at the broad-nosed wer-im in the tree, who made it disappear. "They're in terrible condition."

Obek shared a glance with his companion. "If—and we strongly mean if—what you report is true, we are needed at home. Our Pyrgos-er-Rockies kin will need our help."

"You doubt us?" Felis snarled, his mischievous glint gone. "The dryad's story wasn't enough to convince you?" Felis flexed his fingers, claws flashing as they opened and shut. Na'rina itched to grab his hand and examine it. La'meliai's *curiosity killed the cat* ran through her head and she folded her hands against her waist to keep from doing something foolish again.

"Unsubstantiated rumors," Obek replied. "We cannot act on rumor. It's for our father to decide our next move." He and his companion turned to leave.

"You're a fool," the Wer-Kadis scorned. "We have to find the command center."

"No, Obek's right," the oread rumbled. "It's his father's place to decide for the dwarves." She seemed pleased Obek did not fall into step for the Wer-Kadis.

Before he could respond, a branch snapped and they heard footsteps.

"The view's worth it," said a young boy's voice.

The wer-im vanished. Obek pulled on his companion's sleeve and they rushed from the clearing.

"Hide, Sister," the oread whispered, sinking into the ground with a low shock to the air.

Na'rina grabbed the maple behind her but as her zoi aima touched the tree's, sparks shot into her. She gasped, shocked and frozen in place. *What just happened?*

"It better be worth it," wheezed an older voice, close to the clearing.

The Wer-Kadis pulled Na'rina from the tree with a growl. He wrapped his arms around her and jumped. Her stomach flipped. With ease, he swung them up against the trunk before freezing just as three humans entered the clearing below.

Na'rina's heart, once dislodged from her throat, beat against her ribs in a painful rat-a-tat. She sucked in and held her breath until the beat softened and she could exhale without being heard. The Wer-Kadis still held her tight around her middle as swarms of gray flies swam in her vision.

"Look!" The boy, roughly ten years old, grinned in triumph as he pointed to the valley below.

The two men following him were not excited. One, with thinning white hair, gripped his knees to wheeze, the extra flesh on his face trembling. The other man might be the same age, but it was hard to tell. Wrinkles fanned out from his eyes and mouth but his slicked-back hair, looking almost like a shell, still shone a healthy blond. Both men wore black suits with once-shiny leather shoes. They couldn't be more out of place than oceanids in the desert.

The Wer-Kadis' cheek brushed Na'rina's ear as he leaned forward. His tensed posture spoke volumes. Across the clearing, a blaze of orange, there and gone, flashed amidst the leaves of another maple. Na'rina narrowed her eyes. *There.* She spotted the wer-im where he perched, tensed in the branches. His eyes flicked from the humans to the Wer-Kadis, taking his cues from his leader.

"Can see the whole section," the boy declared, puffing out his chest. He held out his hand. The blond man huffed but pulled several bills from his pocket and dropped them into the boy's waiting hand. The boy stuffed the cash into his pocket, gave a sloppy salute, and bolted back the way they'd come.

The heavy man, still hunched over, wheezed and glared at the boy's retreating back until he was lost from sight. "Least he didn't lie."

The other man shrugged. "We would have known if he did."

He received a hum in response. Without a glance at the view, the men turned to the maple in which Na'rina and the Wer-Kadis hid. A deep growl vibrated against Na'rina's back. Still gripping her waist, he leaned over her shoulder, teeth bared, to brace on a branch in preparation to attack.

Na'rina stared at his teeth. She almost raised a hand to check the spacing between his canines. Wer-im were known for dropping from trees to sever the spines of their prey with one quick bite that slid those teeth between one vertebra and the next. She didn't have to check to know the spacing was perfect. Cold realization drained the blood from her face. He wasn't just being cautious. She glanced at the humans, then across the clearing to that waiting spot of orange hair. She'd never killed or been a part of killing another animal. Before she could think twice, Na'rina placed a trembling palm against the Wer-Kadis' chest and applied pressure. A cold drop of water hit Na'rina's ear. She jerked and another landed on her nose, then another on her forehead. Raindrops glistened on his black hair as the Wer-Kadis shifted to meet her gaze.

"Gah!" the heavyset man exclaimed below as he wiped water from his balding head. The oak from earlier had not been wrong about the severity of the storm. Both men hunched, flicking their suit jackets up over their heads in a futile effort to protect themselves.

"We can't pull it in this," the blond man shouted over the rain. "It'll damage the core."

The heavy man grumbled but followed as his companion stomped away.

Only when they were out of sight did the Wer-Kadis move. He came nose to nose with Na'rina. "Never distract me from my prey." Rain pelted their faces, plastering their hair to the tops of their heads, but Na'rina couldn't move. This close, she could see the thin green outline of his hazel eyes, and felt a great deal of sympathy for a cornered deer being hunted. Finally, the Wer-Kadis released her from his stare and grip to jump out of the tree. He landed on silent feet where the humans stood moments before.

Na'rina steadied herself against the maple with trembling hands. She hadn't thought about what might happen if the Wer-Kadis turned on her. *I can't show fear.* Too late for that. All of the wer-im could probably smell it wafting from her.

"Coming down, Sister?" Having emerged from the ground, the oread called up to Na'rina through the rain.

"In a moment," Na'rina said. She laid her fingertips against the trunk of the maple but didn't dare touch the zoi aima inside. Never before had connecting to a tree's life been painful, and the sparks that sang along her nerves when she touched this one lay fresh in her mind. *Something's not right.* She climbed the branches and discovered a part of the top had been cut off. The lower foliage hid the damage, but as she inspected it now, Na'rina found a hollow hole drilled into the flesh of the tree. A metal pipe lined the inside, but the hole sank farther into the core, beyond the first few inches she could see.

With her thumbnail, Na'rina cut a shaving from the bark. It came away green, proving the desecration to the core was recent. A sliver of the natural core still trickled nutrients to the limbs in a desperate attempt to stay alive, but the leaves were turning brown around the edges. Na'rina's brief contact with the tree gave her a taste of its suffocation. Thankfully, he had no dryad, but his pain was real.

Without connecting with the maple, she ran a thin layer

of zoi aima across his bark, cloying his senses as if he were going numb for winter. She couldn't save him, but this would ease his slow passing. Na'rina worked her way down the tree. When she got close to the ground, she paused. She sensed a sphere of empty space and within it sat something metallic, something with its own kind of energy that tasted of fire and left the bitter flavor of acid in her mouth.

Na'rina lowered herself through the branches to the ground. The oread watched with a curious tilt to her head, indifferent to the rain. Beside her stood a glowering Felis.

"Come, Dryad."

Na'rina ignored him. Trailing her fingers around the trunk of the maple, she sent sparks of zoi aima into it like feelers. With each burst, her fingers burned in proportion to the strength of her search. *A defensive measure?*

"Dryad, it's pouring, if you hadn't noticed."

The burning grew stronger as she circled. It shot little stings into her fingers, into her palm, and finally up her arm and into her shoulder. With a gasp, she shoved her hand into the trunk against the pain and wrenched backward, tearing a fist-sized chunk of the bark away. Beneath lay a panel with two hinges and a lock. A fine line separated the panel from the rest of the mechanism. Too fine for Na'rina to slip her nails into to pry it open.

"Move aside." Felis, now fascinated, nudged her

shoulder with his hip and squatted to study the panel.

Na'rina stumbled. She shot the wer-im a reproving look but it was his turn to ignore her as he withdrew a ring of thin metal tools from his pocket. He flipped through them and then inserted one into the lock. A second, needlelike tool, followed. After a moment of grumbling, the lock popped open. Felis smiled in triumph.

They both leaned close to see what lay inside. A round object, about the size of Na'rina's palm, glistened a soft gray. It could have been a human radio, but Na'rina doubted it. She reached to pull it free.

Felis grabbed her wrist. "Water will damage it."

He pulled a bag of roasted meat from his pocket. He ate a few pieces. "Want some?" He held a chunk out to Na'rina, who recoiled. "*Na?* Okay." Grinning, he moved the rest into a second, half-full bag. She watched as he took the now empty bag, flipped it inside out, pulled the mechanism from its sanctuary, and reflipped the bag around it. Before Na'rina could see more, he stuffed the object inside his jacket.

The oread pointed to the west where the mountain curved away from its view of the highway and the city. "There's a cave that way. We can get dry there."

The wer-im built a small fire and before long its warmth

filled the cave. At first, the flicker of flame brought on the Collective Wisdom with a renewed vengeance that left Na'rina shuddering, but aware of the logic behind the fire—the wood was dead and they needed warmth after all—she'd fought the genetic memory until it was a clamor in the back of her head. Now, warmed by those same flames, Na'rina found herself relaxing. It left her uneasy, taking comfort near a fire, but also drowsy while its heat dried her clothing.

"Where would you search first for this 'command center' you speak of?" the oread asked the Wer-Kadis.

*I still don't know their names.* Of course, neither did they know her name. No one had introduced themselves. *How did we miss such a basic thing?* It wasn't polite and, among nymphs at least, it was a huge oversight. The wer-im, on the other hand, might not care.

"West," the Wer-Kadis said, his husky voice far away, "where the last atta…"

Na'rina slumped, wrenched into communication with her Rina. To everyone around the fire except maybe the oread, it would appear as though she'd fallen asleep, but this anything but slumber.

*Na'rina!* The wail echoed like the distant cry of a wounded animal. *Na'rina!* The call pierced her skull.

*My Rina?*

*They're destroying her!* The image of aspens, toppled and

flayed of their bark, their pale flesh exposed to the sun and starting to lose the sheen of freshly exposed sap, flashed through Na'rina's mind as her grove shared her horror.

*Your mother's dying and her Rina's vanishing.*

*What? Where's my mother?* Panic hitched in her throat.

*She never returned from the north. The silent grove was a trap.*

Na'rina clutched at the faint touch of her Rina. *Where is she now?* Through the mother grove, Na'rina's grove should know where the Mother Drydanda was, but if she knew, she could not hold on long enough to share the location. She heard, *Come home, my Na'rina!* And the contact disappeared as mist in the morning sun.

With a gasp, Na'rina sat upright, almost colliding with the Wer-Kadis and the oread, who leaned over her.

"Sister?"

"I must go!" Na'rina scrambled to her feet but the Wer-Kadis stalled her with a hand on her shoulder.

"Where?"

"Home. Mona'rina needs me!" Na'rina ducked under his arm to snatch her bag. She made it three steps before the Wer-Kadis blocked her path.

"I must go!"

"*Na.*" His voice grew firm.

"She's dying!" Na'rina ducked to the side but he stayed in her way. She dodged and he moved to block the cave's entrance. Desperate, she darted forward to push past him but he locked his arms around her with finality.

"Why?" she sobbed, pummeling his shoulders with her fists.

"I have my reasons," the Wer-Kadis answered as the oread said, "Let her go." The cave floor rolled in warning.

Na'rina latched onto the other nymph's strength. It wasn't a Drydanda's first reaction to force another's hand, but she wasn't without her own resources to do so. Zoi aima rippled from Na'rina's core outward into her palms where she pressed them to the Wer-Kadis' chest. She couldn't touch his lifeblood like she could a tree's, but she could make him feel her own. Her mother likened it to the electric zap some farmer's fences gave when touched.

Zoi aima shot from her hands into the Wer-Kadis. He flinched and stiffened, but instead of releasing her, his hold tightened as he answered the oread's demand to let her go.

"I cannot," he said through clenched teeth.

Desperate, Na'rina gathered more zoi aima into her palms. She cringed this time when the lifeblood shot from her hands. Although her mother had taught her about doing this, she'd never practiced it—she'd had no reason to—and now a dark fear grew that she might kill the Wer-Kadis.

He groaned, but her attack only stiffened his hold. Na'rina whimpered and began gathering a third attack.

About to release it, Na'rina froze when the Wer-Kadis gritted against her ear. "Unless you're willing to kill me, stop."

The zoi aima tingled in Na'rina's palms. *Why is he so determined?* She trembled. *Could I kill him?* Na'rina gagged and tears trickled down her cheeks.

"Let her go," the oread demanded again. Although they were both nymphs, they were of very different elements. Seeing Na'rina stall her zoi aima attack, the oread rolled the earth beneath their feet. A crack echoed through the cave as the ground split in two. The Wer-Kadis lurched back, pulling Na'rina with him. Startled, Na'rina didn't resist but she clung to the sudden hope that the mountain nymph could force the wer-im to release her without Na'rina resorting to killing.

The floor continued to pitch side-to-side. With another crack, a rock dropped from above. The Wer-Kadis swayed and the rock glanced off his shoulder instead of his head.

Several wer-im ran into the cave, jumping the gap in the floor to rush the oread. Na'rina spotted Felis among the group of snarling, scuffling bodies. She cringed as a wer-im smacked the wall of the cave, twisted midair, and landed back on his feet to rejoin the fight.

Her hope flickered. Although the oread was in her element, the wer-im had numbers, which guaranteed them one thing—touch. As with all nymphs, having even a finger on the oread prevented her from entering the ground, where her small attack of rolling earth and dropping rocks would become deadly to the wer-im.

There was a rumbling thud and a whoosh of air. Na'rina risked a glance over her shoulder and her spark of hope flickered out. The oread lay face down, pinned by Felis and two others.

Beneath them the ground continued to pitch, but the cook perched with his knee planted between the oread's shoulder blades. For a second time in the same day, Na'rina watched as a wer-im bared his teeth to attack. Felis' canines glistened within the frame of his gray beard.

"Felis!" The Wer-Kadis stopped him short.

Felis froze. He snarled, but then the snarl melted beneath the Wer-Kadis' gaze. Felis snatched a fist-sized rock and swung it at the back of the oread's head. The Wer-Kadis cradled Na'rina's face, forcing her to look away. Nonetheless, she heard the crack as it connected, and the rumbling ground went still.

The oread lay beside her on the cave floor, her face drawn and her body still. Until she wakened, there was no way to know what kind of injury Felis had caused, but the sound of his rock cracking against the back of her head kept repeating in Na'rina's mind. She was sure, had she been in the oread's place, she would not wake up from such an attack.

"Relax," Felis said again, irritated at her absorption.

"You would have killed her," Na'rina accused.

He scoffed. "Mountain nymphs have the hardest heads in the world. If it hadn't been a rock, it wouldn't have fazed her."

"Why are you holding me?"

Felis gave an infuriatingly ingenuous shrug.

She glared until he moved away. The guards at the mouth of the cave nodded as he strolled into the drizzle of rain. They would, however, stop Na'rina. *Is this some kind of twisted revenge for their banishment?* Perhaps Afre guessed right after all. The Wer-Kadis had let everyone else leave. He'd even given orders to let the oread go after she woke.

Na'rina laid her palm flat against the dirt floor, reaching out mentally for her Rina. She found small shrubs and grass hardy enough to force their way through the rock of the cave, and even felt the whisper of larger trees whose roots traveled deep into the earth. But there was only a vague sense of her grove. Not enough to communicate again without great effort.

Na'rina sighed. *Why is he keeping me here?* The Wer-Kadis had asked nothing of her so far and, after securing her in the cave, disappeared with a few others, effectively preventing Na'rina from asking him any questions. *Who knows when he'll return?*

The oread stirred, muttering low about heavy rain and mud, but she didn't wake. The knot of icy worry in Na'rina's stomach thawed a degree at her movement. After a while, the orange-haired wer-im entered the cave carrying a bottle of water, a blanket, and a small pillow. He set them on the floor and hesitated, staring at Na'rina like she was a pinecone amidst acorns, but then he shook himself and retreated. She considered calling out to ask his name—those green eyes still reminded her of her Rina's leaves—but opted to keep her silence. *Don't be curious.*

She wondered how her mother would handle this situation while she eyed the water bottle. A part of her wanted to ignore it out of defiance, but the hard ground numbed her backside. *I need to move around anyway.* Mona'rina would have found an angle to negotiate her way free, Na'rina decided. She was coming to the conclusion she lacked her mother's skill in this area as well.

Giving in, she crawled forward to retrieve the water, then crawled back to the rear wall of the cave and took a cautious sip. A refreshing sensation washed through her arms and legs as rain would soak into a dry streambed. After one more sip, she tucked the bottle into a crevice of the wall to save for later.

The oread began to snore, the ground vibrating like aftershocks of an earthquake. Na'rina slid her fingertips along the back of the oread's head. Her worry dissolved. Like most nymphs, the oread healed quickly. The enormous lump on her skull was now no larger than a robin's egg. Na'rina slid the small pillow under the oread's head and leaned back against the wall to continue waiting. She gave into sleep, the oread still snoring, some time after the moon rose.

The chirp of morning birds filled the air and the mouth of the cave glowed with sunshine when Na'rina woke. She squinted but didn't see any of the wer-im.

"They're still on guard," the oread grumbled.

"You're awake," Na'rina exclaimed, delighted to find the mountain nymph sitting next to her. "Are you all right?"

The oread grinned with a mocking glance toward the wer-im guards. "It takes more than a rock to harm me."

"If you're all right, why are you still here?"

The oread laid a large hand on Na'rina's shoulder. "We're stronger together, Sister. The Wer-Kadis wants you here and he's given no reason why. I don't like it."

Na'rina threw her arms around the other nymph's neck. "I am Na'rina."

"Now, now," the oread rumbled, patting her back. "Let's do this proper."

Na'rina backed up and composed herself. This was something her mother had taught her. *I can do this right at least.* She laid her fingertips along the oread's cheek bones and welcomed the feel of the oread's callused fingers on her own face. The rush of sensation as they touched foreheads caught Na'rina's breath.

*Age.* Not frail but powerful, etched the other nymph's bones like each year added to her vast reserve of strength. Patience, a bottomless weighted willingness to wait for what she wanted.

*Majesty.* She touched the clouds and sank her foundation deep into the earth, knowing both sky and world. Almost as an afterthought, there came the grit of rock, the salt of the ocean, and the expanse of life that called this nymph's mountain home.

Na'rina had guessed correctly. There was a sense of her mountain far to the west. And by the taste of salt on her tongue, her rocky slopes sat next to the coast. But unlike Na'rina, who could still feel her grove and communicate, the oread could not reach out and speak with her home at this distance. The ache of the separation made Na'rina's own sense of loneliness a small thing. It was isolation so vast, the pain of it seemed to erode the oread's great strength.

*I am Rosharu Oreadanda.* No hint of her potent emotions echoed in the calm of her voice.

*I am Na'rina Drydanda, daughter of Mona'rina.* Compared to Rosharu, Na'rina felt like a child holding out her favorite toy, thinking it was the best thing in the world when, in reality, it was a pinecone next to a Sitka spruce.

"Such potential." Rosharu smiled and ran a rough thumb across Na'rina's cheek. "Mona'rina must be proud."

"They're searching the hillside." Felis' voice shattered the moment.

Na'rina flinched. She'd forgotten where they were.

"For the device?"

Frustration and fear washed over Na'rina at the velvet voice. *He's back then.* The Wer-Kadis could come and go as he pleased but he didn't allow her the same freedom. The thought burned in her stomach, ready to burst into flame. *I might just have the nerve to bury him alive if I get the chance.* Shock caused her to go still. *Did I just consider that?*

Rosharu chuckled, catching her expression. "Angry?"

Na'rina snorted.

"They checked the tree, but they're looking for something else," Felis answered. "Something about a power surge."

"Pack up," the Wer-Kadis ordered. "We have to be gone before they get here."

Felis called to the guards, who rushed in and began packing up what was in the cave. Na'rina shared a look with Rosharu before she turned to stuff the blanket, pillow, and water bottle into her pack. With Rosharu beside her, she did not feel as timid when she joined the wer-im at the mouth of the cave.

They found Felis standing to one side, answering the Wer-Kadis' questions while wrapping a white bandage around his leader's arm with a skill that spoke of long practice. Na'rina looked around and considered making a run for it, but negated the idea. *I might be fast, but there's no way I can outrun them all.*

The group took off east, skirting around Chattanooga until they entered one of the humans' national forests, which allowed them to run unhindered for a while. When they left behind the cover of the trees, however, the human population pressed in and hindered their progress. Near Interstate 85, the

Wer-Kadis split them into groups of two or three to pass over the busy thoroughfare by various routes. Na'rina ended up crossing the chill metal and concrete of a footbridge.

Beneath the rumbling of passing vehicles Rosharu leaned close to whisper, "Four of them are missing."

Na'rina started counting the wer-im, but hesitated when she realized she didn't know the total number of the group.

Rosharu shrugged. "It's interesting, is all. Where did the others go?"

Na'rina shrugged back but determined to pay closer attention. *Another area where I've fallen short as Mamma's representative. I can't even say how many have broken the banishment!*

As they moved farther southeast, the sense of Na'rina's grove weakened until the familiar essence disappeared. She hadn't attempted communication again, but just knowing her Rina could reach her had been a comfort. Her heart wrenched and she stumbled. She almost turned around but the Wer-Kadis appeared next to her. She ignored him—and the instinct yelling at her to run away from him—but inside she felt like a bird denied the open sky.

Her anger grew with her distress at being truly separated from her grove. *How does Rosharu deal with such separation?* Na'rina glanced at the oread. *If my sister nymph can handle it with such grace, so can I.* Na'rina gulped.

She would escape soon, she determined, and return to

her grove.

The Wer-Kadis pushed them hard the entire day, however, and the distance grew. Every time they slowed to travel a more populated area, a tick started in his cheek. The tension built in the group until it sat on a knife-edge, but he kept the wer-im focused and showed a remarkable ability to navigate the towns and cities on their path. The Wer-Kadis wanted something and was determined, it seemed, to reach the coast that day, although Na'rina doubted they could manage it. *What does he want so badly?* Finally, as the day grew later and they passed a sign for Lake Moultrie, he allowed a slower pace.

By evening exhaustion weighed on Na'rina. Not only from the traveling, but from holding her anger to a simmering boil. *Is this the cost of holding anger close?* The travel, however, did afford her time to consider escape plans, and she set aside some as unlikely while holding onto others for their various advantages.

The wer-im finally stopped as the sun slanted through the trees from the western horizon. They'd left the populated areas behind and entered another of the humans' national forests, where they set up a small canvas tent for the two nymphs in a grove of loblolly pines, and then set about procuring dinner. Felis always had meat to cook, so whether Na'rina saw it or not, she knew they were hunting. Shuddering, she turned her thoughts to convincing Rosharu to help her.

*Ick,* a loblolly complained, *do the felines have to be so close?*

*There goes our peace and quiet for the night,* another agreed.

Na'rina savored their grumbling as she settled on the damp ground—it was shockingly more damp here than around her mountain home—beside Rosharu in front of the canvas tent, which gave off the faint smell of musty oilcloth, dirt, and beneath it all but far more disturbing, smoke. Na'rina then laid out her plan for escape in tones low enough, she hoped, the wer-im's sensitive hearing would not catch. Rosharu grinned when she finished.

"Happy to help," she said and left it at that.

Their plans laid, they waited for deeper night. They sat in front of the tent most of the evening, occasionally talking while they waited. With the pines surrounding them but not near enough to touch, Na'rina took comfort in the other nymph's presence. Of course, she could hear them, but she couldn't meld with them without touching them first. She glanced at their dark-skinned trunks, so close, but not close enough. *Soon,* she consoled herself, rolling one of the prickly loblolly cones from palm to palm. Although no explicit instructions had been given, she was sure the tent's distance from the trees was purposeful. The Wer-Kadis knew specifics about her, though she couldn't fathom where he'd learned them.

"He watches you, the Wer-Kadis," Rosharu said, breaking their most recent stint of silence, "though I cannot place his intent."

Na'rina dropped the pinecone to wrap her arms around her knees. "You've known other Wer-Kadises?"

"*Sa.*"

"You don't trust this one?"

Rosharu picked up a twig and began to peel off the dead bark. "I've never known a Kadis who wouldn't put his own good above others." She rolled her heavy shoulders in a shrug but her expression could cut stone. "I can't figure out what he wants from you."

Na'rina shuddered and rested her forehead on her knees. She studied the Wer-Kadis through the fan of her hair.

He sat with several other wer-im. They talked and laughed but they were not merry, just comfortable. Taking a fresh piece of cloth, the Wer-Kadis re-bandaged the large gash on his left arm. Na'rina had been too angry to think about it that morning but now she wondered how he'd gotten injured. The lines running from his hazel eyes to his dark hair shifted as he answered a question. No matter what expression he wore, however, those lines gave his face a severe look.

"Want to know how he got hurt?"

Na'rina jumped and glowered at Felis who gave her a

sideways grin.

*His feet pad like a bobcat's as he slinks by,* a loblolly grumbled.

"You're disturbing the Oreds, Wer-im," Na'rina said in reproof.

"Oreds?" Felis asked, looking around. "I see only one Ored." He pointed at Rosharu.

The mountain nymph scoffed. "I am an o-r-e-a-d, Wer-im. Not an Ored."

Felis' mouth hung open in confusion.

"Rosharu is a mountain nymph, or *oread,*" Na'rina explained. "An Ored is our name for pine and spruce trees."

Felis stared up at the towering trees. "They talk?"

"All the time."

He grinned. "Cool."

Na'rina shared a look with Rosharu. Then she asked, "What happened to the Wer-Kadis?"

It took Felis a moment to respond as he gazed up at the trees. "Power dispute. Some of the wer-im are adjusting to the new Kadis' style. With Tarn leaving, they thought this Kadis might be weak."

"He's new to the position?"

The wer-im's face lit up. He sat on his heels beside her, warming to his subject with a sly grin. "Newish. The old Kadis was taken during an attack." He motioned toward the Wer-

Kadis without looking at him. "Icarus was his protégé and stepped up, but he doesn't want Silas' position when it's possible his mentor's still alive."

A vibration in the ground made him pause to look at Rosharu. She stared hard at the Wer-Kadis, unaware of how she projected her mood into her element. Finally, the silence registered on her and she shook her head. When she looked at Felis, she raised a brow like nothing happened.

He shrugged. "Some wer-im think his insistence about Silas is weakness and challenge him. They think he can't let go of his mentor."

*Silas.* That was the name Tarn mentioned. "You believe the old Wer-Kadis lives?" Na'rina asked.

Rosharu leaned closer, almost pressing against Na'rina's shoulder to hear the answer as Felis sniggered. "*He* believes Silas lives and I," he pointed a thumb at his chest, "am smart enough to know I'd lose that challenge."

"Why does he believe he's still alive?" Rosharu asked.

Felis shrugged again. "Not sure."

Rosharu scoffed, not satisfied.

Na'rina glanced from Felis to the Wer-Kadis and back, trying to picture it. "You wouldn't win a fight with him?"

Felis, like all wer-im as far as she knew, was a proud creature, but he stated his inferiority to the Wer-Kadis without a hint of resentment.

Felis pulled some sort of human wrapper from his pocket and fiddled with it. It smelled of mint but what seemed to hold his attention was the shimmer of the foil in the faint light from the moon. Rumbling dissatisfaction deep in his throat, he stuffed the wrapper back into his pocket. "When our blood runs hot in a fight, most wer-im can't stop and the fight ends when one combatant's dead." He gave Na'rina a meaningful look. "A rare few, however, have such control." Felis paused, wincing. "When Icarus stepped into Silas' position, it was accepted. Peaceful actually, but then he continued where Silas left off with this threat against the mythics. Most wanted revenge, not tactics, hence the most likely candidates for Wer-Kadis challenged him." Felis took in Na'rina's shock and cut his words short. "The Kadis is still here. The candidates, all except Tarn, are not."

He'd killed them. Na'rina tried to fathom such finality.

*Such a waste,* a loblolly murmured.

"He didn't have the control to stop?" Na'rina asked.

"You don't understand," Felis snarled. "He *decided* not to stop. If he had, the others would not have—and four-against-one is not good odds."

"And Tarn?"

Felis snorted. "Is old and plays the game well. As a general rule, the wer-im will not accept a leader who cannot best our other top fighters. Tarn fought so there wouldn't be any question about Icarus' leadership, but Tarn waited until the end of the fight, when the other three combatants had been beaten, before stepping into the challenge. It left Icarus the choice to keep him alive. Tarn stepped into the fight knowing he'd lose it." Satisfaction filled the statement.

"You're certain about that?" Rosharu asked.

"Icarus and Tarn have scuffled dozens of times. When Icarus was younger, Tarn roughed him up a lot. He bares the marks to prove it." Felis gestured at the skin between his thumb and index finger. "But even before Icarus matched him in size, Tarn started to lose their fights. It's been years since the old wer-im beat him. "

Na'rina shuddered. Felis spoke of the scar on his leader's hand as if he envied Tarn for creating it. She glanced toward the Wer-Kadis. He was tying off the bandage on his arm. "Will he scar from that?"

Felis scoffed. "That? Not a chance."

"The other wer-im's dead?" Her stomach rolled.

*My Rina, I feel like everything's been flipped upside down!* She reached for her grove, craving the comfort of her Rina's touch, knowing her words would go unanswered

Surprising her, one of the loblollies answered, *Oh, things are flipped, Drydanda. They're definitely flipped.*

"*Na*," the wer-im sneered, bringing Na'rina back to the conversation, "the Kadis didn't give the fool a chance to push it to a Kadivas—that's our leadership challenge."

They stared at each other until Rosharu's deep voice broke the silence. "From what I understand working as a pride isn't normal, yet you also say this Silas, your old Kadis, led you all. How's that possible?"

Admiration, perhaps even more than what he'd shown for the current Wer-Kadis, filled Felis' answer. "Silas was unique. He paid attention to things. Several years ago he became aware of a mobilization against the mythics." Felis indicated wer-im and nymphs alike. "There's always been a placeholder leader among the wer-im, but usually that cat's a leader in name only. Silas brought his concerns to the Kadis at the time and was ignored. He returned with proof but the Kadis refused to take Silas seriously, afraid to press his authority in order to pull the wer-im into a pride. However, he never counted on Silas challenging him." Felis sighed and his eyes grew distant. "It was an amazing fight."

"You were there?" Na'rina asked, waving her hand in front of his face to draw him back.

He beamed. "One of the lucky few. Watching that fight was a lesson. The earth was Silas' battlefield. Every tree was perfectly placed, every hill gave him the upper ground." His voice faded and his eyes glazed again as he relived the event in his memory.

Na'rina had gotten the impression from Tarn that the

Wer-Kadis' actions were different from what this Silas would have chosen. Yet Felis idolized the old Kadis while following the new one with complete loyalty. The Collective Wisdom did not prepare her for the intricacies of dealing with this species. Na'rina felt a sinking in her stomach. The Wisdom had not been prepared with the idea that they would ever have to deal with the wer-im again. There were huge gaps in its knowledge base. *How can this be when it's a genetic memory passed on by each Drydanda?*

Rosharu shook her head in contempt at the wer-im's story. "What'd this Silas do when he won?"

Felis shook himself. His face lacked the distinctive markings of the Wer-Kadis, so although his eyes sparkled with delight and his beard sported dark stripes, he didn't appear tense. Maybe that was why the Wer-Kadis put Na'rina on edge and Felis did not. *Well, mostly not,* she amended.

"Silas prepared us for the attacks," Felis answered, sober again, "but they brought weapons we didn't expect. What you see here is all that's left of us in Northern America."

"His preparations didn't help?" Na'rina frowned and hugged her knees tighter.

"We're alive," Felis snapped.

"If the wer-im couldn't stave off these attacks, how will we?" Rosharu asked.

Felis didn't answer as he grew still. Na'rina couldn't see him breathing. Then his hand shot out to the side and came back holding a dead rabbit. He'd snapped its neck in one smooth motion.

*Ick! Not at my roots!*

"Why did you do that?" Na'rina cried out.

Felis tilted his head, pointing first at Rosharu. "You eat once a month, maybe," then at Na'rina, "and you live off water and sunlight. Throw in a few berries, some wine and honey, and you're happy." He jabbed a thumb at his chest. "I feel hunger almost every hour on the hour. A drawback of a fast metabolism: I have to eat—often." He started to raise the rabbit to his lips but froze when he caught the Wer-Kadis watching. "Right. *Don't disturb the Drydanda.* How'd Tarn deal with these rules?" He rolled to his feet and stalked into the trees with the dead rabbit dangling from his fist.

Na'rina sensed the Wer-Kadis scrutinizing them. His hazel eyes shone with the reflectiveness of a feline watching its prey at night. Finally, he blinked and looked away. Released from his gaze, Na'rina motioned to Rosharu and they slipped into the tent.

They waited for several tense hours until no sound came from the wer-im outside, the stillness broken only by the chittering of a squirrel or the chirrup of crickets. The noises mixed with the throaty vibration of Rosharu's snore. Her rumbling covered the soft scratching as Na'rina pulled lose the stitching of the seam between the wall and floor of the tent until she created a hole large enough to slip through.

Na'rina lifted the oilcloth and paused. Sensing her hesitation, Rosharu peeked at her and winked without a hitch in her snoring before rolling over with renewed vigor. Na'rina smiled and slipped out. Rosharu would be all right. As long as the wer-im didn't touch her first, the oread could disappear into the ground when they saw Na'rina was missing.

The ground chilled Na'rina's body even as the air beaded her with sap-like sweat. The humidity, so unlike the dryness of her mountainous home, coated her with a second skin. She stayed flattened with her belly on the dirt until she spotted the glittering eyes of the two guards keeping watch on the west end of the camp. Those eyes scanned the woods, pausing here and there to follow the movement of a mouse or the flight of an owl. This might be Na'rina's first real encounter with the wer-im, but in this case the Collective Wisdom kept her from acting a fool. Those guards would see anything that moved more than a twitch despite the darkness.

Rethinking her plan, Na'rina focused inward until she felt the cold wash of zoi aima through her skin, shifting her color to the murky brown found in the bark of her trees when they dried out. It was a sickly clay-mud color, but her purpose was to remain unseen. Thus camouflaged, she waited until those watching eyes turned away. Each time they did, she inched forward on her belly. *To the trees, to the trees...* She chanted the phrase, staving off fear by focusing on the simple task. Over an hour later she laid her hands on the nearest loblolly root between the creeping vines covering his bark.

*Hey now,* the tree grumbled sleepily.

*I need your help.* Na'rina showed him everything in images, thinking faster than the loblolly was accustomed to, but he didn't seem to mind as full awareness flushed through his bark.

*These rascals! Follow my roots. Berra will pick you up on the far side.* Most trees had individual names for other trees, but these were personal and rarely shared, even with a Drydanda. It showed the measure of the loblolly's distress that he named his brother without hesitation.

Na'rina's grove, thankfully, had all the same roots and she didn't hold a private name like others. She was simply Rina, without thousands of individual names. As the loblolly stated his brother's name, Na'rina picked up the tree he meant by his mental image, which allowed her to follow the path the loblolly indicated without asking for clarification.

Zoi aima flowed beneath the bark as the loblolly welcomed her to meld with him. It was a wonder, and a blessing, that the wer-im could not see the seething rush of life. Against the darkness it shone to Na'rina as bright as a torch, but then she saw the layers beneath the physical and the wer-im did not.

Could the Wer-Kadis see it? She resisted the urge to look for him. The rest of the wer-im would see only night-shadowed trunks but who knew about the Wer-Kadis? She had to hope he was either elsewhere, distracted, or asleep.

*There now*, the loblolly crowed, *they've noticed nothing. This way, Drydanda.* Her skin prickled like she walked through a field of thistles as she followed his guidance through his roots. It was a byproduct of traveling through a tree not her own, and she did not fight the sensation. Not all Drydandas could travel this way, but the nature of an aspen inclined Na'rina and her mother toward the talent because they routinely traveled through the roots of their Rinas.

She reached the spot where this pine's root contacted the next one belowground. Above ground or below—it did not matter as long as they touched. She swapped trees and continued on, passing from pine to oak, and back to pine, then cypress, and so on until she lost count of how many roots she'd touched in her journey west. Only when she felt sure the wer-im wouldn't catch a hint of her did she emerge into the thick underbrush beside one of the human's small towns.

*Well done!*

*Honey, you're so clever.*

*Run, Drydanda.*

The forest urged her on. It was time to run—even surrounded by the human population. The wer-im would not have to worry about the slow, cautious pace she'd maintained to escape the forest. They'd race to the spot where she stood and only then would they have to worry about the humans. For her to be successful, Na'rina needed to put as much distance between the edge of the marshy forest and herself before the sun rose.

For once, she relied on speed instead of stealth to traverse the human towns and cities at night. She'd be exhausted by the end of the coming day, but stars forbid the Wer-Kadis catch up to her.

The horizon was glowing by the time Na'rina stopped to drink at a stream near the western boarder of Georgia. Rays of sun shot over the edge of the world to trace her skin and her body drank it in until her skin glowed with delight. Felis only knew the half of it when he said she survived on sunlight. It was as vital as air and water. Sunlight fed the zoi aima within her as snowmelt fed mountain rivers, overflowing their banks with the joy of an overzealous newborn water nymph. Channeling the flush of zoi aima, Na'rina shifted her skin to white again before lengthening her stride into a ground-eating lope.

*I've done it!*

The touch of her Rina had returned during the night but now she soaked in the warmth bathing the bark of her grove. The sun pulled sap and other moisture to the surface of the aspens, juniper, and sage. These scents mixed in Na'rina's senses, making her ache to breathe in the essence of home in person as opposed to smelling them through the filter of her grove. Her

Rina, sensing the direction her long strides carried her, encouraged her to move faster.

Oddly, Na'rina's grove had no details on her mother's whereabouts, which spurred Na'rina on all the more. Something was hindering communication between the Mother Drydanda and her grove, which in turn left Na'rina's grove in the dark. Anxiety knotted her stomach. *I'll be home soon,* she assured herself, although she had little idea what she'd do when she got there.

Around noon, she started seeing signs for the Mississippi border and her heart sank. At her current pace, she wouldn't get past the river before nightfall. To get to Chattanooga, she'd followed a path her mother laid out that avoided much of the human population. But the Wer-Kadis had taken them farther south across unfamiliar land. At this point, Na'rina had skirted enough towns, cities, vehicles, and roads that she'd lost count.

Toward evening, she entered a rare area of open grassland. Breathing in the freedom and speed it allowed, she began to look for a tree to rest inside, but as she scanned the horizon nothing presented itself. Finally, she spotted a small cluster of trees. They weren't ideal as they did not connect to a larger forest, but they could shelter her for one night. She angled toward the copse and the fine hairs on the back of her neck stood up. She glanced behind her.

There—not far away—ran the Wer-Kadis.

His long strides ate the ground between them, shortening the distance even in the brief moment it took Na'rina to glance back.

Na'rina stretched into a reckless sprint. She whimpered, her legs wobbling as she stutter-stepped before catching her balance. Now, of all times, her strength deserted her!

She heard a grunt, far too close, from behind, and strained harder, forcing her knees to keep from buckling even as one of them tried to go sideways.

Na'rina glanced back again and sobbed.

Dark brows lowered, the Wer-Kadis was intent on reaching her before she touched the small grove a few meters ahead.

*He's going to kill me!*

The Wer-Kadis slammed into Na'rina's back and locked his arms around her. They tumbled forward as the ground rushed at Na'rina, far too fast for her to avoid the impact she saw coming. The Wer-Kadis twisted at the last second and Na'rina heard the thud of his shoulder taking their combined weight. A groan sounded beside her ear but he didn't lose hold as they skidded in the dirt.

Na'rina cried out—fingertips stretched toward the roots inches beyond her reach. Even if she could touch them, it wouldn't matter. With his hold, she couldn't meld. Tears pricked her eyes. *Don't let him see.* But she couldn't stop her shuddering breath, and he held her tight as he regained his own composure.

*Now he's going to kill me.*

Na'rina struggled to break his grip on her, and heard a strange sound.

She looked over her shoulder and gaped. "You're

laughing?"

"Ah, Na'rina, for such a delicate thing, you do know how to lead one on a merry chase."

She froze. *He knows my name?* The lines from his eyes pulled upward at her baffled expression and he laughed harder.

"What's so funny?"

"The wer-im will think you almost bested me."

"That's foolish."

The Wer-Kadis sat up, taking her with him. He rotated his right shoulder, displaying the dirt ground into his skin and the blood trickling down his arm. "Is it?" he asked, his tense look returning.

Na'rina huffed and looked away. She didn't like him, but he'd taken the injury in her place. She couldn't fathom why.

"I'm sorry for your pain, Wer-Kadis."

He clasped her chin in a calloused but surprisingly warm hand, forcing her to meet his hazel eyes. "Icarus, please."

Her nostrils flared. A personal name would be too intimate. When it became obvious she would not obey, he let her chin go. His fingers came away with the faint white powder from her skin that resembled her aspen's bark. Curious, he rubbed his thumb and forefinger together.

"What's your natural color?"

She turned her head away.

After a moment, he stood up. "We'll head back in the

morning." When he didn't move away, she looked over to find him offering a hand. The gesture and the glint in his eyes confirmed he'd always be within arm's reach. As long as he could touch her, he could prevent her from disappearing into any nearby tree, and he knew it. *How?*

"Where would you go?" he asked, attempting to be gentle, but his husky tone carried too much knowledge. "This grove leads nowhere. I'd wait for you to give up."

"I'm patient," she countered. "I could wait forever."

He eyed the closest tree, a beautiful young maple with grayish bark. "They are not your Rina. From what I understand, staying too long forces unpleasant changes on the dryad."

*How does he know things only a Drydanda should know?* She attempted to bolt. Faster than even she could see, he moved, and instead of reaching the maple she smacked up against his chest.

"I hate you," she hissed, humiliation heating her face.

"Without a doubt," he agreed without any heat. Gripping her shoulders, he turned her toward the trees, showing he no longer feared her disappearing into one of them. With a gesture, he encouraged her to sit down next to one. Na'rina folded her legs and then went still as he dropped his backpack and moved around, far too close for comfort.

*Girlie,* the maple against her back muttered, *what's all this tension? You could cause me to freeze up with such an air.*

Na'rina ignored him. Usually, she would have smiled at the maple's grandfatherly tone but she didn't want to share her frustration. He would not understand it.

As the Wer-Kadis stepped around her, Na'rina caught what he carried in his hand and groaned. One tufted ear twitched as he saw her distress. The Wer-Kadis dropped the dead branches back onto the ground and sat down against a neighboring maple, as graceful as any feline. She watched, shocked he'd discarded plans for a fire, while he set about cleaning his raw shoulder. Unable to look away, she stared as he peeled the fabric of his shirt away from the drying blood. *That blood could have been mine. Why'd he take the fall?*

Na'rina slapped her palms on the ground to stand up. The Wer-Kadis reached out to stop her, his expression wary.

"I'm not trying to escape!" she chided. "Let me see your shoulder."

After a pause, he relaxed and she knelt facing his shoulder, turning him slightly to catch the light of the rising moon on his injury. The light coated his skin with a silvery sheen while the night still dulled his tanned coloring and helped her ignore the red of his blood. She gently peeled the rest of the fabric away to reveal the wound. It ran down his right side underneath his arm until his belt stopped the ground from grating his hip. Na'rina ripped the remains of the shirt to expose the area.

"Water?" she asked.

He groaned as he leaned to retrieve the small backpack. It had fit snug to his back due to its waist strap and had surprisingly taken little damage during their fall. It looked familiar, if bulkier than when she'd used it. She'd forgotten it in her focus on escaping.

"That's mine," Na'rina accused.

"It was handy," the Wer-Kadis grimaced and opened the pack. From it he pulled two bottles of water, a stiff bristled brush, and a red first aid kit.

*He was so sure of catching me, he brought supplies.*

She snatched a water bottle from him and poured half the contents over the wound, catching what spilled with the remains of his shirt. She recapped the bottle and picked up the brush.

"Need this often?" Animosity sharpened her words as anger smoldered in her stomach. She wanted to cause him pain. She clutched the brush to keep from acting on the impulse. The Wer-Kadis turned his head, watching her emotions, but he didn't answer her sharp question. With a sigh, Na'rina scrubbed his shoulder with enough force to dislodge the dirt embedded in his skin. He continued to study her, and his silent regard brought a lump to her throat. *What does he see? A scared nymph? A naïve, weak creature?* At last satisfied with the cleaning, Na'rina washed the remaining water over his shoulder. She let the skin dry before using the sheers from the first aid kit to cut, wrap, and tape several pieces of gauze to cover his wound.

"This is ruined." She indicated the shirt and sat back on her legs.

The Wer-Kadis shrugged. He turned to root around in the backpack and pulled out a green t-shirt. Na'rina watched absently. *How can I convince him to let me go?* She knew nothing about his intentions, and without knowing what he wanted, how could she negotiate? The pain from her Rina sat in the back of her mind like a lodestone, pulling her west. Without thinking, Na'rina traced one of the lines on the Wer-Kadis' back. His skin wasn't a smooth tan but crossed with darker lines, just like the ones running from his eyes. They started at his spine and, as veins in a leaf, ran along the contours of his ribs until they faded near the curve of his powerful chest. Her finger froze on the raised flesh of a thick scar. It traveled the edge of one of the black lines following his rib cage. His other wounds were mere nicks compared to this one.

He went still beneath her touch. His reflective hazel eyes, now gilded with the silver moonlight, locked onto hers. Surprise tingled down her spine. Na'rina dropped her hand and held it tight in her lap, hanging her head as heat rushed her face. Her mother would scold her for such a lapse in judgment.

"Some lessons," he said, "are harder to learn than others."

Her gaze flicked up to find him still watching. Something told her she'd just peeled the bark off a piece of his past—and she didn't want to see what lay beneath.

Na'rina cleared her throat. "I have to go home," she whispered, hoping he'd hear the plea in her words and not the tremor.

He blinked and the intensity from a moment before became hidden by his familiar inscrutability.

"*Na*, Na'rina."

"Why?" she asked. "What reason can you have for holding me?"

"Several reasons, none of which I'm at liberty to explain." He pulled the shirt over his head.

"My mother's dying! They're destroying her grove!"

"What would you do? Save her Rina? That wouldn't keep her from dying, and you'd be captured in the process. Then what? You'd be as helpless as your mother."

Na'rina's heart clenched. "Healing her Rina would give her strength."

"Strength for what? To last longer under whatever torture she's going through?" The lines on his temples tightened and he leaned his arms across his knees.

"Through her Rina I could pinpoint her location—"

"And walk right into their hands," he interrupted. "You have strength, Na'rina, but you were not willing to kill me, one creature who stood in your way. How would you deal with dozens? Would you be capable of killing them all to free her?"

His words washed over her like icy melt water. *I'm as powerless as an aspen trying to stop a river.*

"I have to do something!" she sobbed. Her Rina pulled at her, begging like a child. Tears streamed down her cheeks and dripped off her chin.

The Wer-Kadis stared, exasperated. When he reached out a hand, she cringed and backed away over her heels. The hand meant to comfort her latched onto her ankle instead. "You stubborn sprite!"

"*Let go!*"

"Stop acting like a sheltered twig."

"Stop telling me what to do!"

"Stop rushing to get yourself killed!"

"That's rich coming from a wer-im!"

"Enough!"

*Enough!*

A spike of pain shot through Na'rina's brain, there and gone. They froze. It had been the Kadis' voice but he seemed as surprised as she by the mental ricochet.

*What was that?*

Then the argument hit her. A blush heated her neck. She was her mother's ambassador and she'd just acted like a century-young child.

The Wer-Kadis blinked as his shock faded into a twitch at the corner of his lips. The swift change startled Na'rina. When he smiled, he was almost beautiful in the same way a sunbathing lynx could be in its obvious enjoyment of the warmth.

"That turned ridiculous fast," he chuckled.

Na'rina's blush deepened.

"I mean you no harm, Na'rina."

"Hard to believe considering. How am I supposed to trust you? You've told me nothing."

The Wer-Kadis bowed his head and loosened his hold on her ankle. His fingers, though his grip remained strong, warmed her skin.

"We can help each other, but I need you to trust me," he said. "I can't say more than I already have."

"Why not?"

He hesitated. "Promises."

*Promises? To whom?* But she knew he wouldn't tell her. "You won't let me go?" she asked again, trying to keep the whine from her voice.

His hazel eyes seemed sad, understanding—almost—but resolute. "Not yet." And he released her ankle.

*This is confusing,* the maple, silent for awhile, muttered.

Na'rina couldn't help but agree. She leaned back against the maple but a thought, driven more by curiosity than need, settled strong in her mind. La'meliai's *curiosity killed the cat* echoed in her mind, but she thought this one question was probably safe: "How do you know my name?"

His nostrils flared in surprise but he only looked at her.

"What? That's covered by mysterious promises too?"

He raised a brow and shrugged.

*Gah!* Na'rina wanted to growl but convinced herself to let it go.

"Sleep, Na'rina," he said. "We have a long day tomorrow."

Sunlight caressed her face and Na'rina drank in the warmth until a shadow covered the beam of light. She peeked an eye open.

"You're interrupting my breakfast."

The Wer-Kadis dropped a brown paper bag beside her and stepped out of her sunlight. "To complement your sustenance."

Na'rina sat up to investigate the warm, yeasty smell wafting from the sack.

"Bread!" she exclaimed, "and honey!" She tore a piece from the loaf and poured the honey over it. The first bite melted on her tongue. Licking honey from her fingers, she caught the Wer-Kadis watching her.

He squatted and broke off a chunk of bread. To her surprise, he poured honey onto the bread and took a bite. He chewed, once, twice and swallowed like it stuck midway down his throat. He spat to the side and took several swigs of water from a bottle.

Na'rina muffled a chuckle against her hand.

"That," he said, standing back up, "will plague my tongue for hours."

"Too sweet?"

He snorted. "No flavor. May as well just drink the honey."

Na'rina ducked her head, still smiling. "Thank you for breakfast," she said, pouring honey onto the rest of the bread. "Where'd you get the food?"

He spat again, and slung the pack over his shoulder, eyeing her as she chewed. "Nearby town."

"You went to a human store? Your markings, don't they stand out? And you left me here—unguarded?"

He eyed her with amusement. "You weren't going to wake for at least an hour." His confidence spoke loud and clear. "As for my markings, humans have what they call 'makeup.' If the contact's brief, a beanie over the ears and some foundation on the face cover my more noticeable features."

"I see." Na'rina finished the bread and rose. It was time to run east again. She tried to hide how much she hated the thought, but as she fell in step beside the Wer-Kadis, matching his easy lope, she could feel him glancing at her. Despite his preoccupation, the Wer-Kadis' long legs ate up distance and Na'rina lengthened her stride to keep pace.

As they traveled he again showed a remarkable ability to navigate over roads and through towns with minimal exposure to humans rushing about their lives. No wonder he'd caught up to her so easily.

The Wer-Kadis stayed within arm's reach, no matter their surroundings, to keep her from disappearing on him. For the most part, there were no trees and Na'rina wondered at his caution. For her to escape into a smaller plant would be unpleasant. *Does he not know that?* He knew about a dryad's nutrition, he knew about zoi aima and her mother's abilities, he even knew how to spot Na'rina in a tree, yet his wariness indicated he lacked understanding of her specific abilities.

Na'rina watched him from the corner of her eye in turn. The points of his canines touched his bottom lip but he didn't have an overbite. She remembered when he'd snarled, while stalking the humans, that the bottom canines also protruded farther out than the others. Top and bottom interlocked for a killing bite.

Na'rina winced. He seemed intent on putting her at ease but his very presence caused her to tense up. Plus, his overall goal stood contrary to her own. She recalled the memory from her Rina of the desecration to the mother grove, its toppled and flayed aspens turning dull as their corpses lay to dry in the sun. In the background of the carnage she saw the skyline of her home.

She stole another glance at the wer-im. *There's no way to escape him right now, but situations can change.* Her breath heaved and she realized that in trying to match his stride she was running almost as hard as she had the day before. He wasn't much taller than her; he just had disproportionately long legs. And powerful, as evidenced by his jump into the tree a few days earlier and the lunge that took her down. *I'll need something other than strength to get away.*

By midafternoon they reached a national forest in the northeastern region of Alabama. The trees called soft hellos to Na'rina.

*Well, I'll be. It is a Drydanda.*

*Girlie, you look beat.*

*Ignore him, honey. You're as beautiful as my silvery bark.*

Na'rina savored the rush of thoughts and life as she passed beneath their canopy. The underbrush grew in close, slowing their progress. When they found a deer trail to follow, she was loath to pick up the speed again. To slow them down, she touched each nearby tree, giving a taste of zoi aima in greeting. The Wer-Kadis darted this way and that to stay close but it didn't take long for his expression to darken.

"Must you?" he protested.

Na'rina stiffened her spine and glared back. "It's only proper to greet them," she said and continued. More of her greetings than expected fell on dormant ears, but she kept that herself. Falling silent was natural to older trees.

Afternoon passed and dusk hovered when Na'rina felt the change. They'd left the larger national forest behind long ago to skirt towns and cities galore, and had entered an unmarked wood where Na'rina again took to greeting the trees.

Timid replies met her touch. But these trees weren't dormant. They were scared. Opening her mouth to mention it, Na'rina cried out and pulled back her hand. Needles stuck out from her fingers like porcupine quills. She raised confused eyes but the Wer-Kadis wasn't there.

*What's happening?* All day he'd been her shadow.

A flush rolled over her as her vision blurred and her legs turned to water. Na'rina sank to her knees.

"What luck!" cried a voice. "They'll be thrilled."

Two figures walked into sight. They blurred as a swarm of gnats narrowed the edges of her vision, but their heavy tread suggested they were human. Hands grabbed her shoulders from behind and Na'rina gasped. *There's a third human.*

The hands pulled her arms back and wound something coarse around her wrists. *Did the Wer-Kadis set this up?* That didn't feel right, but Na'rina couldn't reason why. She heard a growl followed by a thud.

The hands let go. Na'rina tilted sideways and barely managed to free her hands of the half-tied rope before she fell over with a strangled cry. The ground drove the quills deep into her palms.

A slick gurgling came from behind her, but she was too weak to turn her head toward the sound. She lay with her cheek against the dirt, watching the two blurry humans hesitate.

"Thought the felines hunted alone?" one asked.

"Doesn't matter. We don't need it. Kill it."

He raised his hand, taking aim above her.

Na'rina's zoi aima reached for the core of the roots under her body. Nothing happened. Her gut flipped. Never had she been unable to touch the lifeblood within a plant. For the first time ever, she was alone on the psychic plane of existence that was as vital to her as sunshine and water. She strained for the zoi aima now, whimpering as emptiness filled her.

The air recoiled, a concussion of sound that rang in Na'rina's ears, and the human's hand jerked.

*A gun!*

"Missed!" The human aimed again.

*Kadis!* She tried to shout but no sound came from her lips. The swarm of gnats grew thicker as a figure flew over her and collided with the gun-wielding human. *Strong legs*, she thought as the spicy scent of the Wer-Kadis filled her nose. With his hands around the human's neck, he twisted and the same gurgling she heard before emanated from the man's throat. When the wer-im let go, blood spurted down the man's chest as he dropped to the ground. Na'rina's stomach heaved but the bile stuck in her throat like her body couldn't find the muscles to throw up.

The vague shape of the other human took off running. The Kadis spun and leapt, catching the man and driving him to the ground. She knew exactly what caused the crunch when the

Kadis severed the spine.

Then, to Na'rina's horror, he turned toward her. Her fingers twitched as he stalked forward. The world swam and— just as the Wer-Kadis reached her—faded to blessed darkness.

Warmth like rays of the sun on her Rina's powdery bark radiated against her side and back. *Is this death?* A prick like the fiery burn of a porcupine quill shot from her hand up her arm.

*Nope, not dead.*

She felt another prick from one of her fingers and whimpered. Thrilled at the sound from her throat, her elation crumbled when she tried to move away from the pain and nothing happened. She felt as heavy as the stone bench in the Chattanooga park. Likewise, the zoi aima flowing in her body hissed behind her ears with a sluggish sigh. She blinked, and her sight swam like she'd drank too much wine.

Na'rina found herself sitting with her legs splayed on the ground. Another set of knees rose on either side of her and beyond them sprawled the gnarled roots of a large oak. Her arm jerked as another prick zinged through her nerves. Two callused hands held one of hers, one cradled her long fingers as the other pulled at the spines embedded in her palm. She stared at those hands, confused, but then a familiar spicy scent hit her, surrounding her. Everything snapped together.

"Kadis?" she slurred.

"Relax." His warm breath brushed her right ear as he leaned over his task. As he spoke, she registered the heat and rise and fall of his chest against her back.

*He's holding me.* She felt vague surprise, but none of the usual fear. *Is this from the spines? My instincts feel watery. He was going to kill me—but I'm not dead.* She remembered him killing the humans with the ease of a seasoned predator but this created, disturbingly, a warmth in her that corresponded to the heat helping her shoulders relax. Just as he leaned against the oak, she leaned against him. *That should bother me...*

"What hap—" she tried to ask.

"Not sure," he admitted. "Your zoi aima touched a tree with a device like the one you found at the Lookout meeting, and it shot these into your skin." He lifted her hand to indicate her injury. When he pulled the next spine, she winced. "It could've been an ambush," he mused while he worked, "but that raises some interesting implications like how did they know you were going to be here? Or it could have been a defense mechanism to protect the device. But that also means it's a defense mechanism against dryads specifically because I was able to pull the device from the tree without triggering it." His rambling ended on a growl.

She tilted to see his face and her body started to flop

over like a rag doll.

"Careful." He tightened his arms around her. "You don't have your equilibrium back yet." He adjusted their position so she leaned against his left shoulder. Since she could see his expressions while he worked, this suited her.

"Kadis?"

"*Sa?*" He frowned over a stubborn quill.

"For that to work, they would have to know my anatomy."

"I know." The quill came out, shooting a line of fire up her arm. "But were they after you or dryads in general? And how did they know where to place the device? We know humans are involved, but how do they know such specifics?"

She hummed. Any local dryad would greet the trees with a touch of zoi aima. They couldn't sink their zoi aima into the tree or control its lifeblood like she could, but all dryads greeted the forest with a small giving of themselves by brushing the bark psychically. It was disturbing that someone would use the courtesy against them.

"You think they know we touch other trees to say hello?"

"*Sa.* The dryad from the tree you touched is already gone, if it had a dryad to begin with. She wouldn't have survived the desecration to her tree. So why place it in a dying tree unless you're sure others will touch it?"

"Unless it's just to protect the device?"

He rolled his shoulders. "True, but we still come back to the fact it was aimed to work on a dryad specifically. If it were simply a defense, why only aim it at one species?" He pulled out the last spine and set it on a bandana beside him. When he let go of her hand, Na'rina found she could twitch her fingers but not move her hand from his knee.

"How do *you* know so much about dryads?" Na'rina cringed as the words left her. She hadn't meant to voice them but her brain, just like her body, felt slow.

His nostrils flared. "You ask too many questions."

"I've a right to know," she protested. Again the words were out before she could stop them.

"It's not a question I can answer."

She huffed and watched her hand as she tried to move it. The Kadis watched with her. When she could move her wrist, she rotated it in a circle, pleased and surprised her skin still held its white color. It was reassuring that, even after passing out, she hadn't lost the control of zoi aima within her own skin.

"Considering how long you were out, it takes a while to fade," the Kadis observed.

"Long enough for the men to contain me," she agreed.

Now able to move her arm, Na'rina again acted on impulse. She grasped the Kadis' right hand and flipped the palm toward her. Even La'meliai's *curiosity killed the cat* comment didn't cause her to pause. Hopefully he wouldn't react like Tarn and attack her or she'd regret it later, but the wer-im didn't resist as she studied his palm.

The small scar she'd noticed in the web of his thumb and forefinger sliced through from the back of his hand to the palm. It was not alone. The meat of his palm bore several more white lines.

"Tarn?" she asked, touching one of the scars.

The Kadis grunted. "Who told you that?"

"Felis."

"Cat talks too much."

"It wasn't Tarn?"

Na'rina looked up when the Kadis did not respond.

Finally, "*Sa*. It was Tarn."

"Why?" Na'rina wanted to bite her tongue as tension pulled at the lines on his temples.

"He forced fights with me when I was young," the Kadis replied..

The edge in his voice left Na'rina cold. "I thought…" She hesitated but he raised a brow, inviting her to continue. "I thought wer-im often kill each other when they fight."

The Kadis' lips twitched. "We do."

"Then why didn't he kill you?"

"For all the times Tarn and I sparred, these are the only marks he left." He gestured with his scarred hand. "They were training fights."

"I thought you were friends."

"We are now."

She frowned, confused.

The Kadis chuckled. "The wer-im respect me enough to follow me in Silas' place. That respect comes in large part because of my history with Tarn."

Na'rina gave a "huh" and went back to following the scars on his palm with her finger. *What a brutal way to learn.*

Her finger moved from the scars to trace the ridges of his calluses out to the tip of each finger. The heavy calluses bore deep crevices in the middle of each finger from the first knuckle out to the fingertips.

"Out with them," she demanded, massaging the pad between the first and second knuckle.

He huffed but complied, extending his claws, which perfectly fit along the lines dug in his calluses. They started at the first knuckle and curved, not proceeding beyond the tips of his fingers. Na'rina traced one, studying the sharp point and razor edge on the inside of the curve. Even against her white skin, they were pearl in color on top and transparent near the cutting edge.

She glanced at his face and froze. Just as she'd seen once before, intensity glittered in his hooded hazel eyes like he enjoyed watching her.

"Those men?" she asked, needing a distraction from his

stare, although the question carried the image of blood gushing down a human chest.

"*Sa.*" He blinked, shuttering whatever thoughts lay behind his eyes, and retracted his claws. "Against the humans, we made a good team."

Na'rina snorted. "I made a good diversion, you mean."

He shrugged. "It worked."

Why wasn't she revolted by his reply? He'd *killed* the humans. Still holding his hand in both her own, she trailed a finger down the miniscule line left from the index claw.

"Humans are capturing mythics," he pressed. "What just happened proves an alliance could mean our survival."

Na'rina hummed as a lassitude stole over her but her mind couldn't really process his offer. She knew it should bother her.

*All creatures need rest, Drydanda, to heal.* Relief flooded her as she clearly heard the oak's voice. The isolation she'd experience on the psychic plane was fading. *Take some zoi aima,* the oak offered, *I've plenty to spare.*

She couldn't be sure if the Kadis heard the tree, but when she released his hand and curled against his chest to sleep, he placed the palm of her good hand against the massive root and settled his arms around her. As the warmth from the oak and the Kadis mingled, creating a wash of spicy air and oaky musk, Na'rina felt the first twinge of confusion at their proximity. The two shouldn't mix. But the twinge faded as fast as it came.

A chill held Na'rina as it dawned on her that she was rationalizing the killing of those men. It may as well rain ice, it wouldn't make her any colder. *Mamma, I'm sorry.* It wasn't an actual message for her mother though, because this was not something she could discuss unless they were face-to-face. Na'rina continued to replay her mother's lesson from when she was young, trying to apply it to the situation in which she now found herself.

She'd been a child, maybe fifty years old, playing a game with two other dryads.

*"Show your leaves, Drydanda!" called Ale'ored, a small pine dryad, as she ran her fingers across the bark of each aspen she passed.*

*"She's showing off," Brin'ored grumbled.*

*"You're just piqued because she finds you so fast in your spruce," Ale nudged her shoulder.*

*"She only has to search one tree. There are hundreds here!" Brin*

*spun in a circle, indicating the fast-growing grove that added new suckers every year. "And I'm starting to itch ignoring the zoi aima. I want to see like I should."*

*"That would be cheating," Ale said. "You know the rules. No seeing the psychic while we play."*

*Brin snorted. "I'll pitch my cones at you next time you suggest playing."*

*Na'rina pinched her lips to keep a laugh from escaping and giving away her position. Brin always turned surly when the game didn't go her way. As agreed, most of Na'rina's body was outside of the tree she hid against, but it was a great hiding spot. The aspen had split in its growth, creating two large trunks instead of one, and, after changing her skin to match the white bark, Na'rina climbed between the two trunks and lay her body flat on the shadowed side.*

*Brin and Ale were allowed to hide everything but a nose or fingertip inside their trees when they played at the spruce or pine respectively, but with the grove, Na'rina agreed to keep most of her body outside of any aspen she hid behind. Not only did this leave her more visible, but it also gave Brin and Ale more opportunity to touch her and pull her out of her tree—the purpose of the game in the first place. The one hiding was allowed to move as well, but Na'rina had not needed to as Brin and Ale searched for her.*

*Ale stepped beneath a nearby aspen and Na'rina sent a small burst of zoi aima to flutter the leaves against her hair. Ale jumped and clapped her hands in glee.*

"We're getting closer! Show your leaves, Na'rina!"

Brin grumbled and Na'rina dropped a small dead branch onto her shoulder. The spruce dryad jumped, picked up the branch and pitched it away from her like it was a snake.

"We're so close, Brin. Keep looking!" Ale's enthusiasm was hard to ignore but Brin planted her feet and folded her arms over her chest.

"I'm done, Ale. It's been over an hour."

Ale's slender shoulders slumped and Na'rina almost gave herself away by scoffing. Another two steps and Na'rina would have been in sight. Of all times to give up! She waited to see if Ale would persuade Brin to keep looking—this was, after all, Ale's favorite game—but the small dryad knew when to give in.

"Night's falling, Drydanda," Ale called, more subdued now.

"Right here!" Na'rina crowed, emerging feet from the other two. "Look at my hiding place. Isn't it perfect!"

Ale chuckled but Brin eyed the split aspen with distaste pinching her lips.

"Show-off."

The spruce dryad climbed up into the spot to look at it. Or so Na'rina guessed until Brin planted her shoulders on one trunk and her feet against the other. With a heave, she split the aspen to the base before hopping to the ground with a look of satisfaction.

Na'rina and Ale gaped at Brin. Then the Rina's pain lanced down Na'rina's spine.

No one hurts my grove—ever!

*Zoi aima shot from Na'rina's fingertips without the usual, necessary contact with her grove, the lifeblood an angry violet instead of the cool green or blue she'd always seen.* Roots erupted beneath Brin's feet in a rain of dirt, clay, and sharp-edged rocks. The sinewy roots whirled around the dryad, encasing her and then sucking her into the ground with a heavy thu-ump *that shuddered through the grove and Na'rina's slender body.*

Na'rina spun around to find Ale but she was gone, and a tiny, rational part of Na'rina was relieved she did not have another target. *Zoi aima* seethed into the grove, surrounding her like continuous trails of lightening. Na'rina could barely handle the hot pain of the split aspen, much less focus on the subtle shudders in the roots that told her Brin struggled below ground.

Something touched her *zoi aima.* It was so commanding yet so familiar that Na'rina reached for the other Drydanda in greeting despite the red lacing her lifeblood. Mona'rina briefly greeted her before laying her palms to the two closest aspens and pulling at the connection between Na'rina and her grove. The pain seared like peeling fabric off a burn, but this was her mother, and Mona'rina's penetrating green stare told Na'rina she would brook no disobedience.

Na'rina relinquished control of her grove to her mother until Mona'rina lifted Brin gasping and shaking from beneath the earth.

"Take her to her Ored," Mona'rina ordered, and Na'rina noticed Ale standing behind her. She must have run for Mona'rina the moment things turned violent.

Violent. Me? *The thought cooled Na'rina to an icy calm in*

*seconds. But the disturbed ground lay as mute testimony to her complete loss of control. She watched Ale wrap her arm around Brin's shoulders and the two scuttled away like they wanted nothing to do with whatever was about to happen between the Mother Drydanda and her daughter.*

*Na'rina turned her gaze to the split aspen, staring at the weeping innards of the tree. She sobbed. "My Rina."*

*"It is too late now to heal her," Mona'rina said. "You wasted that time." Her mother rarely minced words.*

*Na'rina shuddered. It wouldn't take long for the green and white interior now oozing sap to scar and blacken.*

*Mona'rina wrapped a long arm around her daughter's shoulders. "Let this be a reminder to you."*

*Na'rina bowed her head in shame.*

*"Let me show you something." Mona'rina steered her away from the wounded tree and Na'rina took comfort in her mother's embrace. They left Na'rina's grove and entered the mother grove, continuing until they reached her origin tree. The massive aspen greeted them with a thrum of life so vibrant Na'rina could see the glow of its zoi aima shimmering in the air. The aspen also had a split trunk, although one much bigger than the injured tree in her own grove. The eerie resemblance made her sway in dismay.*

*"You feel her?" Mona'rina asked.*

*"Sa." How could she not?*

*"Touch her." Her mother led her closer to the origin tree. Confused, Na'rina laid her palms and forehead against the larger of the two trunks.*

119

*The powdery surface sent out a warm glow in greeting, filling her with enough zoi aima to make her float if she'd wanted.*

*"Now touch the other side."*

*Na'rina glanced back to see Mona'rina nodding to the smaller trunk, her thin brows raised in subtle command. Na'rina stepped to the side to obey. She'd never touched this part of the tree. For some reason the larger side always drew her.*

*Laying palms and forehead to the Rina, she gasped.*

*"What do you feel?" her mother pressed.*

*"She refuses to respond. She hears, but... It's—"*

*"Shhh," her mother laid a finger to her lips. "Walk with me and greet this half of my Rina."*

*Na'rina laced her arm with her mother's. As they walked, they touched each aspen in greeting. They received no response. Na'rina's skin crawled. The grove's silence rang with an awareness that made her head ache. She had not realized before that she instinctively avoided this part of the mother grove.*

*"This, my daughter, is the result of rash, violent action. I feel nothing from this half and fear I never will."*

*"How?"*

*Her mother smiled with such regret that Na'rina longed to take back the question.*

*"The banishment of the wer-im," Mona'rina said. "They lived with the woods. It was one of their most loved homes. When we forced them out, we altered something we shouldn't have messed with in such haste."*

*"But they killed dozens before we acted against them,"* Na'rina argued, still shocked by her uneasiness as the grove watched, intent on their conversation, but offering no input.

*"Because they acted first doesn't mean violence was the correct way to respond. Today Brin'ored caused you agony before you buried her, but that doesn't change the shame you now feel for your response."*

Na'rina blinked, refocusing as the Collective Wisdom from her own memories faded in time to see the familiar road sign for Lake Moultrie, South Carolina.

This memory stayed imprinted on her as writing on stone although Mona'rina never took her into the silent part of her grove again. At the time, Na'rina went to Ver'rina, her grandmother, in an attempt to understand how the silent grove was possible. She still didn't understand Ver'rina's answer, but then, she understood almost nothing her grandmother said.

Now, as she ran beside the Wer-Kadis, Na'rina wrestled with her conscience. *He killed to protect me.* Did he *need* to end their lives to do so? Probably not. Yet after the drug wore off, Na'rina couldn't escape her relief in knowing those particular humans would never hunt her again. Her stomach rolled at the thought.

He offered an alliance. The dryad nation would hate such a thing, but was it *necessary?* A day earlier, she would have said *na,* but now she wasn't sure.

Na'rina could smell the Kadis' spicy scent as they ran. It lingered in her hair and every time she caught a whiff, it reminded her of her part in the humans' death. But no matter how she considered it, she came to the same conclusion. The men had seen them and had known they were not human. They would have given chase. And they'd made no effort to hide that they wanted Na'rina alive.

With all that in mind, Na'rina couldn't argue with the efficiency of the Wer-Kadis' response. When she returned home, she did not want humans following her. Although the Kadis' intentions were different from hers—and still unknown—his actions aided her goals. It made sense, but Na'rina felt cold within her veins, knowing her mother would not approve.

The sun hung at midmorning by the time they rejoined the group at the roots of the loblolly pines.

*Drat!* one loblolly grumbled. *Thought you'd made good your escape.*

Na'rina sagged against his trunk and wiped away the sweat coating her skin. The humidity was worse here than in Chattanooga, but inside she remained ice-cold.

*You seem conflicted, Drydanda.*

*I almost made it,* she told the pine, keeping only the image of her running in the forefront of her mind. The trees did not need to know about the Wer-Kadis killing people.

The wer-im greeted the Kadis with proud smiles.

Rosharu glowered at him and winced in apology when she met Na'rina's gaze. She shifted as if she intended to stand up, but Felis, who sat next to the mountain nymph, slapped a hand to her knee. Rosharu harrumphed but settled back against the sweeping roots of a bald cypress.

Na'rina's eyes narrowed. Even across the small clearing, she saw the pinkish lines tracing Rosharu's right shoulder and arm.

"What happened?" she asked.

The Kadis' head swung toward her. The alarm on his face faded to confusion.

"What's this?" Na'rina waved her hand toward Rosharu and winced. Her palm still throbbed from where the spines had been embedded.

*She put up a nasty fuss when the Wer-Kadis left to catch you.* There was a note of satisfaction in the loblolly's comment. He sent her an image, since her back was pressed against his bark, of Rosharu throwing clods of dirt and rocks at the wer-im as she tried to prevent the Kadis from following Na'rina. The pine's memory also revealed why Rosharu had not succeeded. Felis. He'd taken the brunt of Rosharu's resistance, but he never let go of her. With that small contact—a hand on her arm, a leg wrapped around her ankle, a finger caught in her hair—he'd prevented her from melding into the earth and hindering the Wer-Kadis.

123

"I didn't mean her harm." Felis raised his hands and pleaded as he watched the Wer-Kadis' confused expression clear.

"Explain," the Wer-Kadis ordered.

Felis flinched. "You told us to keep her from following you."

"Foolish wer-im," Rosharu spat. "Think you can hold the mountains."

"You're still here," Felis shot back but his hand brushed her leg as though to reassure himself he still held the advantage.

"Enough!" the Wer-Kadis ordered. He turned to Rosharu. "You may leave if you wish."

She snorted. "I'm not your charge and, as you know, my reason for leaving no longer exists."

The Kadis shrugged but turned away. "Come, Felis." He held up Na'rina's backpack. "I've something to interest you."

Felis grinned and jumped to his feet to accept the bag. The ground rolled beneath him in a ripple of moss and damp dirt. He yelped, jumping, then glared at Rosharu. She picked up a handful of damp earth and watched it trickle through her fingers, her expression neutral. The neutrality slipped, just a hint at the corner of Rosharu's broad lips, when Felis turned away.

"Join us." The Kadis startled Na'rina from watching the exchange. He held a hand out to her just as he had the day—or was it two days now?—before. She knew better than to run, but neither did she want to be near him. His spicy scent still lingered in her hair, a disturbing reminder of recent events.

"Let her rest," Rosharu grumbled. "Can't you see she's tired of you?"

The Kadis ignored Rosharu. "We're attached at the hip for now," he said to Na'rina. When she tried to ignore him, he raised a brow and asked, "Would you prefer I carry you?"

She stilled. He'd do it. She huffed and pushed to her feet, determined to retain a fraction of dignity at least.

Rosharu moved to follow, and another wer-im clamped a hand to her shoulder to keep her seated. The ground rippled beneath her.

"I should stay with my sister." Rosharu bared her teeth at the wer-im touching her.

"*Na,*" the Wer-Kadis disagreed. "You stay here."

"You do—"

The Wer-Kadis' eyes flared.

"It's all right, Rosharu," Na'rina interrupted. The memory of him killing was too fresh for Na'rina to risk an argument between them.

Rosharu eyed her for a moment, assessing, before she slumped back to the ground.

Felis watched, his yellow eyes pausing on the Wer-Kadis' shoulder and Na'rina's bandaged hand. "That's got to be a great story," he mused, but neither the Kadis nor Na'rina replied.

"I'll be here for you, Sister," Rosharu called out. Her

words held a promise and Na'rina treasured them as the two wer-im led her away.

They walked, staying within the trees to avoid the buildings glimpsed through the trunks on either side. Before long, the marshy land covered by cypress and water tupelo opened onto a cove. Na'rina halted at the edge of the tree line and swayed. They stood on the shore of the ocean where a breeze, blocked before by the trees, cooled Na'rina's damp skin. She'd smelled brininess in the air since that morning when she'd woken free of the senses-altering drug, but she hadn't connected it to the proximity of salt water.

"Beautiful, isn't she?" the Kadis observed.

Na'rina nodded. Below them, a wooden boardwalk ran parallel to the water. Beyond it stretched the beach and then the surf. Several humans walked or jogged, absorbed in the worlds of their music, magazines, or sandy toys. Two children worked on a lopsided castle, their yellow and red buckets half full of sand for more towers.

Sure, they'd traveled through countless towns in the past several days, but they had not lingered. Here, as Na'rina took in the nearness of humanity, it sent shockwaves through her heart. Every instinct shouted for her to duck behind a tree. Mythics didn't spend time around concentrations of humans, let alone interact with them. It simply wasn't safe, but now the two wer-im pulled on dark knit beanies, preparing to immerse themselves in this spot. From the corner of her eye, Na'rina saw the Kadis produce a bottle, then smear several drops of its contents on his face to blend out the dark lines running from his eyes. *So this is the humans' makeup.*

Done with the makeup, he produced an oversized hoodie and held it out to her.

Na'rina grumbled as she slid the garment on, feeling like a child in her mother's clothing.

The Kadis wasn't done. Next he pulled a familiar black ball cap from his back pocket and snapped it toward her.

"Going through my things?" she asked, testy at his brusque demand, but she took Afre's cap, taking comfort in the thought of the faun. She never wore hats. There were a multitude of ways she gleaned information from the environment and the wind across her scalp was one. To suppress the sensation was like covering her eyes and trying to dance through a crowded grove. "It's not like I need to cover my ears like you." Na'rina pitched the cap at his chest.

"Men stare. Wear it," the Kadis insisted, jamming it on her head. She cringed when the feel of the wind through her hair went silent.

"Pushy wer-im." She batted his hands away when he attempted to tuck her hair behind her ears. "If humans are such a concern, why did we travel through city after city to get here? Why are we standing on a crowded beach?"

The Kadis raised a brow and didn't answer but she caught the glance Felis shot at his back. Disguised to the Kadis' satisfaction, they wandered toward the boardwalk and sat down on the far side of the walkway, dangling their feet over the edge. Na'rina groaned when the wer-im placed her between them but she didn't argue. Felis rummaged in the backpack and came up with one of the tree devices.

"Another one?" he asked.

"It comes with a protective mechanism. Look in the bandana." The Kadis motioned to the bag.

Na'rina cradled her bandaged hand. It still throbbed.

"What are these?" Felis held the red bandana close as he examined the quills.

"They stung me," Na'rina muttered.

"Stung you?"

"They shot out of a tree when she touched it," the Kadis clarified.

"Have a bad habit of touching the wrong tree?" Felis teased.

"They were coated with something that made her pass out. When she came to, she was rather loopy... and unable to move. Any ideas?" the Kadis asked.

"A few." Rotating the bandana, Felis studied his new project and stroked his beard.

Na'rina fidgeted. The base of her skull itched and she

rubbed her neck, pushing the ball cap lower over her face. Sandwiched between the two wer-im, she felt claustrophobic. They wouldn't let her move away, but maybe she could gain some space.

She pulled her legs up and crossed them beneath her, shoving her knees against her captors' thighs on either side. Felis glanced at where her knee pressed into his leg, set the bandana on it, and picked up one of the metal quills. Na'rina harrumphed. She'd wanted to irritate him, not help him. The Kadis chuckled and mumbled what sounded like, "Pushy sprite."

The itch returned and her stomach rolled. The feeling reminded her of when a strong wind bowed her Rina's trees. She was watching the two boys build their sandcastles when trickles of sand started vibrating loose from the packed towers. Na'rina swallowed against the nausea churning in her belly.

"Something's wrong," she muttered, hugging her stomach.

The Kadis' gaze didn't leave the rolling waves.

"Something's wrong!" she repeated.

Sandcastle towers toppled and some of the humans looked around. A jogger stumbled and threw out his hands, but when the tremor didn't repeat, he shook his head and went back to jogging. Na'rina gagged, barely keeping her breakfast as bile burned her throat.

"She's hard to control," Felis said with a worried glance

toward the trees.

Understanding hit Na'rina as the disturbance created a deep resonation in the earth. *Rosharu!* Within moments, the disturbances grew weaker, indicating the oread was moving away. She'd promised to be there... Had she known this was coming?

"What are you doing?" Na'rina fumed, turning to the Wer-Kadis.

He rested his arm across Na'rina's knee where it touched him. "Have you ever met an oceanid?"

*"What?"*

"An oceanid, a nymph of the ocean."

"I know what an oceanid is!"

"Have you met one?"

Groaning, Na'rina scrubbed a hand across her face. Her Rina wasn't near the ocean, which made interaction with the water nymphs rare, but as the Mother Drydanda's daughter she'd been included in the few meetings they'd had. *"Sa,* I've met an oceanid," she admitted while wondering if she could somehow help Rosharu. Humans walked not twenty yards away. She couldn't fight the wer-im without creating a scene and even if she could evade them, by the time she got to the clearing it would be too late.

"What'd you think of her?" The Kadis let his arm drop from her knee to lean over and grab a handful of sand. In a trickle, he allowed the grains to escape his fist.

"Onishla was gorgeous," Na'rina replied, twitching as the memory of the oceanid flooded her mind, competing with her worry of Rosharu. The Collective Wisdom brought the memory back in stark clarity. "She had a carrying voice and strong emotions."

*I can't help Rosharu.* Her shoulders slumped. The Kadis' arm returned to rest across her knee. Perhaps it was an attempt to comfort her but she doubted it. He just didn't trust her not to pull a fast one.

"She was tall, with elongated limbs and silvery hair trailing to her heels," Na'rina continued, holding her spine stiff in silent resentment. "She picked me up when my mother introduced us and danced through the trees with me."

Meanwhile, Felis muttered as he examined the gray device and the quills. Rosharu, oceanids, even his Wer-Kadis seemed forgotten. Na'rina scowled at him.

"Strong emotions," the Kadis said. "You describe them well." But he did not explain further as he reached for the backpack and snapped it open. Felis' head swung up and he reluctantly dropped his new toys inside. Without a word, the wer-im rose and turned back toward the tree line, Na'rina scrambling to follow. She ran ahead of them as they entered the woods, but slowed at the warning growl from the Kadis.

Upon entering the space they'd left an hour before,

Na'rina froze and swayed. Chunks of ground lay opened like slanted sink pits. It reminded her of the time she'd seen a meteor shower hit the ground.

An unfamiliar wer-im greeted the Wer-Kadis. "That's one angry nymph. She fought us like a banshee but it's done." As he walked away, Na'rina noticed a large welt growing on the back of his neck.

Na'rina's knees hit the damp earth.

The Kadis knelt next to her. "She's gone, not dead."

*Is he telling the truth?*

Rosharu cared about Na'rina for no other reason than they were both nymphs. Until now she hadn't appreciated how much that care bolstered her. Her mother was trapped, possibly dead, and she was a captive, surrounded by the very species her mother forced from the dryad existence. Na'rina curled up against the roots of a large oak and pulled her knees in toward her chest.

*Is the oread okay?* Na'rina asked.

*Here now, Drydanda, have more faith in your elders,* answered a cypress.

*The world will be well again,* the oak murmured in that all-expansive way in which oaks saw things. Still not comforted, Na'rina willed him to shift his half-exposed roots to cover her body and shield her from the nearby wer-im who watched her. A warm hand landed on her shoulder, and the oak harrumphed as the Wer-Kadis kept her from melding. Instead, the oak covered all but her shoulder, and then he shared the story of his exposed roots, now coated in moss but once rubbed bare by a massive storm. Na'rina lost herself in the rains and lashing winds of his past which engulfed her worries like leaves in a hurricane as she drifted off to sleep.

The warmth of the morning sun soaked into the oak's thick bark. He flushed that warmth into Na'rina, waking her gently to the conversation of the wer-im.

"Can she do it?" asked Felis.

"Silas said Mona'rina can do many things without sinking into the energy behind what she touches," the Kadis answered, "but this isn't Mona'rina." He left the thought hanging.

A pang squeezed Na'rina's heart. No, she wasn't her mother.

*Different does not mean less,* the oak reassured

*But I should not be different, now should I?*

The oak, catching her meaning, grumbled something unintelligible before replying. *Few remember the last time there was a dryad like you. Who knows the truth of your zoi aima?*

"We've gone to a lot of trouble if she can't," Felis worried. "Not sure Silas would approve."

The Kadis growled.

Na'rina clung to the oak's voice, not wanting to deal with the warm hand that still rested on her shoulder.

*You must deal with the present now, Drydanda,* he chided. Reluctantly, she willed his roots to withdraw their protective covering.

"If she can't, she can't. The trouble we've gone to is worth more than what she can *do*." The Kadis shook her. "Good morning, Na'rina," he greeted when she cracked an eye open.

"Let me be." She hugged her knees, stretching her back while at the same time dislodging his hand from her skin.

"Can't." The Kadis didn't seem to mind. He reached into his pocket and retrieved an object, which he held out toward her. Gray metal glinted in the sunlight filtering through the canopy, and she recoiled, cradling her hand. It no longer throbbed but the memory of the pain that stupid device caused was fresh enough.

"I don't want it," she insisted when the Kadis continued to offer her the round object.

"Didn't figure you did." He smiled ruefully and the lines extending from the corners of his eyes lifted. His voice softened, carrying the husky, compelling edge she'd noticed at the first meeting. Although he tried to keep it light, he wanted her to obey. "We need to test your abilities and this is the fastest way."

135

"My abilities?" She shuddered away from the device. "I touch zoi aima. This dead *thing* does not contain zoi aima."

"There's no defense mechanism in the actual device as far as I can tell," Felis told her, missing the gist of her argument. "That was in the tree housing it."

The Kadis set the device on the ground and took both of Na'rina's hands. "What is zoi aima to a plant?"

Na'rina wished he'd missed her point as well because this was worse. This proved on a whole different level just how much he understood about her.

"It's lifeblood," she whispered.

"It's energy," the Kadis said, "and you can feel that energy, manipulate it. It's not much different from flipping the switch to turn on a lamp, or directing energy into a root to make it move. It's possible you can control an electronic device like you do the roots of a tree."

*Is that possible?*

Seeing her waver, Felis retrieved the device and flipped it over to show her the back. It was smooth like a stone tumbled in the ocean's waves, but embedded with several small lightbulbs and a finger-sized depression. "We need to see if you can open this without damaging the innards," he said, excitement edging his voice. "I could pry it open, but it's delicate and I'd lose the stuff inside." He pointed at the round depression. "The lock here is coded to a fingerprint. When pressed, the fingerprint triggers the device to open. From what we know, Mona'rina can feel the electrical pulse that reads the finger and make it think it sees the correct pattern."

*How do they know this?*

Na'rina glanced between them, one smiling with enthusiasm, the other tense, urging her to try with his silence.

"You've no idea what Mona'rina does exactly? All this is theory? What happens if it reads the wrong print? What then? It explodes in my hands?"

The Kadis took the device from Felis and cradled it in his palm, holding it out to face her. It looked delicate against his rough skin. "I'm confident it won't explode." His hazel eyes took in her indecision but he waited, perfectly still.

"I've never controlled the zoi ai—energy—in anything but a plant," she pleaded.

"Have you tried?"

The Kadis elbowed Felis' ribs but the seeds were planted. She never *had* tried. Dryads avoided contact with humans almost like a plague, which extended to the devices they created. What reason would she have to investigate the energy within such a device? Their assertion that Mona'rina could do it, however, did not surprise her, just the fact they knew about it. Her mother could manipulate any type of zoi aima, as far as Na'rina knew—plant, animal, electronic, it didn't matter—but her mother also dealt with the pain behind the connection.

Na'rina's hands shook and she clenched them, trying to calm her nerves.

Plants came naturally to her. It itched sometimes when she touched unfamiliar ones, but that was minor. Animals were another matter completely. That she *had* tried and the result left her with a baked feeling in her skin. Although she never managed to actually touch an animal's energy, she could shoot pulses into a body, like she had with the Kadis when he kept her from leaving. But that didn't compare to sharing. This venture was altogether different. There was no *life* in the metal device. *This is going to hurt,* she agonized.

"You don't have to connect with it, just control the flow of energy," the Kadis reassured her.

*Gah!* Could he read her mind?

He lifted her chin with his hand, forcing her to meet his hazel eyes. "You can do this."

Na'rina gulped, surprised at his confidence. She stared at the round device on his steady palm. Her hand shook as she laid her finger against the depression in the surface. Nothing happened. In heady relief, she sagged against the oak.

"Nothing," she whispered.

"You have to depress the screen." The Kadis continued to hold the object out but there was a gentle, if mocking, curve to his lips.

Na'rina's relief evaporated. Placing her index finger

against the depression again, she pushed. A pulse, like the sting of a bee, raced from the center along a route of twisted wire to the screen beneath her finger. Before she could react, the energy flashed, there and then gone, and the thing beeped a negative. Beneath that stronger burst trailed a trickle of energy that Na'rina followed from the core outward to a small, glowing red light.

The Kadis smiled. "Try again."

"If she can't do it, she can't, and we start over at square one." Felis rolled back to sit on his heels.

"Patience," the Kadis reprimanded, his eyes intent on Na'rina.

Na'rina just stared at the device. The pulse surprised her and she hadn't acted fast enough to trick the device into reading the correct pattern, but she'd felt it. It was almost simple, like repeating the outline of a leaf after it'd been imprinted in mud. "I think I can do it." She reached for the screen again.

The bee sting zinged, creating miniscule concentrations to indicate where the ridges of the finger should lay. She tracked it, nudging it here, pulling it there, altering what the device read by tiny degrees. The device beeped again and the light shifted to yellow. It blinked three times before changing to a steady green. With a metallic *pop*, the two sides snapped open like a clamshell splitting in half.

Felis snatched the device, crying, "Excellent!" Without

even looking at the Wer-Kadis for approval, he wandered away and began dismantling the internal parts.

The Kadis paid him no attention. Instead, he watched Na'rina, who spun away to retch in heaving waves that racked her body. Had she not already been kneeling, they would've brought her to her knees. The Kadis pulled her long tresses away from her face. Na'rina wanted to jerk away but when the nausea passed, exhaustion ruled.

"It'll get easier," he said in a low tone.

"You knew this would happen?" She choked, wishing the words came out stronger as her body fought another wave of nausea.

The Kadis sighed. "As you get better at it, it won't drain you as much."

"I won't do it again." She pulled away, swayed with another flush of sickness, and slumped against the oak.

The wer-im cocked his head. "You must."

She hunched her shoulders against his compelling voice. "*Why?* You've given me no reason to help you."

The hand he'd reached out to encourage her clenched into a fist and withdrew. Na'rina cringed at the intensity emanating from him. In the last few days he'd relaxed, just a little, but now that on-edge expression pulled at the corners of his eyes. This was the wer-im she expected. She'd been lulled into feeling almost comfortable but every instinct in her froze now.

The Kadis shot to his feet and took off.

As soon as he disappeared her original orange-haired escort and another wer-im materialized, leaving her no chance to escape. Those leaf green eyes met hers before moving on to scan the area. Na'rina looked around at the devastated clearing, at the torn-up earth where Rosharu had wrenched rocks from the ground. *If the mountain nymph couldn't force their hand, how can I?*

Na'rina's hand strayed to the leaf at her throat. Its delicate surface curved around her fingers, supple despite its gilding. *What do I do?* She longed to ask her mother, but she felt no connection with her grove, much less the Mother Drydanda. *If Mamma's free, she would have reached out to me by now.* The conclusion had been building inside Na'rina since the Kadis brought her back. Na'rina had felt her Rina pulling at her during her escape, but there'd been no sense of her mother that entire time. A painful certainty now ached in her chest. *I'm alone.*

A Drydanda was never meant to act alone. The leaf warmed beneath Na'rina's touch as though it contained a consciousness of its own but it held no awareness to give her advice.

Hours later Na'rina was leaning against the oak, listening to the murmur of the forest as it breathed in the night's breeze, when, without a sound, the Wer-Kadis knelt beside her. Her heart beat double-time against her ribs as she made out the glimmer in his feline eyes. Anger simmered in that look, controlled but communicated through every line of his body. Na'rina shivered and the nearby trees shuddered in sympathy.

"Follow me." Rolling to his feet, the Kadis ghosted from the clearing.

Na'rina flitted after him, responding to his command. She considered bolting, disappearing into a tree, but before she finished the thought, he appeared at her shoulder, directing her with a nudge here and a touch there, never more than an arm's reach away.

Their path led to a cliff overlooking the ocean. Na'rina glanced down and noticed the boardwalk they had visited. Now, however, the beach sat empty. The Kadis sank into a crouch and watched the ocean crash onto the rocks. He seemed as distant as the dark roaring ocean, just as powerful, just as fierce. Na'rina hesitated before making herself kneel beside him, frightened anew by just how little she understood him.

"We've found him." His husky words were barely audible over the sound of the water.

"Found who?" Na'rina asked.

The Kadis' reflective gaze shifted from the waves to her face. Na'rina swayed and then chided herself for still reacting from instinctive fear.

"Silas."

*The former Wer-Kadis?* Na'rina swallowed. "Tarn mentioned him."

His eyes glimmered, thoughtful with dark emotions. He flashed a vicious smile before returning his gaze to the ocean.

"What do you see out there?" He flicked his fingers at the seething expanse. Even with the rolling of the waves, the water glittered, reflecting the stars and moon. A few ships floated farther out, but she only knew that because of the faint glow from their lights. A human eye couldn't pick them out at such distance.

"A few ships and stars."

The lines on his face tightened and pulled up in what she was coming to think of as his pleased expression.

He pointed to a cluster of lights straight ahead from

143

where they perched. "Those are three ships: the Observer, the Sansabria, and the Erstwhile. The Observer holds Silas. Our biggest obstacle to freeing him is the locks. Mechanisms much like what you opened today but they scan the whole palm. Breaking them sets off alarms and we'd be lucky to survive the venture, but if we can bypass the doors without triggering the sirens, getting Silas becomes easy as breathing." The Kadis leaned forward, like he wanted to jump the distance between the cliff and the ships.

*This is why he captured me?* "You want me to help you rescue Silas—but you're keeping me from saving my mother?" Na'rina couldn't keep the incredulity out of her voice.

The wer-im tensed and she went still. She heard a low rumble, but it cut off as he rolled his shoulders. "Silas studied these humans. He knew they were going to attack. If anyone knows where Mona'rina might be held, it'd be Silas. He might know why they're holding her and how to free her." That reflective gaze shifted to her. "If he can't help you, I'll personally see you back to the Rockies."

*Back to the Rockies.* He already knew where her grove was but a chill ran Na'rina's spine at the reminder.

*Think, Na'rina, think.* She stilled, examining what she now knew. The Kadis *needed* her help. *How would Mamma use this?* Na'rina couldn't figure why the old Wer-Kadis was so important, but clearly he was. She didn't think the Kadis would tell her why.

*No point in asking. How can this help my mother?*

Na'rina couldn't help but remember the men who attacked her and the Kadis. She would encounter more attacks in attempting to rescue Mona'rina, but if she had the wer-im's aid, she might succeed. Anxiety rolled through her but beneath it came a bright flicker of hope. *The Dryad Council will hate this.* She shuddered. *But my personal cost isn't important.* From the corner of her eye, Na'rina caught the Kadis watching her. In the dark, his eyesight was even better than her own and he watched her emotions flitting across her face.

"Not just back to the Rockies," she finally countered. "If I help you free Silas, you help me free Mona'rina."

That grin, that pleased, almost proud grin, pulled at his lips, revealing his long teeth. "Deal."

Na'rina ducked her head, shocked to feel pleasure at his approval.

"Come. You need more practice with the device."

Na'rina swallowed. *I may have just agreed to my destruction.* But she had agreed, and now, she had to try.

Once again the Kadis held out the device on his palm and Na'rina groaned.

"Relax. Use the mechanism's energy instead of your zoi aima. You're trying to pick the lock, not force it."

Na'rina understood the concept but doing it escaped her. She'd retched three times before she figured out how to hold the reaction down but other than that small accomplishment, she'd made no progress.

"How about a break?" Felis suggested, tossing an apple between his hands.

Na'rina scowled at him.

He held his hands up in surrender. "Or not. You can break when you pass out."

The Kadis continued to hold the device, waiting with a tight look around his eyes. Did that look ever go away?

Na'rina couldn't help glancing around at all the wer-im. The longer this took, the more of them that gathered to watch. They knew if she couldn't stop getting sick, she'd be no help in rescuing Silas. The ship's locks would require so much energy that she'd pass out opening them if she couldn't figure out how to stop the drain on her zoi aima. It could be done, the Kadis assured her, Mona'rina could do it. Na'rina kept a bitter smile from touching her lips.

The expressions of the wer-im around her ranged from mocking to hopeful to almost encouraging, but no matter the expression, their eyes weighed on her already worn nerves. Her palms stuck a little when she rubbed them down her legs.

"Relax," the Kadis said again.

"I'm trying, Wer-Kadis. Believe me." Na'rina braced

herself, and touched her finger to the screen. The now familiar energy rushed through the device. It popped open, but the wer-im were watching her, not the metal contraption. She swayed and they groaned, a chorus of disappointment.

"Can you sense the pattern before activating it?"

Na'rina turned to find the orange-haired wer-im at her shoulder, his green eyes wary at interrupting, judging from the glances he shot the Wer-Kadis.

She frowned. "What?"

"You're able to trick it because you can sense what it expects, right?"

"R-i-g-h-t," Na'rina drew out the word.

"If you already know what pattern's needed, can you hold it in place before activating the device and let the energy flow into your pattern instead of shoving it into the desired mold?"

Na'rina tilted her head as she thought about it. "Shoving it into the desired mold" described exactly what she'd been doing. It was reactionary—and dryadic. *What if I'm preemptive?* She almost scoffed. Treat it like a wer-im would, command it to do as she wished, or just assume it would respond because she told it to.

"Stupid idea," another wer-im mocked when the silence lengthened.

The orange-haired wer-im spun to face his mocker, who

stood several inches taller. "You know nothing about electronics."

They hissed and crouched, facing off.

"Enough," the Wer-Kadis ordered. The deep rasp in his voice carried a threat and the two wer-im scrambled apart to obey.

Na'rina hid her surprise. The Wer-Kadis' firm hold might be the only thing keeping them from tearing one another apart. She'd forgotten they were usually solitary creatures.

"It might work," she said to shift everyone's focus, "but I've opened this one so many times I can't tell if the pattern's in my memory or if I can feel it before the surge."

"Hold up!" Felis darted from the clearing and reappeared with another device. "Here's the second one you found," he explained, handing it to her. "I believe they're all keyed to a different print."

Na'rina flipped it over. "Here goes," she muttered, placing her finger on the screen, but careful not to trigger it yet. She reached out. At first nothing met her probe and the sensation of emptiness was as disturbing as the stone benches in the park. There was no *life* to feel, just a cold shell. Finally, her search found the core nub where the energy originated. No pattern existed in that compact center but she found the cold wires the energy followed. Tracing these, she came to a halt just below the screen. Floating there as faint as an old memory hung a fingerprint as if etched backwards on the bottom of the display.

Na'rina released the breath she'd been holding. With a trickle of her zoi aima, she created a mold for the energy to fill. Then she pressed the screen. The energy rushed into the channels of her zoi aima and with it the bitter, acidic flavor of beetle filled her mouth, but then the device popped. No wave of nausea hit her. She held still, waiting for it to crash into her, but nothing happened.

"Ha!" She threw the device into the air.

Felis snatched it mid-air and shot her a reproving glance. Na'rina ignored him. The other wer-im cheered and a few elbowed their neighbors, holding out hands for payment over bets she'd been too focused to catch them making.

"All right," the Wer-Kadis called. "Back to your posts."

The orange-haired wer-im gave her a pat on the shoulder before vanishing with the others. Na'rina swayed in giddiness. The last time she worked so hard to learn something she'd been a child, when her mother introduced travel to her. Being away from her Rina had made her sick at first, too, she recalled. She reached for the first device, which the Kadis still held, but he pulled it away and pocketed it as she protested.

"First." He revealed a bag from behind his back and handed it to her.

"Bread!" She inhaled the faint yeasty aroma coming

from it.

"And honey," the Kadis said with disgust as she dug in. "We'll continue when I return from eating."

Na'rina shuddered, revolted in return, as he left.

The Wer-Kadis did not return for a while and Na'rina began to twitch with boredom. It was a rare occurrence for her. The forest's chatter usually provided endless entertainment, but due to her agreement with the Wer-Kadis, she couldn't focus on anything else. She decided to take a walk. Two wer-im moved to follow, but they didn't stop her from wandering. It wasn't long before she found herself on the cliff the Kadis took her to the previous night. She could not find the cluster of lights that revealed the Observer's location during daylight but she sat on the rocky overlook to watch the gray-blue waves below.

Laughter drifted up from the cove to her left. Two children, a boy and a girl, raced across the sand. Twins. Although the boy had a huskier build, their eyes and facial structures mimicked their mother's, who followed them at a sedate pace. A smile pulled at Na'rina's lips but then it faded as she gazed back at the ocean. What could the humans want from the mythics?

Lost in thought, Na'rina pulled her long hair into a

ponytail at the base of her neck and flipped up the hood of her sweatshirt. *Am I that different from the humans that they'd still notice me sitting up here?* She still wore Afre's ball cap under the hood—which made her more androgynous than usual—but she'd had such little contact with humans that she had no idea if her clothes and distance were enough. Peals of laughter echoed through the cove. The tide's seething from the night before had calmed to a gentle roll that lapped over the children's feet, making them shriek at the cold touch. Na'rina felt a kinship to those restless waves as the disquiet within her refused to calm.

"Back to practice," she muttered, hoping the Kadis had returned from hunting by now. She peered out, trying one last time to see the Observer, but even her eyes couldn't pick out the ship.

Night darkened the trees around them. The Kadis turned Na'rina by the shoulders, inspecting her disguise one last time before they left the clearing.

"Satisfied?" she asked.

He grunted.

Throwing up her hands, she joined Felis and snatched the device he held. The wer-im growled but she ignored him and popped the mechanism open for the millionth time.

"You've got it." He snatched the device back.

*What kind of pitch are you stuck in, Drydanda?* a loblolly asked.

*Not stuck,* she insisted, *I agreed to this.*

*Ha,* the pine scoffed, *your roots must be twisted. It's not safe to float onto the oceanid's home. Our roots don't grow there.*

Na'rina couldn't argue, and she was glad for the interruption when the Kadis approached with another wer-im at his shoulder. She hadn't seen this thin creature before, and the whisker lines on his cheeks fascinated her.

"This is Malon," the Wer-Kadis said for introduction, and the four of them were off. As they ran toward the now familiar cove, the pine's words haunted Na'rina. She hadn't considered the logistics of getting to the Observer. Dryads were not salt water fans, much less swimmers. She could float for hours, but swimming? *Ugh.* Should she mention her shortcoming? A glance at the Kadis revealed an unwelcoming, determined expression. What was his plan? Reaching the water, relief flooded her at the sight of a small boat resting on the sand. Then a thought hit her. *There's no motor.* Even a dryad could swim faster than a rowboat.

"Won't it take all night to get out there?"

"*Na.*" Malon pushed the rowboat into the water and held it steady as they climbed in. After they were settled, he shoved the boat farther into the water and hoped in, comfortable with the swaying motion.

Na'rina looked for oars but found none. Before she could ask about it, a long-fingered hand appeared on the side of the boat beside her elbow. Next came a mass of silvery hair, followed by a narrow face with blue eyes.

"Meet Owasha," Malon said, "and her sister Alaya."

Oceanids! Of all the nymphs, Na'rina found those of the ocean to be the most lithe and intriguing, perhaps because they were so different from dryads. They loved the deep places in the ocean but it wasn't this that held them apart from the other mythics; it was their temperament. Unlike dryads, oceanids did not hold calm or peace as high morals. They were as likely to drown you as speak to you, and they seldom saw eye-to-eye with their land-based cousins. Their tempers could explode at the hint of an insult, igniting fantastic, often deadly storms, to the consternation of their sister nymphs, the naiads or crinaeae.

Owasha and Alaya strung a rope through the oar ring on each side of the boat and disappeared below the water without a word in greeting. Na'rina leaned over to watch Owasha's sleek form. Onishla, the one oceanid she'd met before, had been like herself—a Danda—and able to travel at great distances from her home. Because of that, Onishla was trained to hold her volatile temper in check while dealing with other mythics. Na'rina wondered if Owasha and Alaya would seem wilder without that tempering. The water's surface rushed past where she gripped the side and she concluded, with the oceanid's help, they could reach miles out in no time. It didn't matter where the Observer sat.

"How'd you convince them to help?" she asked the Kadis.

"Some oceanids were captured and taken aboard the Sansabria," the Kadis whispered. "A week after their abduction, the humans dropped them overboard. They hadn't been fed, they didn't comprehend where they were, and they were covered with puncture marks from head to toe. Like your hand after the tree encounter. We convinced the nymphs the Sansabria might have information about their sisters' conditions. We worked a deal to free Silas and gather information about the studies that were done on the oceanids. Malon and Felis will board the Sansabria tonight."

Na'rina gave a silent, "*Ah*," as she stared at the Wer-Kadis' glittering eyes. How involved were the wer-im? For an exiled species they seemed to have a branch in everything. How long had they been breaking the banishment? Her mind whirled and the ocean's spray coated her fingers where they rested on the side. Na'rina frowned as another thought struck her.

"How are they getting past the locks on the Sansabria if I'm on the Observer?"

The Kadis leaned close to her ear. Na'rina stilled as his warm breath fanned her cheek. "They're the distraction."

"Shhh," Malon hushed them and indicated how close they were to the ships.

Na'rina started. She'd been so caught up in trying to understand their situation that she hadn't paid attention to the approaching lights. The massive ship rose like a metal cliff. She tilted her head back, and back, and then sent a plea to the Kadis with her eyes. *How are we going to scale that?*

He leaned in again and merely said, "Stay close."

She swallowed, unsure what he expected of her. They hadn't covered anything about this expedition except that she

155

was required to unlock doors. *Why didn't I ask?* Her mother would have scolded her for such a giant oversight.

The oceanids pulled them alongside the Observer's nose—bow according to Malon—and held them steady. To the left, two massive anchor chains protruded from holes high in the ship's bow. One chain clanked against the rowboat. Na'rina eyed those thick metal links and gulped. She could almost fit *through* one of those things.

Malon tapped her shoulder. "When you get topside, these chains span about the first fifteen yards of the deck. Whatever you do, don't step over them. If they slip, we'll be looking for pieces of you later. There are labs three stories below the main deck and they're holding Silas in room 52B." The wer-im patted her shoulder and leaned away.

"We've gotten to the labs before but haven't gotten inside because of the locks," the Wer-Kadis picked up where Malon left off. "Beyond what room he's in, we have no idea what we'll be facing when we get inside. Follow my lead." He took hold of one giant link of the anchor chain and, when he was sure she would follow, started climbing.

"I've gone insane," she muttered, but she took the chain and started the haul upward. *Just like climbing a tree.* But her senses insisted this was different. The chain shuddered as they climbed but no zoi aima ran through it. And unlike bark, the links were smooth and slick with moisture. She clamped her long fingers tight, ignoring, as best as she could, the sense of cold metal and dead weight.

She continued to climb, her arms quivering. Wind played over her ears and neck, tugging at the cap on her head as the faint whoosh reminded her how high she'd climbed. *Don't look down!* Na'rina closed her eyes tight against the urge to do just that. She didn't want to see the space below her feet or the roll of the waves. Heights had never bothered her, but then again, the ground beneath a tree didn't heave. Enormous white numbers stenciled onto the ship encouraged her that she was near the top. She looked up and saw the Kadis pull something from his belt. Swinging it, he let go and the grapnel sailed upward until it hit the railing with a soft clank.

The Kadis tugged, checking the hold, then climbed up and disappeared over the side. The outline of his head and shoulders reappeared as he leaned over to help her climb aboard. She gripped his hand, grateful for the aid.

Landing on the metal deck, the rubber soles of her human shoes slapped against the deck. The Kadis shot her a warning look and she glared back. He was the one who insisted she wear the stupid contraptions.

She knelt beside the Kadis as they took in the ship—it was a small city of activity—and the nonskid bit into her knees. Na'rina braced her hands, palms flat, on the tacky surface to relieve the pressure. The ship rumbled, hollow as the husk of a scorpion. Her senses scattered, searching for warm zoi aima to latch onto and finding only emptiness instead. *Dead. Utterly dead.* Paralyzing terror shot through her. *Trap!*

The Kadis rose and took a step before he noticed she wasn't following. He jerked his head for her to stay near but she barely noticed the gesture. The Kadis crouched and pried her hands from the metal deck. As soon as he severed the contact, her fear abated, but she still felt ice in the pit of her stomach. *Warmth.* She reached for the only thing she knew contained life, laying her palms against either side of the Kadis' face. Her senses opened to the warmth of his blood pulsing through his body. His pupils dilated but he didn't pull away until she nodded, swallowing, and dropped her hands.

*Move, Na'rina.*

The Kadis gripped her hand to lead her forward. They followed the outside curve of the deck—staying well clear of the anchor chains—until the chains ended and the rest of the vast deck opened up before them. Men wandered all over that expanse. Some were obviously guards but most seemed to be simple workers in plain clothing. The dark hoodie and jeans the Kadis gave her earlier fit right in. The Kadis halted to pull his beanie down even though the foundation he'd already applied hid the lines on his face. He then flipped Na'rina's hood up as he leaned in to say, "We have to pass the smokers to get through the hatch into the ship. I'll probably talk to a few, so follow my lead. And if you have to speak, lower your voice."

Na'rina's legs wobbled as they started forward. *What am I doing?* The Kadis had not reclaimed her hand and she found herself wanting the warmth of his callused fingers. By now they'd walked across the deck and she could see, far in front of them, another pair of figures strolling the aft deck. Understanding dawned. The Kadis was using the humans' normal movement as their disguise.

They approached the door—hatch—leading into the island of metal rising from the center of the ship. Several men leaned on the railing near the door to smoke. The odor carried, and Na'rina gagged.

"What're you up to?" one of them called as she and the Kadis came closer.

"Stretching our legs," the Kadis responded in a smooth Irish brogue. "We've been holed up fixing the electronics on one of the lab doors all day. The stupid thing is locked open and it's had the techies twitchy."

*Where did he learn that? How does he know what they'll expect?* But he must have done his research because the man chuckled and slapped the Kadis on the shoulder as they came within reach. The movement blocked their way forward but hid Na'rina as she lowered her head and coughed.

"Smoke?" the man offered.

The Kadis accepted a cigarette. "Don't mind if I do."

*What?*

"You?" The man held out the pack to Na'rina.

She opened her mouth to refuse and hesitated. She couldn't imitate an accent and her timbre wouldn't sound right.

"She quit recently," the Kadis answered for her.

Na'rina met the man's eyes, smiling her "no thanks." The man stared at her, captivated, until the Kadis snapped the lighter to life and lit his cigarette, breaking his fascinated stare.

Cigarette smoke hit Na'rina's nose and she swallowed the urge to vomit as she turned away to look out over the ocean.

"Quiet day," the Kadis observed, leaning on the railing beside her.

The man joined them. "Too quiet maybe."

Na'rina breathed shallowly, trying not to inhale the floating smoke. *Vile, nasty, repulsive!* The litany ran on but she kept her head down and swallowed the urge to vomit again.

"Too quiet?" the Kadis asked.

"They've made no progress and the deadline's coming up. It's not a big deal for us, but the scientists are nervous. I'm surprised you didn't notice today in the lab."

"Ah," the Kadis said, "I just assumed their edginess was due to the door."

"Nah." The man finished smoking and flicked the butt over the side. "Some suits showed up this morning. Guess they're pressing for results. Makes me glad I'm just a mechanic."

Shrugging, the man headed toward the door. "Back to work," he muttered as he disappeared inside, oblivious to the fury emanating off the Kadis.

Na'rina waited for the Kadis to move, but he continued to stare out at the ocean. Finally, she slid a hand down his arm, pinched his smoldering cigarette from between his knuckles, tossed it overboard, and twined her fingers with his. His tense eyes met hers and his nostrils flared. For once, that look didn't frighten her. It wasn't aimed at her, it was shared.

"Back to work," she whispered.

His grip tightened but he inclined his head and they continued into the ship. For a moment she'd forgotten her fear of the hollow, rumbling vessel. That fear engulfed her anew as they entered the metal shell. Her stomach clenched and Na'rina halted, swallowing hard.

"It's not alive," she tried to explain when the Kadis looked back at her.

"Neither will we be if they catch us." He stepped close, blocking her view of the narrow hallway. "Focus, Na'rina. You can do this." His utter confidence rolled through her the way the first touch of sunlight gave her strength each day. She pulled in a ragged breath and thrilled when the Kadis flashed a pleased grin before leading her farther down the metal hall.

*Silas can help find my mother,* she reminded herself, and continued to run through the reasons for this insane venture as she followed the Kadis. A group of humans approached ahead but the Kadis didn't slow. When they drew near, he pressed against the wall to let them pass. Na'rina did the same but thought she'd faint as she held her breath. The humans filed by single file, shoulders turned to fit the tight space but continuing their discussion without looking at them.

The Kadis gave her a thrilled smile and continued on. He led her down a metal ladder, through several open hatchways, then down another ladder and around a corner. They encountered more humans along the way, but every time the same thing happened. At one point, Na'rina watched wide-eyed as the Kadis palmed the ID badges right off the pockets of two passing humans without them noticing. He handed her one and clipped the other to his shirt.

It wasn't until they reached the third level down that anyone gave them a second glance.

"ID card," the guard demanded with a hand out. He stood before a door—*hatch, Na'rina, it's called a hatch*—blocking their path.

The Kadis handed him his ID. The guard scanned it and watched his screen. He looked up, looked back at the scanner, looked up.

In a flash, the Kadis grabbed the man, spun him around against his chest, holding him with one hand over his mouth and the other at his neck. Stark terror widened the human's eyes.

Na'rina couldn't bear it. Before she could think twice, she slammed an elbow into the guard's chin and he slumped. The Kadis' head swung toward her and his words *never distract me from my prey* flashed through her mind.

"Blood everywhere doesn't help us," she snapped.

The wer-im growled and tossed the body into a side room. He pulled the door shut and locked the hatch. "That'll shorten our time."

*So would blood. Gah! I hate violence!* Na'rina's elbow stung. *At least he's alive.* She tried to console her conscience, but the throb in her arm seemed to accuse her. Climbing down another ladder, Na'rina stopped short. They'd entered the laboratory floor and she felt like she'd just left behind a dark cave and the sun blinded her. Florescent lights glowed above the white and silver walls and shone through massive observation windows. She and the Kadis ducked in unison. Half the floor was visible through those windows from their vantage point and several white-coated forms worked in the rooms beyond. Still crouching, Na'rina pinched a lab coat from a hook by the ladder. There was only one. The name card pinned to the pocket read, "Dr. Sally Henderson."

The Kadis held it up while she slipped out of her hoodie and inserted her arms into the sleeves. He pulled the ball cap from her head.

"Keep your hair around your face," he whispered, then

gestured at the door.

A square plasma screen flanked the door leading into that windowed room. Na'rina wiped her sweat-sticky hands on her pants before she stood up and approached the device. Her heart beat against her ribs so hard the wer-im could probably hear it. Hovering her hand above the screen, not triggering it yet, she searched for the correct print. Unlike with the small tree devices, this one stored several to choose from. With a sinking realization, Na'rina started shuffling through the options. Each print trailed back to an information log. She searched for Dr. Henderson. After several tries, she found a Sally. *Gah! Wrong one.*

Na'rina continued, becoming more nervous the longer she stood in full view. The Kadis waited, crouched by her side. At this point they were winging it—they were now beyond where the wer-im infiltrated before—but that didn't seem to bother him.

*There!* "Sally M. Henderson, Doctor of Neurology." Na'rina formed the print and pressed the screen. The pulse made her gasp as the energy flowed into her pattern and keyed the door with a click and a faint whoosh. She gagged on the bitter taste of beetle, but thankfully, felt no drastic drain in her body. She braced herself anyway before stepping through the passageway.

A long hallway ran before them, dividing the floor in half. On both sides rose waist-high walls topped with windows.

Those walls and windows divided the floor into workspaces, some with computers, some with machines Na'rina couldn't name, and some with small lab tables where white-coated doctors worked.

There were no doors except for the one Na'rina could make out at the other end of the hallway. However, the workspaces were numbered. They started at 1A.

A nervous laugh threatened to escape Na'rina. *This is going to be a long walk.* She strode forward with her hair draped over her cheeks but her hands hung limp at her sides, shaking. Through the windows, she saw some humans holding clipboards. The next time she passed a wall cache she nabbed a board and gazed down at the letters and numbers on it. They blurred as she focused on her peripheral vision.

She stopped midway down the hall, frozen in the sea of windows and lights as the Kadis, crouched against the waist-high wall, stopped beside her, a frown pulling his dark brows together. He nudged her. Na'rina just glanced to her right and then back to the clipboard in her hand, flipping a page as if she were reading it. Getting the hint, the Kadis moved to the side of the next entryway and they listened in on the workspace's two occupants.

"—this stuff do?" one of the men inside was asking while he lifted a vial containing a sapphire liquid up to the light. His hair, slicked back like a shell against his head, caught

Na'rina's attention first but more than anything, his suit stood out—black in an area full of white lab coats.

"We thought it'd heal the water creatures but they didn't last long enough for us to test it. We had to throw them overboard. Haven't caught anymore yet, so here it sits."

The Kadis shook his head and ghosted down the hall, gesturing for her to keep up, but Na'rina lingered.

"I can't tell the board that," the suited man said with disgust. He tossed the vial back to the doctor. On the desk beside him sat several other vials, all labeled and sparkling different colors in the light. "None of these will convince the board to keep you. What else can you show me?" he barked, moving on to the next workspace before the other man could answer. The doctor set the vial into the next test-tube rack and scurried to catch up.

Na'rina stared at the tiny vial. She glanced away and pretended to scribble on the clipboard just as the doctor looked back. When he looked away again, she slipped inside the workspace, nabbed the tiny glass container, and slipped it into her pocket before rejoining the Kadis. He hissed. *Ignore him.* They'd told the oceanids they'd search for information. This wasn't much but at least she could show they tried.

After number 36A the hall ended and another plasma screen blocked their path. Na'rina pressed the screen, hoping Sally Henderson had access to this section. Sweat began to bead on Na'rina's forehead, and then, to her relief, energy pulsed and the door slid to the side. Instead of massive observation windows and workspaces, the hallway beyond was lined on both sides with doors. Each boasted a small, wired glass window but they were opaque enough a person would have to open the door to see inside. As they walked down the hall, Na'rina resisted the urge to pull one open just to see what was so secret.

The hall ended at room 52A. A plasma screen guarded yet another door—a windowless, steel-plated door designed to slide to the side instead of open in or out. In bold type, the door was labeled 52B. Na'rina gulped. Apparently even the humans had some understanding of what they were dealing with—but the question was, did they fear Silas specifically or would they treat any wer-im with such extra caution?

Just as Na'rina reached for the plasma screen she heard the soft *click* of a door opening behind them and froze. Panicked, she met the Kadis' startled eyes. He spun, grabbed the door handle to 52A, and they ducked into the room before anyone entered the hall behind them. A female doctor glanced up from where she stood by a form lying on the bed in the room. The alarm on her face melted as the Kadis pounced, slamming his fist down on the base of her neck. The doctor fell in a mass of lab coat and limbs to the floor.

"No blood," the Kadis muttered.

Na'rina flashed a smile, and then caught the *snick* of the

door to 52B sliding open. She spun, yanked 52A's door open and inserted her clipboard between the tiny gap of 52B's sliding door and the frame before it closed. Na'rina slipped past and into the room beyond.

Na'rina stood in a tiny antechamber, shocked at her luck because whoever entered the room before her had already moved through the second door and hadn't noticed her following. A faint acrid smell filled the small room. Na'rina wrinkled her nose as she approached the thin antechamber door to listen to the humans inside. She crouched beside the hinges, hoping to see through the small crack, but the door sat too tight to the frame.

"Where are we today?" a male voice asked. "Specifics, Doctor."

"We tried waking him," answered a female. "That didn't work, so we attempted to pull the desired result from the body without him conscious."

"And?"

There was a pause. Na'rina got the distinct impression the female didn't want to answer.

"And no dice," she said. "The Enhanced Ketamine

seems to be the one drug their bodies don't burn through but all the others were easy to pull out of their comatose states. This one, however, seems to have adapted to it. It knocked him out, but now his body's generating it on its own to keep him unconscious. It may be a defense mechanism, but without knowing how his body's doing it, I'm hesitant to proceed."

"And you're sure we can't use him without him aware?"

"Yes," the female whispered.

"Then use more invasive measures to wake him. We have to produce results."

"Hector?"

"What, Dr. Simms?"

Na'rina cringed at the irritation in the voice.

"I can almost believe he can speak if he wanted."

"This *animal* would slice your throat if it could. Never have these creatures achieved speech. They scream like any cat—but speech? Careful where your imagination takes you, Simms."

The door thumped from being hit and swung toward Na'rina. She backed against the wall as it almost pinned her.

"But I've studied them. They have the vocal cords and voice boxes!"

The door stopped. "Careful, Simms, or you'll lose this position."

The door swung open again. Before it closed, the doctor

keyed the outside and rushed through it in a huff, followed by the acrid scent.

Na'rina glimpsed the Kadis' furious eyes behind 52A's cracked door before 52B whisked shut again.

"You do have them, you know," Dr. Simms muttered from the other room.

An idea occurred to Na'rina. Dr. Simms wasn't convinced her subjects were just animals. Na'rina could work with that.

Na'rina slipped off her lab coat. Without it, her lithe, long-muscled dryadic body became obvious. That would probably be enough, but Na'rina wanted to be so striking it would leave Dr. Simms speechless.

Focusing inward, she washed a thin layer of zoi aima through her skin and the ashy white faded with a chill, replaced by her light spring green. The color reminded her of the underside of an aspen leaf. As an afterthought, Na'rina pulled her long hair up into a ponytail. She took a breath, rolled her shoulders back, and opened the inside door.

Monitors cramped the room beyond from floor to ceiling. Against the left wall sat a pudgy woman at a tiny metal desk. The woman, Dr. Simms, scribbled notes, only stopping to tuck stray hairs that escaped her chestnut bun behind her ear. This close to a human, Na'rina shuddered at how vulnerable she looked in her lab coat and khaki pants.

Looking away from her, Na'rina stared at the shiny metal slab dominating the center of the room. On it lay the largest wer-im she'd ever seen. Wires were attached to his head, his arms, his chest, even the soles of his feet where they protruded from the white sheet covering him. Fury flushed from Na'rina's head down through her torso like a boiling wave. Only a prolonged second, during which she held her breath to keep it from seething from between her teeth, kept her from expressing her anger. If the sight of Silas like this infuriated *her*, then it was a stroke of fate the Kadis hadn't followed her into the room.

"Dr. Simms," Na'rina greeted the heavyset woman when she was sure the words would not lash out from her, then, as she caught sight of the name plate, "Rebecca."

The woman spun in her chair and her mouth dropped open. After a frozen second, her fingernails scraped the bottom of her desk, searching for the small red button Na'rina could just make out beneath.

"Before you call for help," Na'rina moved to stand on the other side of Silas, "would you like to hear his voice?"

Dr. Simms' hand stilled. "His voice? He has no voice."

"Neither do I," Na'rina smiled at the irony, "according to some."

Rebecca Simms pivoted away from her desk, never taking her wide eyes off Na'rina. "He won't wake up."

Na'rina reached for the first wire. "Neither would I, if this were what I woke up to." She pulled the wire off his skin and one of the monitors went silent. The doctor gulped as Na'rina removed three more monitor wires.

"Then how do you wake him?" she whispered.

Removing two more wires, Na'rina placed a hand on Silas' chest and pulled the metal contraption from his head. A nearby screen turned black with a startled beep.

"Watch." Opening his collar enough to lay her palms on his chest, Na'rina concentrated on the blood in her veins, on the warmth and the zoi aima that made up her life. She didn't need to touch Silas' lifeblood, she just had to raise his temperature and the rate of his heart to burn off the drug keeping him under. It was a process of streaming zoi aima into him instead of shooting it, but the idea remained the same.

At first nothing happened. Na'rina's zoi aima met something sluggish as though she were trying to fill mud with lifeblood. Then Silas' chest heaved on a sigh and the resistance lessened when one of the unattached monitors sang.

Dr. Simms' mouth hung open. As Na'rina streamed even more zoi aima into the wer-im, his hands clenched and his heart thudded heavily beneath her palms, pulsing out a flood of the wer-im's own zoi aima, flushing it through his body in waves. Na'rina marveled at its vibrancy. She wasn't connected to that rushing, churning life, but that didn't mean she couldn't sense just how vital and volatile it was in nature. The monitor sang, its pitch hitting a high note, and then it flickered, warbled and tried to restart, but the overload continued and it blew out with a static pop.

Dr. Simms' eyes flicked between Na'rina and the blown-out monitor. Silas screamed, and the doctor jumped.

Na'rina's heart clenched. She thought she'd killed him for a moment as his heart stuttered, but then the cry rounded out into the gritty roar of a mountain lion and his eyes snapped open—brilliantly green gemstone eyes. Na'rina jerked her hands away and he snatched her wrist before she stepped back.

"Mona'rina?" As he studied her face his brows drew together in confusion.

"His voice!" Dr. Simms gasped, her hands fluttering. "They'll want you both. They said you were in the area but they never thought you'd come here. *Oh, dear*—" she cried as Silas slid off the slab toward her. She shoved backward in her chair but smacked against the desk, well within his reach. He clutched her throat in one massive hand, a snarl revealing his long canines. Dr. Simms gurgled, feebly struggling to pull off the punishing fingers gripping her.

"*Silas!*" Na'rina lunged across the table and grabbed his arm, again thanking her stars the Wer-Kadis wasn't in the room. Silas turned those bright eyes on her, and her heart rate stuttered with a fear he could probably smell. "*Na*, Silas."

He blinked, scanning her face as when he mistook Na'rina for her mother. It was an intense look but she could not say what he wanted to find. His snarl melted into something devoid of feeling. Its coldness made her shiver, but at least when he turned back to the doctor, he no longer seemed intent on slicing her throat.

"Stupid woman," he growled, smacking her temple with his fist.

Na'rina jumped at the harsh *thwack*. The doctor slumped in her chair. *She's still alive,* Na'rina assured herself as she saw the pulse in Dr. Simms' neck.

"My clothes?" Silas asked, now focused in a way that reminded her of the Wer-Kadis. Looking at the light surgical trousers and thin shirt he wore, she agreed he'd stand out once they left the lab deck. Na'rina glanced around and shrugged when she came up empty.

"There's a lab coat." She pointed toward the antechamber.

"That'll do," Silas said. He followed her and shrugged into the coat. The shoulders stretched taut across his back but when he slouched it didn't stand out as much as the thin shirt.

"Your skin," he reminded her, raising a hand toward her face like he might touch her cheek. Na'rina swayed away, shocked at the familiarity. But he was right. A layer of zoi aima returned her skin to ashy white and cleared her head before she moved to key open the door.

This time she didn't have to search for the print because only two, the male doctor and Rebecca Simms, existed. The door *snicked* open. Na'rina glanced down the hall and then dashed into 52A where she smacked into the Kadis and stepped back as he gripped her arms. The depth of irritation in his gaze froze her.

"What part of staying close don't you get?" he asked.

"Icarus," Silas said.

She sagged as the Kadis released her to embrace his mentor like he would a family member.

"What of that one?" Na'rina gestured to the form on the bed.

"Dead," the Kadis warned. "Half dissected."

Na'rina stopped mid-step. She'd been about to look but now her stomach rolled.

"Wer-im?"

"Dryad."

Na'rina's nausea grew and she spun away to find the Kadis behind her. He embraced her as she swayed. She clutched handfuls of his shirt and buried her face in the fabric, for once purposefully breathing in his spicy scent to obscure any other smell.

*"Why?"*

"Come, Na'rina." The Kadis' breath brushed through

her hair. "You can fall apart once we're back on land."

Her fists tightened before she forced herself to let go.

Silas rolled the unconscious doctor back against the wall and pulled off her lab coat.

"You stand out, Drydanda," he said, holding it open for her. She hesitated to step closer to him, then, steeling herself, let him slip the white coat onto her shoulders before she pulled her hair free of her ponytail.

"Let's go." The Kadis held the door and they slipped out. The hall of secret doors shone, mockingly bright now that she had an idea of what lay behind them. She couldn't wait to be free of the metal ship and its cruel experiments. Keying open the next door, she stuffed her hands in her pockets and walked beside Silas while the Kadis, crouching, followed behind.

Silas, although huge and broad-shouldered for a human, had none of the telltale signs that would give the Kadis away. He displayed neither the distinctive lines nor tufted ears. In fact, the only thing marking him as inhuman were his large, brilliant green eyes, which slanted up at the corners. His other features seemed softened; aggressive but not so angular that he resembled a cat. Na'rina couldn't put her finger on why, but between the two, the Kadis seemed more wer-im and Silas other. The fluorescent lights gave his skin a milky brown cast. He garnered such respect from the others of his species, yet her mother never mentioned him. Considering his age, it was likely he'd been involved in the banishment. And even waking from a sedative, he'd mistaken her for the Mother Drydanda. He'd clearly known Mona'rina.

When they finally reached the last door to the labs, Na'rina touched her palm to the screen, heard the *snick* of the door, and then two voices arguing at the base of the ladder. She glanced up but the humans didn't notice them leaving the lab. Na'rina went with it.

"I swear I didn't forget to log out. There's a glitch in your stupid system!"

"It hasn't glitched in months. If you weren't absentminded, you wouldn't have an issue."

Na'rina's heart pounded as they passed the humans on their way to the ladder. She expected second by second for the humans to look over.

"I need to be logged into my station in five minutes. I can't do that if the locks say I'm already in the labs."

Na'rina stumbled. *Sally Henderson.*

The Kadis climbed up the ladder. Silas's claws pricked Na'rina's skin as he grabbed her arm and pushed her to precede him. Na'rina clutched the metal rungs with clammy hands, thankful her sap added to her grip. Behind her, Dr. Henderson huffed toward the door and slapped her palm to the screen.

"See, I—" She cut short as the door whooshed open. "Stupid piece of—"

"It's not a glitch. If you wouldn't..."

Silas followed her up the ladder wearing a wicked grin. *They didn't notice!* Na'rina couldn't believe it. She grinned back as they joined the Kadis.

"Almost there." He held out her hoodie and ball cap and she shucked out of the lab coat before pulling them on. For Silas, he held out a dark brown canvas coat he'd pinched from a coatrack along the way.

They kept moving. Na'rina's need to be away from the ship, now that they'd freed Silas, itched in her skin. The Kadis led the way through doors and up ladders and she marveled at his sense of direction in this dead jungle. Silas followed on silent feet as he stretched his neck and shoulders, enjoying his newfound freedom. *How long has he been a captive?* Na'rina couldn't remember if the Kadis had ever said. Halfway up the last ladder, the ship erupted with sirens and a rumbling that vibrated in Na'rina's skull. Speakers crackled to life, repeating, "All hands to stations."

The Kadis took her by the wrists and hauled her up the last few rungs. "We have to be off the ship before it starts to move!" he shouted, pushing her toward the outside door leading to the smoke deck. Dashing through, Na'rina stopped short. Armed men swarmed the ship. Rifles, Na'rina realized, as the moonlight slid across the weapons' black barrels. The humans rushed to line the railing of the ship. She looked to the forward bow and felt the deep rumbling of the anchor chains against the deck in the soles of her feet. Those chains grated, metal against metal, as they lifted from the water like massive snakes. The Kadis and Silas halted behind her as they evaluated the situation. Watching the chains move, Na'rina targeted the one open area of the deck.

Grabbing her left shoe, she yanked it off and pitched it. The right one followed it over the side. A group of men on the aft spotted them and yelled. The Kadis spun to confront them but Na'rina seized his arm with a sharp "*Na!*" She tugged him in the opposite direction—toward the channel between the moving chains. Malon's warning about finding pieces if the huge links caught them echoed in her mind. With that danger, the men wouldn't step over the writhing chains to block them, so the key lay in speed. She and the wer-im needed to run. They needed to be past the men before they aimed those rifles.

If that wasn't enough, they needed the momentum to vault over the ship's bull nose and leap into the ocean. It had to be a powerful lunge. Na'rina pictured the anchors coming up and the ship moving forward. The Kadis wouldn't have an issue clearing the ship with his powerful legs, but she and Silas needed speed.

She stretched her legs into a sprint and the nonskid bit into the soles of her feet. *Faster.* Men blurred around her. *Faster.* One of the chains paused, caught on something, and broke free.

It lurched, writhing into a snake curve at Na'rina's feet. She skipped over it and when she landed she felt the faint thud of two others landing behind her. *Faster!* Na'rina raced toward the railing and jumped. Planting a foot, she pushed off and soared out over the ship's nose, rolling into a dive as the wind tore her cap free and whistled past her ears. One thud of her heartbeat, she was air born, and the next, she slammed into the icy water.

The freezing ocean slammed into Na'rina. Breath rushed from her lungs, and she fought to swim for the surface. *Where's up?* Hands grabbed her shoulders, pulling her deeper. Na'rina flailed as the pressure on her body grew painful.

*It'll crush me!*

She thrashed but then the hands clasped her face and a mouth met her own, forcing air into her chest.

The blurry face clarified and Na'rina saw the silvery hair and blue eyes of Owasha. Na'rina clung to the oceanid as the water *thrummed* and the ships above began moving, beating clouds of bubbles in their wake. Owasha clasped Na'rina's face again and breathed more air into her lungs. Only when the ships were gone did Owasha swim upward, hauling Na'rina with her. As they broke the surface, a cool breeze chilled Na'rina's scalp and she sucked in a delicious gulp of air.

She glanced around for the others but they were nowhere in sight.

"Do you swim, Dryad?" Owasha asked.

Na'rina looked back to Owasha and recalled the vial in her pocket, wondering if it was still there—and intact. "Not well," she admitted.

"Good." The oceanid plunged her below the surface and held her there.

Na'rina froze, shocked. Her lungs began to scream for oxygen and she thrashed against Owasha's arms. It did no good. Owasha's grip only tightened in her hair. Finally, the oceanid returned them to the surface, night, stars, and ocean spinning as Na'rina's vision narrowed with black gnats. She sputtered and drank in as much air as possible.

"Where is she, Dryad?" Owasha demanded.

"*What?* Who?"

Owasha dragged Na'rina back under the water, then hauled her up again, pulling them nose-to-nose. "I could kill you."

"You could—but why?"

The grip tightened further, bringing tears to Na'rina's eyes.

"She's close enough to the water I can almost taste her filth," Owasha sneered. "Where is the oread?"

*Rosharu?*

"The wer-im," Na'rina rasped. "They drove her away."

Owasha dunked her again. "Lies! I feel the vibration of her steps. She searched the shore where the boat was docked.

Why?"

"I don't know!" Na'rina snapped, coughing up water.

Owasha pulled her under and they sank. Na'rina's zoi aima flushed to her skin to warm her and fight the pressure of the cold ocean. It carried a flush of rage so strong she vented zoi aima out her hands to keep it from splitting her skin. The oceanid flinched. *Enough of this!* Clapping her hands to Owasha's temples, Na'rina shoved zoi aima into her head. The oceanid's hands convulsed and let go long enough to latch onto her throat. Na'rina shot out again but the zoi aima went wide as another set of hands forced them apart. The water around them hardened, encasing Na'rina and Owasha in separate marble-like spheres.

*Alaya!* Na'rina braced for another attack. It didn't come. Instead, Alaya guided their globes upward. When they broke the surface, Na'rina's globe turned liquid again and sluiced back into the ocean. She gulped air, exhausted. *If they attack me now, I'm done for*, she thought, and tilted onto her back to float.

"Let me finish!" Owasha cried, trying to push her sister out of the way.

"You threaten a Drydanda? Have you gone insane?" Alaya shoved Owasha backwards.

"I can smell the oread on her."

"Drydanda have amnesty among all mythics! You want the Dryad Council to exact punishment? To force you onto dry land for a bitter end? Calm down, Sister. The Drydanda boarded the ship to help us."

Owasha spit, sending up a small geyser where her saliva plunked into the ocean. "Our sisters are beyond help. I will never give safe harbor to her," she shot a finger at Na'rina, "or any Drydanda who smells of mountains." Owasha dove and disappeared.

Alaya's shoulders slumped.

"Thank you," Na'rina croaked.

"Don't." The expression on Alaya's silvery face was bitter, not sad, as Na'rina expected. "Bringing the oread this close to the ocean was asking for trouble."

"*Why?* Perhaps I expect nymphs to be peaceful because I'm a dryad, but Rosharu's been kind to me."

Alaya flinched at the name. She eyed Na'rina with consternation before scoffing, "Peaceful? Kind?" She seemed to chew on the words as she pulled Na'rina's floating form toward the shore.

"You think I'm naïve," Na'rina stated.

"*Na*, Drydanda," Alaya disagreed. "Naïve is the wrong term. You seem to be untouched by nymph history. That's dangerous for you."

Na'rina's feet touched sand and she stood to walk the rest of the way. Alaya followed her out of the water and Na'rina couldn't help a small smile. *Oceadanda.* Just like a dryad could not travel far from her tree unless she was a Drydanda, an oceanid could not leave the ocean. Alaya was one of the ocean's few leaders. This explained why Owasha did not attempt to break Alaya's water globes. She might argue with her sister, but she could not overpower her.

"Dangerous for me?" Na'rina asked.

Alaya gestured back at the ocean and shrugged. "Our long, sordid history clouds our wisdom. You're in a unique position to avoid all that and see us for who we are."

Alaya turned to stare at the distant lights of the ships as they disappeared from sight. Alaya sighed and moved to reenter the ocean.

"Wait!" Na'rina patted her pockets. Wonder of wonders, the tiny vial remained intact. "We didn't find much to help your sisters but one of the doctors made this to heal them. It's untested," she warned, "but it might be of use to you."

The Oceadanda cradled the vial in her long fingers. "A part of me knew the wer-im did not plan to help us tonight. It is their nature to be single-minded and they were after their own answers." The tide lapped at her feet like it called to her. In the darkness, she was a silvery wraith against the gray, seething waves.

Felis and Malon had boarded the Sansabria, but they didn't have a Drydanda with them to open the doors. Anything they did, then, would have set off alarms. As the Kadis had said, they'd been a distraction, not a search party. Na'rina wasn't about to insult Alaya by denying that.

Alaya smiled goodbye and then she was gone, a silvery flash in the water.

For a moment Na'rina just stared at the spot where the Oceadanda had been standing. *What history is Alaya referring to?* Flashes of the Collective Wisdom tumbled through Na'rina's mind, but none of it gave her answers. Her world was expanding, shifting, changing at an alarming rate and the odd council meeting or ambassador trip had not prepared her for the intricacies in dealing with the other mythics.

Too exhausted to put together the pieces, her knees gave out and she crumpled to lay on the wet sand. Her neck throbbed and swallowing grated her sore throat. The night felt unreal. A giggle escaped her. Stretching her arms above her head, Na'rina lengthened her spine and pointed her toes to relieve the ache traveling all the way from her hair to her heels.

She tilted her head back to gaze at the boardwalk, wondering about the wer-im. In her upside-down state, the trees beyond looked like the world's hair flipped over to hang free. Had they cleared the ship? Had Alaya brought them to shore before helping her? *Are they even alive?* Na'rina rolled over and pushed to her feet as her elation evaporated. Dark gnats swarmed her vision. She braced herself to keep from falling over, blinking until her vision returned to normal.

Sand stuck to her clothes and skin. She brushed at it

while scanning the cove. Driftwood, scattered across the beach, reached like bony fingers into the dark sky. Otherwise, the shore lay empty. After days of being under constant supervision, the stillness felt eerie.

"Hello? Wer-Kadis? Silas?" The crash of the waves drowned out her voice. He'd promised to help free Mona'rina! What if he'd abandoned her, or they hadn't—

*"Na'rina!"*

She turned just as the Kadis caught her by the waist, lifting and spinning her in a circle. The world blurred and Na'rina hung onto his shoulders as his spicy scent filled her head. She soaked in his elation just as she would the heady high of the noonday sun. Hiccupping giggles, Na'rina buried her face against his neck until they passed.

"I wasn't sure you'd made it."

"Alaya dropped us ashore up the coast," the Kadis explained, lowering her to the sand. Na'rina clung to him in a sudden desire to hang on. For a brief moment of shared elation, she'd felt connected, like when she stood within her Rina.

"You risked a great deal this evening, Drydanda," Silas interrupted.

Na'rina forced herself to step back from the Kadis to address Silas. "You can return the favor."

The big wer-im's eyes shone, but he wasn't watching her. The disapproval in his gaze was aimed at the Kadis. The Kadis went still under that scrutiny but then he lifted his chin in defiance.

"First we need food and rest," Silas said, breaking the stare. "You're looking wane, Drydanda, and for a creature who starts out ashy white, that's saying something." He held out an arm for them to walk with him.

Na'rina woke to splotches of sunshine playing across her face as the breeze rustled the leaves of the red oak towering above her. The shape of the leaves reminded her of a turkey's foot. She smiled. Although different from her Rina, the oak's zoi aima also held a sweet tang that filled her with the desire to dance.

Instead of returning to the demolished clearing, they had moved farther inland before settling in the previous night. Na'rina glanced around her. No Kadis, but Silas lay curled in a ball still asleep. His light brown skin shone translucent in the sun. His time in the labs must have dulled any deeper color he'd once had. She watched the older wer-im wake, stretching and arching his back before opening his brilliant green eyes. If anything, they looked more vibrant in the sunlight.

"Good Morning, Drydanda."

"Morning, Wer-Kadis."

"I am not the Kadis. Call me Silas."

Na'rina tilted her head. "I thought you were the Wer-Kadis before—"

"It is Icarus' place now."

"Wasn't he just filling in for you?"

Silas smiled but his expression carried something hard. "He may see it that way, but now it is his responsibility."

Na'rina shook her head and her hair fell around her shoulders. She knew, without knowing how, that this would not be welcome news to the wer-im. They expected Icarus to pass the leadership back to Silas, but if Silas refused to accept it? *How will they respond?* Strangely enough, she suspected the Kadis would take it the hardest.

"They expect you to lead."

Silas turned his face into the sunshine and closed his eyes. "We shall see."

"See what?" Felis appeared from behind where Na'rina sat. The Kadis followed him.

"Nothing," Silas said. "You ask too many questions."

"You rarely answer them," Felis shot back.

Their banter, light but edged, struck Na'rina as oddly informal. But then she remembered, they rarely acted together as a pride. Although Felis respected Silas, feared him even, their social structure was not as—honed—as that of the dryads.

Silas eyed their group. "Where's Tarn?"

Felis stole an almost guilty glance as the Kadis, but he just walked over to Na'rina and held out a paper bag. Na'rina looked between the three wer-im before accepting it. She peeked inside the bag and was delighted to find it contained a variety of berries.

"I've given him a task," the Kadis finally answered.

"Bit vague," Silas noted, frowning. "How long?"

"Awhile. Felis, show him."

A poignant silence fell as Silas and the Kadis stared at each other. Finally, Silas looked away from his protégé, and gestured for Felis to show him one of the devices. The Kadis settled beside Na'rina and chewed on a piece of meat. Was he as unconcerned as he seemed? Faint lines crinkled the corners of his hazel eyes. Was he angry, ashamed, hurt? Na'rina couldn't tell. She almost blurted out what Tarn had said to her, but decided to hold her silence.

Silas took the device and pulled it apart piece by piece, laying each section on the ground with sure movements. Getting down to the core, a round disc, he rotated it in his hands, inspecting it before laying it flat on his palm. The disc began to glow and a corresponding vibration echoed in Na'rina's chest. Silas growled and the disc glowed brighter. He stood and, with the same gritty roar she'd heard in the lab, he pitched the core against a tree. It shattered, tiny pieces whizzing in all directions. Na'rina cried out and shrank back, hand raised protectively. When she chanced a peek around, she saw several metal shards lodged in the bark of the red oak.

*Ouch,* the oak grumbled. Thankfully his thick bark took the abuse with little sign of damage. Silas yanked the pieces free, cursing as he ground them into the rich dirt.

"You have more of these?"

"Two more," Felis answered.

*Where did he find another device?* Na'rina didn't chance asking the question.

"Destroy them," Silas ordered.

"But—"

"Destroy them," the Kadis reiterated before the older wer-im flew into more of a rage.

Hands up, Felis backed away before pivoting on his heel and disappearing into the trees.

*Should I make myself scarce, too?* Before she could decide, the Kadis flicked the paper bag in her lap with his finger. "Eat. He'll calm down shortly and explain."

Only then did she notice that the Kadis was finishing his breakfast. He must have been eating the entire time. He scraped the last bit of meat off a bone, then went to bite into it. Catching her watching, he stopped and slipped it into his pocket.

Na'rina shuddered, imagining the crunch of teeth against bone. Although he'd stopped short, her mind went there anyway. "You're saving that for later?"

He eyed her, then nodded.

"Why?"

One eyebrow went up, but Na'rina just waited for an answer. Alaya spoke about being open to understanding the other mythics. This was as good a place as any to start.

"Calcium," the Kadis answered. "We derive calcium from bones."

It was so logical she could only utter, *"Oh,"* in understanding. She'd heard dryads speak of the practice in reference to the species' violence, as if their nature demanded they destroy their food down to the marrow. Yet it was for the nutritional content. *How easy it is for us to misunderstand one another.* Uneasiness settled over Na'rina like a cloak. *What else do I not understand?*

The Kadis flicked the paper bag again and Na'rina realized he'd been watching the play of emotions across her face, reading her with those knowing eyes. Embarrassed, she looked inside the bag. With a thumb and forefinger, she picked out a metal shard that had punctured the flimsy paper and landed in the berries.

Silas grimaced, took the shard, and pitched it over his shoulder before settling cross-legged in front of them.

"What was that?" she asked.

Silas smirked. Red tinted his cheeks still but the rest of his expression spoke of calm. The rapid change put Na'rina on edge. *How does he not get emotional whiplash?*

"Someone's putting out feelers," he explained, accepting a cut of meat from the Kadis. "The device registers energy, or zoi aima, and transmits the location when a surge triggers its power source."

Dread hit Na'rina. How many times in practicing opening the devices had she sent out a beacon? *Here I am. Come get me.* Then Silas' words registered. Only a Drydanda sent her zoi aima into a tree not her own.

"That means it targets Drydanda," she whispered, frowning. "But why would you care? The Drydanda banished you."

Her words were ill-thought. Silas flinched, and she wished she could eat them. But, as he kept doing, that brief shock of pain on his face transformed into a flash of teeth, meant to be a smile, and he tore off a bite of meat instead of answering. While he chewed, he seemed to consider his response. As they waited for him to continue, the Kadis leaned over to look inside the bag of berries. Na'rina held it up. He reached in, took a handful, and tossed them into his mouth. Then he reached for a few more.

"Whoever constructed the devices had to understand the Drydanda's abilities," Silas explained. "That suggests either the humans know more than we expected—or a mythic is helping them." He held up his hands like he weighed both sides, and then he shrugged. "Plus, the devices have been placed here on the East Coast, where no Drydanda has been born in centuries. Are they unaware of that and are throwing a wide net or," here, he pointed at Na'rina, "did they know a Drydanda would be here now? No matter how I look at it, these humans know too much. They captured me and are now after you. There's plenty to piss me off."

Na'rina swallowed. *I am a target.* Her hand froze in the act of pulling berries from the bag. The Kadis nudged her hand and she popped the handful into her mouth, grateful for the gentle way he'd reminded her to move. "But what do they want from me?"

"I haven't figured that out yet." Silas finished the meat and stuffed the bone into his pocket. Perhaps he'd seen the Kadis do it before, but somehow, she doubted it.

The Kadis broke the ensuing silence. "The Mother Drydanda is in trouble. How would you like to go about helping her?"

Silas' nostrils flared. "That would be up to you."

"You are Wer-Kadis," Icarus countered.

"I am not."

"You are."

Na'rina set down the paper sack and pressed her back against the red oak. *Here they go.* Her lungs constricted as the two eyed each other. Silas' bigger build would give him an advantage in a fight, but Icarus reminded her of that eerie stillness just before a storm. She couldn't guess who would win in a fight and she did not want to witness one to find out.

Silas flashed that grin—the one underscored by resolve. "I will not take back that responsibility." His eyes flickered toward Na'rina, then away. He snorted, breaking the taught stillness as he shook his head and rose. "Walk with me."

The Kadis considered for a long moment before rising to join the older wer-im. He was so difficult to read that Na'rina could not fathom his reaction to his mentor. Shock? Confusion? One thing, however, caused her to slump in relief.

*They didn't fight.*

*They will,* the red oak assured her.

Her hands shook as she picked up the sack and tried to pop a raspberry into her mouth. It dropped into her lap. Scooping it up, she caught Felis entering the clearing, holding the destroyed pieces of the devices.

He glanced around. "Where'd they go?"

"On a walk." Na'rina's voice came out airy, but steady.

Felis shook his head. "Strange ones, those two."

She agreed but, with the other two absent at the moment, she had a more pressing question. "Why is Tarn such an issue?"

"He's loyal." Felis shrugged. "With Silas' capture, Tarn was the one to watch Icarus' back before Icarus even knew he needed it."

"Ugh. Challenging him for leadership was watching his back? Nope, don't answer that. I've heard the logic." Na'rina threw up her hands. "Okay, explain this instead. The Kadis ordered Tarn to stay with La'meliai but Silas doesn't like that decision. Why?"

Felis gave a devilish grin. "Silas figured he didn't need to worry about Icarus as long as he had Tarn to advise him. Now he's finding out his protégé doesn't always fall in line." Felis paused, scratching his beard while he considered. "I think Icarus played it right. Leaving Tarn behind made it look like he was weaker. Some tried to oppose him and now he knows who those wer-im are. It strengthened his position in the long run."

"Complicated," she said.

"Yeah," Felis agreed.

Darkness, misty with the stirrings of hidden animals, had fallen by the time Silas and Icarus returned. Their soundless reappearance made the hair on Na'rina's arms stand on end. Smoothing the sensitive hairs, she shrank back into the shadows, hoping to remain unnoticed.

Silas headed straight for her, however, while the Kadis never looked her way. Na'rina stared after him as he paced to the far side of the small clearing. *What happened?*

Silas cupped her chin and forced her to look at him. She flinched, startled, but he did not release her.

"Na'rina Drydanda, *nothing* can interfere tonight. Understand?"

Na'rina's stomach sank. His words raised gooseflesh along her arms.

"Understand?"

"No interference," she whispered.

His gem-like eyes narrowed. "Give him your complete

support."

"What?"

"Give Icarus your complete support."

Na'rina grabbed his arms and his muscles quivered under her fingers. "We just saved you. You can't throw that away."

Silas stood, breaking her hold, without responding.

"Silas, please!" Na'rina pleaded but he turned away, sweeping into the center of the clearing without looking back. He raised his hands in a demand for attention. Na'rina gasped as dozens of eyes peered out of the darkness. The wer-im had gathered.

"Tonight," Silas announced, "we two, who have known the taste of Wer-Kadis, will decide the flow of leadership from this point forward by the Kadivas. No interference is permitted. To interfere is death. The winner must prevail unequivocally— either in the death of his opponent or in his complete subjugation."

Growls rumbled in response and the forest held its breath like a tiny creature startled by the passing of a predator. Excitement edged that wariness. Only Felis seemed disturbed by the pronouncement. "They'll kill each other." He moved to step forward.

Na'rina seized his arm, stopping him. He growled and she slapped him across the face. Felis gaped. *What's gotten into me?* She pulled back, shocked at the sting in her palm.

"You know the rules," she hissed, forcing him to sit. "You interfere—they'll kill you."

"This is a disaster." Felis sagged. "They have to fight, but one of them is about to die."

"Maybe not," Na'rina said, hoping the Kadis wouldn't throw everything away after saving Silas.

Felis just gave her a withering sneer.

Na'rina groaned. If either wer-im died tonight, her best chance to save her mother would turn to dust. She looked away from Felis just as Silas and the Kadis rushed each other, claws drawn and teeth bared. If there'd been a call for the Kadivas to start, she'd missed it. She cringed, raising a hand to cover her eyes, but then she went still, watching in horrified fascination. Na'rina knew it wasn't the clash of their bodies that would haunt her memory but the tearing of flesh. This wasn't just a show so the wer-im would accept Icarus' leadership. Blood dripped from slashes across arms, backs, and chests as Silas and the Kadis danced around each other, their skin glistening with sweat in the silvery light of the moon.

A chill traveled Na'rina's spine. The Kadis had fought similar fights in the Kadivas after Silas' capture. As far as she knew, he bore no scars from those challenges. As blood dripped from his chest now, she grasped how severe his injuries would have to be to leave marks. Even as she watched, the scratches across his chest began to close. They'd leave no trace.

Na'rina cried out as they charged again. Crashing into each other, they hit the ground in a shower of debris and rolled, covered in dirt as it stuck to their wounds. It was obvious Silas and the Kadis were evenly matched.

Felis pulled at her sleeve "Drydanda, what are they doing?"

Na'rina frowned. *His* leaders were fighting, but then she followed his eyes upward. The limbs of the trees swayed in the breeze—but no wind kissed her skin with the warm scent of earth or leaves. And yet the branches creaked, swaying and scraping against one another almost like a grove of widow-makers.

Na'rina laid a curious palm to the nearest root. With a cry, she jerked away. "They're *angry*." Anger seethed through oak and pine, ash and maple in an all-encompassing radius around the clearing. They *hated* the wer-im in the clearing.

A thud followed by cracking limbs brought Na'rina back to the fight. Icarus fell through the branches of the pine Silas threw him against. He twisted to land on his feet. The boughs above reached, bowing the tree's trunk in their desire to capture him before he moved away.

Na'rina slapped her palm against the red oak's trunk and shouted, *Na!* Every tree within psychic earshot shuddered. Their shock zinged into her skull and settled into a throbbing headache, but the tree reaching for Icarus straightened.

"What are they doing?" Felis repeated when Icarus again came close to the pine and it bowed, missing catching him only due to its bare lower trunk. Its upper branches waved in frustration.

"I don't know!" Na'rina admitted.

Icarus lunged at Silas, those powerful legs giving him a startling amount of distance and force. His shoulder slammed into Silas' chest with a thud that Na'rina felt in her ribs and the two tumbled over each other, kicking up dirt and leaves. The trees shuddered, branches creaking as though they, too, felt the impact. They fought Na'rina's control when the wer-im rolled over their roots.

*Do they know something I don't?* Na'rina hesitated, and a pine's branches reached for the combatants.

"Na'rina!" Felis gripped her arm and his claws dug into her skin. "You must stop them."

"Why are they reacting like this?"

"Does it matter?" Felis shook her. "You can't let them interfere or it'll invalidate the Kadivas."

But the forest never acted without reason. Only twice had she seen a tree behave on this level without the direct influence of a dryad. Both times the pine feared for his dryad's life. Na'rina scanned the area for a nymph hiding within any of the nearby trees. It was unlikely she would have missed seeing one before now but nothing else made sense. *Nothing.*

As the Kadis vaulted off another oak, the tree snapped his gnarled limbs around the wer-im's torso, sending leaves fluttering to the ground in a shocking disregard of his new growth. There was a whoosh of air from the wer-im's lungs.

"If he dies, the wer-im won't help Mona'rina!"

Felis' words sent a shock through her. *Mamma, this makes no sense.* But Felis was right. Once the forest calmed, Na'rina would demand an explanation, but for now her mother's survival mattered more.

Na'rina jumped to her feet, laying her palms against the trunk of the oak closest to her. Fire shot into her bones. Her knees wobbled and she nearly fell over. *So much anger!* It burned along her nerves and made her bones ache.

*Enough!* The command ricocheted through the nearby root systems until it reached the tree holding Icarus. Silas paced, watching but not taking advantage of his opponent's vulnerability—and staying well away from the trees. With a shudder, the oak released his prisoner, and Na'rina wondered if this was what it felt like for Mona'rina when she took over another dryad's tree.

Icarus dropped through the branches and twisted midair to land on his feet. Instantly, the wer-im went at each other again. Anger surged through Na'rina's palms, coating the oak's zoi aima with a reddish tinge. Blood thudded behind her ears as she tried to soothe the tree. Her eyes glazed under the strain and the violence in the clearing blurred and became an echo of bloody growls.

Silas and the Kadis rolled toward the perimeter, over a mass of exposed maple roots. A howl reverberated inside the living wood as the roots shifted to capture the wer-im.

*Na!* Na'rina shouted, heart pounding.

*You must give him your complete support.* Had Silas known the trees would react? Her stomach knotted. The forest sensed her lack of concentration, snatching on the chance to slip past her control.

*Na!* Everything shuddered.

The forest stiffened in shock and their roots stirred, disturbing the ground in a faint quake.

Silas' head swung toward her. His brilliant gemstone eyes glowed with a desire for blood she'd seen before in the unreasoning eyes of true, mindless predators. He stepped toward her. Icarus spun him, catching him off guard and planting him on his back. A howl, a gritty, high-pitched yowl of frustration ripped out of Silas's throat.

Na'rina swayed. She'd started to trust the wer-im on some level, maybe because they always held their violence in check with a disarming, self-effacing awareness. But here, Silas wanted blood. The coldly reasoned wer-im was not in evidence.

*Hold!* She sent the command deep into the roots. *We*

*must not interfere. My mother's life depends on this!* The forest groaned, torn between its lust to capture the wer-im and a deep desire to listen to her, a Drydanda.

Silas planted his feet against Icarus' chest and shoved, sending the Kadis flying.

He landed near a pine, which tensed.

*Be still!*

The tree didn't move to capture the wer-im. Free, Silas spun toward Na'rina, but before he could attack, Icarus pulled him back.

"What's the matter with him?" Felis wondered.

Na'rina couldn't respond. Silas' vengeful intentions were now clear. He meant to attack her—even to the detriment of defeating Icarus. *Why?* Na'rina trembled as Silas again tried to launch himself across the clearing at her. Icarus yanked him off balance and a gritty howl ripped from the jewel-eyed wer-im's throat as he hit the ground. Silas held Na'rina's eyes in an intense, unwavering glare.

His irises quivered.

The trees shuddered. Na'rina felt it course through her limbs, unable to tell if her own shock caused it or if the forest was reacting to the change in Silas. His brilliant green eyes blinked and the irises quivered before snapping to thin slits.

Na'rina's blood chilled.

The older wer-im convulsed and then, as molten metal

flows into a mold, Silas' body lengthened, the nose and mouth pulled out while his forehead rolled back and his ears became rounded hollows. A deafening cheer rose from the spectators but Felis repeatedly whispered, "It can't be…"

The mountain lion turned on Icarus, swiping a paw across his face and neck and opening the left side of the wer-im's head. Icarus' body spun and he crumpled. Silas pivoted on his hind legs and the moonlight shifted across his tawny fur. The texture looked mossy—but Na'rina didn't have time to puzzle over that as Silas' muscles coiled and he sprang.

*"Icarus!"* Na'rina screamed and slammed her forehead against the oak's bark with a shock at the base of her skull. The tree accepted her melding with a soundless concussion to the air. Disoriented, Na'rina still felt the shudder as Silas slammed against the trunk where she'd stood an instant earlier. Before he could rise, a dark shape landed on his back and locked arms around his leonine chest. Silas tried to break free, his long teeth gnashing at his captor's hands. In a flash, those strong fingers slid upward in a locked position behind the lion's head.

Na'rina gaped in numb disbelief as Silas writhed and Icarus held on, seemingly unaware of the blood streaming from his torn face as his eyes glowed in determination. Silas' movements slowed. Then, in a last effort, he jerked his head back, attempting to escape Icarus' locked hands. Icarus held on, his lips pulled tight over his teeth, gritted in resolve and red with blood. It made a grisly mask on his sharp features.

The two finally fell still and a soft whisper reached

Na'rina's ears. She couldn't make out Icarus' hushed words to Silas despite the tree's sharp senses but his husky timbre soothed, rolling from the wer-im in warm tones. The sound contained a calm power unlike anything she'd ever felt. Silas fastened his jewel eyes on Na'rina within the tree.

*Silas can see me, too?* Somehow, it didn't surprise her that this wer-im could see the psychic. His deep chest sighed under Icarus' hold. It felt as though Silas looked into her soul with those glowing eyes. His irises quivered and Na'rina's stomach rolled when they rounded out into his natural gaze. His leonine body relaxed and flowed into his arms and legs, the snout separating into mouth and nose, the ears shifting back to the sides of Silas' head. "Still unwilling to make the difficult choice?"

Na'rina suspected the question was meant for Icarus alone, but the oak's senses picked up the soft words.

Icarus gritted out. "I will do what's needed and no more." Na'rina caught the answer but then his voice pitched too low again for the oak to make out words.

A few moments later, Silas exhaled and called in a clear voice, "I submit to our new Wer-Kadis."

Cheers vibrated through the oak. The Kadis released the older wer-im and stood back. His eyes glazed and he swayed.

"*Na!*" Na'rina shoved outward so fast the tree instantly released her. She caught Icarus as his knees buckled. She staggered under his dead weight, and her hands slipped on the blood covering him. "Help!" she gulped, fighting not to drop him. Several hands lifted him and, before she had a chance to say anything, the wer-im shuffled Icarus out of sight.

Na'rina stared at the blood glistening on her arms and reached up a startled hand when something trickled down her cheek. Her fingers came away red. It must have dripped from Icarus' head. She swallowed hysteria and glanced up to find Silas watching her. She froze. Perhaps she'd been wrong to gauge the Kadis as the more dangerous of the two. But no, Icarus bested the older wer-im. And yet Silas had tried to kill her. It seemed more accurate to say that Silas was more dangerous to *her*.

From where Silas sat on the ground, he tilted his head, watching the play of thoughts across her face. Several wer-im cleaned his wounds, but he'd barely lost any blood compared to Icarus and the procedure seemed a nuisance to him. Silas swatted at one wer-im to leave his face alone and started to rise. Na'rina spun away, terrified of facing him without the Kadis. *Please let him be all right*, she thought and took off. The wer-im didn't attempt to stop her.

Na'rina's stride lengthened into a heedless run through forest shadows, the skitter of nocturnal animals going silent as she flashed through their nightly rituals. An owl hooted its surprise, and, as Na'rina ran, Icarus' blood dried on her skin. It made her feel defiled.

Inside, her pulse throbbed with the need to be away. It

overrode her logic until the sound of running water drew her. Na'rina skidded to a stop at a river's edge, dropped to her knees, and dunked her head in the water. No naiad greeted her intrusion, so she had no way of knowing what river she'd found, but the chill of the water cleared her racing thoughts.

*I can't run.* For the first time in days, she was wer-im-free, but it didn't matter. Although they no longer haunted her steps, they held something far more precious to draw her back. Or more specifically, Silas held something far more precious. *Information.* Na'rina shuddered and pulled her head from the river. Water streamed from her hair but she ignored it as she fought off the memory of Silas' feline face.

*I have to face him again.* It was a terrifying reality. *But I don't have to face him alone.*

Icarus wanted to keep her alive and he'd won the Kadivas. Recalling the control he'd exerted over the larger wer-im despite his injuries brought a deep sense of calm to Na'rina. His injuries would take time to mend, though, even with a mythic's ability to heal. The sight of his bloody face flashed in her mind. Those slashes were as deep and as wide as Silas' lion claws and would be particularly slow to heal.

She would wait to return then, until she was certain Icarus was conscious and well. The pride wouldn't go anywhere until he recovered, which gave her at least a day.

Na'rina scrubbed her arms in the chill river, Icarus'

blood tinting the water red as it ran off her skin, carrying the stain into the current. Once it ran clear, she sat back on her heels and plucked at the shoulders of her shirt. Bloodstains already hardened areas of the fabric, but she hadn't brought a second one with her. Sinking back onto the spongy ground, she wrapped her arms around her knees and listened to the night sounds resume. A raccoon carried her babies up into an oak across the river, her soft chittering carrying over the running water. Somewhere in the forest a fox calling its high-pitched greeting barked and was answered by another farther away. A family perhaps.

"I miss you, Mamma," Na'rina whispered, her voice a soft breeze that didn't bother the night creatures. A few weeks earlier, she and her mother had danced in her grove with their heels beating the rhythm of the flutes into the earth and their hearts delighting in the shushing whisper of fluttering leaves. Here the only sound to comfort her came from the chatter of the river.

Behind her, the cypress and water tupelo watched, she could feel their awareness, but they didn't call a greeting. Perhaps they knew about her recent encounter with their upland kin. Their silence made her loneliness sharper. It wasn't like she'd found that many dryads in her travels, but the forest was always there. Even if it was a single tree within a human city, it still offered her a connection. She would have chatted with the river naiad if she'd appeared, despite how bouncy they tended to be. Or had the naiad grown dumb like so many dryads?

Na'rina had not realized just how many of her kind had given up on living outside their trees until this trip. Her mother said pockets existed where they helped one another stay aware. In the Rockies, there were several such areas where it was harder for humans to intrude, but as she traveled east, she'd only found one such place, near the eastern border of Kansas. After that she'd found La'meliai and a few dryads who remained aware but were no longer able to leave their trees. No pockets, just lonely individuals. The dryad world lay quiet. Na'rina hugged her knees tighter. *Maybe I just missed the others.* After all, she'd only seen a portion of the East Coast and, if they'd caught a whiff of the wer-im, they would avoid the species. Na'rina hoped that was why she felt so alone.

Her thoughts left a queasiness in her belly. If the dryads were being quiet because of the wer-im, they'd seek the Drydandas for leadership. *What will they do when they don't find my mother or me? Will the Council step in?* She had no idea.

The Council was set in their ways, and they hated the wer-im with a nearly blind passion. Even now, Na'rina fought down the images of the Collective Wisdom flashing through her mind like a knee-jerk reaction when she thought of the wer-im, and she hadn't lived through the banishment. Personal memories, as the Council would have regarding the wer-im, were always stronger. With a hidden menace targeting the dryads, to move against the wer-im would pull her species out of their natural cover, leaving them even more vulnerable.

*What would you do, Mamma?*

"Ditch the wer-im?"

Na'rina's head snapped up at the rumbling voice. She looked around to see the heavy shoulders and curly hair of Rosharu as the oread appeared from amidst the trees.

Eyeing her, Rosharu snickered. "Which one did you slaughter?"

Na'rina barked a laugh. "None of them."

Lowering herself beside Na'rina, Rosharu pinched a piece of Na'rina's bloodstained sleeve. "Red blood. It's not yours, so which one did you beat to get away?"

Na'rina shrugged, but her heart beat hard against her ribs at the thought of talking about the Kadivas. "It's a long story." She wondered again why Silas had turned against her after telling her to support Icarus. Na'rina shook her head. She had other questions—ones Rosharu could actually answer.

"Why do the oceanids hate you?"

Rosharu tensed but then rolled her shoulders with a bitter chuckle. "It's ancient history." She ran a hand through her curly hair but her pinched lips belied the casual gesture. "Unfortunately, we have long memories."

Na'rina hugged her knees tighter and waited, letting

silence encourage elaboration. It was a tactic her mother taught her.

Rosharu sighed. "An oread girl was born near the ocean and grew up playing with the oceanid children nearby," she said. "Some say she wasn't aware of the differences between oread and oceanid until much later. When she matured, the oceanid boy she'd always played with asked to handfast with her. They were young and didn't understand how both their species would hate the idea. Their union was denied outright." She scoffed. "But again, the two were young, impetuous, and decided to handfast in secret anyway. They were like you and me—Dandas—able to travel far from their elements. They ran, even though it took them from their homes." Rosharu paused, considering her next words. "It didn't work. The oceanids captured the girl, drowned her, and threw her body at the foot of her mountain. This fired the oreads into a rage that boiled their mountains. The boy tried to reach his love's body, but he was buried and killed in the lava that overflowed with the oread's fury."

Na'rina continued to wait as Rosharu's eyes glazed. After a moment, she shook herself and the ground gave a heavy shudder. "It would be disastrous for the two species to continue such outright violence. The other mythics would step in to prevent such a thing, but the feud continues below the surface. We throw our elements at each other. Their storms erode our mountains in bits and pieces. We, in turn, push up new islands or erupt and add land to our bases."

Na'rina rolled the story around, looking for the leaves and buds to flesh it out. An oread's memory was legendary for details, but this story contained nothing but bare bones for something Rosharu had lived through.

"Owasha wanted you, not just an—" Na'rina sucked in a breath as the ground lurched.

Hard lines etched Rosharu's face and she dug furrows in the dirt with her fingers. Na'rina swallowed her question. She did not want to risk the fragile friendship she had with Rosharu.

Looking for a new topic, she plucked at her bloody shirt with a groan. "Ugh."

Rosharu blinked and the ground's shuddering subsided. As though nothing happened, a wicked grin spread across her broad face. "Don't have a clean one?"

Na'rina shook her head in dismay.

"Follow me." Rosharu grabbed her wrist and pulled Na'rina to her feet before she understood the oread's intent.

"I need something human," Na'rina said.

"I know." Rosharu started jogging, and pulled Na'rina along at a run.

"But human shops aren't open at night."

Rosharu gave a hearty chuckle. "True, but we're not 'going shopping.'"

Rosharu led Na'rina out of the forest and onto a highway. They turned to follow it northeast. The sprinkling of traffic meant they couldn't run down the paved path, but they flitted along beside it, ducking away from the lights long before human eyes could make them out. Rosharu's long stride slowed to a walk as they approached a town. Laid out before them were sprawling lights, as if a giant child had stumbled and dropped her glitter. Its sparkle nearly rivaled the night sky, but Na'rina found the velvety black of the heavens far more attractive than the architecture of the humans.

"This way." Rosharu took off again.

Na'rina lengthened her stride and felt the impact change against the soles of her feet when they hit sidewalks instead of dirt. No wonder humans produced special shoes to run; they destroyed the natural shock absorption of the earth.

Rosharu halted. Na'rina stopped behind her and swayed in place to slow her momentum. Gazing for a time into a darkened alley, Rosharu finally led the way into the narrow thoroughfare. Smooth concrete changed to broken rubble beneath their feet. Na'rina winced, catching a toe, and paid more attention to where she placed her feet. Without the shoes she'd pitched over the side of the ship, every sharp edge in the cracked pavement bit into her soles. Rosharu didn't seem to notice the difference and Na'rina hurried to catch up. Just before they reached the end of the alley, Rosharu flipped the lid open on the last dumpster. Instead of the trash Na'rina expected to find, the bin contained discarded household goods. A lampshade lay half buried beneath the broken pieces of a couch frame that held several overflowing cardboard boxes of clothing.

Rosharu pointed at the brick wall the dumpster butted up against. "Secondhand store."

Na'rina gave a silent *Ah* and joined Rosharu in rifling through the boxes. In short order she found a deep red V-neck shirt and jeans that hung past her heels but, after rolling up the hem, fit fine. Rosharu studied her with Na'rina's bloody clothing under her arm.

"You'll do," she conceded, "but these will cause questions, so we'll dispose of them elsewhere."

"We'll be long gone before anyone finds them," Na'rina argued.

"Humans like to test things and wer-im blood produces very nonhuman results."

"Right." Na'rina deferred to Rosharu's vast experience. Glancing at the sky, she grimaced to see the velvet night turning to the dull gray of dawn.

"I need to get back," she muttered, heart sinking at the reminder that she'd have to face Silas. *I also have questions for the forest. I'll focus on that and maybe the answers will help when the time comes to confront him.*

217

"You escaped. Why would you return?" Rosharu asked.

"I made a deal with them. They're going to help me find my mother."

"In exchange for what?"

"I've already fulfilled my half of the deal."

Rosharu snorted. "What makes you believe the Kadis will hold to his half?"

Na'rina stared at her with a sinking sensation.

"Did anyone witness your deal?"

She couldn't voice the answer. No one had heard her deal with the Kadis—but then, he'd spoken of it after rescuing Silas. Surely, he meant to follow through?

Rosharu read her face and sighed. "Maybe we can rescue Mona'rina together. Maybe—"

"What have we here?"

They spun around and Na'rina swallowed dismay. Three men were closing in on them. She turned to flee but stilled and swayed as two more blocked the far end of the alley.

The labs on the Observer flashed through her mind. *I will not be dissected!* She eyed a fire escape ladder but its lowest rung hung well above her head. She looked for something else—and her hesitation cost her as the men drew closer.

Rosharu rumbled a low curse and prepared to face off with the group of three.

*Why doesn't she sink into the ground?* Na'rina remembered

the cracked pavement. *Maybe it's too thick.*

Following Rosharu's lead, Na'rina snatched the closest thing to a weapon, a chunk of the broken couch frame, and cringed. She'd do whatever she had to if it meant avoiding the ships. *I've been with the wer-im too long. Their fight instinct is rubbing off.*

Na'rina barred her teeth as she hefted the piece of wood, and one of the men laughed. "Feisty."

Their sour sweat assaulted Na'rina's nose. Another man chuckled and reached for something on his hip. Na'rina closed her eyes and swung, hoping her dryadic strength would catch him off guard. Anticipating the *thump* of wood against flesh, she stumbled when her swing met air. Bracing against the dumpster, she opened her eyes and gaped at the crumpled form on the ground, blood gushing from his throat. One of his companions lay behind him in a similar state.

Na'rina gagged.

"What would you've have done with a piece of wood against that?" a voice asked.

Raising startled eyes, she encountered leaf green ones topped by a shock of orange hair.

The wer-im pried the piece of couch frame from her numb fingers and pointed to a gun lying beside one of the downed men. Na'rina jumped when the wer-im tossed her makeshift weapon back into the dumpster with a clang. "It's a tranq gun like we've seen from their other attacks," the wer-im answered as he eyed Rosharu. "We're not sure how they found you, though."

"I thought you'd finally let me out of your sight," Na'rina said, still staring at the bloody man and the gun.

He gave a cynical chuckle. "Not a chance, Drydanda."

"We don't need your help," Rosharu interjected.

Was Rosharu right? Could they have won without the wer-im showing up? Staring at the five men and that gun, Na'rina shuddered.

*We would have lost this fight,* she admitted.

The wer-im sneered. "You're not welcome, Oread."

Did he mean Rosharu didn't deserve the wer-im's help or that her presence wasn't welcome? Na'rina couldn't decide. The two glared at each other, and for a startling moment Na'rina thought Rosharu meant to fight the smaller wer-im, but when he looked away and offered Na'rina a hand, the mountain nymph merely sniffed in disdain.

"We need to get back, Drydanda, before the Wer-Kadis begins to worry."

"We don't need them, Na'rina," Rosharu said. She didn't say more but Na'rina knew what she was offering: Ditch the wer-im. Now would be the time to do it if she wanted.

The warm, coppery smell of blood filled the air. Na'rina's stomach turned. It only hardened her resolve. "I made a deal," she told Rosharu. "I want to see it fulfilled."

Rosharu snorted. "Hope they honor their part."

Na'rina bit her lip, but accepted the wer-im's hand. When he led her from the alley, two other wer-im materialized to follow behind. Rosharu stuck with them until they left the town's limits.

"Stay sharp, Na'rina," she called before veering off. The edge in her voice stung. Na'rina watched her disappear as a sense of loss hit her.

To distract herself, she addressed the orange-haired wer-im. "I don't know your name yet."

He smirked and left her hanging. *I should've expected that response, I guess.* Shrugging off his rudeness, Na'rina kept pace in silence and, as they returned to the forest, she marveled at how the morning gray softened the colors. This time of day always inspired a calmness that she loved, and they traveled at such an easy pace she felt free to gaze around.

She snuck another peek at the wer-im. He lacked the powerful legs of his Kadis and seeing him up close revealed his blunt feline qualities. He seemed less wildcat, and more pet. Perhaps he acted fierce because his looks wouldn't do it for him. Na'rina chuckled before she thought better of it. He shot her a sideways sneer. *Great. Making fast friends.*

She blushed but grinned and decided to press her luck. "Are you a George? You look like a George."

His lip curled.

*Nope, not George.*

By the time true sunrise lit the horizon, she'd been through Alex, Cody, Roger and Steven, all to no avail. When they reached the clearing of the Kadivas, two wer-im occupied the area, neither of whom Na'rina recognized. Relief washed through her at Silas' absence.

"Thank you, Eli," she said lightly to the orange-haired wer-im and caught his scowl. *Not Eli either.* She shrugged and turned to focus on the now silent trees who acted up the night before, choosing to begin with the oak. Laying her palms flat against his rough bark, she greeted him with a gentle, *Good morning, Dry,* using the formal name for oak trees as a way of adding weight to her words.

He didn't speak. Instead, his apology flushed through her as he shared his zoi aima, treating her as he would a branch and sending water and nutrients into her body. The pulse brought a flush to her cheeks and a tingling to her fingertips. She directed the zoi aima down through her body until it reached the soles of her feet, where she returned the warmth to the roots of the oak. Another pulse tingled in her nerve endings. Even though the process was slow compared to her Rina, the inexorable flow warmed the roots of her hair and felt smooth as honey. The flow contained the deep *thrum* like a baritone voice and Na'rina remembered that Drys were some of the first trees to house dryads. They held within them such history that she could spend decades soaking in their age.

*Why did you want to interfere?* she asked.

The zoi aima sharpened.

*Answer, Dry. Why?*

The zoi aima cut off without warning like a slap to the face. Na'rina stepped back with a gasp, tears pricking her eyes. *Maybe another tree?* She approached a pine.

*Good Morning, Ored,* she greeted, again using the formal name for pine and spruce trees, but he refused to even acknowledge her. She stepped away, ignoring her tears as she stared up at the pine's long trunk. As she stood, fighting frustration, a whisper tickled the soles of her feet. The subtle but familiar zoi aima touched her the same way a crisp mountain wind would chill her skin.

*Rina?*

Na'rina inhaled as the consciousness of her grove, far distant, whispered through her blood. It had taken her grove a few days to extend through her fellow trees to find Na'rina. Pride swelled in her, and no small amount of concern. The effort involved in reaching this far could harm her grove if she wasn't careful.

*Are you all right?* Tension edged her question as it occurred to her there might be more danger at home.

*Are you?* the multi-toned voice fluttered.

*Of course.*

*I smell salt water and blood on your skin, and feel tears in your eyes. These do not indicate honesty in your words, my Na'rina.*

*I sense fear and weakness in your voice,* she scolded back. *Neither of us, then, is in the best of shape.*

There was a sullen silence before her Rina took up a new subject. *The Drys and Oreds do not wish to speak with me either, but they cannot hide their angst. They fear for your mother and someone else, but who they withhold from me.*

Na'rina stilled in shock. Who would they fear for on the same level as her mother? *Even I, the daughter of the Mother Drydanda, don't warrant such concern from the forests.*

*Na'rina,* her Rina cut into her thoughts, *the mother grove is weak.*

*Are they still destroying her?*

*Something has halted the machines that were cutting her down, but she bleeds from wounds too large to heal without your mother.*

The pain Na'rina sensed from her Rina made her bones ache. *Thank you, my Rina.*

*Na'rina, do not cry. No matter the loneliness, you are never truly alone.* The mental touch disappeared, leaving the taste of sunshine and fresh leaves in its wake.

"Does she sleep standing up?"

Na'rina swayed and then stilled.

"*Na,*" came the answer with a wry lilt. "Only the crazy ones do that."

*Silas!* Was he his reasonable self—or the blood thirsty one? He sounded reasonable, but it could be a trick.

"Come, Na'rina, the Wer-Kadis asks for you."

Na'rina hid her cringe. She opened her eyes to find one of her wer-im guards in a tree, and Silas standing not five feet in front of her, his gemstone eyes intent on her face. She swayed but managed to not step back.

"What are you searching for?"

Silas' brows shot up, but then he shrugged. "You resemble Mona'rina strongly."

"She is my mother."

"Undoubtedly."

Na'rina frowned, confused by their conversation.

"Come," he beckoned, changing the subject. "Icarus awaits."

She eyed the hand he offered until he withdrew it. He shrugged as he turned. She followed, wondering that he didn't comment on trying to kill her the night before. Perhaps angry wer-im tended to lash out at other creatures besides their intended opponents, but she doubted it. In his enraged state, he'd singled her out for a reason strong enough to distract him from the Kadivas. She wanted to ask him. He appeared calm at the moment, but that could change without warning—and *Curiosity killed the cat.* She bit her tongue.

"This is unusual, Silas." Felis met them, stepping out to

block their path.

"Unusual?" Silas asked. "The Kadis asked for the Drydanda and I've brought her to him."

"Don't play dumb." Felis sneered. "It doesn't suit you."

"You think I'm intent on harming Icarus?"

Felis frowned but before he could answer Icarus called, "It's all right, Felis."

Felis stepped aside, muttering, "You were never one for rules."

"Rules?" Na'rina asked.

"If a challenger survives the Kadivas he's removed from the pride for a while to prevent him from attacking again," Felis explained, glaring at Silas' back. "It creates too much upheaval to have challenge after challenge after challenge."

Na'rina suppressed a shudder as memories, sharp and vivid, of the previous night flashed through her mind.

Silas bowed slightly to the Kadis when he came into view. Na'rina had been wrong about how long it'd take him to heal. As Icarus turned, red lines stood out against his dark complexion along the left side of his face—he'd have permanent scars from Silas' claws—but as far as Na'rina could tell, he'd bear no other marks from the Kadivas. *What kind of fights left the other scars on him then?*

Those hazel eyes, however, were clear as Icarus took in those approaching him. "Did the wer-im accept the—

unorthodox—Kadivas?" he asked Felis while giving Silas a reproving look.

Felis snorted. "The acceptance was unanimous, although if you hadn't let Tarn live in your previous Kadivas, the wer-im would probably have demanded a rematch. Your precedent saved you."

"Good," Icarus said, then pinned Silas with a look. "But my precedent can change. Clear?"

A tick started in Silas' jaw, but he bowed his head in compliance.

Na'rina stayed still. She wanted to ask the Kadis about her mother, wanted to make sure he'd follow through on his deal, but this was the first time he had to enforce his authority over Silas. She did not dare interrupt that.

Icarus ran a hand over his face. His fingers paused on the puckered red lines. Na'rina cringed. How strange the scars must feel.

"All right, then. What must we do, Silas, to help the Mother Drydanda?"

Na'rina's relief made her sway. *Rosharu was wrong. She does not understand this Kadis.*

Silas hesitated, shot an indecipherable look at Na'rina, and shook his head. "I'll go to her grove. From there—"

"*Na*," the Kadis interrupted. "We do this together."

Silas' nostrils flared. "I'll be faster alone."

227

"You do not have the abilities the Drydanda does. We do this together."

Silas' lips snapped shut. A gleam came into his eyes as he studied Na'rina. "Perhaps you're right," he said, squatting down. He reached for a stick and began to etch a rough outline of the U.S. in the dirt. "Before I was taken, I received reports of five command centers. One in Vermont, one in Florida," he listed, placing an *X* over the general locations, "another two in Washington and lower California, and one in the four corners at the juncture of Colorado, Arizona, Utah, and New Mexico." Silas considered his sketch before continuing. "I suspect they have Mona'rina at the last location, but I've nothing but its proximity to her grove to support that. I propose breaching one of the eastern centers in hopes of confirming Mona'rina's location first."

*Why does he always call my mother by name? Why, in fact, does he want to go to her grove alone?* Then his suggestion hit her. *Breach one of the centers?* Na'rina thought of the ship and ice settled in her stomach.

Icarus knelt and took the stick from Silas.

"Two more centers have been found." He drew an *X* on the lowest point of Texas and another on the Tennessee-Arkansas border. He pointed at the last location. "This one's a day's travel if we take a small group."

Na'rina stared at the Tennessee border. She traveled

past that area on her way to Chattanooga not more than a week ago. "How do we find the information once we're there?"

"We've been breaking in and copying their records. With you, we can bypass breaking in and have you pull the information from the outside." That gleam still lit Silas' eyes as he spoke.

Na'rina frowned, not understanding what his plan would require of her but getting a sinking feeling it would involve more human electronics. "I don't follow," she admitted.

"I'll teach you," Silas said.

She cringed. Noticing, Felis gave her a teasing smile and she scowled.

"It'll have to do," Icarus said, ignoring their exchange. "*We'll* start after lunch with your training and leave in the morning for the Tennessee center."

Na'rina wasn't the only one to catch the Kadis' emphasis. Silas frowned at Icarus with what looked like frustration over his insistence that they work as a group. As for herself, she appreciated Icarus' willingness to walk this road with her, both because of her struggle with her new abilities and because she didn't want to be left alone with Silas. Somehow, those hazel eyes communicated that he understood both.

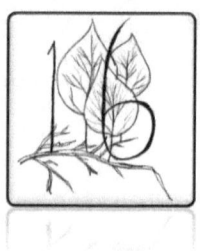

Perched in the top of an oak tree, Na'rina soaked in the warmth of the sun for her lunch. A small stream had provided her with water before she climbed the tree and now her body flushed with a contented glow. With her eyelids closed, she savored the green tint the light brought to her lids. Below, the oak shuddered as someone else entered his branches. Na'rina congratulated herself on noticing the subtle movement as Felis climbed up to join her.

"The Wer-Kadis is ready for your training."

"And what if I've not had my fill?" tilted her face into the sun.

Felis grunted and started to climb back down the tree. "The sooner you train, the sooner we help your mother."

Na'rina sighed, opening her eyes. "Felis?"

He stopped mid-move among the branches and raised a brow.

"What *is* he?"

Felis' yellow eyes dilated. "What do you mean, Drydanda?"

"Wer-im are not shape-shifters, we both know this. So what is Silas?"

He leaned against the oak's trunk, his stocky shoulders wedged between the branches. "I've never seen it before, Drydanda, but the stories say some wer-im can change into the feline they resemble."

"How? If you've never seen it, then it must be rare. How—why did Silas change?"

Felis smiled a toothy grin that heightened the bobcat resemblance. "Blunt, aren't you? Apparently great emotion or need can alter the wer-im to his feline form. As to what triggered the change last night, you'd have to ask Silas."

Na'rina's nostrils flared. "Can he do it at will or is it spontaneous?"

Beginning to descend the tree again, Felis answered over his shoulder. "The change is usually uncontrolled. However, with Silas, I'd say he planned it somehow."

Na'rina climbed down the tree after him.

*Planned it?* He'd been so focused on catching her, he'd lost the Kadivas even in his altered shape. Could he have planned such a thing? It'd require an amount of control while fighting she wasn't sure possible for such a hot-blooded creature. The wer-im pride would retaliate if they thought a challenger had thrown the fight. Was that why he'd changed, to make his effort seem unquestionable? Was Silas capable of orchestrating the shift in power with such care? Her instincts shouted, "*Sa!*"

Na'rina delved into the Collective Wisdom, noticing Silas had not triggered any images when she'd first seen him. He should have if he'd been part of the banishment. She sifted through the genetic history, fighting the fire she always saw when it was connected to the wer-im, when something else occurred to her. The Collective Wisdom carried no specifics about the banishment. No leaders were pictured, no faces or names. It was as devoid of detail as Rosharu's story.

"Thoughts to share?"

Na'rina jumped. She'd followed Felis in her preoccupied state and almost ran into Silas.

"No," she blurted out. "I'm just worried for my mother. Her grove's been sorely wounded."

Silas' expression shifted from inquisitive to pained, almost angry. "Tell me."

Na'rina flinched.

"Silas," Icarus warned.

"I need to know, Wer-Kadis, to gauge the damage to the Rina." The logic was at odds with the burr in Silas' voice.

"I see toppled aspens flayed of their bark," Na'rina whispered, ice growing in her stomach as she voiced the horror.

"They're dry by now—stacked in piles—but no one's come to take them away." Na'rina's eyes glazed while she recalled the images, but she jerked back to the present when Silas reached to take hold of her shoulders. She swayed away from him before he touched her.

Silas' hands clenched and he dropped them. "I know the images pain you."

"I am fine, Wer-im."

Icarus shot Silas a warning look. "There's a town a couple hours northwest of here," he said. "It should be suitable for you to learn." He spoke to Na'rina but he watched Silas still.

"You received these images directly from your Rina?" Silas asked, ignoring Icarus.

"*Sa.*"

"How long ago?"

*What?* Na'rina glanced toward Felis and Icarus, but Felis gave a confused shrug and Icarus simply seemed resigned.

"Originally, about a week ago. Most recently, today."

Silas' eyes widened in shock and then a disturbing smile split his face. "*Today?* Mona'rina must be proud!" He spun and walked in the direction of the town Icarus had indicated. The Kadis slung a black duffle bag over his shoulder and fell into step with Silas with the resigned look still on his face.

Na'rina huffed. Of all things she hadn't expected this. Felis gave her a perplexed look.

"I never understand those two," he complained.

"Neither do I," Na'rina admitted. "Why does Silas care how far my Rina can reach?"

"Your tree spoke to you today? Was it a message passed on through others like a Sedessan would pass on information?"

Na'rina gave him a scathing look. How did Icarus and Silas know so much and Felis nothing at all? "I spoke *directly* to my Rina, the consciousness that is my *grove*. She's talented."

"Grove? Like a bunch of trees?"

"Aspen grove. It's all the same organism underground." This was like explaining to a child.

Felis mouthed the word "grove" and kept walking. "You dryads are a complicated species."

"Look who's talking." She elbowed him. Perhaps she was responding to all the tension she'd been dealing with, but it felt good to tease him.

Felis scoffed. "How dare you!"

"I dare."

He stopped dead, brows furrowed. "Bold," he grumbled, but started walking again.

"Coming?" Icarus called as they caught up to him and Silas. The twinkle in his hazel eyes made Na'rina think he'd seen the exchange.

"You wer-im take yourselves too seriously," she said, flitting forward past Icarus to touch the nearest tree in greeting.

"Do not!" Felis protested.

"When was the last time you danced?" she asked.

Felis started to answer but was drowned out by Silas' snort. Na'rina ignored them as she flitted forward, half dancing as she went.

The town Icarus mentioned turned out to be a rambling city. They stopped on a hill overlooking the cluttered sprawl to don better clothing to cover their nonhuman features. Na'rina stared at the buildings below. Such places always seemed ugly. Icarus nudged her shoulder and held out a tan corduroy jacket and a military style ball cap. *Again? Ugh.* Once she'd pulled on the clothing, he handed her a bottle of water and a yellow bandana. She raised her brows in confusion. "Wash your face."

"Why?"

Icarus ran a quick finger over her cheek and Na'rina flinched. He held out his index finger, showing her the white powder left from her skin.

"Oh." She knelt to wash her face while the others outfitted themselves.

Icarus faded out his facial markings and pulled on a ball cap of his own, tucking the tops of his tufted ears beneath the brim. Although the makeup and the cap softened his feline features, he still resembled a lynx. The predator hid; he didn't disappear.

This became all the more obvious when he examined the fresh scars trailing his left cheek and temple in an oval pocket mirror. His jaw twitched and he grimaced in a flash of annoyance. The ball cap couldn't hide the lower, thicker, two lines that stood in stark red contrast to his healthy skin. Any human who looked at those ragged wounds would know this was a dangerous man. Icarus carefully applied more makeup. He managed to dull the redness but nothing would hide the damage.

Troubled by his frustration, Na'rina looked away as she finished scrubbing her face.

Felis was trying on sunglasses. He held up two pairs, asking everyone's opinion. Icarus pointed at one without looking away from his oval mirror, while Silas indicated the other. Felis grunted.

Silas snatched for the pair with the darker lenses. "You'd look ridiculous in those."

Felis jerked back, surprised, and tensed to fight.

Shoving the bandana in her pocket, Na'rina sidled up to Felis and snagged the lighter lenses from his fingers, sliding them onto his face. Leaning back, she studied him as she turned him right and left by his shoulders and made humming noises.

"Definitely this pair," she announced. "The frames have a nice shine."

Felis pulled the glasses off to check and hummed, mollified, before handing Na'rina the darker pair. She passed them to Silas, who slid them on to hide his gem-like eyes as he turned away.

Na'rina's stomach relaxed. Last thing she wanted to see right now was a skirmish between the two—especially over a pair of glasses. Absently she ran a hand over her face. White powder came away on her fingers.

"Great," she mumbled.

"Hmm," Icarus agreed. "Why didn't you tell me it'd instantly come back?"

"Never had a reason to wash it off before, Wer-Kadis."

He scowled. "Hold still." He pulled out more human makeup from the duffle and daubed it on her face.

She flinched. As soon as the liquid touched her skin, she sensed the ingredients were plant-based. *Ugh!* "You know what they make this stuff out of, don't you?" she grumbled as he moved on to apply eye shadow to her left eyelid.

"Don't dwell on it," he mumbled, concentrating.

"Considered going into business?" Felis asked, watching the Kadis put finishing touches on Na'rina.

"Shut up," Icarus replied.

"No really, I can't even tell she's got—" Felis snapped his lips shut at the look Icarus shot him.

"Where to?" Silas asked.

The Kadis took off, his long strides barely resembling that of a human in his irritation. Na'rina hesitated, but then, catching Silas watching her, she hurried after him. As they neared the human residences, Icarus slowed his gait and Na'rina fell in step beside him.

Icarus' eyes narrowed in determination, pulling the lower scars taught. The cap on his head twitched as he tried to move the ear closest to Na'rina. *What does he notice that I don't?* Na'rina wondered as they walked. *He always sees more than I do.*

"I didn't have another pair of sunglasses," he said under his breath, "so keep your head down."

Na'rina shot him a surprised look but dropped her head, trusting his judgment. Entering a human city in broad daylight—to linger around humans—was a new experience for her. Was she as obviously *other* as the wer-im?

Several blocks up, they stopped at a bus stop where three humans already waited. A man in a gray suit never looked up from his cell phone. The other two, who looked to be a brother and sister in their late teens, glanced over but continued their bickering. Na'rina picked up the words "Dad," "drinking," and "luggage," but she missed the rest as Icarus' plan dawned on her.

"We're riding a bus?" she cried, her stomach knotting.

"Lower your voice when you talk," Icarus admonished. "We can't reach the business district today by walking."

Na'rina heard what he said but her brain stuck on the bus ride. She'd never ridden in a vehicle before, much less one filled with humans. Recalling feeling trapped in the bowels of the hollow ship, she swallowed panic.

*Hold it together!*

Na'rina noticed the siblings had fallen silent while her brain skittered. The girl was staring at the powdery white residue on her hands. Shoving them in her pockets, she kept her head down and encouraged her stomach to stay put until the bus pulled up. Icarus passed them money as the bus arrived and they stepped aboard after the three humans. The enclosed space smelled of metal, plastic, and human sweat. Na'rina shuffled to the closest seat. Maybe looking out the window would distract her from the dead metal rumbling under the soles of the horrid shoes Icarus had provided her.

Silas sat down beside her and Na'rina went utterly still. His scent, which disturbingly reminded her of the juniper that grew in abundance around her Rina, lingered. Na'rina stared at her ashen face reflected in the window. Was Silas' juniper like Icarus' spice—a way to lull his prey, or draw them in? Its sharpness almost masked the solid wer-im smell of all three of her traveling companions.

"Tell me of your mother." The words were soft. Icarus and Felis could hear from their seats across the aisle, but Silas' voice was too low for human ears.

239

Na'rina had an unreasoning desire to ignore him, but they were trapped in this rumbling husk and she expected Silas would not let his question go unanswered. She swung around, sitting with her back against the wall of the bus. At least now she had Silas in sight. Across the aisle and back two seats, the human girl from the bus stop stared at her and Na'rina slouched behind the backrest of her blue seat.

"Why should I, Wer-im?" she asked, keeping her words as low as his.

"We were not always enemies," Silas grumbled. "And I've not heard news of the Drydanda in years." He sounded sad, but his dark sunglasses masked his emotions.

"Why would you care?"

"Mona'rina and I were—friends—at one time."

"Funny," Na'rina replied, "she's never mentioned you."

He flinched. She'd meant to hurt him but she hadn't expected much of a reaction. The result wasn't as satisfying as she'd hoped.

"Does she mention any wer-im by name?"

"*Na.*" This reminded her the Collective Wisdom held no specifics. *Does he know about that?*

"I wouldn't think so." He gave a wry grin. "I did not know she had a daughter."

Na'rina didn't answer. How could she? Her upbringing said anything she told him would be a betrayal. And yet, in the last few days, she'd found her knowledge to be skewed, deceiving even, about these creatures. *What's true and what's created by bitter resentment from a bloody war?* Her upbringing supposedly prepared her to deal with situations like this, but Na'rina didn't know how to sort out the pieces, let alone her misgivings about this wer-im in particular.

"Whom did she find to handfast with?" Silas pressed.

Na'rina hissed, and then clapped a hand over her mouth. Icarus met her eyes across the aisle and the whites of his claws retracted as he affirmed she was okay. He gave her a searching look before turning his head away. It put his face in profile, but he'd pulled his cap up to uncover his ear to listen more closely.

"You're digging," she accused.

"Curiosity. It's a hazard of my species." He gave a smile intended to be self-deprecating. It unnerved her. "But I know what personal cost Mona'rina suffered for the banishment. The dryads would never have forgiven her for ignoring our violence, but her banishing us tainted their view of her. Some speculated the Drydanda would die out because no one would handfast with a Drydanda stained by violence, no matter her strength."

Na'rina clenched her fists against her stomach. Silas hit the problem square. After Na'rina buried Brin'ored, some claimed she *proved* the bloodline was failing. Few things still brought her mother to anger anymore, but that claim had. It haunted Na'rina, because that anger carried a depth of pain she didn't understand. Mona'rina ordered the Dryad Council away, too distraught for a time to listen to them.

"She wasn't," Na'rina blurted out.

*"What?"*

"She was never handfasted."

Silas' brows rose above the dark frames. "You came to Icarus' meeting as an ambassador. The Council would never accept that if you weren't legitimate."

*Knowledgeable indeed!* Her stomach rolled but Na'rina raised her brows in mimicry of his own gesture. If he knew so much, let him figure out the details. "I'm legit," she whispered.

The wer-im's jaw tightened. "That doesn't happen."

Na'rina snickered. "Neither do wer-im shape-shift."

"Her grief—"

*"Sa."* Seeing he grasped the reality, she felt compelled to explain so he didn't misunderstand. "After the banishment, the dryads shunned her. Not permanently, they needed her too much for that, but to prove they'd never allow her to handfast. She went into shock. She calls it grieving, but she separated consciousness from her grove without the buffer of distance. It terrified her Rina. Fearing for her sanity, her Rina seeded without the spark of her mating. The seed took within a day. My grove is almost twenty-four hours older than me."

"A dryad dies when a tree seeds first," Silas said in horror.

"Usually."

"You're a True Born descendant." He slumped into his seat.

Drained, Na'rina pivoted to look back out the window. At least the conversation had distracted her from the bus for awhile. Now she gripped the edge of the seat, trying to ignore the vibration in the soles of her feet. *True Born.* The term implied an exact ability flow. What her mother could do, so could she. Except that wasn't true. The Mother Drydanda held several abilities Na'rina did not, like tapping into an animal's zoi aima. The term also implied an intensification of ability in the descendant, which again had not manifested in Na'rina. In fact, her mother's abilities exceeded her own in most things. Perhaps the Council saw the truth; perhaps the bloodline degraded instead of intensified, became unstable.

*Am I unstable? Would I even know it if I was?*

"What about Ver'rina and Levi?" Silas asked. "Surely they didn't shun her?"

Na'rina froze, her fingers going numb from gripping the edge of her seat. *Grandma and Grandpa?* "Ver'rina cannot leave her tree," she said, not looking over at the wer-im. "And Levi?" She shrugged. She'd never met her grandfather, but somehow that had never seemed important until right now. No one ever seemed to bring him up. *How naïve I've been! Who was Levi? And who does that make me?*

The bus jerked to a stop and Icarus rose. Na'rina and the others followed, again trailing the human siblings as they stepped off the bus. Na'rina felt giddy as her feet hit the sidewalk. No sensation of life stirred beneath her feet, but at least the ground wasn't moving. Her relief dissolved, however, as the noise of the city enveloped her. Na'rina hurried through the growl of vehicles, the chatter of humans, even the slap of shoes hitting hard concrete to catch up to Icarus, who led them down the busy street and into a cell phone store.

Once inside, she gasped for breath, trying to ease the tightness in her chest. The cool, quiet interior of the store brought her calm after wading through the mass of humanity.

"Looking for anything specific today?" a short, balding man asked, approaching, and Na'rina realized he was addressing her.

"Just—" She lowered her tone and tried again. "Just looking, thank you."

"Wonderful, wonderful. We have a sale today on all new model phones. It includes unlimited data and…" the salesman rambled on and Na'rina's mouth went dry. She couldn't learn a new skill with him chattering in her ear. The tiny store offered no privacy and the man was now touching her arm, directing her toward another display.

"Excuse me," Felis interrupted, adapting a heavy drawl. "I've got a phone here—"

"I'm with another customer, sir. If you'll—"

"Oh, I'm with Chuck." Na'rina grinned and watched the man's face go blank. She gestured toward Felis, who drew the man away, going on about the problems with his phone.

Icarus, who had been standing against the wall with his hat pulled down, head lowered over the screen of a phone, joined her once the salesman was engaged in conversation with Felis. Na'rina swayed at the comforting yet disturbing spicy scent that came with him as he moved. It should've sparked an instinctual warning in her. It didn't.

"Over there." Icarus guided her with a hand against her back to the glass display case where Silas stood. The older wer-im was staring into the case of resale smart phones but subtly pointed to the counter behind the case, where the computer the store used as its register sat.

"The goal," Silas murmured, "is to access the customer files without touching the computer."

Na'rina gaped. *What?* She snapped her teeth shut but the rest of her stayed frozen. Icarus clearly felt the tension in her back.

"You can do this," he encouraged. His body shielded her from the salesman's view.

Across the room, Felis was raving about a silvery phone case he'd found. "I can see myself in it! How'd they make it that shiny?"

"How?" Na'rina asked under her breath.

"Have you ever entered your Rina without touching her?"

Na'rina swallowed. *Once.* She remembered her anger at Brin'ored. The harsh concussion to the air, the push of roots, then the *thwamp* as she pulled the dryad into the ground all rushed through her. She'd told herself *never again.*

"I see from your face you've done it," Silas said. "This is the same concept—but without two consciousnesses."

"What do you mean?" Her voice trembled.

"Entering without touch requires a spark of some sort—anger, a need to protect, or even joy you crave to share—except there's no consciousness to reach toward your spark. Instead, you span the distance entirely with your zoi aima, to fulfill a need to feel the energy in the computer. You have to *feel* that need."

She didn't *want* to feel the computer's energy, much less *need* it. "I—I can't. It's dead. It's—"

"It's a way to your mother," Icarus said.

So simple. *I do have a need.* A desperate one.

Na'rina laid her sweaty hands on the glass display—they'd leave a residue—and stared at the back of the register. Except for the one time, she'd always needed contact to touch something's zoi aima. The small fingerprint scanners from the trees were the first time she'd communicated without "completing" the contact by touching palms and forehead. *Just another step.* One gigantic step. She pushed outward on her zoi aima, using the metal frame of the display case as a physical and mental anchor. If she'd poked a stick into mud, the feeling would be the same. The green and blue swirling glow of her lifeblood created a haze to her psychic eye as it reached, slow and sluggish, across the counter. Na'rina's stomach clenched. This was a real extension of herself even if most others couldn't see it. Sparks zinged through her palms where they rested on the metal frame.

"That's it," Silas murmured. "Just a little farther."

*Can he see it?* Icarus probably could since he saw her within trees, but could Silas? He'd seen her in a tree as well. Her vulnerability nearly choked her, but outwardly she ignored the gem-like gaze that watched. The computer sang with electricity. It felt different from a plant's zoi aima but similar to the palm scanners, only more powerful with a constant stream coming from the wall. *Here goes.* She touched that stream. Bitter acid, like chewed beetles, again coated her tongue, strong enough that she fought the urge to gag. Energy sizzled along her nerves, sensitizing the glass and metal beneath her hands, and the fabric of her clothes on her skin. Icarus touched a hand to her back—she hadn't noticed when he's withdrawn it—and it sparked with a zap.

"Silas?" Na'rina could hear Icarus' husky voice in the

background as she dug into the computer.

*Files.* Names flashed by, phone plans and invoices and—

A spark zapped her palms. "Ouch!" Na'rina stepped back and swayed. Black gnats swarmed the edges of her vision and the world tilted.

"Catch her!"

Blinking, Na'rina looked up. The faces of Silas and Icarus were joined by Felis and the salesman. "Should I call for help?"

"No," Silas responded.

"Epileptic," Icarus added. "Just need to get her outside. We'll call her doctor later. Maybe her medication's off."

The salesman nodded and opened the door as Icarus carried her out.

"I'm fine," Na'rina protested when he didn't set her down but continued to carry her beyond the salesman's worried gaze. Once around the corner, he set her on a metal bench.

"You sparked like a transformer. I'm not sure you'd know fine right now."

Na'rina glowered but accepted the water Felis offered. For a random moment, the water bottle reminded her of her backpack and she wondered where it had ended up. Taking a drink, she stared at the nub of a root sticking up between the sidewalk seam, wishing she could meld with it to escape the city. Before her eyes the ground lurched and cement chips jumped like grasshoppers on the sidewalk. Water splashed down her front as Silas sat down hard next to her and Icarus took a step back to brace himself.

"Earthquake?" Felis asked.

"Didn't feel right." Silas sent a look at Icarus, jumped off the bench, and darted around the corner before Na'rina could figure out what the look meant. Icarus hesitated, then followed him.

"Icar—" Felis called out and the square of cement beneath the bench tilted free from the rest of the sidewalk. Felis tumbled and disappeared into the sudden hole in the earth.

Na'rina grabbed onto the bench as it slid, with her on it, after him.

Na'rina's stomach lurched. In a strange moment of clarity, she pushed free of the bench and landed on her feet. She caught sight of a tunnel just as Felis cried out, but when she looked around for him, the sidewalk rumbled above and all light disappeared.

"Felis? *Felis?*" Na'rina scrambled around in the dark until she found Felis on the ground, the bench lying across his torso. She shoved it aside. "Are you okay? Felis—*wake up!*"

"You want him awake?"

Na'rina froze and peered into the darkness. The soft breathing of not one, but two other creatures made the fine hairs on her neck itch.

"I told you things didn't look right." This voice was female.

"How were we to know? I wasn't chancing a fight with that thing."

"He's not a thing," Na'rina said. She felt along Felis'

arm, up to his shoulder, chin, and mouth, relieved to feel his breath brush against her palm.

A light clicked on.

*The siblings from the bus?*

"Hello, Drydanda," the two said in unison.

"What's going on?"

"The Council put out a search for the Mother and Daughter Drydandas," the girl answered.

Na'rina rocked back on her heals, finally seeing the slight brown mottling to their skin and the narrowness of their bodies. *How did I not notice?* That narrowness would fill out as they grew, but it was more angular than the human frame. *Silas' questioning must have messed with me not to see this.* "Dryads don't usually go into cities," she mused.

"We use the underground network here," the boy explained, gesturing to the tunnel, "but because of the Council's orders, we've been searching more populated areas. A city was your last known location."

They fidgeted under Na'rina's scrutiny. A rich, dark brown flushed through the girl's skin, replacing her more neutral tone with an even, beautiful chocolate. If she walked around the city with that lustrous skin, people would stare. The girl tried to change back to the lighter tone, but it only held for a moment before firmly settling. Na'rina didn't need the small acorns hanging from the girl's earlobes to tell her what kind of dryads these were. Oak dryads. Young, healthy Drys. And one a male. The rarity in that was a marvel—and sent a spark of hope for her species through Na'rina.

"What can you tell me?"

They looked at their toes, hesitant.

"What else?" Na'rina pressed.

Their eyes darted toward Felis and the hand she rested on his shoulder.

The girl bit her lip. "Rumors only, Drydanda. The official message just said to get you home."

"What rumors?"

"Wer-im breaking the banishment and threatening the dryads." They spoke again in unison.

*Twins*, Na'rina thought. *Born to the same tree.* Then the situation dawned on her and she groaned, scrubbing a hand over her face. The Council, in a knee-jerk reaction to the return of the wer-im, had inadvertently exposed the dryads. These two roaming the city in broad daylight proved that. Perhaps the old Council *was* capable of making rash decisions—if spurred by fear.

Her eyes settled on Felis, still unconscious. His animated expressions were missing, but laugh lines trailed from the corners of his eyes and mouth before disappearing into his gray beard. The black stripes in his beard, like mutton chops, were reminiscent of Icarus' facial lines. Na'rina admitted, if those two wer-im were representative of their species, then their hearts seemed to be in the right place. She'd agreed to an alliance, but now she had to put substance to it beyond what was personally required of her. Could she give her word concerning the wer-im after knowing them such a short time? *If I don't, what will the Council do? Can I still save my mother?*

*Na.* The dryads were strong but they lacked the wer-im's tactical mentality. Plus, except for herself, dryads couldn't travel farther than fifty miles or so from their home trees. That restriction alone would make finding Mona'rina difficult. *We need the wer-im.* Na'rina ached. This decision would convince the Council she was unstable, a degradation of the Drydanda bloodline. Na'rina fought the tears pricking her eyes. One thing she knew for certain. Her mother would make the same decision in her position. *Any sacrifice for the good of the dryads.*

"Listen," she said, standing up and approaching the twins. "We're isolated because of what we are. That isn't usually a problem but right now it is." They swayed as she placed a hand on their shoulders. "The Council does not know what threatens us. Have the wer-im broken the banishment? Obviously." She waved at Felis and the girl flinched. "But not for revenge. Look at me, I have not been harmed. My mother, however, has been, but that's not the wer-im's doing. The Wer-Kadis came to warn us, but he was too late. Now he and his pride are helping me find the Mother Drydanda *and* helping me figure out what *is* attacking us."

The boy's dark eyes flashed. "But if it wasn't the wer-im—"

"Then what?" the girl whispered.

"What's happened?" Na'rina asked.

"They've disappeared."

"Who?"

"Our elders. They went out to dance on the new moon, like always, except in the morning, they were gone and their trees were silent." A sob escaped the girl and her brother drew her against his side. "That's why we sent word to the Council in the first place," he explained. "They told us to find you."

Na'rina backed away to lean against the wall. *More silent trees?* The similarities to the grove her mother went to investigate were too strong. *The elders are dead.* She knew it with a gut-wrenching certainty, but she didn't say so aloud. As she thought it through, Felis' eyes flashed beneath his lashes. Shaking her head, Na'rina waited for his eyes to fully close again before turning to the twins.

"Can you send word to the Council for me?" Na'rina didn't want to contact the Council directly. They'd order her home, which would open an issue about leadership. The Dryadic Code required any descendant to stand in, in the absence of the Mother Drydanda, but in ignoring the Council, she created the opportunity for them to name her unfit. It would give credence to their desire to name themselves more capable and lead everyone into a drawn-out struggle for control.

"We can," the boy answered, his arm still around his sister's shoulders.

"Tell them you found me. Let them know I've negotiated the aid of the wer-im to find the Mother Drydanda and to figure out who is attacking mythics. Also, I ask them to send word for all dryads to withdraw into their trees until we know what's after us. We are too vulnerable out in the open like this."

"They will not like that, Drydanda," the boy said. "I felt their fear and hate in the message. They want the wer-im gone."

His hesitation was mild compared to what she might have faced if he were older. *Will the Council vote to remove me from leadership?* It was possible, but not enactable until she returned home, and they couldn't order her back without direct contact. She might pay for such maneuvering, but it couldn't be helped. *I'm trying, Mamma.*

"Send them the message," she replied. "They won't express their anger at you. And make sure to stay in your Dry until contacted."

"Drydanda?" the girl hesitated. "How else can we help?" She stretched her fingers out as though to take Na'rina's hand.

No older dryad would make such a gesture toward a Drydanda. It pulled at Na'rina, but she couldn't accept the offer.

"I must travel far. It's not something I can ask of you." She smiled to soften the words. "But stay alert. You know how to contact my Rina?"

They nodded.

"If you hear or see anything, pass it along. The more we know, the better."

"*Sa*, Drydanda."

Na'rina turned to "wake" Felis.

"Drydanda?" asked the girl again. "They say the wer-im killed hundreds before they were banished. That they set trees on fire and gloried in them burning."

Na'rina paused, her hand over Felis' shoulder. The wer-im's jaw tensed but he kept still.

"How—how can you work alongside them?" The words came rushing out. The girl was afraid of second-guessing a Drydanda.

Na'rina sighed. Such fears echoed her own. "I was not alive for the banishment," she admitted, "but my home region was one of those hit the hardest. The effects lay heavy around my grove. So believe me when I say I don't make this decision lightly. In the short time I've known the wer-im, I've seen many things I wish I hadn't. What I have not seen, however, is violence without purpose. I don't know what their purpose was all those years ago, but I suspect there's much we don't know about that time." Na'rina turned toward them. "I can't ignore our history, but I also can't afford our isolation when we don't even know who is attacking us."

The siblings bowed their heads, a sign of deep respect. It hit Na'rina like a fist to the stomach. When had she ever received that gesture apart from her mother? *Never.* Emotion tightened in her throat as she shook Felis' shoulder.

"I think I've a couple cracked ribs," he groaned, sitting up.

"We're sorry," the boy said. "We didn't know we could trust you."

Na'rina looked up at the living roots and vines that had been woven together below the humans' sidewalk. She recalled the nub of a root peeking through the crack in the cement above ground and now understood the dryads arranged the roots to hold the sidewalk in place, and to lower it, when they wanted. Na'rina suspected they had numerous access points like this.

She pointed it out. "Rather clever."

"Not the word I would've used," Felis groused.

Na'rina swatted his shoulder and stood. "How do we get out of here?"

The boy pointed. "Follow the tunnel. There's a door that will drop you out under the bridge on the edge of the city."

Na'rina thanked them as she helped Felis rise. They turned to leave when another thought hit her. She turned back to the twins. "One last thing. When you spoke with the Council, what did they say about using my Rina to contact me?"

The twins stared at their toes again. Felis growled and they jumped, shooting him glances.

"What did they say?" Na'rina pressed.

"They tried contacting your mother," the girl finally said. Na'rina could imagine how well *that* went. They'd take one look at the devastated grove and refuse to touch it. "They said the grove wouldn't speak with them because of her pain."

"And my own Rina?" Na'rina asked. She could feel a headache building behind her temples.

"The Daughter Drydanda's grove refuses contact," the boy quoted in a low voice, and Na'rina could guess which Council member he was mimicking. "She must be in grave danger. Do not try to search her out through her Rina. Such efforts might kill her."

Na'rina's breath seethed out her nose and she spun away before saying something she would regret. They never touched her grove—of that she was certain. *They're lying.* Until recently, she would not have thought them capable.

"They refused to say more," the girl added.

A dull ache throbbed behind Na'rina's eyes. In her mother's absence, the Council had chosen to cut the Daughter Drydanda off from the dryad population. *Why?* The answer she came to was staggering: *They want to drive the wer-im out—no questions asked.* The only way to do that, without a Drydanda, was to control the dryads. They would have to order the dryads to work together to banish the wer-im, which would expose every last one of them. *They'll get us all killed.*

Felis pulled her attention back to the present. "Drydanda, this does not sound good."

Na'rina met his gaze. "Your Kadivas is a far simpler, honest way to take power."

He straightened up, brows raised.

"The Council lied about attempting to touch my grove," she told the twins, not voicing the rest of her suspicions. This was the only solid fact she had—but it was enough.

The siblings fidgeted, disturbed.

Na'rina hesitated. If she didn't do something now, the Council might start ordering action against the wer-im and expose more dryads to the humans. *I can stop them, but it's drastic.* She took in the twins' open faces, trusting attitudes, and swirling zoi aima. The lifeblood blended between them, a result of being twins, in a thick, rich coffee-colored fog. They offered trust and sincerity melded with the stability of all oaks. *I can work with that.*

Na'rina walked back to the twins and held out her hands. Without hesitation, the boy set the flashlight on the ground before he and his sister clasped hands with her. Tilting her head forward, Na'rina touched foreheads with them. Like touching a tree, the contact opened her to their flow of zoi aima. It swirled, chocolate to her blue and green and filled with the heady oak smell of their Dry.

*In the Dryadic Code it states, when leadership is passed from the Mother Drydanda to her daughter, the daughter may choose her own Council.* The pulse within the twins quickened. *My mother is incapable of leading at this time.* She showed them the toppled aspens, the logs stripped of their bark, and the fiery pain emanating from the mother grove. The girl's hand trembled and a shudder traveled the length of the boy's body, but neither pulled away. *Therefore, I step in until she is returned to her proper place. In doing so, I choose my own Council. I choose you two along with La'meliai from the forest above Chattanooga. I leave open the last two positions until a time when I have considered more.*

Zoi aima, not her own but her grove's much headier pulse, shot from Na'rina's hands to encase the twins' arms. It circled their skin from their hands to above their elbows and then retreated, leaving in its wake tattoos of branches and the folded buds of aspen leaves. The girl gave a hiccupping laugh but she spoke with her brother when he said, "We accept and serve with honor."

Na'rina pulled back, but before she released their hands, a flutter shot through her and into the twins. *Welcome to our Council,* her grove greeted them and then disappeared, leaving behind the faint scent of aspen and a sweet taste on Na'rina's tongue.

"Send word to La'meliai. Then send out a message for all dryads to withdraw into their trees. They are my eyes and ears now. Have them contact you and then pass it along through my Rina. And let the former Council know I'm well," she added as an afterthought.

Typically, Council members had to be present at the choosing of their replacements, so this wasn't a clean change of power. Na'rina almost snorted. This Council always protested a single new member. She had no idea how they would respond to their complete replacement. But it was her right—even if it was unorthodox.

The twins bowed and backed away. "We support you, Drydanda. We'll do as you've asked." They disappeared in the darkness, leaving the flashlight on the floor.

Na'rina slumped against the wall.

"Don't see *that* happen every day," Felis said. "Now, let's get back. I've a feeling the Kadis is about to start a full-fledged search for you, which won't be pretty."

Stooping to pick up the flashlight, Na'rina followed the wer-im down the tunnel.

"Nothing is as I thought," she said.

"That's the way of it." Felis shrugged. "Think you've got it all figured and—*bam!* Your world's turned upside down. Take Silas. I never thought he'd let go of leadership."

Na'rina shuddered. She definitely didn't have Silas

figured out. "I may have just started a civil war."

"Did you have a choice?"

"I don't think so," she whispered. If a Council member died, he or she was replaced, but never had the entire Council been replaced by a new Drydanda. That clause in the Dryadic Code had never been used. The dryads feared such upheaval.

*I'm not natural.* She was too rash, too "hot-blooded" for a dryad. The flashlight revealed the door where the tunnel ended, stemming the flow of such thoughts. Felis turned the hatch and the door swung open.

"Local dryads keep it well oiled," he noted with approval.

Na'rina followed him out to find the sun dipping below the horizon. She enjoyed the last rays on her skin until the skyline of the city and the bridge above them were encased in the gray of dusk. While she stood there, Felis climbed onto the bridge and took a look around. When he came back, he was scowling. "Dryads can't send us in the right direction, can they? They dropped us north of the city instead of west."

"We didn't ask for a specific location, Felis."

He grunted. "Let's go. We'll have to skirt the city to meet back up with the Kadis."

They climbed from under the bridge and headed away from the city lights before swinging southwest. Na'rina wasn't sure how they were going to find the other wer-im, but Felis didn't seem concerned, so she didn't ask.

*My Na'rina?*

Na'rina stumbled and caught her balance. Felis shot her a questioning look but she kept running and he went back to leading the way.

*Rina?*

*Your mother's Council has been informed of your decision.* The words came through with a certain wry humor. Her grove sent her an image and Na'rina almost laughed. Ser'ored and Ray'ored stood before her *seed tree*, the center of her Rina's awareness. Both pine dryads, their hair stood in green spikes around their heads. They were old beings, but unlike many aged dryads, neither had fallen into the temptation to sleep within their trees. Ser'ored stepped forward with a hand toward the seed tree. He hesitated.

"Do it, Ser," Ray'ored said.

"I don't see you stepping forward," he shot back.

Na'rina slowed, then halted. Felis growled but she sensed him standing next to her, waiting.

"I was the one who said it was a bad idea to force Na'rina home. She's too much like her mother."

"We have to deal with the wer-im now and she's ignoring the danger." Ser'ored grimaced and his nostrils flared. As they bickered, the connection with her Rina trickled away and then came back weaker.

*We can't wait for them to make the contact. Can you touch Ser'ored?*

*Sa.*

Na'rina groaned as her Rina's strain flowed through the connection. Felis gripped her arm to keep her upright. At one time she would've flinched but she felt no danger now. A thin white root shifted to rest against Ser'ored's bare toes. He jerked away and Na'rina almost cursed him.

*Try again.*

Her Rina tried as the two old Council members watched in shock. The grove shouldn't be able to move without its dryad present. Not without a strong need, like what she'd seen at the wer-im's Kadivas.

*Show them what they're dealing with,* Na'rina encouraged. With a shove from the earth, her Rina surrounded Ser'ored's ankle. Na'rina swayed. Ser'ored shrieked, tried to step away, and fell onto his backside when the grove didn't release him.

*Greetings, Ser'ored.* Na'rina didn't waste time waiting for him to speak.

"This isn't possible. We just heard you're still in the east."

*I am. My Rina thought it important to show me your presence in the grove. What brings you here?*

"We are concerned for your safety. The wer-im must be telling you all sorts of lies to convince you to work with them."

*I fear honesty has not been a strong trait of either species.*

"You're calling us liars?"

*I'm saying that a new threat faces us and if we can't get over our enmity, we'll be killed by an enemy we don't even see.*

"They *are* filling your head with weird tales." Triumph sparked in Ser'ored's eyes.

Na'rina felt it then. If she continued to debate, she'd never succeed. He wanted to be right so badly he wouldn't hear a word she said. *I have seen things I wish never to see again;* she recalled the ship and had her Rina pass the images on. The dissections, the labs, the military setup. Maybe it'd give Ser pause…Maybe.

*I fear for our people. I stand by my decision to ensconce the dryads in their trees and elect my own Council. When I return, it will hopefully be beside my mother. At that time, she will retake her authority and you may deal with me as everyone sees fit.* Na'rina cut the connection before they had a chance to recover from their shock. She'd moved fast enough. They had not thought to order her home. One less grievance to add to their list of her wrongs, because she would have ignored such an order. The world around her swayed. She blinked and worked to focus on Felis' worried gaze.

"There's something not right about you, Drydanda," he said. "Are you okay?"

"None of us is exactly 'normal,' Wer-im, but I'm fine."

"Okay." He released her arm. "Let's go."

She lengthened her strides to keep up as he tried to

make up lost time. Something dropped from a tree behind Na'rina. She ducked and spun around to find Silas standing there. Felis launched himself and then pulled his attack short by twisting to the side when he saw who it was. He landed on his side with a protracted *o-o-f,* followed by a hiss through his teeth as he cradled his tender ribs.

"Hello," Silas said.

Na'rina flared her nostrils and spun back around to enter the clearing ahead, where Icarus dropped from another tree. He grasped her shoulders. She swayed back but couldn't go far.

"What happened?"

Na'rina hesitated.

*You vouched for them. Plus, Felis already knows most of it.*

Icarus' expression lifted in his "pleased" look as she relaxed. He let her twist away when Silas entered the clearing, and they all sat while she explained about the oak twins and the Council.

"Rather ugly at home," Felis confirmed.

Silas studied Na'rina as if he were dissecting her brain. "You elected your own Council?"

Na'rina just lifted a brow.

He gave a low whistle. "Ugly indeed." But contrary to his words, his bright eyes held a look similar to Icarus' pleased expression. He reminded Na'rina of a cat about to eat a mouse.

"The dryads are safe at the moment," Icarus said, giving Silas one of those meaning-laden looks. Someday, Na'rina would decipher those looks. "For now, we head toward the Tennessee command center."

He held out a bag to Na'rina. Peeking inside, she found bread and honey.

"Want any?" she teased, smiling her thanks.

Icarus made a disgusted *yuck*.

Na'rina chuckled and tore into the bread.

First the ship, then the bus, and now a car? In the dark, the green exterior looked like a beetle—easily crushed along with anything inside it.

Na'rina's stomach dropped and her hands grew sticky. "Why can't we just run there?" They could run faster than the car, so why would he resort to the use of such a contraption now?

"We'll be less noticeable in a car, and crossing through cities won't slow us down." Icarus placed his warm hand on the small of her chilled back.

Silas ignored her. Opening the car door, he slid into the back seat on the far side.

"It's a deathtrap-on-wheels," Na'rina protested. "Does Felis know how to drive?"

Felis shot her a hurt look from the driver's seat. "We won't crash."

"But it's a, it's—"

*"Na'rina."*

She stilled. One patient word but it carried so much.

"Right." With a deep breath, she squared her shoulders and slid into the back seat while Icarus climbed in front. Silas flashed his teeth in what he must have meant to be an encouraging smile and Na'rina shuddered. Having to sit next to him only strengthened her dread.

The car rumbled forward and Felis turned onto a main road. Na'rina tried to tune out the sense of rattling metal but there was nothing to hold onto—no pulse of zoi aima beneath her soles, no bubbling laughter from a tree, not even the unbroken warmth from the sun to dull the knowledge in her core that she sat in a brittle cage. Trees and buildings rushed by her window and her temples throbbed in time with the flash of street lamps. A hand touched hers and she jerked. Swiveling her head, she found Silas watching her, an unspoken, indecipherable question on his face. She raised her brows.

"Mona'rina recovered after the banishment?" The question came out soft, but it carried a need so raw everyone in the metal deathtrap tensed. For Na'rina, it was like the conversation in the bus never ended. *What drives him to keep asking me?* Simple curiosity couldn't explain this intense interest in Mona'rina.

"Obviously," Na'rina answered warily.

"And her grove?" Silas leaned closer. She felt like a

mouse under that stare. "It healed as well?"

Icarus shot his mentor a warning look from the front seat. Silas ignored him.

Na'rina pressed tighter to her car door. The intensity in Silas' eyes reminded her of how he'd looked just before the Kadivas.

"I may have vouched for you, Wer-im," she responded in a breathy voice, her heart pounding, "but the state of our groves is our own business." He already knew Mona'rina's grove had been attacked recently. *Why does he care if the mother grove healed after the banishment?*

"You don't under—"

"*Silas!*"

"I—"

Icarus snarled and Silas snapped his mouth shut, his eyes dilating.

Na'rina hugged the car door. *What does Silas want from me?*

Silas' jaw twitched until he finally conceded through clenched teeth, "*Sa*, Wer-Kadis."

Tension simmered in the silence until Felis grumbled his irritation and the strain faded with the sound of his voice. The night dulled the sense of motion outside, and with it the throbbing in Na'rina's head. She caught the road sign announcing their entry into Tennessee, but for the most part she rested her temple against the doorframe and gazed at the sky, ignoring everything around her.

She thanked her stars for Icarus' intervention. Without him, Silas would continue to pressure her. Her stomach knotted as she considered her situation with the Council, or rather, the Councils. Her decision pitted young dryads against some of the oldest, most respected of their kind. Well, not all young, she admitted. La'meliai's almost dormant state before their contact indicated great age, but that didn't mean she knew anything about the subtleties of ruling. *I should know those subtleties—but all I've done is blunder along like a newborn giant, smashing everything without regard for the consequences.* Na'rina sighed.

"Bored, Drydanda?" Felis asked with a teasing lilt.

"Can't dance in a car," she grumbled, picking up on his attempt to lighten the mood.

"There's music." He hit a button and soft rock filled the air.

"Music?" Na'rina scooted to the center of the backseat, ignoring inadvertently bumping Silas, and leaned forward to see the radio controls. "There's actually something good about this contraption!"

Icarus pointed out the station control and volume buttons for her.

Na'rina scrolled through a country station, then jazz, then something that announced itself as "oldies."

"How'd you get to the meeting if not by a car?" Felis asked.

"She ran." Silas' voice was sharp and Felis flinched.

"Oh, what's this?" Na'rina asked, covering Silas' dark mood and the irritating, meaning-laden silence that followed it.

"More country," Icarus answered. "You're supposed to wear a seatbelt."

"A what?"

Icarus pulled out the strap that crossed his body with his thumb.

"See," Na'rina cried. "Deathtrap-on-wheels! Even the humans know it." She returned the radio to the soft rock station and slid back into her seat to buckle her belt. Intermixed with the music she picked up Icarus' low chuckle.

Picturing the wind playing through her Rina's leaves, she listened to the music and imagined dancing in the grove. The sense of the car faded as her pulse slowed to the tempo in her head. Her breathing softened, mirroring the deep rhythm of sleep, although she remained aware of her surroundings. *When the world spins beyond control, reconnect with who you are.* Her mother's words floated through her mind. She'd never understood what Mona'rina meant. Now it seemed so clear.

"What's she doing?" she heard Felis ask. Always curious Felis. She imagined him stroking his beard as he looked in the rearview mirror.

"Grounding herself." Silas' response didn't send the usual thrill of fear through her in her current state.

"She's marbling."

Na'rina heard Icarus turn in his seat to look. She almost chuckled. Something about her skin fascinated him and a small, rebellious part of her took pleasure in not telling him her actual color.

"Is this—"

"*Na*," Silas said. "She's not naturally two-toned."

They wanted to ask more, but even in her current state Na'rina felt Silas' continued dark mood. She immersed herself back in the music and let the wer-im stew in silence.

The music disappeared, and Na'rina snapped into awareness. As the engine died into silence, she felt a stillness not altogether natural. They'd reached the center on the western border of Tennessee. Icarus got out of the car and opened her door, his eyes gleaming at her surprise. Wind brushed her skin, bringing with it the scent of maple and sassafras and something akin to heated stone. Despite the warm night, however, her skin pricked with goose flesh.

"The center's down the road," Icarus said. He held out the familiar hoodie and a new ball cap.

Na'rina pulled the hoodie over her head while Icarus donned his own black beanie and dark sweater.

"Kadis?" she whispered, trying to speak quietly enough for the other two not to hear.

His reflective eyes glinted, serious and intent.

"I—" she hesitated, then tried again. "At the phone store, I sparked and passed out. What if that happens again and they come after us?"

He framed her face with his hands. He was warm, always warm. Na'rina wanted to lean into him, but swayed and stayed in place.

"That's why I'm here," he answered softly, though his voice held that familiar rasp. Why *I'm* here, not why *we're* here? "I will protect you. I promise."

A spark flared from Na'rina's core. Surprised, she grabbed his wrists and the spark ran into him. It felt strangely like the flare that rushed into the oak twins when she selected her own Council. Silas hissed, but Na'rina almost missed it under the flutter of her Rina rushing from the soles of her feet up through her hands.

*Hello, Kadis.*

Icarus' irises constricted but any response he could have given would have gone unheard. Her grove's contact stayed brief, leaving the familiar sweet taste on Na'rina's tongue and the scent of fresh leaves.

"*Icarus.*" Silas' voice came out strangled.

"Let's go." Icarus released her and turned away without acknowledging Silas.

The older wer-im looked stricken before shaking himself and moving to follow.

*What was that?* Her Rina didn't respond. Did her grove watch constantly now that she'd stretched far enough to contact her? *Probably.* Could her Rina speak to *anyone* through her? Na'rina had always thought only dryads could hear the trees, but Icarus heard, too.

It took her a moment to follow the others. The forest's life surrounding the hard-packed dirt road returned to her in a rush, dulled only slightly by the soles of her shoes. The tangle of undergrowth grew right up to the fence of the complex that Icarus lead them toward; its black scrollwork reminded Na'rina of a cemetery. She suppressed a shudder but the trees closest to her shuddered in response anyway.

"You're projecting, Drydanda," Silas warned.

"I'm aware, Wer-im."

Felis gave them a sideways glance and pointed ahead. "The scouts found a spot against the fence where the main power lines are buried and dug up a chunk to expose the lines."

*When did Icarus send scouts?* Na'rina stepped closer to listen to the discussion, realizing he probably organized the scouts before they left for the phone store. *He trusted I'd figure out the computer. Why does he have such faith in me? What if I fail?*

"The main power lines?" Silas asked.

"*Sa,* we—"

"This is stupid," Silas sneered. "The Drydanda could go up like a torch if she draws too much energy."

*Go up like a torch.* Silas' words raged through Na'rina's mind like flames, heightening her instinct to run. "How do I control it?"

Silas shook his head. "We need something smal—"

"The scouts couldn't find anything," Felis said, backing up a step when Silas snarled.

*How did he keep from destroying the wer-im with his sporadic behavior?*

"How does she control it?" Icarus clapped a hand on his old mentor's shoulder.

Silas swayed on his feet. Oddly for a wer-im, the motion seemed to settle him. He stilled and his jewel eyes focused on Na'rina. She met that gaze but struggled to suppress a shudder. The trees quivered anyway, rustling their leaves.

"Focus on exactly what you want and stream only as much energy as you need. Control just that. Since you can't control the whole stream, flow with it."

*That's supposed to be helpful?* She had plenty of control when it came to her body, and yet she sparked over connecting with a tiny computer. Na'rina studied her hand, at the white skin that was naturally green. She'd held the color for weeks now. *Surely I have enough control.*

"That's the concept," Silas said, as if reading her mind.

*Gah! How does he know so much?* Na'rina clenched her fingers and shoved her hand in her pocket. "Where are the power lines?"

Felis led them around the fence. The foliage grew thick and Na'rina brushed her fingers along the trunks of the trees they passed. The aged bark felt brittle. She tried a soft hello but nothing responded, not because they refused, but because there was no consciousness to answer. Tears pricked her eyes.

Felis stopped short. He took a handful of underbrush and pulled it away, and Na'rina swallowed her sorrow when she saw the brush had been pulled up by the roots earlier and laid here to hide the large hole beneath.

"Sorry, Drydanda." Felis gently set the bush aside, as if that made up for tearing it out by its roots.

He hadn't been the one to uproot the bush, the scouts had, but she scowled at him anyway. A sassy response, however, was beyond her as she truly took in the command center. From the road it'd looked like a large building, but from here she saw several buildings made of brick that stooped like small mountains from the ground. The ships had been huge, but this complex was a city in comparison—and according to the wer-im's intelligence it was one of many such centers.

"What is this place?" She didn't expect an answer but Felis responded anyway.

"Our intel says all the complexes like this belong to a company called Intela Corp. They're research facilities that make medical equipment and drugs."

"We're *truly* just lab rats to them." Hysteria pitched her voice into a higher register.

Icarus laid his hand on her shoulder and followed her gaze to a building sitting apart from the others. Smokestacks billowed steam from its roof, proclaiming a separate power source from the power lines.

"If the information's in there," he said, "you can retrieve it like you did in the phone store. The added boost from the power line should make it possible. Come, I'll lower you in."

Na'rina hesitated, then accepted his hand.

"Control," Silas reminded, as she lowered herself into the hole with the exposed lines.

*That's helpful.* She scowled, her stomach rolling.

Icarus climbed in behind her and she raised a brow.

"You pass out, someone's got to lift you out."

He'd lifted her into a tree before. This would be nothing if he had to pull her out. The safeguard made Na'rina feel a bit better as she knelt and the musk of disturbed earth surrounded her. The exposed power lines radiated a kind of dry friction. Just hovering her hands over them made her palms tingle in pain.

"Control," she mumbled and laid her hands on the lines. Energy, bitter and acidic, eddied back into her.

"Lights are flickering," Felis called from his position above the hole.

Na'rina pushed back against the flow and sparks flared out her toes, bringing the smell of burned rubber from her shoes. She hadn't even started to use the energy yet.

"Na'rina?"

The sound of his voice grounded her. Icarus knelt and placed an arm around her shoulders, and she let the warmth of his body combat the cold energy threatening to flow into her from the lines. But it wasn't safe. If she sparked again, she might kill him.

*Don't spark again.*

"Control," she whispered and bowed her head to touch the line. A strangled cry of warning sounded behind her. She recognized Silas' voice, but some part of her knew that to control herself in the energy flow she had to connect with it— not just direct it as she'd done before. White filled her vision. Her body flushed cold compared to the life-filled zoi aima she was accustomed to, and the river of electrical currents swept her in. She'd fallen in the Colorado River once in the spring when the snowmelt turned the water into a torrent of debris and pulling current. The disorientation she felt now was just like being in that swirling, swift-moving river. Except the river had been simply cold. This made her body break out in a sweat like stark terror.

"Flickering a lot!" Felis' warning whispered in her mind.

The river flowed forward and then split in multiple directions. She picked the left branch at the last moment and careened down a smaller channel until the energy shot off into dozens of tiny currents. She was overloading those circuits, flickering the lights.

*Rein it in, Na'rina.* She heard a familiar hum. A computer. *Don't fry it.*

She slowed to where the energy washed around her like chill rain. The lights stopped flickering and the computer hummed like a contented feline in front of her. She crept forward, picking up her pace little by little to match the exact flow into the computer. It buzzed when she entered it. Na'rina sucked in her breath and held it while she waited.

*Can I hold my breath as conscious energy?*

That's what it felt like. She released the breath when the computer didn't explode. *Files. Thank the stars, it looks like a grove of trees.* And it did. The twisting network reminded Na'rina of the swirling mass her grove looked like belowground, many parts but one massive entity.

*Employee lists.*

*Drug names and research.*

*Study types.*

*Doctors.*

*Species under study: plant or animal.*

It all looked normal. No wer-im, dryads, oceanids. Would they call the mythics by their true names?

*Daft! What would they call Mamma?* None of the names even hinted at a mythic. The research appeared mundane. She paused over a supply list:

Diphenhydramine—antihistamine.

Lidocaine—local anesthetic.

Chlorhexidine—antiseptic antibacterial agent.

Ketamine—general anesthetic.

Enhanced Ketamine—Zeta site special (tranquilizer).

Propofol—general anesthetic.

Orphenadrine—skeletal muscle relaxant.

Na'rina swayed and the computer warbled like she'd given it a bad command. Dr. Simms had named Enhanced Ketamine as the drug they'd used against Silas. *Zeta site?* She pulled every reference she could find but the only mention came from the directory. Na'rina's stomach sank. The small map in the directory labeled the building with the steam billowing from its chimneys as the Zeta site. *Of course.* She shot out a pulse of zoi aima from her body into the ground, hoping her Rina watched and would catch the information she gleaned thus far. As she pulled away from the computer, her nerves burned. Bile, along with that horrid acid taste, filled her throat and Na'rina took a shuddering breath to hold her stomach in place.

"Silas?" Icarus' voice whispered.

Na'rina wished she could warn him to move away, but if she pulled back enough to speak, she'd never convince herself to do this again. The nausea intensified as she searched for the building that the directory listed as closest to Zeta. She wasn't sure it mattered but the less actual distance she had to reach across the better, in her mind.

*Theta building.* She found the smaller building. Although tiny, it contained enough energy to power the larger projects conducted at the center. Not in use at the moment, the power cells sat along one wall, waiting. With a bracing breath, Na'rina drew from those cells. A hum built in her body, similar to the high-pitched thrum of a hummingbird's wings, and her hair stood on end. Like fire across her nerves, the energy swirled in reds and violets. She drew more and the hum turned deafening.

"It's glowing. Kadis' claws! What's she doing?"

*Always curious Felis.* Na'rina almost smiled but the pain sensitized her skin to the point she could feel each small hair stir on her neck.

"Focus, Na'rina." Her stomach clenched at the nearness of Icarus' voice.

She pushed her zoi aima beyond the walls of the Theta site, reaching with her energy-enhanced lifeblood for the Zeta building. Vulnerability rolled in Na'rina's stomach. The

282

computer store had made her feel as exposed as a newborn faun when she'd reached across the small expanse of the counter to touch the computer with her psychic mind. Now she was laid bare, open to pain, joy, hunger, and thirst. As her zoi aima quested through the vast open air between one building and the next, the life of everything nearby weighed in as a dense mass. With all that life came its associated desires, the dark secrets, the ambitions and fears—of trees, of plants, of animals, humans and mythics.

*Mythics? Not just the wer-im?*

Something swirled nearby with a destructive desire like an avalanche hovering over a mountainside. Na'rina shied away and her reaching zoi aima brushed against the power of the Zeta site. Grasping ahold, she shielded out everything else to focus on the site. A large part of her did not want to know what that darker mythic was—never had she touched something so ominous. The files pulled her attention. By their sheer depth, it was clear the humans had been at their work for far longer than the mythics realized. And they were ordered in a way she never would have considered:

<u>Predators</u>

- *Wolves:* possibly extinct. Myth only vaguely resembles reality. Natural prey is the Bovidae Sylvani (mythical faun), cattle, deer, and swine. Most have dark fur—

Na'rina moved on before she became too engrossed in the humans' findings.

- *Felines:* More types than at first surmised. Solitary creatures. Teeth spaced for separating vertebrae of larger species such as humans, apes—

She shuddered and moved on. She wanted to know more, understand what Intela Corp knew of the wer-im, but didn't have the time to view the entire file.

- *Energy Minds:* draw or release energy. Attempts on subject: electrocution, placed in power cell, vacuum.

Nausea climbed the back of Na'rina's throat again. Dryads were considered predators. A picture of Mona'rina, the "subject," opened with the file. "Location: Four Corners." They'd shorn her mother's beautiful dark hair close to her head and attached wires like what they'd done to Silas. More wires, more than Na'rina could count easily, connected to her body. The Mother Drydanda's deep green eyes were open wide, but an unusual brown laced through the green and her irises expanded to almost cover her whites.

Na'rina knew, without the explanation below the photograph, what torment the picture documented. With the power line fueling her, her own irises expanded to cover her whites—an attempt of her body to assist in seeing the energy— but, whereas Na'rina pulled the energy in of her own volition, it flooded Mona'rina.

A spark heightened Na'rina's awareness. Something moved within Theta's walls—something neither human nor healthy—but familiar. It moved through the brick of the building the way Na'rina moved through the power line, the brick acting as an extension of the creature's being.

- *Energy Mind*
- *Liquid Mind*
- *Mass Mind*

So much information—but time was up. The creature stopped in Theta's wall behind a breaker box. Delight, malicious and hysterical, flushed from it.

*Na!* Na'rina backed against the flow of the power line, trying to escape as the creature extended a heavy hand out of the wall and opened the box to expose the switch for an entire wall of dormant cells. The energy of the power line pushed against Na'rina's efforts to get out the same way a river would press a swimmer going upstream. The flow went *into* the research center, not outward.

Electricity sparked along her skin in waves and Icarus released a throaty roar that vibrated in her core. Clawing outward, pressing hard against the energy, her zoi aima crossed the fence line but she couldn't take her hands off the power lines before the hand flipped the switch. Raw energy flooded the line, fluctuated, then hit Na'rina in a bright flash. She lost all sight, psychic and physical.

*Icarus!* She pivoted to hold him protectively just before fire and energy exploded outward from her in a shower of earth and foliage. Debris rained through the air with a deep concussion. Na'rina caught no hint of Silas or Felis.

*Did I kill them?*

As everything stilled, her senses reached out, but the world came to focus in glittering shards and fragile pieces. The Kadis' body drew her down toward the blasted-out earth. No pulse, no warm zoi aima, fluttered against her hands. Icarus, usually so warm and vital, slipped from her numb fingers as she crumpled to the ground.

Na'rina's cheek rested against a cold, smooth surface that smelled of bleach and concrete. She cracked open her eyes and winced, not because of any light—she was surrounded by darkness—but because moving caused stabbing pain through her temples. She touched her face with a trembling hand. *What's wrong with me?* The trembling radiated through her torso, and when she shifted to sit up, pain shot through her chest. It reminded her of when Brin'ored split her aspen in two. Na'rina gasped and slumped back down, breathing between clenched teeth.

Na'rina peeked her eyes open again and the throbbing in her head intensified. *Use your other senses,* she chided herself. *It's pitch black anyway.* She closed her lids tight and took in the feel of the room. It only took a few seconds to find she was in a cube with a small bench. One wall contained a circle of tiny indents, but she felt no door in the otherwise smooth walls.

No wind caressed her scalp and no zoi aima teemed

beneath the soles of her feet. Never before, not even when wearing shoes and a cap, had she experienced such complete deadness. Her chest grew tight.

*There has to be a way out.* Na'rina steeled herself and stood up. Shaking, she reached upward to explore the ceiling, which was only about a foot above her head. Her fingers encountered a circular groove, but she couldn't get any leverage on it. She pushed against it, but nothing moved. If it was some kind of door, she wasn't sure how it opened.

Moving on, she splayed her palms flat against one of the walls, and reached outward with her zoi aima just as Silas taught her. *Nothing.* Her reach felt like it struggled through packed cotton. If an electronic lock existed beyond the smooth walls, she couldn't find it.

Na'rina's shoulders slumped as she dropped her hands.

Icarus. *Will he come for me?* She stilled, pulling the pieces of her memory together until they made an agonizing, gut-wrenching whole. Her knees buckled and she hit the floor as a sob choked her. There'd been no heartbeat and no zoi aima within his deeply vital body.

*Na,* Na'rina shuddered, *Icarus is not coming.*

The implications of that terrible fact left her breathless. She fought to pull air into her lungs against panic. Without a Drydanda, the dryads would turn on the wer-im, perhaps even blame them for her loss. And now, without the Wer-Kadis to lead them, there was no reason for the wer-im to hold back if the dryads attacked. The banishment would seem tame if such a confrontation erupted.

"Mother, what have I done?" Na'rina pushed to stand again but her body rebelled. As she lay prone, her fingers searched for the leaf necklace, seeking that small connection, but her fingers met bare skin. The chain and delicate leaf were gone.

Her hand flopped to the floor. It began to dawn on Na'rina just how much zoi aima she'd expended searching the Zeta site. *I need food.* But without water or sunlight, she may as well wish for the moon.

———————

Warmth touched her hand, climbed her arm and kissed her face. Na'rina's eyes flew open to catch the movement of the ceiling. The circular groove shifted to the side, letting sunlight stream down a long shaft in the ceiling to touch her where she still lay on the floor.

*It must be almost noon. How long have I been here? A day? Two?* Desperate for the light, Na'rina crawled fully into the weak, glass-filtered sun and sucked in the sustenance as fast as her body could handle.

A tiny spot on her chest warmed and then grew hot, as

if she held a flaming stick against her skin. Searching with her fingers, she found ridges just below her collarbone on her left side. Na'rina traced the outline and sobbed. By tilting her chin down, she could just see the glowing outline of an aspen leaf below her skin. *I didn't destroy it, I absorbed it somehow!* Filled with relief, she lay her head back on the floor.

Na'rina struggled to lift a hand to rub at her eyes, and paused to stare at her skin. It was no surprise that she'd lost control of her coloring, but her natural soft green had dulled to almost brown, a clear sign of being singed by fire or electricity. Shaking, she scrubbed away a scab on her arm. As soon as it flaked off, her sappy blood began to flow. A shudder traveled down her spine.

This, more than anything else, spoke of how drained she was of zoi aima. She should be healing fast enough that when the dry sap broke away there was healthy skin beneath. Na'rina searched within, testing the lifeblood flowing through her. *I'm dying.* The blue and green swirl of zoi aima, vital to her existence, centered on her heart and nowhere else. It explained why she fought even to lift her hand, let alone stand up.

She lay in the stream of filtered light with tears streaming from the corners of her eyes. It was weak food, but it was nourishment, and she desperately needed it. Slowly, her body began to heal the worst of her wounds. *Do they know they're feeding me?* As though they heard her question, the cover in the ceiling stirred with a dull groan and started to move.

"*Na!*" Na'rina cried, struggling to her feet, but the cover closed, taking the warmth and the light with it. Only the leaf, pressing small lines like veins on her chest, stayed warm enough for her to feel. Sliding back down the wall, she sat and rested her head on the bench.

Something stirred, a sound so soft at first she thought her imagination created the vibration out of sheer need. *Voices?* The sound grew closer and Na'rina's stomach clenched. She knew that voice.

The far wall slid open like the sliding doors on the ship, and a familiar acrid smell wafted into the room. *Dr. Hector.* She was sure of it although she didn't get a good look at him when she'd freed Silas.

*Stay relaxed. Don't show your fear.* At least there were no trees nearby to mimic her distaste as Dr. Hector stepped into the room. The door whooshed closed and a small light in the wall clicked on, illuminating one side of his slender face.

"Enjoy your snack?" The corner of his mouth twitched, but he didn't smile. He sported a dark goatee and slim glasses that didn't hide the spark of intelligence in his eyes.

The room was small enough Na'rina had to crane her neck backwards to see his face. *Ugh.* Na'rina braced to stand.

"No, no," Dr. Hector said. "Stay seated."

She paused. *Why?* She pushed off the floor and

collapsed in convulsions as energy shocked her shoulder and left her body shuddering on the floor.

Dr. Hector held up a small metal box with a black button on it. "See, we placed a device in your shoulder. Nifty little thing that feeds off any energy you have stored and shocks you with it. You could fight the convulsions but, considering you're the power source, it will kill you. Relax, and the device turns off. It's your way of controlling it. I, of course, can turn it off—and on—as I choose." He pocketed the box and crouched over her. "You're tiny for such a powerful creature," he mused. "You wreaked havoc on our systems when you took out the main power line. Not to mention the crater you left." Again, his mouth twitched. "Now this little device," he said, pulling a different metal box from another pocket, "will explode in about two minutes."

He placed the box into her limp fingers. "Contain it."

*What!?*

He stood, stepped back, and leaned against the door with his arms folded. Although the space was already tight, a sheet of protective glass slid out of the ceiling to separate them. He nodded at the box and actually smiled.

*He's serious.*

She wrapped her fingers around the dark gray device and found that it fit in one hand. No zap came from her shoulder at the small movement. Seeing her questioning look,

Dr. Hector held up the control box and pointed to the black switch. It was turned off. Na'rina sat up. *He said contain the explosion—not stop it. Does he know I can stop it if I figure out how it works?* Better not to find out. She'd directed the power from the center in an attempt to protect Icarus. *Perhaps I can do the same now.* Where to direct it?

Defiance, pulled from a well of frustration and fear, swelled within her. Na'rina stood up, wobbling, and braced her shoulders against the back wall, facing the protective glass while cradling the box against her stomach.

As with the tree devices, feeling the energy inside was easy. No timer ticked away the five minutes, but the energy built like the humming within a beehive.

*Thirty seconds*, Na'rina gauged. The hive vibrated, growing stronger. This would hurt, but wouldn't be deadly. At least, she didn't think it'd kill her.

*Ten seconds.* Eagerness made her step forward, once, twice, before bracing her feet on the ground as she prepared to direct the explosion. It was oddly like telling the sensor device what print to read.

The air went white. No sound, no feel, nothing. She flew backwards, smacking into the wall with a bruising thud. A high-pitched ringing sang in her ears, but even with that overarching sound, she heard the splinter of glass. The protective wall spidered into a sheet of cracked crystal. No sooner had Na'rina slouched to the floor then her shoulder spasmed and shock waves convulsed her body.

*Relax.* She couldn't. Her body fought the waves washing through her. *Relax!* Still Na'rina couldn't get control of her limbs. She smacked the bench with the back of her hand and her heel hit the wall. Her head cracked against the floor, and then everything stopped as suddenly as it started.

"Can't have you dying just yet." Dr. Hector's voice pierced her skull, rolling around her head like the flashes of light she saw before her eyes. "I'll leave you to think on what you did wrong."

---

He thought she'd learn not to target him. *Fat chance.* Her mistake was missing her chance to kill him. *What a violent thought.* Very un-dryadic.

*I don't care.*

Na'rina reasoned that what she did wrong was forgetting to counter the force of the blast. In the hole, when she'd held Icarus—her throat constricted—when she'd *tried* to protect him, she directed the explosion outward, equalizing it by sending the energy out in a circle around her. In the cell, the blast punched off of her as the backdrop, throwing her back and lessoning the force behind the explosion. That single blast could have killed

Dr. Hector, but she'd blown her chance.

She wanted to cry—or curse. Her fingers brushed the smooth floor on either side of her. They'd removed the spidered protective glass and installed a new piece that currently hid, recessed in the ceiling. For a smooth room, there were a lot of moving parts. Na'rina's right hand stopped when she discovered a rough edge, a crack in the floor. She traced her fingers along the crack, finding it extended about six inches. A humorless chuckle escaped her mouth, followed by a shock from her shoulder that brought tears.

She'd thought the doctor had left it turned off because she could move her hands. Perhaps it only registered the tension in her core but Na'rina decided not to test her theory. Instead, she held her hand over the ridge in the floor and reached beyond for a tree to pass along a message. Nothing touched her, nothing responded. Tears continued to trickle from the corners of her eyes, down her temples, and into her hair.

———

The ceiling opened, bathing the floor in delicious warmth. It touched Na'rina's upper torso, but the rest of her lay shadowed beneath the bench. Shifting to curl up in the light would trigger her shoulder. Instead, she flooded her skin with as much green as she could manage and whimpered as her body began to heal. Relief was short-lived. Not five minutes passed before the ceiling closed again.

The wall swished open a moment later to admit Dr. Hector with his acrid odor. It was the smell a diseased oak emitted right after being cut down, she realized. The door closed and he leaned against it.

Na'rina didn't move although, with her position, she looked at him upside down.

He pulled out the control box and flipped off the switch. Na'rina still didn't move.

"Hmmm. The green makes sense," he mused. "Like any plant, it aids photosynthesis, but what allows you to store and manipulate it after that?"

Na'rina remembered the dissected dryad on the ship. He'd insisted to Dr. Simms that the creatures they studied weren't sentient or capable of speech. But he must be aware she understood him or he wouldn't have given her orders earlier. Now, however, his questions felt rhetorical. Na'rina held her tongue, figuring the less intelligent he believed her to be the better.

"The other one that survived transport like you made a lot more noise."

*Survived transport? That has to be Mamma. Made?* Past tense. Na'rina's stomach clenched and then rolled with a desire to throw up. *Is she dead? Na.* The files she found were recent. They never mentioned Mona'rina was dead. Na'rina clung to the belief that her mother was still alive.

"Shall we try this again?" Dr. Hector pulled another little box from his lab coat. *Do they always make ugly, gray boxes?* She caught the box when he tossed it. He stepped back and the shield of glass slid down from the ceiling.

Na'rina's eyes pricked. *Again?*

"Tried to kill me last time," Dr. Hector said, pointing a warning finger at her. "I assure you, you won't succeed, and if you try again, I will turn on the device in your shoulder and let you die."

*I've lost my chance.* Na'rina hid her tears by sitting up and placing her back to the doctor. As before, the device gathered energy, but this time the sensation stung her fingers. It didn't exude the destructive intent as before but it gathered energy for something—

As Na'rina's fingers tingled it dawned on her what she was holding. A second before the device went off, she pitched it into the farthest corner of the ceiling, where it hit with a dense *thunk.* There was a crack like thunder, and Na'rina's body convulsed as the device sucked all the energy, including the zoi aima from her core, from the room. Breath wouldn't enter her lungs. Her body felt dry from the inside out. Just as the device was finishing its horrifying job, she snagged a wisp of zoi aima and focused on it, holding it within the leaf beneath her skin. When the box shut off, that tiny swirl of life trickled into her core. Her heart gave a lurch, stuttered, and kept beating, sending out aching pulses through her chest.

"Clever." Dr. Hector's laugh bounced around the room like an angry hornet.

Na'rina heard him flip the switch on the device in her shoulder, turning it back on. Then came the swish of the protective glass sliding home into the ceiling before the door clicked open and shut.

*He's gone—for now.*

She lay still, although her insides quivered and her breath came in shallow gasps. *I thought Dr. Hector wanted to study me but this is torture. Is this payback?*

Na'rina longed to speak with Icarus. Again, her memory replayed his limp body falling from her hands as his lifeblood failed to warm at her touch. It haunted her. *He trusted me and I failed him.* She felt utterly alone like no dryad was ever meant to be. Na'rina finally understood how a dryad could will her zoi aima away instead of enduring isolation in a tiny cell.

Time meant nothing in the dark. Na'rina stayed alive by instinct, cradling the spark that kept her breathing, for they hadn't reopened the ceiling to let in precious sunlight and her tiny store of zoi aima was ebbing away.

At last, the door swished open. The back of Na'rina's eyelids brightened from the light that turned on, but the illumination couldn't feed her and she didn't stir. Not even his acrid scent registered.

"The monitors tell me you're alive," Dr. Hector said. A change in pressure, air moving against her skin, warned her before his fingers brushed her cheek. "Judging from your coloring, 'alive' is being generous." He pushed on her cheekbone, rolling her head to the side. "Cold, papery texture like peeled bark, coloring has darkened further, started to brown, similar to an aspen tree dying."

*Is he recording this?*

"Bones have not started to protrude, perhaps due to no dormancy before death." The litany continued, droning against

Na'rina's brain like a nest of bees.

"Can it be revived?" A voice popped with static from the grill in the wall. Na'rina had discovered the grill during her initial search of the room, but she'd paid no further attention to it.

Dr. Hector took his time answering. "Possibly, although this creature seems incapable of anything more than what we have already discovered. It adds no value to our research."

*Story of my life.* Of course they learned nothing more from her than they had from Mona'rina.

"Instructions are to revive and study."

"There's no point."

"This is not negotiable as per the director. The clean energy project could hinge on these creatures."

Dr. Hector's protest seethed out between his teeth unspoken. His monotone returned as he continued recording. "It is unknown at what point an energy mind can no longer absorb energy and revive itself. I postulate for Study 1 of this experiment that the energy mind may indeed still be able to absorb energy, but at a slower rate than the norm due to the changed coloring in its skin. First test will be sixty seconds of sun. If no change occurs in the energy mind then the time will increase in increments of sixty seconds. Records show no more than five minutes are needed to effect a change. If nothing is recorded by five minutes, the energy mind will be determined to be beyond reviving and will be disposed of. First sixty seconds starts now."

The ceiling hissed. Na'rina held her breath, waiting for the precious touch of sunlight on her skin. Warmth kissed her face but no sunlight lit her eyelids. Her ability to absorb any nutrients in such conditions was negligible.

"Let it be noted that the day is overcast and no direct sunlight is available. Experiment will continue as we've found energy minds don't need direct light. We will expand out to six segments instead of five to compensate for the difference."

Six segments, a minute each, of indirect sun filtered down a tube in the ceiling? Even if she'd been well, such insubstantial food would barely be enough to restore the nub of zoi aima she'd been holding in her core.

On cloudy days, dryads entered their trees and relied on the tree to absorb the nutrients needed. Or they ate berries or honey, or even bread. Anything to supplement. *Does he know I can eat human food?* Na'rina struggled to say something, anything, to show those behind the grill that she was alive. Her facial muscles refused. She'd gone partially dormant to extend the zoi aima she held. *Need more.* Na'rina opened herself to the warmth on her face. She tried washing her color to a solid green but there was no more in her body to work with.

The light taste of rain filled her mouth as, little by little, her body absorbed sustenance but then the warmth faded as the ceiling closed.

"No change noted in the first sixty seconds. Monitors register nothing by way of increase energy or brain activity. Second increment starts now."

Na'rina focused on the hiss in the ceiling and the faint warmth that followed. The taste of rain returned like sweet nectar. Soon, the tang of honeysuckle coated her tongue. She tried to intensify the flavor but it faded, along with the warmth on her face. She hadn't heard the ceiling closing. A chill, fueled by dread, spread from her center. The intake of sunlight was too slow to make enough of a difference.

"No change," the doctor droned.

*Surely their sensors are sensitive enough to detect some change!* Perhaps not, Na'rina agonized. Without the telltale flavor of rain and honeysuckle in her mouth, she wouldn't notice much change either. *Four more increments. Make them matter.*

The ceiling hissed.

Na'rina wanted to groan at the inadequacy of light that filtered down. The clouds must have shifted, further covering the sun. The rate of absorption slowed until she barely tasted rain, much less honeysuckle. If her face hadn't gone dormant, Na'rina would have wept, but instead the pressure built behind her eyes until her head ached.

The increment passed and Dr. Hector droned his observations. The next two increments passed with no noticeable change, the doctor's words becoming more monotone with each recording.

The ceiling hissed. *Last segment. Make the monitors sing.* Na'rina's skin tingled in anticipation but nothing came—no warmth, no taste, just a creak, thud, creak, and then silence.

"Ceiling has malfunctioned," the voice crackled from the grill.

"Last segment will be abandoned," Dr. Hector replied. "There have been no changes up to this point. Another segment will make no difference."

"This is unorthodox. The director will not be pleased that this study was abandoned."

"This creature has proven incapable of furthering our study."

"Your reasoning being that this one is younger?"

"It doesn't matter. The director set a deadline and we don't have time to continue this experiment until this creature matures. Our best chances for success lie with the older mind. Note it in my study and have this thing disposed of. The director may question me directly if she chooses." The door swished open and closed and the artificial light went out.

*Disposed of?* A scream she couldn't voice tightened her throat. *Mother, I'm dying.* Na'rina had fought the knowledge up till this point, but she had nothing to hope for now. *So alone. Is this how you've felt since you've been taken?* How had her mother

303

survived for so long? Na'rina thought the mother grove had been attacked to weaken Mona'rina, but there was no contact with her Rina in the cell. It wouldn't have mattered if the grove was healthy if they had no connection for it to strengthen her mother.

What if there could be contact? Any contact? Na'rina's thoughts stuttered. *What if I've overlooked the simple things?* She'd reached for a tree earlier, but there were dozens of other, smaller sources of zoi aima stretching through the earth. When she had reached through the crack in the floor she'd attempted to get a message out, but what if she tried for more? Not just messages, but putting will to whatever plant she found? Like when she'd touched Ser'ored with her Rina, physically separate from the grove but still directing its will, making it *move.* If she were inside another plant, like with La'meliai's ash, she could control it. And she'd moved her grove while separate from it. The next logical step would be to try a plant life not her own.

*Just another step. Another giant step.*

She craved Icarus' encouragement more than ever now. His belief that she could do whatever she put her will to always steadied her. But in her mind, his body fell from her hands again and again. *I'm alone*, she choked. Then, right on the heels of her despair, she remembered her Rina's words: *You are never truly alone.* Na'rina's heart ached at the memory of her Rina. It was gentle rain compared to the tempest of Icarus' death, but it was an insistent rain. *You are never truly alone.*

Na'rina's hand already lay, by chance, over the crack in the floor. Being dormant prevented her from moving and therefore setting off the device in her shoulder. If this didn't work, the effort alone would kill her, but how else would she use her last reserve of zoi aima? Na'rina reached into the earth in the same way she had reached the Zeta site building. She didn't search for a specific plant now. Anything large enough to help her would do.

The smell of damp earth swirled through the psychic touch. The rich soil harbored dozens of small roots—grass, bushes, vines—and then a tree, a sickly, rotted tree. She shied away from touching it, knowing any contact with its zoi aima would make her ill. Then it hit her why she'd found no trees before: all of the trees surrounding the center were unaware. They would not have responded to her call because they lacked consciousness.

Na'rina passed over the grass and bushes because they were too small to help. She needed something with its own vast store of zoi aima. She paused over a vine. It was a kudzu that had climbed an entire wall of the building housing her. Na'rina marveled, for a moment caught up in the plant's slow but purposeful lifeblood. It reminded her of a stream that would carve away part of a mountain to claim its spot in the world.

*Let me help*, the kudzu stretched, eager. He sent a myriad

of images, clarifying his intent. If she asked, he'd give everything. Na'rina sensed something else. Behind his already inexorable strength swirled more. A familiar zoi aima that tasted of sunshine and leaves.

*My Rina?*

*She'll help me grow!* the kudzu chortled.

*There you are, my Na'rina,* the grove breathed. *I've been searching for you.*

Hope blossomed in Na'rina. In her dormant state, she could not give or take lifeblood from a plant other than her seed tree. Even now, sending out a stream with her consciousness was sapping her small store. But with her Rina giving extra to the kudzu, his potential growth increased tenfold. All Na'rina had to do was direct him. As she had willed La'meliai's ash to heal faster than was natural, she could will the kudzu to grow at rates he could not manage on his own. If the vine found her within the building and carried her outside, perhaps she could still absorb sunlight, but she would not know for certain until she lay under the cloudy sky.

As she processed this, the kudzu trembled with joy, sharing the pressure he felt from the grove's presence like water pressing against a dam. He thrilled beneath the weight of it, inviting Na'rina in as freely as a tulip opened for the sun. Such welcome made it easy to cross the psychic line from being a separate entity to accepting the kudzu as hers to control.

Her dormant body lying on the cell floor faded, replaced by the cold brick where it touched the vine's skin. Even with the overcast sky, he soaked in warmth and moisture from the air. Na'rina quivered at the heady mix of the kudzu's zoi aima that craved growth as much as sun and rain, and her Rina's stronger lifeblood with its swirling, almost angry need to free her.

Na'rina took in a steadying breath through the kudzu's skin. It tasted of fine dust. *Find my cell.* She pictured her room with its small window in the ceiling. It wasn't much to go on, but the vine stretched to comply. "Impossible" was not a familiar concept to him, and he attacked the building with enthusiasm. After climbing the wall to extend across the roof, the kudzu shot out branches to explore every crevice, hole, grill, and pipe he came across. The Rina laughed as she fed it zoi aima. Pulling on that lifeblood, the kudzu moved deeper into the building through the grates he pulled free.

Sound—screams, the grate of metal on metal as hinges were pulled free, the rumble of bricks being torn apart and crushed—filtered through the thick skin of the vine in a muffled deluge. He was not used to sharing his experiences, and Na'rina found the mass of ground he covered made it hard to sort out each new part of the building he found. It was her Rina who caught the familiar acrid smell and directed her attention to a narrow hallway with pictures of waterfalls on the white walls. Dr. Hector raced down the hall, a short blonde female at his heels.

"It's still coming," she babbled. "You said the energy mind was incapable of anything more. Are you sure this is a result of—"

Na'rina lost the words as they turned a corner. *Follow them.*

*Gladly.* The kudzu shot down the hall and around the corner. The hall ended with a single door and a biometric reader like what she'd seen on the ship.

"Doctor? *Doctor?*" The blonde woman tugged on his arm, staring wide-eyed at the kudzu. He didn't turn but raised the butt of a flashlight and swung it at the scanner.

*Na!* The vine shot forward but not fast enough to stop him as the scanner shattered with a metallic crunch. Finally Dr. Hector turned to face the writhing mass of kudzu barring their escape from the hall.

"Will it kill us?" The woman clung to him.

"Doubtful." He leaned against the door and folded his arms, just like he did when he studied Na'rina. "Everything we know about them suggests they're peaceful." His mouth twitched. "I'm not even sure the energy mind is aware of what the vine's doing. I suspect it's merely responding to the mind's need."

Na'rina wanted to strangle him. In response to her thought, the kudzu formed an image of the thick vine wrapped around Dr. Hector's neck. There was a question inherent in the picture. All Na'rina had to do was say, "*Sa.*"

She gagged. *I'm not violent,* she insisted, but the denial rang hollow. Almost like a shrug, the kudzu offered a different option, and showed itself forcing a way between the wall and the door to break the mechanism and shove the door open.

*Sa.* Na'rina seized the less violent option, but Dr. Hector stood in the way. He pulled out a large knife and hacked at the vine. Stabbing pain lanced into Na'rina's mind.

*Contain him!* she directed. The kudzu shot forward.

"Doctor!" the woman screamed, pulling at the branches encircling his legs, waist, and arms. The large knife clattered to the floor. Her cries became a shriek when the doctor ended up strapped to the ceiling in a web of vines. Even through the dulled senses of the kudzu, the wail echoed in Na'rina's ears.

*Make her stop!*

The vine shot toward the woman. She fainted.

*Perfect.* Na'rina's relief was palpable. *Now the door.*

The kudzu seemed to grin. A tiny new sprout grew and pain shot through Na'rina's connection with the plant. Despite that, the kudzu giggled. He slid the sprout between the wall and door, and with a massive draw on the Rina's zoi aima, it thickened into a large, bloated limb. The door groaned, buckled, and sprang open with a dull thud.

*Ha!* Satisfaction filled the word, but when the kudzu turned his focus on Na'rina's dormant body on the cold floor, he froze. Mottled brown and green, she resembled a mossy log.

*For being so close to death, you've a strong will.*

*Any Drydanda could do this.*

*Nope, not true. Another already failed.*

*What? Who?*

Like a petulant child, the kudzu shot sprouts in all directions. His focus dissipated along the new growth, and she had no hope of forcing an answer. Calling out only weakened her further. She stopped and waited for the vine's focus to come back. It rejoined her just as she thought she'd lose the will to direct it.

*Now my shoulder.* After she knew to search for it, the tiny metal device they'd implanted beneath her skin created a cold nub that throbbed like an itch she couldn't scratch.

*Nasty bit of work,* the kudzu grumbled. Glass shattered and sprinkled the floor as another shoot broke through the ceiling window. It lifted Na'rina from the floor to expose her back. Her body flopped like a doll, but since there was no tensing of muscles it did not activate the device. *Sorry, Drydanda. This isn't going to be pretty.*

He placed a thin sprout, like a thorn, against her shoulder and dug into her skin. Sappy blood flowed down her back, but she felt only a pinching on her left side. He dug farther and Na'rina twitched. Shocks rocked her body and traveled into the kudzu the way lightning ricocheted through her grove's roots. To her surprise, the vine held tighter, absorbing the shock with determination. As her shaking subsided, the sprout closed around the cylinder that was no bigger than her fingernail. Withdrawing from her shoulder, the kudzu tightened around the device until it cracked. When he relaxed, pieces fell to the floor.

*Now carry me—*

Na'rina pictured the overcast sky but her connection with the kudzu stuttered as her last bit of her zoi aima faltered. Darkness closed in as she instinctively reached to pull lifeblood from the dozens of vines they'd used to search the facility. Nothing happened.

*Your dormant state prevents you from absorbing other plants,* her Rina softly reminded her. *One last will, my Na'rina, to get outside. Maybe you can still take in sunlight.*

Na'rina fought to remain aware. *I canno—*

*Try, my Na'rina.*

She imagined open air, trees, and a cloudy sky. Maybe the kudzu understood, maybe not.

*My Na'rina?*

*Huh?*

*I've found the faun, Afre.* Another section of vine hovered over the huddled form of the faun Na'rina met weeks ago. His furred legs were matted and patchy and his ears lay back against his head, submissive in an unnatural way. Broken.

*Get us out,* she whispered with a last surge of will.

*My pleasure.* As the kudzu moved toward Afre, he withdrew into the corner but didn't fight when the shoot lifted him.

The faun blurred in Na'rina's vision and a moment later she became aware of her body again. A burning in her shoulder hit her with the reality of her bleeding open wound, but her agony couldn't escape her parted lips. It didn't matter that she was aware, her muscles hung limp and her throat barely drew breath.

*I'll make it outside only to die on the ground.* Na'rina had given everything to reach the sunshine but she was certain she could no longer absorb it. *I need my Rina.* But her grove lay miles to the west. Without actual contact, the grove couldn't break Na'rina's dormancy.

The faint touch of sun kissed her skin and a psychic sigh ran through Na'rina. *I tried, Mother.* Dulled though her senses were, she felt the mat of leaves and dirt against her back as the kudzu laid her on the ground, and the play of wind across her skin was comforting. *At least I'll die surrounded by the natural world.*

"You told me, 'Don't anger the Drydanda.' For sky's sake, she just crushed a building! Why didn't you warn me?" The familiar teasing drew closer with each word, jarring against Na'rina's resignation toward her death.

*I've gone insane.*

"*Enough.* She's gone dormant. We need to move."

*My insanity has a cruel edge.*

"She looks terrible."

*Thanks, Felis, it's good to see you too.*

Hands slid beneath her shoulders and knees and lifted her. "Silas, how do we stop her bleeding?" Warm breath fanned across her face with an unforgettable spicy scent. *Icarus' lifeless body fell from my hands.* Na'rina's heart constricted. *This can't be. I killed him.*

"Felis, hold the fence," Silas ordered and Na'rina's equilibrium wobbled as she was shifted around. The fence brushed her arm and she realized they must have cut a hole in it to get inside the compound. "We'll control the bleeding back at

313

the car."

"Why are you bringing the faun? Isn't he kind of useless?" Even in their hurry, Felis had questions.

"The Drydanda spent her zoi aima getting herself *and* the faun out. She must have her reasons."

*Why does Silas care?*

"Security's moving to secure the perimeter. *Let's move.*"

They picked up their pace. Lightning flashed from Na'rina's shoulder into her core and limbs, ending as a throb in her head.

"Felis, open the doors," Silas ordered.

The jolting grew worse as Na'rina was jostled into a seat. Her side grew cold as someone grabbed her from the left and slid her sideways. The smell of heated fabric and metal surrounded her. *Gah! The car.*

Then warmth returned to her side as the car door thudded shut. An arm went around her torso, pulling her close and that spicy scent filled her senses.

*Is it possible? He had no pulse.*

She recalled Icarus' warmth when she woke after the spines knocked her out. Her breath stalled in her lungs.

"How do we stop the bleeding?" Icarus' husky voice asked again as his breath fanned her right ear.

*He's alive!* Even with her dulled senses, there was no mistaking it.

Wheels grated, spitting dirt, as the car started moving.

"Let me see," Silas said.

She was tilted forward and a chill ran down Na'rina's right side.

"Something tore into her," Silas stated. "Pinch her skin together. Her blood's sticky but the skin's not able to bind and heal like it should. Give it some help and it'll seal off after a bit." Needles shot through her shoulder.

"Got it." She tilted back and that blessed warmth returned to her right side. "How's the faun?"

"I'll live," came Afre's weak voice from the front seat.

"We made it away clean," Felis said. "Where are we going, Kadis?"

"Colorado," Silas answered. "We've done all we can until we get to her grove. It'll be a close call to get her there before she dies."

*They're taking me home.*

For the first time since Na'rina left the research center and felt the sun on her face—sun she couldn't absorb anymore—hope blossomed within her. She welcomed the pressure of tears behind her eyes.

There was a pause as everyone else registered that Na'rina might die before they could get her home. Icarus pulled her tighter against his side as if his vibrant zoi aima could stave off her slow ebb. It couldn't, but she clung to his warmth anyway.

"Just to be clear," Felis blurted out, unable to stand the tense silence, "are all dryads so secretly dangerous?"

"You're aware all nymphs exist in a plane not totally physical?" Mockery edged Silas' question.

"*Na*, wasn't aware." When the silence threatened to take over again, Felis asked, "So that's a *sa*?"

Silas sighed, exasperated. "Only the Drydanda can control plants not their own, although all nymphs have their Drydanda-type leaders."

"They all can crush buildings?"

Icarus snorted but it was Silas again who answered. "They all can crush buildings if they wanted."

"How?"

Icarus took pity on Felis' need for a distraction. "Oceanids would use water."

Na'rina recalled Felis' muttering during the Kadivas—a nervous response perhaps—while Icarus' voice vibrated against her ear. "Not just open water, anything containing moisture. Clouds, storms, rivers. Oceadandas, Oreadandas, Naiadandas. They *all* have their things, but they're rare and usually peaceful."

"Is there something special about this one?"

"The potential's there." Silas didn't elaborate but Na'rina knew what he meant. Being a direct descendant, True Born, should make her stronger.

"She's kinda papery looking, like—"

"Felis."

"I don't mean to be rude, it's just that she's always so striking, but without movement she's—"

"She *can* hear you." Icarus' voice held both warning and exasperation now.

"She can? Really Drydanda, you're beautiful. I meant no offense. The brownish-greenish-whi—"

"Felis!"

"Right." Silence followed, palpably awkward until Felis broke it again. "I, ah… I get going to her grove but doesn't that present a problem with the Council thing that went awry?"

"It does." Silas sounded like he faced the window. "But the Council can't act on what they don't know."

A new anxiety knotted in Na'rina's stomach at the reminder but then she told herself to relax. *I have to live long enough for that to be a problem.* Her body focused on the warmth seeping into her from Icarus.

As Silas and Felis talked, Icarus settled his lips beside her ear. His breath fanned across her skin, faint but clearly there. *Alive!*

"Hang in there, Na'rina," he murmured. She soaked in the sound, fighting the sleep pulling at her. "Hang in there," he repeated. "You get better and I'll find you bread and honey, or berries—or you can enjoy that honeyed wine that's still floating around your backpack. Just hold on."

*Afre's wine?* She'd forgotten about it. *It survived this long?* But she didn't really care about the wine despite how wonderful it'd taste. She had so much more to fight for. As Na'rina relaxed, she let her awareness drift away.

Na'rina's stomach rolled with disassociated movement and everyone's voice bounced around the car like echoes in a cave.

*What woke me?*

She breathed in, savoring the spicy scent surrounding her as she clung to Icarus' whisper when he shared how far they'd traveled. He'd done this periodically, though it became harder each time to understand his words as her zoi aima grew watery. But she knew when they left Arkansas and had a vague idea when they entered Oklahoma City. They passed through Texas and New Mexico. Then she heard the blessed words, "We're entering Colorado." Determination surged through her. *I'm so close.*

This half-contact with the world lasted right up until they turned toward the mountain pass that housed her grove. The car slowed and then stopped with a crunch of gravel under the wheels.

"This is going to be fun," Felis grumbled.

"They close the pass in the winter. We're a week, maybe two, early of them opening it."

*How does Silas know this?*

"You mean we have to hike in carrying them?"

"We'd have to hike in anyway to avoid the Council." Icarus' voice brooked no argument and Felis heeded the tone.

"We're avoiding the Council?" Afre asked.

Felis snickered. "The old Council's playing dirty. The Drydanda began the election of her own Council when she found out they were lying to take control from her."

Afre grew quiet at that.

As soon as they opened the car doors, the scent of wet aspen and earth infused the air, carrying a chill that spoke of recent rain. A few degrees colder and it would've been snow. The desire to see her home had Na'rina straining against the sodden log feeling fettering her. Nothing happened. She breathed deeply instead, settling for taking in the sweet aroma of home while Icarus carried her from the car. *Soon, I'll be better soon.*

"Why don't these trees work?" *Always curious Felis.* "I thought she belonged to the whole grove or the whole grove belongs to her. How do you say it? Is she—"

"We need the seed tree," Silas cut in.

"Oh."

Na'rina could feel Felis' desire to ask more but his curiosity quailed under Silas' dark tenor. They headed up the dirt road on foot.

"Felis, scout ahead."

Na'rina waited for him to respond but then perceived he must already be off to do as ordered.

"I can walk, Wer-im." Afre sounded strong. He'd looked so broken in the cell, but hearing his confidence, she could picture him as his old self.

"You sure, Faun?" Silas asked. "You're not steady."

"I need to be on my own two legs."

*That's not the old Afre.* This Afre held an edge in his voice even though he was speaking to a natural predator. Their pace slowed to accommodate the faun but Na'rina picked out the soft clop of Afre's hooves. The farther they went, the steadier that sound became.

"Dormancy outside her tree is rare for a dryad, dangerous," Afre noted.

"It's rapid starvation," Silas grumbled. "A Drydanda's control of zoi aima is the only thing keeping her alive."

"Your knowledge of the Drydanda is—unexpected." It wasn't an accusation, Afre wasn't stupid enough for that, but it was probing.

"How old are you, Faun?"

"Few hundred." For a faun, that was vague.

"Not old enough then."

"Old enough to know what you are."

Silas snorted. "You think?"

Icarus' growl vibrated against Na'rina's ear. They fell silent for several minutes before Afre's voice broke it again. "Then tell me Truth."

*Oh Afre.* The fearful faun she'd spent an afternoon with would never have boldly pressed the wer-im like this.

Icarus growled again before Silas could answer. "You know she can hear us, Faun. It isn't the time to tell her that truth."

Na'rina wanted to scream. Icarus so easily saw through Afre's attempt to help her.

"She has to be told before she realizes her potential. Changing a dryad after that is difficult," Afre warned. "If you want her to welcome you, the full truth might be necessary."

"Tree's up ahead," Icarus ignored Afre's warning.

"There's a dryad headed this way," Felis said. Na'rina had no idea when he returned. "Saw him pass over the ridge to the south on my way back."

Their steps quickened and Icarus' gait became rougher as they left the road. Everyone's steps crunched when they hit patches of snow that hadn't melted yet in the higher elevation of the pass.

"There, that tree," Icarus said.

Na'rina didn't need any help to sense her Rina, though. Her seed tree's closeness echoed inside her like the shimmery vibrations of a small bell. The smell of fresh growth swirled in her nose and Na'rina longed to touch the budding leaves.

Icarus let her legs swing free and supported her weight by passing his arms under her shoulders. "Place her palms on the trunk and tilt her forehead against it," he instructed someone. "Felis, check on that other dryad."

*Welcome home, my Na'rina.*

Unshed tears throbbed behind Na'rina's eyes but the discomfort dulled as the ache of distance washed away. It ran over her, a steady spring rain, starting at the roots of her hair and flowing down to her toes.

"This could take some time," Silas cautioned.

Her hands sank into the tree, shooting needles into her shoulders. Na'rina gasped as the wash of zoi aima worked its way into her dormant limbs. Like a dam breaking under the spring thaw, it flushed the dormancy away with a healing that was anything but gentle. *It hurts!* She'd never experienced pain when entering her Rina. This was almost mind-numbing.

*You're not supposed to go dormant outside of your tree,* her Rina chided.

*Didn't have much choice.*

They both knew she spoke the truth and so her Rina accepted that with silence. Na'rina would have died days earlier otherwise. Neither one wanted to contemplate the narrow miss.

"This is taking too long," Icarus stated when Felis returned to inform him the other dryad was a few minutes away.

"We can't separate them without Na'rina willing it."

*Na.* Na'rina ached at the thought of separating from her Rina but she couldn't sink into the grove any faster and she couldn't risk the Council finding her here, especially with a wer-im holding her. *Let me go,* she whispered. The Rina shuddered but released her. The separation felt like she was peeling off her skin. Na'rina cried out, a tiny sound in comparison to the pain, but Icarus clamped a hand over her mouth to muffle the sound.

"Knew she could hear us," Felis said.

Na'rina's stomach lurched as Icarus launched them into the branches of the tree. "Try again, Na'rina," he encouraged once they were in the branches. With one arm he held her torso and with the other he placed her forehead and palms against the bark again. The Rina pulled in her hands and relief washed through Na'rina.

"He might still see you," Felis warned from below.

"Distract him."

"And show my whiskered wer-im face? You sure?"

Afre stepped in. "I've got this. Make yourselves scarce."

The wer-im on the ground disappeared. Within minutes of them scattering, Ser'ored arrived at the seed tree. Through her Rina, Na'rina saw his spikey green hair and heavy rounded joints, features that mimicked his pine's long, deep green needles and the knots that spotted his trunk. For his age, Ser'ored moved with a comfortable grace. When he noticed Afre leaning against a tall pine, he stopped and swayed, staring at the faun in open, but not welcoming, curiosity. Afre gave him a partial bow, the slight curve of a mocking smile on his lips. He'd chosen his position well and Ser's back was to the seed tree.

Na'rina's hands and elbows sank into the tree and her shoulders followed a moment later. Fiery needles shot through her but she continued to will the melding to move faster, before Ser turned and spotted them.

Finally, Ser stepped forward. "The Drydanda is not here." He gave no greeting, no introduction, and the abruptness of his words more than anything showed his slowness in responding to even this small surprise. Na'rina had always regarded the Council as wise and capable, taking their measured responses to indicate well-considered words, but they were never the ones to interact with other species. The Drydanda always acted as the face of the dryads to the outside world. *Maybe this is why.*

Afre tilted his head. His ears swiveled where they peeked from his curly hair. "I know. I came to inform the Drydanda of the fauns' support."

A breeze whispered through the grove, but Ser swayed

like a heavy wind pushed at him. He must have just realized how much influence Afre held, Na'rina noted with a spark of satisfaction at Ser's consternation. If Afre was indeed influential, it meant he'd just made a mistake, complicating the Council's maneuvering for power.

*Could Afre promise such a thing?* She couldn't tell anything from his expression but she doubted he'd reached his father before being captured. There hadn't been enough time for Afre to travel home and then be captured. The fauns probably didn't know a thing about what had happened at the meeting in Chattanooga, much less anything about her actions since.

"You're at the wrong tree." At first Na'rina thought Ser meant to point out her seed tree and she tensed, but he gestured toward Mona'rina's grove instead. "I'll show you."

Afre hesitated and his internal dilemma played across his face. Following Ser would get them away from Na'rina, but Afre knew the dryad wasn't being truthful.

"You assume too much," he called after Ser.

Na'rina groaned internally as Ser turned back toward the faun. Her body hid three-fourths of the way into her tree, but Icarus remained exposed. Trusting the grove had a firm enough hold on her, Icarus climbed over to the next branch, moving out of Ser's line of sight.

"Where are my manners?" Ser's tone shifted to an ingratiating sweetness. "I'm Ser'ored of Mona'rina Drydanda's

Council." He held out a hand to Afre.

Afre accepted the hand, his tufted fingers holding firmly as he said, "Afre son of Oba-Afren."

"Oba-Afren? King Afren has been informed of what's happening?"

Considering the fine line he walked, not a hint of tension touched Afre's expression. She would not have expected the faun to be so talented at such interactions, but she had obviously sold him short in her first estimation. He was, after all, the Oba-Afren's son, trained like herself to lead someday.

"The Oba-Afren knows of Na'rina Drydanda and is aware of her mother's troubles." Afre gestured at his matted legs and emaciated body. "If Mona'rina Drydanda is in a similar position as I myself was until recently—a captive of humans for experimentation—she needs all the help you can find. The question is, why would you cover up your situation? Fauns have always been your allies. Why would you not reach for our help?"

Na'rina stilled. *Afre's confronting Ser?* Her Rina showed her Afre and Ser'ored from multiple views. The faun's face stayed calm, set in displeasure, but as he leaned back against the pine, he slid his shaking hands into his back pockets, hiding them.

"I simply show solidarity for my people," Ser answered after a pause. "Mona'rina's trouble is not common knowledge, and we do not want to panic the dryads. Unrest among us now would leave us vulnerable."

Afre's ears swiveled. He shook his head as if saddened. "Again you offer honeyed but dishonest words. Your people know of Mona'rina's capture and the other species flock to her daughter, trusting her to step in to respond to the threat on Mona'rina's life. They trust her and yet, you do not? Is it a wonder she elected her own Council when support from the old one is lacking? I came here to convey support to Na'rina when she is in company with the wer-im, the faun's natural enemy. Consider that, Ser'ored of the Council. I support her, and the wer-im, because I've tasted the danger attacking us. Perhaps you would do well to look into that threat before you undermine your ability to counter it."

*Captivity really has changed Afre.*

Ser'ored gaped. Fauns always spoke truth, which tended to sway people because fauns were trusted not to spin reality. But rarely did they chastise another creature while telling that truth. A faun said how it is, not how it should be. The dryad's mouth snapped shut.

"I trust you'll convey that without my help." He spun on his heel to leave.

"Your pride will get you killed," Afre said softly.

Ser's back stiffened but he kept walking.

Now fully within her seed tree, Na'rina sighed as the

327

needles of pain receded. The grove folded her closer, swirling zoi aima through her, bringing with it the tangy awareness of tart budding leaves and the fresh scent of wet aspen and earth. *Focus on healing.*

Finally, as she opened her eyes, her sight shifted from the psychic of her Rina to the physical, and the world washed green like the first shoots of spring. Her mottled brown and black faded as mist into the grove and her skin became a healthy celadon. Na'rina stretched, making the aspens within a hundred-yard radius quake.

*This is how it should be,* the Rina spoke with deep satisfaction.

Na'rina heard a chortle and the Rina showed her Afre. Now leaning against her seed tree, the faun watched Silas and Felis return from hiding.

*That one has more backbone than any faun I've ever seen.*

Na'rina agreed.

Felis rushed to engulf Afre in a hug. "You vouched for us!"

"Let go, you overgrown kit!" Afre bleated in surprise.

The wer-im swung him around like a kid holding a kitten. "Can I keep him?"

Icarus and Silas laughed but poor Afre shook like a leaf.

*Take pity on him.*

*With pleasure.* The Rina snaked a root through Felis'

ankles and he shot his arms wide as he fell.

Afre landed on the ground with an *u-m-p-h*. As soon as he hit the dirt, the Rina circled his slim waist, pulling him against the seed tree's trunk and guarding him.

"Think that was a *na*," Icarus chuckled, helping Felis up.

Felis pouted. "I was just joking, Drydanda."

Although the awakening of Na'rina's dormant body took moments, full recovery required almost another day. As the sun rose to warm the powdery bark of the seed tree, they breathed in the zoi aima those rays produced as though drinking a river of water. Lifeblood eddied in waves of green and blue that caressed Na'rina's skin. Though healed, she loathed the need to leave her Rina. An awareness, like the fine hairs rising on her arms, brought her eyes up to meet Icarus' hazel gaze. He watched the seed tree with his shoulder blades braced on the same pine Afre leaned against the day before.

*That one changed something within us,* her Rina remarked.

*What do you mean?*

*When he promised to protect you, it changed something. I felt his anger and shame at your captivity like burning brands. I do not think the older wer-im approves.*

Na'rina recalled the rush of zoi aima when Icarus promised to protect her, before she breached Intela Corp.

*You willed that, even if it wasn't conscious,* her Rina clarified.

*I need to understand, to know, what Icarus and Silas know.*

*Your mother's grove could explain but her Rina won't speak until she's safe.*

*So it comes back to freeing her.*

*Your Grandmother might have answers.*

*She's dormant.*

*Ver'rina can no longer leave her tree, but she's not gone.*

Na'rina shuddered and the aspens followed suit. Icarus tilted his head in feline curiosity.

*Ver'rina's not helpful.*

*She's a wealth of information if you understand her.*

Therein lay the problem. As with many dryads, Ver'rina had withdrawn into her trees hundreds of years ago. The seclusion of remaining within her grove had twisted her perception until she spoke in ways few could decipher.

*I'll consider it.* Na'rina savored the last moment within her Rina and then withdrew, exposing her renewed skin to the sunlight filtering through the leaves. A chill wind played through the trees, carrying the scent of snow, but instead of comforting her, it brought a sense of vulnerability that threatened to make her shy.

"Green," Icarus noted.

"Problem, Kadis?" Na'rina rolled her shoulders with an audible pop.

"Not at all." The corners of his eyes lifted in that pleased look that took away the tension lines on his face.

"Thank you for keeping your side of the deal beyond..." Na'rina hesitated, unsure how to express her gratitude.

Before she could say more, Afre bolted into the clearing, skipped well outside Icarus' reach, and hugged Na'rina in an embrace that left her breathless.

"Thank heavens, I'm no longer alone with these creatures!"

Na'rina laughed. "They still pestering you?"

"That one," he pointed at Felis who'd just come into view, "keeps talking about what he'll do if he catches me."

Felis gave her an ingenuous look.

"You can't pull off innocent when you're never guiltless," Na'rina stated, keeping her arm around Afre's slim waist. She could feel his ribs.

Felis pulled a hurt look but didn't get to defend himself as Silas interrupted, asking Na'rina, "You find her?" Of course his first question pertained to Mona'rina. Na'rina should have expected it even if she still couldn't understand the older wer-im's need to know about the Mother Drydanda.

"You were right about the Four Corners location," Na'rina answered, adding, "and there's something else," before Silas and Icarus could start talking about strategy. "A mythic's involved. Perhaps more than one."

"Go on," Icarus encouraged, the tense look returning to his face as he pushed away from the pine.

"Intela Corp has files dating back to before the banishment. Research on dryads mostly, but there's information that could have only come from a mythic."

"Like what?" Silas leaned forward, his expression so intent he appeared angry.

"Like a dryad's connection to her tree. The humans have no way of knowing about our psychic connection but there's theory about it in the notes." Na'rina paused. What she was about to say next made her body ache. She pushed away the memory of Icarus' body falling from her hands. "Also, the surge of energy that made me, uh, explode from the power line was caused by a mythic in one of the walls."

There was silence as they absorbed her news.

"Several species could do that." Icarus broke the moment, taking it in stride like he usually did.

Silas rumbled agreement and paced, deep in thought. "We have to get Mona'rina out. With a mythic involved, it changes what they might do to her."

"If the Four Corners facility is similar to the one in Tennessee, I think I have a plan," Icarus said.

Silas ignored him, still deep in thought.

While they were talking, other wer-im arrived at the seed tree. They had seemed to disappear after the Kadivas, but

Na'rina realized Icarus must have kept them busy with other tasks and they now waited to learn the next move ordered by their Wer-Kadis. Those reflective eyes watched Icarus, not Silas, and Na'rina breathed easier knowing he still held his place of leadership.

Icarus indicated he was leaving for a short time, but told most of the wer-im to stay in the grove, hidden, until he returned. The wer-im scattered, happy to protect the Rina while their Wer-Kadis was away. With the forest suddenly empty again, two unfamiliar wer-im approached.

*I've never seen them before*, Na'rina said.

*Their group arrived weeks ago to protect the mother grove*, her Rina said. *They're impressive. With only the four of them they've managed to repel those men who tried to cut down the grove—twice—all while avoiding the Council's notice.*

*Really.* Na'rina recalled that just after she'd learned about the desecration of the mother grove Icarus disappeared, only to return with a diminished number of wer-im. That seemed so long ago now. *He always plans so much farther ahead than me.*

*Grandmother might have answers.*

*You know the last time she told me to listen to the world sing and try to eat the wind?*

Her Rina fell silent. Neither one of them understood what Ver'rina meant when Na'rina asked about entering her grove without touching it. Shame kept her from broaching the topic with her mother after her lesson in the silent grove, which left Ver'rina as her only choice if she wanted answers. Her grandmother didn't care about the physical world anymore, and hadn't asked why Na'rina wanted to know. Even still, the effort had been useless. Without planning it, Na'rina spun to follow the southern ridgeline back toward the east.

Afre, who'd sat down while the wer-im made their plans, did not follow her from the seed tree. *He's remarkably good at sensing what people need.*

Her Rina murmured comfort as she walked and Na'rina touched every trunk she passed, gleaning strength like picking flowers, until she almost floated with the support her grove provided. The heartening flow of zoi aima kept her moving right up until she found the stumps left behind by the men who cut through her mother's grove.

They protruded from the earth like the raised quills of an angry porcupine. Nearby, tucked within the shade of the forest, lay a pile of logs, stripped of their white bark and dry from exposure. Na'rina's stomach heaved. Only a force of will kept the bile down. She sank to her knees to lay her palm against the nearest aspen stump. A burning traveled up her arm, locking her elbow and shoulder into tight knots until she felt, through the pain, the grove connected to its roots.

*Hello, Drydanda Daughter*, the mother greeted.

*Let me ease your pain*, Na'rina begged.

The grove refused. *Find your mother.* The command resonated as if the mother grove could *force* her obedience. Then she withdrew, like turning a shoulder, and Na'rina received nothing but a vague awareness that told her the grove remained watchful, but would not speak further.

Na'rina rocked back on her heels.

Behind her came the soft clop of a hoof hitting a rock. Na'rina tilted her head but didn't look over until Afre came to kneel beside her.

"You're right about a mythic's involvement," Afre said. "Only one of our own would know the difference between your grove and your mother's. If they just wanted the wood, they'd have cut into your grove. It's closer to the road."

She'd drawn the same conclusion.

Afre pulled her against his side. He smelled of the sagebrush and pinesap he was chewing. "You are always so serious, Drydanda. It is not natural."

"Hard to be carefree with—" she waved a hand, fighting tears.

They sat for a while, the smack of his chewing pinesap the only sound in the bright but scarred day. Finally, he gave her a squeeze and chanced a timid smile. "Race me back to your seed tree?"

Despite the weight constricting her heart, a smile tugged at Na'rina's lips in answer. Afre, so timid and fearful when she first met him, was now taking care of her. He must have known that staring any longer at those stumps and logs wouldn't be healthy and challenging her to a race was his way of helping. She loved him for it.

Ducking under his arm, she spun and took off into the trees. Behind her came a startled, *"Ha!"* and the sharp strike of his hooves as he launched after her. Soon she caught the flash of his curly hair from the corner of her eye. They raced through white trunks and low-hanging branches, and the grove's laughter lifted Na'rina's spirits.

For a moment they were joined by the flicker of dark hair and long legs. Then it was gone. Rather than triggering instinctive fear or the Collective Wisdom's memory of fire, the glimpse reassured Na'rina. When she had stopped thinking of Icarus as wer-im and started viewing him simply as Icarus, she couldn't say.

The feeling, that shimmer like a tiny bell, pulled Na'rina back to the race and she lengthened her stride to pull ahead of Afre. The faun grunted and gave a last effort that sent him sailing out of the trees. He collided with the seed tree and they collapsed laughing.

"Think you won, Faun."

"Think *he* won." Afre pointed to Icarus, perched in a pine tree above the clearing.

"*Na.* He wasn't competing."

Felis, sitting against an aspen a few yards away, eyed them. Na'rina raised a brow and her Rina, taking in her mood, brushed a branch across his hair. He jumped and turned away, pointedly not looking at them again.

By evening, Na'rina had resigned herself to riding in the green deathtrap-on-wheels again. Felis shot her a grin from the driver's seat, perhaps thrilled they'd soon be out of her grove and back into his element. She scowled and turned away to wave to Afre through the window.

The faun had announced his plans to stay behind, saying he could get a better feel for the Council's maneuvering while they were gone. She couldn't think of anyone better for the task.

"You've earned yourself a strong ally in that one," Icarus commented as they pulled away. "We wer-im are blunt instruments, physical fighters. Afre can attend any Council meeting because there's no guile in him and fauns are clever and accepted almost everywhere. They've long served as advisors."

*You are not simply a fighter*, Na'rina thought, *you're as clever as Afre. What makes you different?* "He lied to Ser," she said aloud.

"He misguided Ser, but you'll notice he never said Oba-Afren knew of current events."

Na'rina opened her mouth and then hesitated. "That's a

fine line for him to walk."

"Think Mona'rina's strong enough to break open her cell?" Silas interrupted, fiddling with an aspen twig as if he'd heard nothing of the conversation.

Na'rina shook her head. "I spent a few days in a cell. She's been imprisoned for weeks."

The twig snapped. Na'rina cringed. It was dry and long dead, but still.

*"Silas."* Icarus snapped his fingers to draw the older wer-im's attention. He waited until Silas met his eyes to continue. "Focus on here and now, not then."

Na'rina had no idea once again what Icarus was referring to but Silas drew a breath that stuttered like he had broken ribs. "Here and now," he agreed and continued to mutter the phrase throughout the almost six-hour drive. In the last hour he fell silent, the two halves of the twig still clutched in his fist. The color of his gemstone eyes darkened and Na'rina scooted tight against the car door.

Felis stopped at a gas station outside the Four Corners Monument. "The center borders the monument on the eastern side where Colorado and New Mexico meet. They'll notice an unfamiliar car approaching, so we'll continue on foot from here."

Na'rina pushed open the door and sighed when her feet touched the warm ground. Icarus handed her a pair of shoes from a black duffle bag in the trunk of the car. Na'rina held them up like they might bite her and wrinkled her nose.

"Color, Na'rina," Icarus whispered.

"Oh." Focusing inward, she ran the thin layer of zoi aima across her skin. Putting on sunglasses, Icarus paused to watch the change.

"Does that hurt?" He seemed sincere.

She shook her head. "It's cold at first. I think because it dampens my ability to absorb sunlight." *Funny, I don't hesitate to tell them things anymore. I really have thrown in with them. What would Mamma think?* A lump formed in Na'rina's throat at the thought of her mother's possible disapproval—and the idea she might see her soon. Na'rina pulled on the shoes and then donned the ball cap and sunglasses Icarus set on the car for her.

"Here." Icarus beckoned her closer to apply makeup to her face. Na'rina held still, studying the scars on his left temple and cheek, only half-hidden by makeup. Time had dulled their angry redness, but even a glance would pick up the length and width of those scars. Na'rina laid her fingertips against the lowest line. Icarus stilled.

"Does that hurt?"

"*Na.*" He caught her hand and held it against his face before going back to his task.

"Really, Kadis, you could go into the makeup business," Felis teased across the top of the car, a glint in his yellow eyes.

He'd pulled on a cap of his own and shrugged into a brown jacket. "You could specialize in foundation and conceal—"

"Shut up," Icarus said, "or I'll paint you as a clown and make you a distraction."

Felis closed his mouth and pulled his fingers across his lips. When Icarus still glared, he ducked his head to toss the black duffle over his shoulder. With everyone disguised, Icarus led them out of the small town. As usual, they followed the road from a distance.

According to Icarus' scouts, the research center sat away from any well-established human habitation just like the one in Tennessee, but the group still wanted to appear as human as possible. Once they left the town behind, they picked up the pace, keeping at a steady jog along the highway, with about a hundred yards in between them and the road. It let them avoid eyes from passing cars. It meant, however, they had to skirt buildings and fence lines from time to time. At the rate they moved, humans would detect a blur, if they noticed anything at all, but it still made Na'rina nervous. They skirted another town and picked up Highway 160 heading south toward the Four Corners.

She relaxed a degree when they turned onto a side road heading toward the state border, and the traffic and human structures fell away, replaced by a smattering of stunted trees. That relief, however, shifted to dread that rolled in her belly the closer they drew to the research center. Like in Tennessee, the trees here lacked awareness and their presence felt heavy, almost sodden. When they left the road to approach the fence surrounding the complex, she noticed that not only were the trees silent, but the vegetation had been sprayed, wilting everything around them.

"They're not chancing another incident like what happened in Tennessee," Na'rina observed, pointing out the browning edges of a bush. The biting smell of heavy chemicals turned her stomach even more.

Icarus hissed and before Na'rina could react, he snagged her waist and spun her around the far side of a tree. Too startled to move, Na'rina braced her palms against his chest and felt the heightened thud of his heart. Finally, she looked up to give him a confused frown. He pointed. High in a tree a camera pivoted, elongating and then shrinking back into the tree.

Na'rina's chest tightened and her breath caught. "Think they saw us?" she whispered.

Icarus waited, his eyes scanning before he shook his head. "No alarm."

Na'rina tilted her forehead against his chest as relief made her unsteady. Warm, violet zoi aima whirled at the contact, almost close enough to touch. She didn't attempt to connect with it, however, knowing it would change the sensation from vibrant to fiery. Without this wer-im, she'd be back in a cell in no time.

As Silas and Felis looked to him for direction, Icarus pointed at the camera, his own eyes, then ahead. The two moved away.

"Close call," she said. "Can we actually get her out?"

Icarus framed her face with his hands, tilting her head up to meet his hazel eyes. "We can do whatever we set our minds to," he said. "It is the nature of wer-im and dryads together."

Na'rina shook her head. "You know I don't understand that."

He looked like he wanted to say something but then his lips thinned. "Trust me?"

Again he asked for trust without facts. Nevertheless, Na'rina nodded.

"You'll understand soon enough," he promised.

"I'll hold you to that."

He flashed a grin as Felis and Silas returned. Silas gestured for them to follow and, in starts and stops, they wound around stunted trees, behind bushes, and down into small, dry creek beds, guiding them to the fence while avoiding the cameras. At the fence line, they lay against the ground, hidden by a patch of dying juniper. The bush browned and drooped toward the ground, but offered plenty of concealment. After a moment, Na'rina spotted what she wanted. She pointed it out with a shaking hand.

As in Tennessee, this center's buildings were made of brick and two of them sustained their own power. Of the two, one boasted windows on the roof, where multiple glass circles reflected the sunlight. Na'rina shuddered. *Do they call that building the Zeta site as well?*

Icarus retrieved the black duffle from Felis and pulled from it a pair of cutters and a contraption with a suction cup at one end and a pivoting arm that ran in a circle. "Glass cutter," he whispered to Na'rina.

To everyone, he outlined a plan to scale the building and, in teams of two, to cut into the cells through the windows until they found Mona'rina. Na'rina studied the windows on the side of the roof facing them. She counted ten, but there might be a few she couldn't see as the building slanted away. That made it twenty to twenty-four cells, twelve for each team, which equaled a lot of climbing in and out of window wells.

She pointed out the numbers.

"Can you get into the rest of the building from one of the cells?" Silas asked.

Na'rina shook her head. She hadn't been able to in Tennessee and doubted it'd be any different here. "The cells are insulated. My escape in Tennessee was due to a crack in the floor."

"Then climbing in and out of windows it is," Icarus said. "We'll wait till dark."

The group settled under the bush. This was worse than moving. With nothing to occupy her mind, Na'rina envisioned all the dangers. When she pictured herself in another cell, her body started to tremble. To hide the telltale movement, she crossed her arms and laid her head down but her mind still tried to run through the risks. *I was never meant to do things like this.* Beside her, Icarus pointed to a pair of men patrolling the fence. *Guards.* They carried long guns that Na'rina couldn't name.

"Should we move?" Felis whispered.

Icarus held up a hand. His lips moved, calculating something and finally, he shook his head. From the duffle he pulled out black knit beanies and black and brown makeup. "Smear this on your faces."

Na'rina sniffed at the makeup, cringed, and passed it along. She focused on her coloring and mottled it on her own.

"Lucky," Felis said.

"Stay down and don't move." Icarus' voice rasped low and calm, the same as if they were strolling through the woods. Na'rina tried to soak in his composure.

A few moments passed before the tread of heavy boots reached them, followed by voices. It dawned on Na'rina what Icarus had calculated. They'd approached the center in the late afternoon and now the sun was sinking toward the horizon.

Being on the east side of the complex, they lay in the long shadows cast by the buildings. The longer they hid, the darker those shadows became. By the time Na'rina saw the movement of boots out of the corner of her eye, the remaining daylight barely lit the edge of the western horizon.

"Hold up," one guard said.

Na'rina tensed. The fence bowed outward under someone's weight, and Icarus braced his palms on the ground, ready to move should the guard call a warning. Na'rina wondered what he was planning. Razor wire topped the chain link fence that tilted outward. Icarus might be able to jump it, but there was a good chance he'd catch on the wire instead.

"They don't like us smoking on duty," the other guard protested.

Harsh smoke mixed with the acrid scent of burning chemicals followed the *snick* of a lighter. Na'rina gagged, swallowing hard to keep her stomach in place. *Don't move.*

"Why do you think I waited till we were out here?" the smoker retorted. "Docs are driving me crazy: 'Those shrubs dead yet?' 'Patrol the fence again.' 'Make sure nothing moves.' 'Anything on the cameras?' You'd think we were under attack."

The fence bowed farther as the second guard joined his partner. "They study some crazy stuff."

The smoker muttered agreement and inhaled on the cigarette. He exhaled heavily. "Yeah, they do. Maybe one of the experiments got loose."

Na'rina almost snorted. Maybe it was the tension but it occurred to her, *she* was the escaped experiment. *Watch out, escaped dryad will turn you green! Or make you explode.* She sobered. She hadn't asked how the wer-im survived her last mishap. She should have. An urge to glance at Icarus hit her but she resisted it as the fence rebounded. The guards' boots passed by on the other side of the fence and they didn't stop again. It was dark enough now that, unless they moved, the humans wouldn't spot them.

Icarus waited until the guards were long gone before pulling the cutter from where he'd hidden it under the duffle. The *snip, snip, snip* of the links being cut seemed loud but the guards didn't reappear.

Icarus held the fence up for Na'rina to slide beneath. Once all four of them were through, he covered the cut section by pulling chunks of the dying juniper through the links until the only way to see the opening was to push on the fence.

"Stay low," Icarus cautioned and led the way toward the building. They made slow progress, avoiding cameras and guards in much the same way they'd gotten to the fence, except now they hid behind power boxes, trash cans, and ducked around building corners. While she had worried the evening away, the wer-im must have been studying the complex because they knew camera locations, guards' movements, and the time between each pass.

*Glad they're on my side.* The thought shocked her but then she admitted its truth. *I'm not natural.* She followed the wer-im around the side of the building with the roof windows and stood back while Felis swung a grapnel. He released it with a whoosh, followed by a thump from the roof. When he pulled on the rope, it went taught. *Maybe it's okay I'm not natural. I couldn't do this on my own.*

Silas scaled the rope and disappeared over the edge of the roof above. Na'rina headed up next. Near the top, Silas grabbed her wrists to haul her up the last few feet, and she resisted pulling away. They had to be out of sight before the guards passed again. She needn't have worried. The other two scaled the rope in less than a minute and pulled it up behind them well before the guards reappeared. The residual warmth on the roof from the day's sun soaked through Na'rina's human shoes as she waited.

"Take the far side." Icarus handed the other two a rope and a glasscutter.

"Oh!" She'd forgotten about the sliding door in the ceiling that covered the windows in the cells. She explained her oversight. "You'll have to pry it open."

"Couldn't have mentioned this earlier?" Silas asked.

Icarus smacked him in the chest with a crowbar he pulled from the duffle and pointed for them to go.

"Sorry," Na'rina whispered, flushing.

"There are always missed details," Icarus replied. "That's why we plan for things to go wrong." His voice remained a calm rasp and there was no way to tell if her oversight fazed him.

She sighed but couldn't untie the knot in her stomach.

The first window sat five feet from the corner of the building. Staying low, they cut it open and lifted the glass free. Icarus chimneyed down the window well with the crowbar tucked into his belt. Na'rina cringed when the door below snapped open. She felt the thump in her hands where they rested on the roof. Icarus pivoted his bracing hold enough to peek into the room below. Without commenting on whatever he saw inside, he climbed out and moved on.

Na'rina stared at the cut window. "Anyone in there?"

"Empty." Icarus cut through the next window without looking up.

*Thank my stars!* Na'rina hadn't considered it until she'd seen Icarus looking into the first cell, but now she couldn't let go of the thought that there would be other prisoners. The wer-im wouldn't help them but it gnawed at her to leave the others behind. *Not enough time to help them all.* She knew it was true but she had to ask. "Icarus?"

He froze over the third window.

"What about the others?" She gestured at the windows, unable to say prisoners.

"Na'rina, your heart will get you killed," he muttered.

Na'rina cringed at the burr in his tone but she lifted her chin. *I won't be ashamed of my heart.*

"We don't have time to free them tonight." It was what she already knew but his words still stung. "But with your mother's help, we might be able to shut down Intela Corp."

*Shut down Intela Corp.* The words sparked an aching desire within her. *I want them gone.* As usual, her emotions played across her face in rapid succession. Seeing her resolve harden, Icarus flashed her a smile before disappearing down the next window well. He didn't come back up and Na'rina peered down into the cell.

"It's a lab," he whispered, handing up the crowbar. "Tie the rope and throw it down."

Na'rina hurried to do as asked and, when the rope hit him, Icarus dropped into the room. He vanished from sight and then came back.

"Join me." He disappeared again.

"Kadis?"

He didn't answer. Na'rina lowered herself, grumbling until her eyes adjusted to the dark inside. Screens lined one wall. As Icarus turned them on, they showed prisoner cells.

"See her?" he asked.

Na'rina scanned the screens, holding tight to her hardened resolve as she saw each was labeled at the top. *Zeta cell one, Zeta cell two, Zeta cell three... Just like in Tennessee, this is the Zeta site building for this research center. They must all have a similar layout.* Some prisoners huddled on the small benches, making it hard to tell who or what they were. The first one was too big, a hulking shape more round than tall. The next appeared to have horns curling above his or her rounded ears.

"So many," she whispered, touching a screen displaying a faun. She'd thought them near extinct until she met Afre.

"Focus, Na'rina," Icarus reminded her.

She kept moving although each image strengthened the growing ache inside her.

"There," she pointed a shaking hand. The Mother Drydanda's mottled skin made her distinct as she roved from one wall of the cell to the next. Her lips moved as though she held a conversation with the empty air and the hands she waved displayed skin stretched against her bones.

"Please be okay," Na'rina said aloud.

"Her grove can help her." Icarus took her elbow, pulling her back toward the window well. At that moment, it snapped closed and bolts slid in place to lock it like on a ship's hatch. Their rope, cleanly cut, fell to the ground with a plop. Everything else still sat on the roof with the black duffle.

"The door?"

Icarus was already moving when she spoke but he froze with his hand over the knob. His hesitation lasted a split second before he spun and hit the ground, taking Na'rina with him. The door swung open, followed by a *pop* that whispered through the room. A harsh metallic and glass *thunk* drew her eyes to a dart embedded in the computer screen above her. She peeked around the desk and Icarus yanked her back. The look on his face reminded her of his warning long ago: *Never distract me from my prey.*

"They're using darts," she warned.

Icarus nodded and disappeared around the desk. Na'rina peeked again. The wer-im took down men as they came through the door, cracking a head against the wall, taking legs out from under the next, slashing at a third, who dropped his gun from limp fingers. His movements blurred but the number of men seemed limitless. As soon as one fell, two more took his place. Only the funnel of the door kept Icarus from being overwhelmed.

A click sounded behind them and Na'rina turned to see the back door opening. A warning cry would distract Icarus. *I'm not a fighter.* Several darts zipped overhead. Another glance told her they'd missed—but Icarus couldn't avoid them all.

*I have to fight.*

The men pouring through the back door fanned out along the wall, their focus on the wer-im. Na'rina crawled under an exam table and tipped the instrument stand over with a crash. The tray was a small and flimsy shield, but she clutched it in chilled fingers and stood to face the line of men.

Someone cried out in surprise, but Na'rina didn't pause to figure out who saw her. Two wide tables stood between her and the attackers. Jumping onto the nearest one, she vaulted the second and slammed into the chest of the man closest to the door. He stumbled backward, smacking into the wall. With the metal tray pinned between them, Na'rina clamped her hands over his temples before he recovered enough to shove her away. Zoi aima pulsed from her palms in a lightning strike that left her with an after-image of the man's glowing form. Eyes rolling back into his head, he slumped at her feet. Without hesitating, she smashed the tray, edge first, into the next man's head.

The third man saw her coming and pulled the trigger of

his dart gun. At the last second, Na'rina swung her makeshift shield up and the dart glanced off the rim and ricocheted into the ceiling. His eyes followed its path and before he looked back down, she backhanded him with the tray, his head cracking against the wall. Na'rina clamped her free hand onto a desk lamp, intending to hit him again, but he didn't move. She turned to the next man but instead of meeting his eyes, Na'rina looked down the barrel of a gun.

*Not fast enough.* But she didn't need to be faster—just unexpected. Energy tingled against her palm from the lamp still clutched in her hand. It called to her. Losing focus on the dark barrel, she pushed the electricity back into the wall with a rush of static in her senses.

The gunman frowned, and then the outlet at his knees exploded.

*How's that for an explosion, Dr. Hector?*

One man remained. Wiry, he held his gun in an unwavering grip. Already he'd backed up to keep clear of the outlets. As soon as Na'rina met his blue eyes, he squeezed the trigger. Instinct brought the shield up in time to block the dart. It *thunked* against the metal and Na'rina peeked around the rim, disturbed by the dent left in the center of the tray. Too late she saw the man fire a second gun he pulled from the holster at his waist. The dart sunk into her skin, stinging like a wasp, and her muscles jerked before her face and right side went limp. *Didn't expect that.* The tray crashed to the floor as her knees gave out. *Sorry, Icarus.* As though he heard her, his husky voice called her name from a distance and she slumped onto the tile.

Na'rina's fingertips tingled but her body responded sluggishly, just as it had when she'd been hit by those defensive tree spines. *I'm in another tiny cell!* Terrified, Na'rina struggled to reach out and explore.

"Kadis?" she whispered into the hollow room. Finally, her hand moved, sliding across the floor to encounter a smooth wall. Dread curled inside. Above her head, her fingertips encountered another smooth surface. *"Icarus!?"*

No response.

*Don't panic.* Breath rasped in and out of her throat until she calmed herself enough not to hyperventilate. *You're never truly alone, Na'rina.* She searched for zoi aima or the sharp tingle of an energy source beyond the cell walls, but the world came back dulled. *Stay calm. Try again.*

Last time she overlooked the kudzu because she'd been too narrow in her search. Now she reached out in a general way, sifting through the leaden bits that met her touch. Disappointment threatened to overwhelm her when she encountered no plant life—but there was *something.*

Na'rina honed in on the warmth she sensed on the right side of her cell. A tingling ran over her skin in the same way sunlight kissed her Rina's bark in the morning. Physically, the pitch-black cell surrounded her, but that faded as she opened herself to the zoi aima beyond the wall. Violet swirls highlighted the backs of her eyelids, carrying a spicy scent.

*Icarus.* The distance between them couldn't be that great since the insulation in the cell didn't hinder her sense of his zoi aima. He was close, and the knot that had been tightening within her stomach loosened.

The door hissed open and Na'rina sprang to her feet, ready and willing to fight to get to Icarus. She swayed as the light clicked on and familiar brown eyes met hers.

"Dr. *Simms?*"

"Oh dear, it is you." Dr. Simms shook her head as she stepped into the room and the door closed behind her. "I hoped you'd escaped with the other ones."

*Other ones.* The words sang hope to her. "Did they succeed?" she whispered. "Please, was it worth this?"

"Did they free the other one like you?" Dr. Simms smiled sadly. "She's barely alive, but yeah, they succeeded." Na'rina swayed, her relief heady, and almost missed the woman's next words. "They're going to kill you. The final experiment was ordered by the higher-ups as soon as they heard of your capture. They want to know how much an energy mind can take before you explode." She looked away and fluttered a hand at Na'rina. "I wish you hadn't been captured."

"Is that why you're here?"

"Wanted to see if it was you," the doctor admitted. "You confirmed so much for me." She shrugged awkwardly and turned to leave.

"Do one thing for me?" Na'rina reached for the woman's shoulder but didn't touch her.

"I can't free you."

"I know. Just, since I'm going to die, can he be in the room with me? The wer-i—the man they captured with me?"

Dr. Simms studied Na'rina, her small gold earrings glinting in the harsh light. "They discourage us from seeing you as sentient, but after the ship I just couldn't ignore the intelligence in all their eyes. I *knew* they understood me, but none of them would say anything." Tears shimmered on her lower lids. She swiped at them with the back of her hand. "He's dangerous and they'll argue against it, but I'll try."

Na'rina smiled, letting her relief cover her face.

Dr. Simms looked stricken. She opened her mouth, then snapped it closed, spun on her heel, and left. The light vanished with her, leaving the afterimage of the woman's white lab coat imprinted on Na'rina's eyes. Her shoulders slumped and she turned to lay her palms and forehead against the cool wall. Welcome warmth washed over her body and his comforting spicy scent played through her senses. If only she could communicate with him, but she'd never been able to connect with an animal's zoi aima. For now, sensing him was enough.

Icarus was moving. Na'rina picked up on it when his zoi aima shifted, passing in front of her cell. She moved, following him, and ended up standing in front of the door when it hissed open. The guard gave a strangled cry and swung the butt of his long gun, but Na'rina swayed away and stepped back before he struck again.

"They're herbivores, dimwit," the guard behind him scolded.

"It put Sipes into a coma!"

They backed Na'rina against the wall, cuffed her hands behind her back, and marched her down the hall to a circular lab whose walls were lined with sensory computers. It resembled the lab on the ship so completely that Na'rina fought the Collective Wisdom as it tried to replay the memory.

"Least we got the calmer one," the guard muttered as they passed another pair of guards who sported long, parallel bleeding cuts on their arms and faces. Na'rina almost smiled but her face fell when the guards backed her up to a vertical backboard, uncuffed her, and tied her—limbs, torso, and head—to the stiff brace.

Dr. Simms approached in her peripheral vision. "Put them across from each other."

They pivoted Na'rina until she faced Icarus, likewise bound.

"I'm sorry," the Doc whispered as she studied a page on her clipboard. "It was the only way to get you into the same room." She set down the clipboard and began placing sensors on Na'rina's temples. Vibrations ran through the device but when Na'rina reached for the electricity powering the sensors, they went dead and a screen on the wall to her left sang.

"It won't work," said a familiar tenor behind her. A faint acrid scent filled her nose. Na'rina tensed and Dr. Hector chuckled. "Yes," he said. "I'm here. Your kind is my specialty. I go where you go. When you escaped, they flew me here to study the other creature like you. Fortuitous, wouldn't you say?"

He came into view holding a little gray box. *Why always a gray box?* He held it up to show her the dial on the front. "You appear greatly healed. Marvelous! Last time I intended to kill you because they're probably using my research as a weapon anyway. All that energy, you know. But such regenerative capabilities! Now those I can work with." He smiled with too many teeth. "I could cure cancer, help war victims regrow limbs, slow aging—but the boss demanded to know how much you can take before you die." He scoffed, disgusted. "Maybe you'll survive even this—and I'll cure the world with you."

A growl filled the room and Dr. Hector met Icarus' eyes.

The doctor chuckled, though faintly this time. "Dr. Simms' idea," he said with a wave, "to include you in the experiment. Apparently, you have similarities in brain activity. We'll see if that equates to similar abilities. Although," he turned to Dr. Simms and shrugged, "I've never seen his kind offer much in the way of study."

Na'rina tuned out Dr. Hector's boasting and stared at Icarus across the room. She had no desire to hear more. *Why did they capture Silas if a wer-im doesn't offer much to study?*

Icarus looked away from the doctor to meet her gaze. His hazel eyes were narrowed, pulling the lines and scars at his temples tight, and his long canines bared. Handsome—and wholly the predator.

*Silas isn't completely wer-im.* In Icarus she could pick out the features that likened him to a lynx: the tufted ears, his facial lines, even the sound of his voice. With Silas, his unmarked skin hinted at something else. All wer-im displayed some sort of defining markings. Malon had his whiskers and Felis his black-striped beard. But if Silas was *other*, how had he shifted? She couldn't reconcile the mountain lion with the unmarked, volatile creature he presented to the world.

As she held Icarus' gaze, his snarl faded although the tension around his eyes stayed.

"Shall we begin?" Dr. Hector held up the gray box and turned the dial to the first setting with a distinct click.

A snarl tore from Icarus' throat as his eyes widened. His color heightened like he'd been burned, likely his blood pressure spiking.

Na'rina's eyes watered as cold electricity pumped into her body, singing along her nerves like fire licking at a tree's bark.

Attempting to absorb it jumbled Na'rina's senses into random bits. Dust in the air, insulation around the room, the click of Dr. Simms' heels, acrid stink, flowery perfume, singing static with the bitter taste of acid, the beep of a machine, and a familiar spicy warmth that simmered above her body's usual temperature. Na'rina snagged onto that warm spice, isolating it even as its heat spoke of Icarus' pain. She continued to hold his gaze while Dr. Hector clicked the dial up a notch.

Irises flickered in their hazel setting.

Na'rina gasped. *Strong emotion or need,* Felis had said. *Could it be so straightforward?*

Icarus' eyes wavered between the round irises she knew and the slits of a cat's gaze.

"Interesting," Dr. Hector muttered. He scribbled in a notebook, then clicked the dial to the third notch.

The slitted gaze solidified and nausea hit Na'rina as the tufted ears shifted, wavering between their usual placement on the sides of his head to back and farther up. *How painful that must be!* Her own body screamed as the muscles along her back contracted into tight knots. *Stay focused. It's my fault he's here.* When she asked Dr. Simms, she'd only cared about not dying alone. She hadn't considered the pain she'd cause Icarus. It sickened her.

*Maybe I can help him.*

The electricity sang, growing higher in pitch by the second, sensitizing her senses to a keen edge. Na'rina reached for the current being fed into Icarus just as she had the computer in the phone store or the kudzu vine, intending to draw the humming stream away from his body. To her psychic senses, her green and blue zoi aima floated through the air with a reddish tinge caused by pain.

As it encountered the wer-im's body, his seething lifeblood lashed out. Grasping ahold and bypassing the electricity altogether, it pulled her in, establishing a full connection like she'd experienced with the kudzu. Always before such an attempt had burned in her skin and she'd failed to connect, but the familiar warmth twined through her zoi aima like the fingers of a friend grasping her hand.

*How?* Na'rina wondered and her Rina's comment—*that one changed something in us*—floated through her memory.

Then Dr. Hector clicked the dial another notch.

Electricity surged through them, coming at her from

both sides, but it was the change in Icarus that hit her like a storm bending her trees. As his lifeblood washed through him head to toe, his ears rolled back and his mouth elongated into the arrow-shaped snout of a lynx. The rest of his body followed, almost liquid as it shifted within the bonds holding him.

"Hector!" Dr. Simms shouted the warning too late.

Icarus' hands narrowed and slid free of the straps. His freedom flushed in Na'rina's veins, heady and disorienting. *Can't touch an animal's energy.* But that wasn't true. With a lynx's heightened hearing she heard Dr. Simms gasp and then scurry away. Na'rina almost licked her teeth to feel the sharp canines, and the stretch of hands from fingers into paws shot phantom growth pains down her wrists. But it was the power in his legs as Icarus leapt across the room at Dr. Hector that thrilled through her. She'd never experienced the excitement of the chase before and she marveled at the singular focus and the rush of adrenaline. All was filtered through her zoi aima. *How much stronger must the thrill be for Icarus?*

The energy shut off. Na'rina's muscles relaxed but horror filled her when Icarus convulsed, changing back in the middle of lunging at Dr. Hector. The image of the doctor she saw through the wer-im's eyes blurred as his muscles contracted.

A guard by the door raised his gun.

Na'rina pushed zoi aima into Icarus, desperate to help him. Pain lanced through them both and Icarus, shifting fully lynx again, hit the ground as the shot zinged over his head.

*Sharing energy requires balance.* Her mother taught her that as soon as she'd learned she could touch other plants. A lack of balance killed whatever she touched. Na'rina hesitated. *I could kill him.*

Icarus convulsed again on the floor and the doctor's boot slammed into his side. Pain radiated in Na'rina's ribs, echoing the wer-im's torment. *I have to try.* She shut out the room by closing her eyes and relying on the steady beat of Icarus' heart to guide her. His warmth curled around her, welcoming the contact.

Na'rina breathed a stream of zoi aima into his violet lifeblood until she reached a harmony, the perfect balance, for his body to flow back into the lynx. Something solidified; his motions became crisp and perfect, well-tuned to his current form. His heightened hearing whooshed in her ears before she picked up the click of the guard reloading his gun. It was mixed with a grunt of surprise and an acrid stench, so strong through the lynx's nose that it burned in the back of Na'rina's sinuses. Although her eyes remained closed, she saw Dr. Hector's dismay as the lynx rose. Through the cat's eyes, his skin took on a pasty pallor and the pulse in his neck beat harder. Icarus' growl vibrated through her ribs.

Dr. Hector's impressive calm, that disturbing detachment that chilled Na'rina to the bone, broke. He hurled the control box at Icarus' face and fled through the door behind him. It clicked with the telling sound of the lock being engaged. Through her zoi aima, Na'rina felt Icarus' decision not to follow him for now. She wanted to cry, to push Icarus to chase the doctor because she could almost taste the relief of not having to worry about him again. *Focus, Na'rina,* she scolded herself, *Icarus knows what he's doing.*

She narrowed her attention to maintaining the zoi aima required for Icarus to remain a lynx. The muscles in his legs bunched and lengthened and blood rushed through him as he spun to find the next threat. He darted under the nearest table just as another shot whizzed over his head. A moment later, he pounced on the guard who pulled the trigger. Not wanting to feel the wer-im sever the man's spine, Na'rina retreated to the beat of Icarus' heart. That steady thud stayed at its perfect, faster rate until a flowery perfume hit her senses. *Rebecca Simms.* The woman was the only one left.

*Not her!* She didn't know if Icarus heard her but plants could when she connected with them, and it stood to reason so could he. He yowled a gritty roar, frustrated at her reining in the thrill of his hunt.

*She helped us.*

He sat back on his hind legs, watching the doctor tremble against the wall where she'd tried to hide between two machines. With reluctance, Na'rina withdrew her zoi aima, allowing his heart to return to normal. Separating left her chilled. Na'rina kept Dr. Simms in sight as Icarus shifted back.

"Icarus?"

"Her suggesting that we both be part of the experiment is helping us?"

*He heard.* Na'rina shied away from considering that for the time being. "She can also get us out of here," she replied in a voice that wavered no matter how she tried to steady it. "With Dr. Hector getting away, we need to go before he alerts someone."

Icarus didn't argue as he came to release Na'rina from her bonds, catching her as her bloodless legs threatened to collapse under her weight. His body emitted more warmth than usual. Na'rina basked in it before pushing away.

"Doc, we need a way out."

"You, you're not going to…" Dr. Simms waved at the body of a guard.

Na'rina didn't look. The copper and salt smell of blood was already assaulting her nose, causing a rolling nausea. She'd helped Icarus this time, a willing participant in the killing, but that didn't mean she liked it. *It was necessary.* She approached Dr. Simms and knelt in front of her to block her view of the room.

"All we need is a way out."

"You escape again on my shift and they'll kill me."

Icarus hissed from across the room and Dr. Simms

whimpered, biting her bottom lip.

"We're going to escape with or without you." On impulse, Na'rina took the doctor's small, pudgy hand. "But if you help us, we'll get you off the grounds."

Icarus growled but Na'rina shot him a warning look. The woman's hand trembled. It was the first time Na'rina had ever touched a human and the Doc's fragile fingers made her own feel over-long.

"He doesn't like me."

"He doesn't like being experimented on," Na'rina corrected, "but he won't hurt you unless you give him a reason."

Rebecca Simms squeezed her hand and braced herself to stand. Na'rina helped her up, and was surprised when the Doc didn't let go.

"This way." Dr. Simms led them to a side door that opened to another lab, window wells and all. To avoid notice, they kept the lights off and relied on the glint of pale moon peeking through the circular windows in oval patches. Rebecca threaded her way past several tables toward a door on the far side of the room, still holding to Na'rina's hand.

She had no choice but to stop when Na'rina went still midstride.

"The door's over there." Dr. Simms pointed in confusion at the far side of the lab.

Na'rina swayed but didn't look.

"Na'rina?" Icarus' breath fanned across her ear from where he stood behind her.

"That's your blood." She pointed at what caught her attention. It was the shirt she wore, ages ago it seemed, to help her blend in when she entered Chattanooga. He snatched it and brought it to his nose. "I was wearing it at the Kadivas." Na'rina's mind raced. *What did I do with the clothes from that night?*

"They asked me to test the blood against the tranquilizers we've been using. They wanted to kno—" Dr. Simms froze as Icarus growled, moving to step around Na'rina.

"*Na.*" Na'rina dropped Rebecca's hand and turned to face Icarus. A part of her mused that she must be destined to stand between the Kadis and his prey. The rest of her focused on the wer-im glaring at the trembling doctor even as Na'rina pressed him back with her hand on his chest. The restraint was not registering.

Taking a chance, Na'rina held his face to mist her colder zoi aima into him. They connected without resistance. If she had any doubts about sharing thoughts, they were gone. Instead of resisting her contact, his mind seized ahold of hers and began to dredge up memories, throwing them at her in quick succession. Na'rina gasped.

*The earth snapped closed over Brin'ored while Na'rina's zoi aima writhed blue and green tinged angry red...*

*The little gray box exploded in her hands, sucking almost every ounce of life from her...*

Dr. Hector's intelligent, bespectacled eyes studied her like an insect to be opened up on an operat—

"*Na!*" She shoved Icarus, sending him crashing into a table and herself into the unsuspecting doctor, who caught her with a cry. Na'rina shuddered as if someone cut through a tree in her grove. Never had Icarus hurt her on purpose. For once, the Collective Wisdom hit her with an image that made sense.

*A tiny woman wearing a brown dress reached up to slide her fingers into Mona'rina's hair at her temples. As the Sedessan messenger's palms connected with the Mother Drydanda's skin, Mona'rina went still.*

The Collective Wisdom shifted and Na'rina knew she was looking through her mother's psychic eyes.

*A dark, mirror-smooth lake lay at her feet. It displayed shifting images of a park in a large city. Chattanooga, Mona'rina gathered as the Sedessan showed her the city limit sign. More images came. Images of danger, of a meeting of dwarves, of the path to take to get into the city. It was a call to meet. Mona'rina struggled to focus on the call, but just beyond the visible part of the mirror-smooth lake lurked ghosts from Mona'rina's past, a silent warning. It was the Sedessan's nature to harvest memories from those with whom they connected. Everyone knew this was the price for using such messengers. Everyone also knew not to attack them for this reason. A Sedessan could drive you mad with your own worst memories. Mona'rina shuddered. A stranger should not know such memories.*

The Collective Wisdom stopped and Na'rina shuddered

just as her mother had. Realization dawned, turning her face into a shocked mask as she stared at Icarus.

"Na'rina." He reached toward her, his expression more vulnerable than any she'd ever seen from him. It tore at her, pulling in the opposite direction of her realization.

*"Get us out of here."* Her voice trembled and she wasn't sure who she was addressing, but both Icarus and Rebecca responded. They rushed from the lab into a dimly lit hallway. Dr. Simms stopped them before they hit the exit door at the end of the hall.

"This goes to a smoke deck but there are cameras. If you can get us past them, we'll be home free."

Icarus pushed the door open an inch, studying the area. He complained sotto voce, *"If* I can get us past them?" Then louder, he asked, "How fast can you move, doctor?"

"Um, human jog?" She waved a deprecating hand at her short legs and out-of-shape body. "Compared to you two, slug slow."

Na'rina clapped a hand over her laugh. Icarus scowled but Rebecca flashed a nervous smile.

"Sorry," Na'rina whispered.

Rebecca squeezed her hand. "It's most likely you succeeded in getting in here because the gaps between the cameras don't take into account your speed." She shrugged but Na'rina saw the doubt forming in her mind.

"We said we'd get you out," Na'rina insisted, "and we will."

"How?"

"Herbicide," Icarus said, letting the door close. "Do you know where to get a can or two of the herbicide they're using?"

"There's some—"

"Go get it."

"We'll be right here," Na'rina encouraged. "We gave our word."

The doctor hesitated, then hurried off down the hall with her heels drumming the floor in a faint tap-tap that faded when she turned the far corner.

"Herbicide at night?" Na'rina asked, not looking at Icarus.

"I can smell it. They're spraying the grounds."

Na'rina leaned against the wall to wait. It hadn't occurred to her until now that the doctor could be raising the alarm, but she quashed the suspicion. It felt wrong somehow. Cracking open the door again, Icarus rechecked the intervals between the cameras. He caught her watching and raised one dark brow. Na'rina didn't want to doubt the doctor, especially to Icarus. She shook her head and looked back down the hall.

"She didn't alert anyone to our escape," Icarus said.

Na'rina swiveled her head toward him. *Is he still in my head?*

"I can hear the click of her heels," he explained. "She's coming back weighted down. And she never stopped to talk with anyone. Can't fault your judge of character."

"She was in Silas' room on the ship," Na'rina wasn't sure why she said it. He hadn't seen inside 52B and she'd never told him about it. He let the door go, gazing at her. He wasn't angry, just wholly interested. "She let me wake him up because I told her he had a voice."

"The other one, the male, was he in Tennessee?"

Na'rina's breath caught. *How does he know that?* Then it dawned on her. He'd seen it in her memories of the exploding gray boxes and the doctor studying her. Not only that, he'd experienced it with the terror, pain, and loneliness she'd felt at the time. Of course he'd make the connection. Such details came as second nature to him. Now more than ever Na'rina understood that about Icarus. She nodded, unable to voice the rioting emotions assaulting her.

Rebecca appeared with a pack on her back and another one cradled in her arms. Na'rina's eyes dropped to the woman's high heels. Human shoes were bad enough, but these—these must be made for torture.

Na'rina relieved the woman of the pack in her arms. "My stars, this thing's heavy." She slung it over her shoulders and buckled the belt to help distribute the weight. The doctor might not be fit but she held a surprising amount of strength.

"All right," Dr. Simms said, standing straighter without the second pack. "What now Oh-Fearless-Leader?" She addressed Icarus, her sudden cheeriness in stark contrast to her earlier fear.

*Is she sick?* Na'rina leaned closer to gauge her skin tone and temperature. *Nope, not sick, just on an adrenaline high.*

Icarus frowned, the expression pulling the lines at his temples tight. "We time it right to get off the smoke deck without being seen. Then we'll settle into the rotation of people spraying the grounds and work our way out toward the fence."

"There are only two packs," Na'rina pointed out.

"Each group has a guard."

"How can you tell?" Curiosity lit Rebecca's face.

"Footsteps," Icarus admitted after contemplating the woman with open consternation. "Military style boots and tennis shoes. They sound different. Now go." He opened the door wide for them to pass. Na'rina darted outside. Three steps and she reached the low fence. Swinging her legs over the top, she ducked down into the foliage as soon as her feet hit the ground on the far side.

Rebecca squeaked behind her. She tried to swing over the fence and caught the pack on the wrought iron, which left her hanging with her heels inches above the dirt. Before Na'rina could help, Icarus pulled the pack free and pushed Rebecca out of the way to make room for him to leap the fence without touching it.

"Man, can you two move!" The doctor's voice was light but quivery.

"That camera," Icarus indicated a pole to their right with a black machine mounted on top, "when it's pivoted all the way to the right, we'll move. About halfway to the fence, we'll turn and walk parallel to it so when the camera picks us up, we're in line with the other groups spraying the grounds."

Rebecca's breath hitched as she eyed the distance. Na'rina smiled encouragingly at her.

*"Now."*

Determined to follow through on her promise, Na'rina clutched Rebecca's arm, slowing her pace to stay beside the woman.

"Faster," Icarus urged.

"I can't." Rebecca's upbeat spirit fell as she wobbled under the extra weight of the herbicide on her narrow heels. Now that they were beyond the manicured lawns of the research center, the ground became uneven. Na'rina glanced at Rebecca's heels again. Hopefully no one got close enough to spot those black spikes.

Icarus grabbed the woman's right arm and she cried out in surprise. "Grab her left," he told Na'rina. She strengthened her grip and, following his lead, lifted the woman just high enough to carry her. Rebecca giggled.

The camera swiveled back toward them.

"Here." Icarus halted. They set Rebecca down and turned to walk parallel the fence that sat as a hulking gray grid in the silver light of the moon. "Guards are always in front. Follow me." Icarus led the way.

"He's different," Rebecca commented with a gesture at the wer-im's back. While they walked, she pulled out the hose on her pack and pointed it at the ground but didn't spray any herbicide, for which Na'rina thanked her stars. The residue in the air from the other crews already burned in her sinuses.

"What did they want to know about his blood?" Even in the dark, she could see her shirt sticking out of Icarus' back pocket. Remembering what happened that night sank a rock into the pit of her stomach. She'd met Rosharu after the Kadivas. Had she dropped the clothing when they'd been attacked in the alley? Na'rina hoped it was that simple. The other nymph had stood up for her. The possibility that Rosharu might have played her—

"I came to the study late," Rebecca answered. "After what happened on the ship, they transferred me here. From what I understand, the tranquilizers failed on some of the felin-speci-person-whatever. We were instructed to find out why and alter the tranqs to work on a broader range of blood types."

"Did you succeed?"

Rebecca shot her a glance and then looked away.

"Great," Na'rina muttered.

"I helped formulate the new tranqs," Rebecca said. "Maybe I can figure out a way to counter them."

"Why would you want to help us?"

The Doc sighed. "I joined Intela Corp because they were making such huge breakthroughs. What a great line to have on my resume! Especially if I could be one of the doctors named on a breakthrough. But then I was assigned the study on your friend on the Observer and you confirmed my suspicion that he was sentient. Afterward, I started to hate what they wanted me to do. I never signed up to torture anyone. Now, perhaps, I can still study you without hurting you."

"You could help Felis," Icarus interjected from ahead of them. "He's been studying the—" Icarus stopped and they followed his lead. A moment later three figures appeared, approaching from the opposite direction. The breeze wafted the herbicide they were spraying. Na'rina swayed and resisted turning away but the chemical burned in her nose, down the back of her sinuses, and into her lungs. Her stomach heaved and she clamped a hand over her mouth.

"You're part plant?" Rebecca asked.

*So much study, yet so little understanding.* Na'rina spun away to retch.

"Shouldn't have eaten that sandwich," Rebecca chided in a raised voice. "I told you it looked suspicious."

The ploy might have worked but Na'rina stared at Icarus through the curtain of her dark hair. He wasn't wearing a ball cap or beanie. If his tufted ears didn't draw attention, the markings on his temples would. They stood out like deep black scratches on aspen bark.

Na'rina pitched her voice into a lower octave. "Excuse me." She stumbled toward the fence, where the shadows were darker, before retching again. Familiar hands grasped her shoulders to steady her. With shallow breaths, Na'rina focused on Icarus' spicy scent until it blocked the chemical enough for her to stumble further into the shadows. As soon as they left the current of wind carrying the herbicide, her stomach calmed.

"You're not supposed to go near the fence," the approaching guard called.

"Yeah, we know," Rebecca replied, "but she doesn't want Matthews to see her throwing up. You know Matthews? He's the head of the chem lab. We go back in to use a bathroom and she'll have to—"

Sirens pierced the night. Floodlights rushed the grounds to the fence line with blinding brilliance.

"*Breakou*—" The guard swallowed his shout, his eyes glued to Icarus' face.

Rebecca, who stood closest to the guard, smacked her elbow into his chin with a loud thwack. His head snapped back and he crumpled. The two techs stared at the plump doctor in surprise, and never saw Icarus coming.

"No blood!" Na'rina didn't shout it soon enough. She spun away before the image of the wer-im slicing their throats became imprinted on her mind, but Rebecca froze wide-eyed as blood splattered across her face. Too late, she squeezed her eyes shut.

Na'rina ran over to her.

"I knew about the claws." Hysteria edged Rebecca's voice.

"Knowing about them and seeing them in action are two different things." Na'rina cleaned the woman's face with the sleeve she tore from her shirt. "Let's go. There'll be more blood if we don't move."

The Doc peeked an eye open, then smiled shakily. Na'rina gave her an encouraging grin.

"Over here," Icarus called. He'd found the cut in the fence and held it open for them. "Drop the packs and run. Don't worry about the cameras."

They cleared the fence and raced away from the complex, but no matter how Na'rina pushed Rebecca or tried to help her stay on her feet, the sounds of pursuit behind them grew louder. The Doc yelped, hitting the ground hard. Dragging Rebecca to her feet, Na'rina pulled her along and kept running only to pull up short as a motorcycle swerved in front of them, tires spraying up a cloud of dirt. Na'rina stepped between the biker and Rebecca. *Where's Icarus?*

Felis shoved open the shield of his helmet. "What's up with the human?"

"*Felis!* Where's my mother?"

"Silas took her in the car and headed back to her grove."

Icarus appeared behind Felis. "Take the human. We'll meet you at the grove."

Rebecca stared like a deer in headlights at the motorcycle.

"*Go.*" Na'rina pushed her toward the bike. "Felis, take care of her."

Felis grinned, the mischievous glint in his yellow eyes shining full force. "Of course, Drydanda." He gunned the bike and took off, Rebecca clutching at his waist.

Icarus seized Na'rina's hand and pulled her into an all-out run. Unhindered now, they flew past brush and stubby trees, but the growling motors of the pursuing bikes still tailed them. Trees and buildings blurred. When they hit the highway, Icarus turned to follow the road. It was all Na'rina could do to keep pace with the wer-im's powerful stride.

As they sprinted northeast, Icarus studied each vehicle they passed with a calculating eye. *What is he looking for?* He grinned when a semi's bulk came into view. Drawing even with the massive vehicle, Icarus swerved to run behind the trailer.

"Grab the metal latch braces," he shouted.

Na'rina's heart lodged in her throat as he gripped her waist and gave her a boost when she jumped onto the rear door of the gigantic death trap. Her fingers clamped onto the latch and she pulled her body in against the door, which vibrated with the turbulence from the road and the truck's engine. Moments later Icarus sailed over her head. His landing thudded on the roof. *Ridiculous legs!* Only Icarus could have made that jump. His head appeared over the top edge of the truck. He reached down, offering her a hand, and Na'rina stretched upward until he could grab her trembling arm to haul her onto the roof.

"Stay down," he cautioned.

Na'rina did as told. She flushed zoi aima to her palms, forcing herself to sweat and using the sap to hold onto the roof. As the rev of engines grew louder behind them, she couldn't resist peeking over the side as she lay on her stomach. Five large headlights, like giant fireflies, followed the truck down the highway. One swerved into the oncoming lane, panning the light over the road before moving back behind the semi.

"They're still looking for us." Icarus pulled her away from the edge and they crawled forward on the truck, Icarus' slightly extended claws scratching on the metal. The wind whistled above them but it wasn't too loud to hear when the bikes finally sped up and passed the semi. With their engine noise gone, it felt quiet despite the roaring of the air passing over the truck.

Icarus chuckled. "Never a dull moment with you."

Na'rina frowned, in no mood to laugh as the rush of their escape faded and all the recent events hit her like a storm. "Silas has my mother," she blurted.

"He'll take care of her, Na'rina."

Silas' attack on her was still too fresh in her memory for her to be comfortable with the older wer-im having her mother.

"How do you know that? He tried to *kill* me."

"Trust—"

"Why should I trust him, or you? You tell me nothing and the things I'm figuring out on my own are not reassuring."

Icarus growled, bowing his head as he stretched his fingers, extending his claws, and then retracting them over and over again. "I've made promises, Na'rina. Promises I can't break. I swear it'll make sense soon." His reflective eyes begged her to understand.

Na'rina didn't want to admire his stubbornness but she did. His word meant something. Growling back at him, she changed the subject. "How did you all survive in Tennessee?"

Icarus chuckled. "Luck, mostly."

Na'rina waited. *His limp body dropped from her hands...* She shoved the memory down, shuddering.

"The others backed away when you started to spark," he admitted. "They were outside the blast radius. Once the debris settled, Silas stayed back to keep watch and Felis ran in to get us out, if we survived. He hauled me out first." Icarus' face set hard around the mouth and eyes. "He went back for you but you were gone. Neither Silas nor Felis can explain how. You just vanished."

The story didn't answer what she most wanted to know. She'd felt no pulse or zoi aima from his body when she'd collapsed. Both physical and psychic senses confirmed he'd been dead before she dropped him. "You were dead."

"My heart stopped," he acknowledged. "That's why Felis grabbed me first. But it's not impossible to restart someone's heart." The scars on his cheek pulled taught at the words, and Na'rina stared at them, stricken.

*I'm worse than Silas. I didn't just leave scars—I stopped his heart.*

"I'm sorry," she whispered.

Icarus snorted, then grinned. It made her breath catch. "Never a dull moment," he repeated, then said, "but enough of that," thus closing the line of questioning with a warning glint in his eyes.

*Gah!* Na'rina breathed down her frustration and thought over her next question. She could picture the panic on Felis' face when he found his Kadis without a pulse, and then when he returned to the pit to find her gone. *Vanished.* Anything that happened above the pit would have been spotted by the wer-im. That narrowed the possibilities for how she was captured.

Na'rina recalled the twisted mythic inside the wall of the Theta Site that turned on the power cells. Even now, the memory washed her body in cold sweat. Could such a creature pull someone underground or hide a person? Her sweat stuck her palms to the metal of the semi's roof and her breathing struggled through a tight throat. Icarus couldn't answer that question.

He'd already said Silas and Felis had no clue about how

she'd disappeared. Pushing down her claustrophobic response to the idea of being submerged in the earth and not in a root system, Na'rina turned to the question she'd first meant to ask. "The tranquilizers that captured Silas didn't work on you, did they?"

He stilled. "*Na.*"

"Why?"

He lifted a brow. With the Collective Wisdom's response earlier, she doubted her suspicion was wrong, but she struggled to voice it aloud anyway. On the tiny chance she *was* wrong, she didn't want to insult him.

"I won't be angry," he said.

"You're part Sedessan." It had fallen into place when her mother's memory of the Sedessan messenger hit her on the heels of Icarus' mental attack in the lab. The lines on his face could be a lynx's marking, but the ones on his back and chest were common among Sedessans, too. Then there was the fact that he *saw* her within the trees when she melded with them. A wer-im could not see the psychic, but it would be second nature to a Sedessan.

Another realization hit her. That was how he'd known her name! He'd pulled it from her at some point when he touched her. It might well have been when he'd caught her escaping. *Oh!*—that weird mental ricochet after they'd argued. He'd slipped briefly in his frustration and shouted on the psychic level.

With a finger under her chin, Icarus tilted her head toward him, forcing her to meet his eyes. "I didn't mean to hurt you." He knew his mental attacked had clued her in. Sedessans were perfect messengers because of their ability to guard their minds from other psychic creatures. They pulled a mythic's darkest memories and threw them against the psychic touch like a shield. Not ready for her contact in the lab, he'd lashed out, catching himself a moment too late to stop the mental thrashing.

"Sedessans are dark," she muttered, trying to reconcile the Icarus she knew with this new knowledge. Few mythics dealt with Sedessans unless they had to, and often such dealings left one feeling like she'd seized the tail of a snake. The species had a twisted sense of humor and a shrewd mind that turned negotiation into a test of mental acrobatics.

Icarus barked a laugh. "And wer-im are violent. We aren't defined by the generalities of the species. Sure, my mental defense when I wasn't prepared was a Sedessan attack. Doesn't mean I'm going to drive you mad."

"How?" she cleared her throat and waved a hand to indicate his wer-im facial features. "You look wer-im."

"Blood always runs true to the gender."

"Your father was wer-im." Na'rina mulled that over, but then the topic reminded her of something else. "But Silas is other. He's not solidly wer-im-looking."

Icarus huffed, exasperated. "I can't tell you. Blood runs true to gender—with some minor exceptions. That's common knowledge."

"His father was obviously wer-im. His mother was something powerful or elemental." Na'rina's mind raced with possibilities but then Icarus clasped her hand and grinned.

"Can't touch an animal's zoi aima, eh?"

She opened her mouth. What could she say? "Didn't think I could," she admitted, looking away. *Am I weaker than my mother or just inexperienced, still growing into my capabilities?* She'd always believed being True Born weakened rather than strengthened her, but now she couldn't be sure. *Why didn't Mamma teach me to connect with an animal's zoi aima or touch the electricity within a human electronic?* Now that she considered it, her mother never even hinted it was possible. With everything Na'rina learned in the past few weeks, she *was* more than capable. Perhaps her mother thought the consequences of learning such things were too high.

"Na'rina."

She snapped out of her musings. "Why can my grove sense you?" the words passed her lips of their own volition. Icarus' fingers twitched around her hand. *Ha! Need to catch him by surprise more often.*

He brought her hand to his lips and breathed a kiss onto her knuckles. She froze, not just because the gesture was unexpected, but because it misted warm violet zoi aima in through her hand, sending a tingle along her skin. Taking in her shocked expression, Icarus flashed a feral grin—and rolled off the side of the truck.

"Icarus!" She pulled herself to the side to find him racing beside the semi. He waved for her to join him as he stretched his legs into a ground-eating lope.

*Never a dull moment indeed!*

They alternated between running and walking as they crossed the mountains along the Collegiate Range until they reached the pass housing Na'rina's grove. With the white aspens and the occasional pine or spruce surrounding them, Na'rina pulled off her shoes and reveled in the tickle of roots beneath her feet. Icarus smiled in amusement but didn't comment when Na'rina sighed. *Home.* Her Rina radiated a contented hum.

*The Mother Drydanda's safe.*

Until that moment, Na'rina had not acknowledged how much she missed the glow of contentment that sang through the leaves. Her steps took her toward the mother grove. Although her Rina almost shouted that the mother was recovering, she needed to see it, to touch the mother tree and know its dryad ensconced inside. As she came into view of the large seed tree, a hum met her. The deep thrum vibrated through the roots, out to the surrounding trees, and up into Na'rina's feet while the leaves rustled without a breeze as if a phantom sylph played through them. Laying her hands on the trunk, she tilted her forehead against the powdery bark. Within, she found the concentration of deep blue and green zoi aima that spoke of her mother's presence. The hum originated there.

*Can you speak with me?* Mona'rina didn't respond but the grove misted zoi aima into her with a plea for patience. Disappointment stung Na'rina but she responded with an *of course* before she stepped away. Mona'rina could not answer her questions until she was stronger. She should have expected that.

"Thank you," she said to Silas, who leaned against a nearby tree with his arms crossed over his broad chest.

He tilted his chin in acknowledgment but then smirked. "I didn't do it for you."

Na'rina swayed, caught off-guard by his open hostility. Icarus, who'd trailed her through the grove, frowned, but she responded first. "You follow the Wer-Kadis. Of course you didn't do it for me." That was only logical. Even from the beginning, he'd seemed hesitant to work with her on Mona'rina's rescue.

"Did Felis make it back with Dr. Simms?" Na'rina asked.

Silas sneered. "The human woman? They were chattering like children last I saw. Said they were headed into the nearest town for some supplies. We break Mona'rina out of a research facility and then bring one of the doctors back with us? Not your smartest move." Silas addressed this last comment to Icarus.

*"Unacceptable!"* The shout interrupted whatever response Icarus was about to give. The hum from the mother tree Na'rina felt in her soles stuttered, then picked back up.

She spun around to find Ser'ored, his spikey hair a vibrant green with anger, striding toward her along with Ray'ored and Pal'rina. Na'rina hadn't seen those two in a while, but she knew the members of her mother's Council. Ray's hair didn't hold the vibrancy of anger, but the tension in her shoulders indicated the dryad had worked herself up to this confrontation. Seeing Pal'rina in the group hurt. Of all the Council members, she'd been the most understanding of Mona'rina and her actions. Unlike the rest of the Council, she'd never looked at Na'rina sideways like she might be a sign the Drydandas were failing. Meeting the other dryad's pale green eyes, she recognized the unshed tears glistening there.

Pal'rina's sympathy vanished beneath a mask of cool detachment when Icarus moved to stand at Na'rina's shoulder. He stood close enough for the warmth from his body to register against her cooler skin. Although Pal'rina attempted detachment, her jaw tightened with disappointment. The ache it produced in Na'rina was similar to when her grandmother didn't approve.

Silas did not move from where he leaned with arms crossed, contempt in his eyes, but a twitch of amusement played at his lips. Na'rina suppressed a shudder, startled as always by the swift shift in the wer-im's emotions.

"*Wer-im here!?* It is against our basic laws. Mona'rina would be horrified! We have to drive them out again!"

Na'rina kept her hands at her sides although they grew sticky at Ser's shouting. He'd always been the spokesman of the Council, but she'd never seen him show such lack of wisdom. *If the wer-im indeed intended us harm, he just handed them reason to attach!* She was very glad they were not, in fact, hostile. *Mamma, how do I handle this?* She'd hoped to avoid a confrontation until her mother stood at her side but that hope was gone now.

"Mona'rina is home by the help of the wer-im. You may ask her about her horror when she is well enough to speak for herself."

The dryads shook their heads in unison.

"You stepped beyond your authority in working with these monsters. This atrocity must be addressed now," Ser answered, stabbing his finger at the ground. "Usually we'd allow you council with your family, but we cannot wait for Mona'rina when the violation against our law stands before us."

"Ver'rina—"

"Cannot leave her tree anymore. She is incapable of meeting in the Circle." Although Ray said this with sadness, her words killed Na'rina's hope.

Without family, she'd stand alone to face her accusers. While she stood in the Circle, family connected her to the

Collective Wisdom that was meant to guide her. Without them to back her up, her actions would be ruled unwise and unguided, making her unfit to lead as she'd been doing in her mother's absence. This was the Council's power play. If they succeeded, her own Council would mean nothing and leadership would revert to the old Council. Then they could banish the wer-im again and expose the dryads to the humans.

*I have to keep the dryads safe—but how?!*

Silas stepped up to her other shoulder. "I'll stand as her connection to the Collective Wisdom."

Shock froze Na'rina. She was certain Silas understood the dryad's governing structure just as he understood everything else, but how could he claim to be her connection?

Na'rina felt Icarus stiffen, but she couldn't tell if it was in surprise or anger as cold washed over her. She swayed, dizzied by Silas' pleased, tight-lipped smile.

"You have no place in the Circle, Wer-im," Ser responded.

Silas' grin became feral. "Always so sure of yourself, Ser'ored? I've every right to a place by Na'rina Drydanda's side in the Circle."

He turned and in a single step, stood beside Mona'rina's seed tree. His hands made an audible slap against the trunk on the side of the smaller split, the side that had been silent for Na'rina's entire life. So shocked a breeze could have toppled her, she raised a hand to cover her gasp as the wer-im's forehead sank against the powdery bark in the same way all dryads connected with their trees. With a whoosh, he disappeared into the mother tree.

The hum grew. It vibrated the leaves and pine needles from surrounding trees until they littered the ground. That hum pushed at Na'rina. She swayed backward, and Icarus put his arm around her to steady her, muttering, "Now it makes sense for you."

In a terrifying, confusing, and earth-shattering way it did. All the little details Silas and Icarus knew about the Drydanda. Silas' overbearing interest in Mona'rina—*his twin sister.* Icarus' refusal to tell Na'rina anything because this secret was big enough even the ruling Dryadic Council hadn't known about it. Such a secret was not Icarus' to tell. If the earth had shuddered hard enough to dislodge her roots, Na'rina would have felt the same disorientation she did now.

Silas had not known about her, which meant he'd been separated, without contact with his grove, for longer than she'd been alive. That explained the grove's silent, watching stare she'd experienced on the day her mother walked her through that half of the grove after the incident with Brin'ored. It was connected, somehow, with the banishment of the wer-im. That part still didn't make sense to her, but the grove's massive exhale of relief did. It shook the grove in a wave, washing from the seed tree out over the mute side in a psychic rush. Na'rina's ears popped and rang with the onslaught that rushed back to the seed tree as the half that had been disconnected for years expressed her agony and relief.

*Finally.*

*Complete, after so long.*

Na'rina had never comprehended how the mother grove lacked this sense of completeness. She wavered on her feet and leaned against Icarus to keep from collapsing in front of the gaping Council members. Their shock, terror, and plain unresponsiveness confirmed their ignorance until now. Dryads, as a rule, were slow to respond to sudden change.

"No one knew?" Na'rina whispered.

"Close held secret," Icarus admitted as he rubbed her shoulders, warming her icy skin.

"But you knew?" Why had Silas told anyone, much less a wer-im unrelated to him?

"Long story," Icarus answered. "Simple answer, he understood my mixed blood, and needed help to protect Mona'rina, but I didn't trust anyone. It forced his hand."

"You didn't trust anyone?" The words were spurred by curiosity, but more than anything, her brain was mud and it was the easiest thing to hold onto.

A soft chuckle answered her. "Another long story, and this is not the time to tell it."

Na'rina nodded, fitting other pieces together in her head as her shock began to fade. *How did I not see it?* As though it were yesterday, she recalled Silas pulling apart the radio-like mechanism from the trees and it glowing. It'd registered the zoi aima coming from him and she never realized it. She'd even felt the vibration at the time.

A whoosh preceded Silas as he emerged from the tree. His too bright green eyes surveyed everyone. If nothing else marked him as a dryad, those eyes did.

"Grandfather Levi was wer-im?" Na'rina asked Icarus but Silas answered.

"Is wer-im." He shook himself. "Shall we proceed to the Circle?"

*Is wer-im? I can meet my Grandfather?* She didn't have time to consider that further as Silas sniggered into the silence. "You insisted," he reminded the Council. "Waiting for Mona'rina is not an option." He held out his hand to Na'rina.

*Be bold,* her Rina encouraged.

As though he heard the Rina's encouragement—perhaps he did—Icarus nudged her toward Silas. With a gulp, Na'rina took the older wer-im's waiting hand.

"You *did* throw the Kadivas," she whispered as her mind continued to run through every instance she'd interacted with this wer-im. The tree's reaction when he and Icarus fought now clicked into place. And her command to not interfere, a command Silas heard, angered his heightened wer-im rage, tipping the balance for him to change.

"Shhh." He winked.

Na'rina's head ached with overload. Silas hadn't needed the anger to change, she corrected her conclusion, he'd needed the distraction to make sure Icarus won without the wer-im nation noticing he'd given his protégé the edge. She knew now, from aiding Icarus' change, that it occurred when added zoi aima heighten his heart rate. Since Silas could control his own zoi aima, he could change at will. His mixed blood augmented his abilities. She twitched with the desire to pull away from Silas but his grip tightened and he pulled her a step closer to tuck her fingers into the crook of his arm. He directed them south toward the location of the Circle. His skin was cool for a wer-im. In this way too, he resembled a dryad.

*How'd I miss it?*

"You've chosen your full Council, Na'rina?"

Na'rina shook her head, bringing her focus to the task ahead. *My Council.* She had put off choosing the rest of the members because she wanted her mother's input.

"Pick the rest before we reach the Circle. This won't work otherwise."

"What won't work?"

"Taking over complete leadership of the dryads."

Na'rina stopped short. "That belongs to my mother. I'm

only standing in."

"You don't have a choice now. If Ser had left well enough alone, it would have reverted to Mona'rina and her Council when she recovers." Silas' nostrils flared in irritation but then a satisfied, tight-lipped smile took its place. "Ser wasn't willing to wait, so now it's all or nothing." He started walking again, pulling her with him.

"Then whom do I pick?" she asked, wondering if she wanted his advice. "I have to present a well-rounded Council but I don't know many dryads who qualify."

"Can't be family." Silas shrugged. "You've got slow, but solid instincts, Drydanda. Listen to them."

So much for sage advice. Instinct told her to be untraditional with her choices—but would such a move take root or rot? Memory said there wasn't anything in the Dryadic Code against what she wanted to do, but then, the Code wasn't written with the idea that someone might pick Council members *outside* the dryads. Then again, there were plenty of dryads to choose from when the Code was written.

"Drydanda!" She stopped as Afre ran to join them. She hadn't seen him since returning, but news of this magnitude traveled fast. At the sight of his face, the knot in her middle loosened a fraction. He clasped her hands and kissed the air by her face in traditional greeting before starting to talk. The Council was far enough behind to see the gesture, but not hear his words.

"They'll call for a vote of the forest," he said. "Since you named dryads on the east coast, you have to call their presence to you." He released her hands and, with two fingers, touched the golden leaf just below her collarbone where it sank into her skin in Tennessee. Although it lay beneath her skin, the edges and veins embossed the area like a small heart. At Afre's touch, it bubbled up and came free in his fingers. He pressed the delicate leaf into her palm. "It's a part of you," Afre said. "Use it."

"I don't know how to call them." *I'm in over my head.* Normal dryads couldn't travel more than fifty miles or so from their tree. She had to show she could bring the oak twins and La'meliai's consciousnesses to her to prove the Council could convene but no Drydanda had ever chosen a Council that couldn't physically meet.

"Way over my head," she muttered.

Silas pushed her forward when she didn't start moving again.

*Is he trying to be encouraging?*

"Our mixed blood makes us unique, stronger," Silas' tone stayed even, but forceful. Something about their unique blood carried deep emotion for him it seemed. "It's why Ver'rina and Levi hid my and your mother's connection as twins. Too much power in one place if someone wanted to control us.

Being True Born, your wer-im blood will augment your dryadic abilities. If anyone can call a Council's consciousness, it's you."

His aligning her with his own disturbing nature did not calm Na'rina, but they reached the Circle before she could mull the truth of his words over and question him further.

The Council formally met at the Circle, a flat section of ground covered in long grass and encircled by one of each of the local trees. Aspen, blue spruce, fir, ponderosa pine, one by one Na'rina picked them out.

Silas stepped into the Circle with a mocking lift to his lips.

Icarus turned her by her shoulders before she followed the older wer-im. "You can do this, Na'rina." He held her gaze. He knew her doubts. Perhaps her Rina shared them with him or perhaps he felt them, she couldn't tell which, but he *knew* them.

"I can't do this." Na'rina clutched handfuls of his shirt.

He touched his forehead to hers and flashed before her mind's eye the memory of them fighting together in the Four Corners center, of her connection with the phone store computer, of her getting Silas out of room 52B, and more. As fast as he showed each memory, they vanished, but their imprint stayed like the after-image of lightning on her eyelids.

"You can." He gathered her hands, kissed her chilled knuckles, and pushed her into the Circle before he backed away into the trees. Na'rina wanted to pull him into the Circle with her, but they would never allow it.

Grass, unnaturally green and full for the elevation and dryness of the region, tickled her feet and legs, and the smell of sage, pinesap, spruce, and juniper mixed together in a familiar aroma of the high places around her home. The trees, their roots poking through the grass, greeted her. The fir giggled a low welcome, the aspen gave her hello alongside the fir's greeting, and the pine's tangy scent swirled with his gruff, *Here to disturb our peace, are you?* His greeting was consistent with his character and it was just as comforting and familiar as the others' welcome. This was the purpose of the Circle, to put her into direct contact with the forest.

Silas guided her to a spot near the aspen. "Soles of your feet touching the roots," he instructed.

She suppressed her desire to pull away when he moved to stand behind her and placed his hands on her shoulders. As it was, a chill coursed down her spine. He'd thrown the Kadivas, instructed her to support Icarus because he knew the trees would react to his danger, changed on purpose, tried to kill her in order to split his focus and let Icarus win—all as part of his plan. Her instincts insisted he could still attack, but she couldn't figure how that would help him now, or why her instincts would not relax.

Ser stepped into the center of the Circle. Na'rina glanced back at Silas to find a smile—half-sneer, half-toothy show of excitement—still pulling his lips upward. She kept a shudder at bay but the chill within her morphed into ice until her skin erupted in goose bumps.

"Mona'rina's Council calls into question the effectiveness of Na'rina's new Council," Ser'ored began.

Ray'ored stood to Na'rina's left in front of the thick ponderosa pine. Pal'rina stood to her right, one tree displaced to stand by the fir since Na'rina stood at the aspen. While she'd been distracted by Silas, the other two Council members had arrived. Fre'ored rested his shoulders against the spruce's trunk, sinking in amongst the branches. His eyes drooped, a sure sign he desired to be within his tree rather than standing in the open air. The last member of the old Council, tiny Lab'ored, sat on the ground, unperturbed that Pal'rina stood in front of his tree. He found a large root from the fir sticking out of the ground and perched with his legs across it, resting his hands beside his hips to touch the exposed bark. His glazed eyes indicated he was listening to the fir instead of Ser.

Pine, spruce, aspen, and fir, but what of the oaks and elms, the cottonwoods and the ash? There had to be a better way to represent them all. Na'rina could only pick five members, but here stood her proof the old Council was a poor representation of the Western Hemisphere's dryads. And that was who she and her mother were meant to lead in time of need.

A Drydanda or two were born every four or five

hundred years. Just enough to keep them connected when, by nature, they could not connect themselves. But the dryads were dying. Na'rina's travels revealed that to her with crystal clarity. *Here's why.* The Council knew nothing beyond their small sphere. There were more dryads in the circle than she'd seen in months because she now stood in the portion of the Western Hemisphere that stayed connected. *We might have known about the attacks on the mythics much sooner.*

"...within the next two hours, Na'rina Drydanda must call her Council to meet here in the Circle." Ser's words pulled her back. *He's only giving me until sunset?* "Family prepare her for her task."

Silas' fingers twitched on her shoulders and Na'rina flinched at the prick of his claws.

"Take the center of the circle," he instructed.

"You've done this before?"

"No Drydanda has ever called a distant Council before."

He gestured for her to sit in the center where the Circle's roots intersected. Na'rina pulled up her pant legs to put her in direct contact with the nexus. Silas knelt in front of her.

"Collective Wisdom guided you to this point." He spoke loud enough for all to hear. "Now it leaves you to prove the wisdom has been shared and you know how to use it." As a last thought, he added, "Give of yourself, Drydanda." Then he rolled back on his heels, stood and returned to the aspen before she could grab to keep in him place. The family representative was supposed to stay with her. *What's he doing?*

Na'rina gasped as the roots beneath her lifted out of the grass and laid across her legs. It was too late to call Silas back. He held her startled gaze. Those gemstone eyes shifted, slitting like a cat's, and then returned to normal. *He planned this.* Knowing it didn't tell her why.

*He is not welcome by us as your guide.*

Na'rina's heart beat double time. *Us?*

*We are the life beneath your feet, the rustle in the wind, the forest that gives you life. We are the first dryads of this region.* The words did not come from the trees themselves, but from inside of them, in the same way La'meliai spoke to her within her ash while she'd cried about her pain. The Circle's dryads, ancient beyond even what the Collective Wisdom could recall, were still aware, part of their trees to the point they could not leave them, but aware separate from them. Most dryads eventually went dormant and faded into their trees as La'meliai would have done had she been left alone. *But this?* This was unheard of. The roots tightened across her legs as others moved up her back to cover her shoulders like rough-skinned hands.

*Why is he not welcome as my guide?*

*He is more "other" than dryad.*

Silas must have known this. The clever wer-im played his hand to get her into the Circle even when he knew she would have to stand alone once there. By backing out before she contacted the Circle, he left that window open. The old Council did not know he could not be a guide.

*Without my guide, will you help me call my Council?* she asked the Circle.

*To prove yourself, you must do this alone.* The response was flat, not cruel but also not sympathetic. Connected as they were with her, they could observe everything she attempted to do but would remain detached. Na'rina fought the cold clutching her chest. She sat alone but watched like a fish caught in an eddy.

*You are never truly alone, my Na'rina.* Her Rina's tone rang sweetly in her ears after the Circle's response. *Plus, your wer-im's here.* The picture of Icarus sitting against her seed tree came. The hint of his spicy scent mixed with her Rina's sweet tang and the images he'd shared imprinted themselves on her mind's eye.

*Can you find the oak twins?* Na'rina didn't even know their names. How had she gotten this far without such details?

*I don't need their names.* There came a vast stretching and Na'rina followed her grove as she pieced together a connection with the twins, who resided somewhere in the Northeast. Another set of aspen roots shot them north. Scrub grass, dandelions, juniper, cottonwoods, sage brush... The sense of movement reminded her of riding in a car, except she remained aware of the plants along the way. She felt the kiss of rain on the dandelions in Wisconsin and the fading sun on the ash tree's bark as they drew farther east. A field of clover nudged them north, sharing the nipping pain of rabbit's teeth on their tender stems that left Na'rina with the urge to rub her arms until they drew closer to the coast and the sense of strength and new growth on a massive oak overwhelmed all other senses.

"Drydanda!"

Na'rina expected to speak with the twins within their tree but her Rina pushed her zoi aima into the open air.

*They see the mystical.* Her Rina shrugged. *You touch zoi aima without physical contact. I can project your image for another nymph to see.*

Na'rina went to touch her stomach and her hand passed through.

"Drydanda? Are you well?" The girl stepped closer and raised a hand, then hesitated.

Na'rina straightened, hiding her surprise behind a mask of confidence. She raised her hand to lay her transparent fingers against the oak girl's hand. Palm to palm, warmth passed between them, warmer than Na'rina's own body. A spicy scent filled her nose and she swayed.

*Rina?*

*I pull from what he offers.*

Tears pricked Na'rina's eyes. She blinked them away as she held out her other hand to the oak boy. He joined them without hesitation.

"We have nothing to report, Drydanda," he said.

"That is not why I've come. My Council must meet or the old Council will reclaim control."

"We will come," the girl said. "Where are you?"

Na'rina shook her head. "Too far for you to travel physically."

The twins glanced at each other. "Then what must we do?"

Na'rina couldn't help but smile. She chose to approach the oak twins first because they were young and willing to try new things.

*I can project them in the circle as I project you here.*

"You feel my grove?" More warmth passed from Na'rina's palms and the twins nodded. "Join with your tree and let my grove carry you to me."

Na'rina marveled at their trust as they melded with their beautiful oak. Her Rina connected the root systems that would carry their consciousnesses to the Circle, so she waited for the grove to convey them.

Nothing happened.

*My Na'rina, the oak will not let them go because he will not be able to feel them when I move them. He's terrified.*

Why hadn't she anticipated this? Even being Drydanda didn't make leaving her grove easy. Na'rina laid her palms and forehead upon the tree's side and he jabbered protests, not even observing custom enough to greet her.

*We'll be completely separate like the ocean from the sky, like the vast heavens from the depths of the sea, like...*

How could she overcome such an ingrained response?

*The first hour is almost past, my Na'rina.*

Na'rina fed a stream of zoi aima into the oak, slowing his racing thoughts as she tried to think. *Give of yourself* Silas said. *How?* Her palm tingled and she pulled it away from the oak to look. Against her skin rested the golden leaf. She'd clutched it so tightly that it now cracked around the edges like a dry leaf. The oak needed something to reassure him the twins would return. Na'rina cringed as she tore a piece off the heirloom. With the tiny sliver of gold nestled in her palm, she sank her fingers into the oak, opened her hand and withdrew the contact, leaving the leaf inside.

*I'll return them,* she assured the oak *This is my promise to bring your dryads back.*

Without warning, the oak let go. Pain ripped through Na'rina, something akin, she imagined, to being shot. The oak's loss left a searing hole in her chest. *This is what you feel when I leave?* Na'rina asked her grove, gasping to keep from screaming.

*Every time.*

Her Rina must have shielded her because she never experienced such sorrow before. *I have to do this again?* But she knew the answer even before her Rina responded. This is what Afre and Silas meant by their advice to give of herself, this sharing of the oak's sorrow.

*Each separation will grow stronger as more of the leaf is given.*

That did not comfort her, but with the first hour already gone, Na'rina couldn't dwell on it. *To La'meliai, please.*

The Rina enveloped her, drawing her back into the zoi aima she used to reach through other root systems and, with that cool embrace, the pain dulled. As they passed through various plants, Na'rina tasted salt in the air and shook off dizziness as a heavy wind swirled from the ocean to lash the stems, trunks, and branches they traveled through.

*Brace yourself,* her Rina warned a moment before she projected Na'rina next to La'meliai's ash. Na'rina stumbled as the searing pain returned.

"Drydanda!" Tarn reached to catch her but she passed through his hands and crumpled to her knees. Grunting, the wer-im shook his hands like she'd left water on his fingers. A silvery laugh filled the air as La'meliai's thin form emerged from her tree.

"He does not understand the nonphysical plane you now inhabit, Drydanda-Sister." The thin dryad laid her fingers against Na'rina's cheek.

"I feel your hand!" She leaned against the touch, nearly breaking into tears.

"I knew when your Rina informed me of your Council designation that you would have to call me. I have been practicing my ethereal abilities." Her beautiful smile contained excitement and patience. The bones at her wrists still pressed against her skin from her long-dormant state but her narrow face glowed.

*This is aging with grace,* Na'rina thought, and pushing to her feet she gestured at La'meliai's tree. "Time to join me in the Circle."

Tarn stepped between her and the ash. "I've my reservations about this."

"Please trust me, Wer-im."

Indecision held him in place, but then he moved aside. She touched an insubstantial hand to his shoulder as she stepped past, sending out warm zoi aima to give the feel of her hand.

He shuddered. "Unnatural, Drydanda."

"Quite unnatural, Wer-im." She tore another piece off the golden leaf, took a deep breath, and placed it within the ash.

*Thank you, Drydanda, for this honor.* The Meliai accepted her promise as she enfolded the golden piece close to her core. Compared with her stiff formality, the gesture seemed childlike, and beneath the brave words pulsed the thinly veiled terror she held in check.

"Stay with the Meliai, Tarn," Na'rina said. "She will quake with La'meliai's absence."

The wer-im tilted his chin. "She explained it to me." He climbed into the ash's branches. She'd expected a response like Felis might give, but this easy acceptance held none of Felis' sassiness.

*This is what Icarus gave up. This calm friend.* Tarn's unruffled attitude seemed to match the ash, to complement her steady thoughts.

Her Rina moved La'meliai without warning. Na'rina's stomach heaved as her body flushed in waves of fire and ice, bringing fever to the gunshot wound. She nearly braced a hand against the ash before she remembered she'd just sink through it.

*Almost there.*

*Where now, my Na'rina?*

*The ocean.* A startled pause answered, and Na'rina pictured the cove where she first met Alaya. *Can you get me there?*

*I can, but she is not a dryad.*

*But she is a Danda in her own right. An experienced leader.*

*So is Rosharu. Why are we not looking for her?*

Na'rina hesitated, feeling a twinge of uncertainty and unease. Rosharu befriended her when she needed it but... *Oreads are rare,* she told her Rina. *We need someone used to governing a larger group.*

*They will never accept a Council member of a different element.*

*The old Council doesn't have to—the Circle does.* At least that's what Na'rina hoped a vote of the forest meant. The Circle's dryadic consciousness beneath the tree's defied the norm, and their awareness instead of dormancy spoke of wisdom and experience few nymphs understood. Surely they'd comprehend the need for a more rounded Council when the current one allowed most to die in dormancy. If there weren't enough dryads anymore to provide the connection they needed in their leaders, they had to look elsewhere.

Although Na'rina felt her grove's misgivings, the Rina didn't voice them as she moved them to the coast. Usually, she'd insist her Rina share her thoughts, but right now Na'rina didn't have the time. The rays of the sun were hitting the Circle from the western horizon back in the Rockies.

Her Rina projected her onto the cove. With a storm raging, the cove sat empty as waves pounded the sand. Na'rina thanked the heavens she wasn't physically present as the spray washed through her insubstantial form.

"Alaya!" She knelt and sank her hands in the surf to stream zoi aima into the ocean. It was just as likely Owasha would feel the call, but Na'rina hoped Alaya's sister was too caught up in the fury of the storm to be bothered.

Alaya appeared above the waves, which split to rush and seethe around her. "You're lucky my sister is far away. She would not hesitate to drown you." Her frown gave her slim features a severe cast but she tilted her head in curiosity as well. "I see you're learning, Drydanda. It's been ages since I've seen one of your kind project. Why do you call me?"

"You wisely counseled me before. Such wisdom is needed now." Na'rina paused while a wave smashed into the shore and washed through the oceanid. From the rioting motion in Alaya's eyes, Na'rina knew some of the fury in the storm was caused by the oceanid, but it wasn't aimed at Na'rina. "Something threatens all of us and we are divided. Help me bring us together. Join my Council."

"With the friends your family has embraced in the past, you would ask this?"

*Friends?* Alaya's protest was not what Na'rina had been expecting. No images rushed to her in correlation with the ocean nymph. Usually the Collective Wisdom seemed eager to fill in past experiences but now it remained silent.

"You don't know?" Alaya perceived, exasperated. "How have you dryads survived when you don't even tell your own of the past? Where is your Collective Wisdom now?"

Na'rina shook her head, frustrated at the gaps she kept finding in the genetic memory. "I don't know. But we are cut off and dying. Please help me change that."

"If I leave, Drydanda, I cannot balance my sister's storm. This meeting must be quick."

"It will be," she promised, shocked at the oceanid's acceptance when clearly there was bad blood in their past. But as she gazed into Alaya's roiling blue eyes, she could not believe the Oceadanda meant her, or the dryads, harm. The last rays of sun touched her physical body back in the Circle. She held out a hand for Alaya to join her on the beach.

Alaya stepped out of the waves and Na'rina tasted salt when the oceanid took her transparent hand. "Then offer of yourself to the ocean and brace yourself for its sorrow. Even your Rina's pain does not compare."

*Don't focus on that!* Knowing the pain would be shattering would make her hesitate. She held the rest of the golden leaf in the water. *My promise.* Waves curled around her hand and she opened her fingers to let them carry the piece of her away. Beneath her feet, the sand shook with a vibration that rolled through Na'rina's ribs. The searing hole left by the oak and the ash tore wide in her with a howl. If Alaya did not return, the ocean would forever seek revenge. *I promise,* Na'rina repeated, and then her Rina swept them away. No amount of distance would buffer the ocean's sorrow that flooded Na'rina.

The Circle materialized. Na'rina took in Ser's narrowed eyes, Ray's gaping mouth, Fre jumping up in surprise, Lab beating on the root beneath his legs like an excited child, but she couldn't focus as her vision blurred. She slumped and would have hit the ground had the roots of the Circle not held her to her sitting position. Ser's lips moved but a rasping sound filled her ears and Na'rina realized it came from her own throat.

*Icarus offers strength.*

Her Rina shared a blessed second of warmth and then the ocean overwhelmed her again, colder still for the tiny reprieve. La'meliai knelt in front of her, obscuring everything else. Her opaque features held sympathy mixed with worry as she cradled Na'rina's face in her long-fingered hands that, as happened at her Meliai, pressed tangibly against her jaw.

"You are here, Drydanda-Sister," the ash dryad said. "You are not drowning. Feel the Circle beneath your legs, feel your Rina..."

The words faded but not because of the ocean. *Feel.*

415

Na'rina clawed at that one task, sinking her consciousness into the ground and the nexus of roots beneath her. The Circle did not resist as she entwined her zoi aima into their swirling lifeblood, an anchor from the storm raging within.

The torment subsided to a dull roar.

Na'rina resurfaced. Over La'meliai's shoulder, she saw Alaya facing Ser'ored, keeping him at bay. La'meliai rolled back onto her heels but continued to cup Na'rina's face until she reached up to clasp the ash dryad's hands in silent thanks.

"She has woken," La'meliai announced.

Ser'ored stepped around the oceanid with a huff. "Your Council is not complete, Drydanda."

Alaya trailed mocking fingers across his cheek as he passed, leaving salty droplets on his skin. He brushed at his face but the drops remained.

"I do not have to call those who are already here," Na'rina answered, fighting the desire to shy away from his glare as he towered over her. Entwined in the Circle's roots, she couldn't stand up to face him at eye level, but she refused to let him see her distress.

"You cannot choose family or old Council." Ser looked around. "Who else is there?"

"Afre son of Oba-Afren."

Lab's falsetto gasp was the only protest as the faun entered the Circle. Perhaps when he saw Alaya, Afre guessed her last choice, because he did not hesitate. The old Council, including Ser, did hesitate. Fauns were welcome everywhere; it would be uncivil to deny him—but to welcome him into a Dryadic Council?

Ser finally found his voice. "As an observer he is, of course, welcome. But we will not accept him for your Council. Even the oceanid is pushing, but a physical creature? You cannot call him psychically. This we cannot allow."

"Fauns have always given counsel. Why is it wrong to make what everyone accepts official?" Fre'ored asked, a considering look on his broad face. Na'rina did not know Fre'ored well—his spruce took root miles to the south at the outer reaches of a dryad's travel range—but her mother trusted his logic above the other Council members. She always claimed Fre's world existed in day and night.

"And what if the faun is down on the southern tip of the continent when the Council's needed?" Ray protested.

"A full Council's only needed during war. Three members are acceptable at any other time," Fre pointed out. "Fauns are peaceful creatures like us. The oceanid is much more volatile."

Alaya hummed. The low sound echoed as though it carried across water. "Balanc—"

"You are not one to speak of balance when you can barely maintain it among your own kind!" Ser lashed out.

"And you've done better? Hiding? Changing history or ignoring it?"

"You know no…"

Afre knelt and whispered in Na'rina's ear. "Call for a vote of the forest."

"But they'll vote against you," she protested. *Everything's unraveling.* She knew the old Council would have their objections. *But how can I convince them when they fail to see the need for change?*

"Trust me," Afre spoke with grim assurance as he grasped her hands, his brown eyes shining with determination. "I counseled you out of fear in Chattanooga and I'm grateful you didn't listen. Now I counsel out of knowledge. Call for a vote."

"I call for a vote of the forest," Na'rina raised her voice.

Everyone fell silent for a moment, and then they all spoke at once. Ray and Fre debated whether she *could* call for a vote. Lab muttered to the fir and then a silly grin split his face as he leaned back to watch. The oak twins' heads tilted as they listened with consternation written across their matching faces. La'meliai and Alaya faced Ser as he raged, waving his hands and shouting about what a spectacle this was.

"Wait till he denies you." Afre indicated the pine dryad, who sneered at Alaya.

"*Not your way?*" the oceanid snapped. "You've challenged her right to pardon the wer-im, to bring them here.

She must prove her Council but you refuse—"

"The forest already rejects this foolishness," Ser interrupted. "With such a fiasco, a vote is not needed!"

In the silence following Ser's shout, the Circle's roots groaned and stretched. They opened their hold around Na'rina's shoulders.

*Stand, Drydanda.*

Na'rina gasped. The voice, heard on a psychic level before, now resonated in her bones like a dwarf's bass drum. Pushing to her numbed feet, she caught herself on the roots sticking up out of the grass. Her grounding in those roots told her of their slow awakening to the physical world as their movement washed chill zoi aima up through her connection like cold rain on her skin.

Her movement caught Ser's attention. "We reject this farce of a Council. The forest has spoken!" He spun on his heel to stalk away.

"That is not your decision, Ser'ored." This time, Na'rina was not the only one to hear the voice reverberating through the air. Ser spun, his eyes searching. No birds chirped and no squirrels chattered. In the stillness, Ser's harsh breathing rasped.

The spruce's branches parted to reveal large, dark eyes peering out from among the needles. Fre, who'd been leaning against that trunk, stumbled toward the oak twins. They tried to catch him out of reflex but he passed through their hands and landed on his backside, where he stayed, mouth agape.

Na'rina swayed when the aspen opened green eyes and grinned at Silas. He touched the powdery bark like a beloved face.

The pine lifted his thick roots to Ser's shoulders and turned the dryad to face him. "You presume a place you have not achieved. There is too much self-interest for the old Council to decide if a new Council is ineffective. Subside and await our choice, Ser'ored." The pine pushed Ser to the side where the other trees directed the old Council members to gather. Lab giggled when the fir's root lifted him, still sitting, and moved him to join his companions.

Na'rina's Council gathered behind her in a tight knot. Afre, although he'd known about the Circle's awareness, stared at the trees' faces with a look of awe.

"Face me, Drydanda," the aspen ordered and the leaves of the nearby aspens quivered. "Tell me of your choices. Why does this unconventional Council represent the Dryads better than the old one?"

Na'rina's mind went blank.

Seeing her panicked gaze, Afre whispered, "Think of the Dryadic Code."

The Code stated what qualifications each Council member must fulfill but she couldn't recall the details. She shot Afre a terrified look. *We've come this far and my memory's going to botch it.*

The faun squeezed her fingers. Stepping around her, he bowed to the aspen. "I provide the roots to ground the Council. I am not a dryad," he said with a self-deprecating smile, "but a dryad's existence makes it difficult to interact with the other species who share this world. It is easier to create harmony when you're not restricted to your roots. I can bring knowledge to this Council and open doors to leaders located elsewhere, so peace may be maintained." Afre stepped back.

*He quoted the Code,* Na'rina realized. *One member must ground the Council just as the roots ground a tree.*

Taking a cue from Afre, Alaya stepped forward. She did not bow but lifted her chin. Na'rina bit her lip. Would the Circle find the oceanid disrespectful? The aspen tilted toward Alaya, brushing her silvery hair with her leaves.

"Speak, Oceadanda."

"Years as long as your own," Alaya spread her hands wide, continuing and quoting the Code as well. "I provide the water to feed the Council wisdom. Consider my life a testament to the wisdom I offer. None older exist within the waves."

La'meliai trialed her fingers across Alaya's shoulder as they exchanged positions. A sign of deep respect. Water droplets graced La'meliai's fingers when she bowed but instead of shaking them off as Ser had tried to do, the ash dryad cupped the droplets like precious gems in her palm. "I see the cycle of the seasons. The young, the prime, the aged and almost dormant. I know a tree's life. Except for yourselves, none knows the dryad's lifecycle better than I do. I'm the trunk, as it were, neither buried below the ground nor falling away in autumn."

Na'rina blinked away tears. Perhaps instinct guided her choices because, truth be told, she had not consulted the Code in her rush to complete the Council.

La'meliai stepped back and Afre pushed the oak twins forward. They shared a bewildered look while they bowed. As oaks, they remained calm, but when they straightened up, neither spoke, and their dark complexions held a pale tint.

Na'rina stepped up behind them. "We stagnate without new growth and change. Here we have the branches and the leaves—"

"Acorns," the girl whispered.

Na'rina held in a smile. "The cones, the leaves, the acorns. That which keeps us connected to the change in the world." With a step back, Na'rina pulled the twins with her and rejoined the group.

Ser'ored stepped forward to face the pine. "I will present for Mona'rina's Council."

The pine's chuckle rumbled underground and even the exposed roots trembled. "Your service as a Council speaks for itself, Ser'ored. Words cannot speak louder than years of actions.

Await our decision."

Ser stared with his mouth agape. Fre grabbed his arm to pull him back to the rest of the group. At the last moment, Ser recovered enough to bow but it was shallow and his eyes darkened.

The Circle conferred through their roots. The ebb and flow of their words brushed Na'rina's grounding but its motion was a touch of wind without sound. Time passed and the moon rose, bathing the Circle in shadows and light. After a while, Alaya began to shift from one foot to another. Her eyes grew distant and Na'rina made out the movement in her irises.

"The storm grows worse, Drydanda," she whispered. "If I do not return soon, Owasha will pitch her fury at the land. It will kill many."

Na'rina's stomach clenched. The Circle—so isolated—viewed time and the needs of others differently. She had no idea how long they'd take to make their decision.

"Why would your sister attack the land?"

Alaya sighed. Her eyes focused and then went distant again. "Do you know what happens if an oceanid dies and his bones do not return to the water?"

"*Na*," Na'rina admitted.

"It leaves the oceanid's psychic mind in torment, crying for his dried bones to be returned to the salt water so he can be at rest. Owasha desires to wash his bones back into the ocean."

"His bones?" the oak boy asked.

Before Alaya could answer, the trees groaned and then bright eyes opened all around them.

"Our vote is cast," the pine intoned. "The new Council stays." At this, the oak twins cheered. "However," he looked pointedly at the twins, "their trial of effectiveness will be handling the current threat against the mythics. If they handle the threat, they will remain the Council. If they fail, the authority reverts to the old Council."

Ser'ored rumbled his protest but the rest of his group disbursed into the darkness. He confronted Na'rina on his own. "If you fail, I will make sure you are banished with the wer-im." He pushed through the group and disappeared.

Na'rina shuddered.

"Can he do that?" the twins asked, horrified.

"With a unanimous vote," the aspen answered for Na'rina.

"I must go." Alaya brushed her fingers over Na'rina's cheek. "Dig into your past, Drydanda. I fear it is all connected." She disappeared, leaving the taste of salt on Na'rina's tongue. With her return to the ocean, the howling sorrow within Na'rina's chest subsided to a dull ache. A moment later, her palm tingled and she opened her hand to find a piece of the golden leaf glowing against her skin.

"May we go as well?" the oak boy asked.

"Of course." Na'rina touched them with warmth on their transparent faces. "Thank your Dry for me."

They smiled and disappeared, leaving Na'rina's palm glowing stronger.

La'meliai cupped Na'rina's face. "Instinct led you to choose this Council. It will lead you through this trial if you trust yourself." And she was gone as well.

The weight of sorrow lifted and a floating sensation suffused Na'rina. The now fully restored golden leaf glowed until her fingers turned ruby in color. Then the light dulled and the leaf returned to its golden hue. Testing, Na'rina held the delicate heirloom to her chest, just below the collarbone where it rested before, and it sank into her skin, leaving the thin outline to which she'd grown accustomed. She detected the slight store of zoi aima within the leaf, the nub that saved her life back in Tennessee.

"She's right." The words rumbled in Na'rina's bones. She turned to meet the shadowed green gaze of the gnarled pine.

"How are you possible?"

"Dryads have many life phases. Dormancy is a risk of the last one. If you overcome it, the dryad becomes the tree." His branches rustled in an up and down motion. "Trust your Council, Drydanda. You were led to them for this time and place." He closed his eyes and her grounding disappeared. It wasn't a violent separation but the push was enough to tell her to let go. She withdrew with an odd mix of tangy pine, sweet aspen, soft fir, and sappy spruce swirling through her senses.

Afre clapped, dancing from hoof to hoof. "Amazing! History in the making!" He rushed forward to thread his arm through Na'rina's. "This calls for celebration." For a moment, she wondered where Silas went, but Afre kept pulling her away from the Circle clearing.

"I'm tired, Afre," she protested, albeit weakly. The past several days had been a constant rush and she couldn't remember when she'd slept last.

"Nonsense," Afre insisted. "We've had hard knock after hard knock. It's past time we enjoyed ourselves for an evening."

When they entered her grove, he released her arm and raced to retrieve a flute from beside her seed tree. Fauns valued few physical possessions but they loved music. He placed the delicate pipe to his lips and launched into a tune that reminded Na'rina of the haunting mix of night noises, like the hoot of an owl. Still weak from his captivity, but taken with the music, Afre leaned into the melody, filling the forest with sound before springing into a dance.

Na'rina breathed it in as honey to her soul. Mythics began emerging from the forest shadows, at first cautious, but then drawn by the pure notes of the flute to dance with one another regardless of species. Na'rina joined them.

Drums began thrumming from the forest like the deep rumble of a distant avalanche. Na'rina couldn't see who played them, but the beat reverberated off the grove's trunks and through the soles of her feet.

An auloniad, a meadow nymph from one of the northern fields, spun into the grove, her hair whirling about her lithe frame. She giggled as the naiad from the Grouse Spring Creek danced in behind her, touching the ground on the balls of her feet. Her flowing blue-silver hair intertwined with the auloniad's golden tresses as they twirled, creating a wave of blue-silver and gold under the soft light of the moon.

Spotting Felis, they danced around him, trailing their fingers across his shoulders but never stopping long enough for him to take their hands. He laughed and spun along with the local nymphs.

He glanced her way and Na'rina mouthed the question, "Rebecca Simms?" The last she knew, the woman had been working with Felis on the tranqs, but there was no sign of her among the dancers. Felis grinned and mimed sleep before spinning back to rejoin the auloniad and naiad.

Other mythics, attracted as bees to honey, wove their way through the trees, creating a halo in the air with their varied zoi aima. Golden wisps mingled with green layers and the warmer mist of violet and red. Na'rina stopped, awestruck. She tasted the freshness of spring water, new grass, and warm sunshine that was as much a part of each species' zoi aima as the bark on her aspens.

*If only it were this easy to create peace among them all.*

A wave of dancers passed by, then leaf green eyes and orange hair spun back, clasping her hand and pulling Na'rina back into the dance. For once, the small wer-im was being bold, and she still didn't know his name.

"Aubrey?" she asked, striking up their guessing game again. He snorted and sent her twirling toward a new partner.

Na'rina twirled back. "Alexander?"

He barked a laugh and sent her spinning toward the auloniad before she could suggest another name.

Exhaustion forgotten, Na'rina wove among the dancers until the laughter of her Rina drew her away and into her own dance with her grove. Brushing the trunks with her fingertips, she closed her eyes and exchanged drops of zoi aima until her senses swirled with the intoxicating tang of aspen.

A warm hand grasped hers, sending her into a spin around a nearby trunk. Eyes still closed, Na'rina circled back, keeping her hand outstretched until it was reclaimed. This time she was pulled into an embrace and a familiar spicy scent filled her nose. She felt neither warning alarm nor instant fire from the Collective Wisdom, just a sense of belonging. His spice interwove with her tang of aspen as naturally as juniper and pine.

Cool wind played through her hair as Icarus guided her by the gentle directing of his hands and the tempo of their soles. His warm breath brushed her check as the sway of his hips told her the rhythm. Her pulse beat in harmony. They danced until the flute and drums faded into a distant echo and time lost all meaning.

Na'rina opened her eyes to find them standing at the far edge of her grove. In the bluish glow cast by the moon, Icarus' hazel eyes glinted.

"I'm not supposed to do this," he said and kissed her.

Na'rina froze, then leaned in as the embrace flushed warm, violet zoi aima into her body. Her hands found his face and she deepened the kiss, savoring the spicy lifeblood seething through her palms and lips all the way down to her toes. Her senses opened until the chill of the night raised gooseflesh along her arms, the rustling of wind in the leaves swirled in her ears, and the distant music rushed along her nerves. She stepped up onto his feet to create a circuit and washed her warmed, tangy zoi aima back into him. Icarus shuddered.

"*Na'rina!*"

They broke apart. Na'rina shivered as the severed

contact left her cold inside and out. Judging from Icarus' tight expression, he felt the break just as strongly. Reining in the emotion pouring through her, Na'rina hugged her stomach before turning to face the Mother Drydanda.

Mona'rina carried the essence of command the way a lion padded through the forest. It took a moment for Na'rina to register the brown and tan mottling covering her mother's face like camouflage and the stubble of her shorn hair.

"You brought them here? You know better," the Mother Drydanda scolded.

Na'rina's chest tightened as she bowed her head. She'd braved so much to save her mother and lead the dryads. Her mother's disapproval stung. *I did what I had to.*

Mona'rina took her posture as submission because her next words were softer. "Send the wer-im away. He's not welcome here."

Na'rina ground her teeth. Finally looking up, she met her mother's brilliant stare. "Not welcome? Is Silas not welcome at his own seed tree? And what about us? Wer-im blood runs in our veins too. Should we be banished as well?"

Mona'rina swayed from head to toe. For the Mother Drydanda, it was as close to shock as she'd ever shown. Na'rina stepped toward her but Icarus placed a restraining hand on her shoulder. "She may not be well."

Her mother's mottled skin displayed illness like mold on

leaves. If more than weakness created the discoloration, Na'rina would contract the sickness as soon as she touched her. Squeezing Icarus' arm, she moved forward anyway with her hands outstretched.

Mona'rina eyed them both, as if seeing Icarus for the first time. Finally, she took Na'rina's hands. Zoi aima whispered through the contact and a mossy flavor coated Na'rina's tongue. It carried no bitter sickness. Exhaustion, however, swirled through Mona'rina's lifeblood, thinning her vitality to a watery sap. She appeared assured and proud, the confident Drydanda, but her coloring hinted at the truth. Her mother remained standing by will alone.

"You should be resting," Na'rina said.

"And stay out of your way while you elect a new Council?"

Na'rina swayed. "You were gone. Your Council blamed the wer-im and tried to take over. I needed the wer-im to rescue you, and we still need them to handle our current threat. I did what had to be done."

Mottling swirled through Mona'rina's green eyes. Na'rina wanted to shrink away but her mother's fatigue only strengthened Na'rina's belief that what she'd done *had* been necessary. "We've much to discuss, Mother, but you need rest," she insisted.

"She's right." Emotion washed through Mona'rina's zoi

aima at the sound of Silas' voice. The tall wer-im appeared out of the darkness to set a hand on his sister's shoulder.

"You've upturned a rock with no idea what lays beneath it," Mona'rina said to Na'rina.

"How am I supposed to know what you've never told me?" Na'rina shot back, then bit her tongue. Her regret faded when no guilt touched her mother. If anything, their connection hardened into a wall. A trickle of feeling still transferred from Mona'rina's zoi aima, but it was guarded. *She's lied to me my whole life, and feels no shame.*

"Did you ever expect me to take your place?" Na'rina asked.

Silas snorted. "Little late for that."

"You pushed for this," Na'rina snapped. "If you didn't want me to elect my own Council, you could have stood by and let me go without a family connection."

Mona'rina swayed and dropped Na'rina's hands to turn toward Silas. "You helped her?"

"Think about it, Mona—"

"You helped her elect her new Council?"

"I gave us a chance to be a family again!"

Her mother's grove should have filled her in on the details. *How is it she doesn't know that Silas helped me?*

*Mona'rina did not wait for the whole story,* Na'rina's grove explained. *Her grove lead with the fact that you'd selected a new Council.*

*Your mother left the seed tree to find you before her grove could tell her anything else—and she hasn't been listening since. Na'rina, I think she rushed to find you out of fear, but she's weak. Exhaustion's clouding her thinking.*

As if to emphasize the grove's guess, Mona'rina stuttered while arguing with Silas. He flinched when she shot a hand out toward him, but it was only to catch her balance. Mona'rina swayed, then crumpled.

"Mona'rina?" Silas caught her just as she fainted. "Strong-willed, feisty dryad," he grumbled, lifting his sister into his arms.

"She'll want to settle this," he said, glaring at Na'rina. "Try not to make any huge decisions before then." Then he strode away.

Na'rina's breath shuddered out of her, whispering in the silence. "She's incredibly weak."

Icarus murmured agreement. "Do you know why I respect you?"

Na'rina swung her head around to stare at him where he leaned against an aspen. The grove hummed at the contact.

*What? I like him.* Her Rina mentally shrugged.

"You never hesitate because a choice might hurt you," he said as though he didn't hear the grove, though he probably did. "You've been scared at times, sure, but the personal cost to saving your mother and taking care of the dryads never matters."

"They're more important," Na'rina said.

Icarus chuckled without mirth. "Do you know a wer-im's purpose?"

Na'rina shook her head, confused at his mood as he pushed off the tree to approach her. Tension edged his eyes but she didn't feel any fear as he laid a gentle hand against her cheek.

"We have an instinct to protect," he said. "Call us the champions of the mythic world. Each of us searches for something or someone we can trust in and when we find that idea or person, we vow to protect and the vow binds us. Silas chose Mona'rina when they were very young. I thought Silas was the one I would eventually choose, but something always held me back."

"Why are you telling me this?" Na'rina asked.

"I want you to understand. Originally, I kept you from running to help your mother because Silas taught me to protect the Drydandas. He insists you're vital to the mythic world and with your mother having been captured, that left you. But you were determined to help her, and as frustrating as that was, I couldn't help but respect your loyalty and sense of responsibility. The night we infiltrated the center in Tennessee, I chose you. I made my vow."

"You barely know me," Na'rina protested. "I barely know you."

Icarus chuckled. "If you don't want me here, that's up to

you, but I don't regret my choice."

She stared at him. Although she'd known him a short time, she found no part of her wanted to send him away. "Your Sedessan side concerns me more than the wer-im," she admitted, dropping her eyes. "After all, I'm half-wer-im."

As always, he read her emotions as they played across her face and he tilted her chin up to meet his hazel eyes. "I don't know why your mother never told you your history, but I've never met a mythic more able to adapt. As for my being half-Sedessan," he grinned, "Sedessans exist here," he touched his temple, "and you are uniquely capable of getting to know that part of me." He kissed her again, but this time kept the touch sweet and brief. Then, still cradling her face, he tilted his forehead against hers. "May I show you a bit?"

She nodded and images began to dance through Na'rina's mind.

*Icarus held the hands of a small girl and, although tears streamed from her hazel eyes, her face held anger, not grief.*

*"I hate her!" she shouted.*

*"Sa," Icarus said, tracing the faint lines running from the corners of her red-rimmed eyes out into the hair at her temples.*

*The girl grabbed a tan shirt from her nightstand and held it against the side of Icarus' face. Only then did Na'rina understand that the dampness on Icarus' neck was the trickle of blood. In the mirror, she caught their reflection. Icarus was young, barely older than the girl. But he was not concerned about his appearance and, as Na'rina saw the memory through his eyes, her own gaze was drawn back to the hazel eyes of the girl.*

*"She marked you," the girl sobbed.*

*"It's okay."*

*"It's not. The Sedessans will make you an outcast."*

*"That's kind of the point," Icarus said. He took the shirt from the girl's hands and held it to his ear. The pressure sent out a spike of pain, but he held it tight anyway. The fabric smelled like the girl, smelled like home, with traces of cinnamon and cumin.*

*As Icarus backed away, the anger on her face shifted to grief.*

*It was damp and cold. Icarus shivered in the cave as he clutched the now ratty shirt. It no longer smelled like home, but he pretended it did. Hunger clutched at his stomach. Sedessans didn't hunt like forest predators since they interacted with humans on a regular basis. But now he couldn't go into the city and risk running into a Sedessan, not with the scar he bore. So he was learning to hunt, but it was slow-going. His stomach growled.*

*He stilled as a shushing noise, a faint sound he was learning came from the pad of footsteps, approached the cave.*

*A large figure darkened the entrance and it was a moment before Icarus' eyes adjusted to the change in light. When he did make out the creature, fear sliced through his hunger.*

*Bright gemstone eyes studied him. Then the wer-im reached out a hand. "Come," Silas said. "You need to warm up."*

*Icarus hesitated, and then accepted the hand.*

*Tarn rushed Icarus, claws out, with a sneer pulling at his lips. A barb of angry determination stung Icarus' chest.*

*The bigger wer-im closed in with a swipe. Icarus yowled as those claws sliced through the meat of his hand before catching on his own claws. Breathing in the pain, he pulled the wer-im close and pivoted his hip into Tarn's midriff for a throw that sent him flying through the air. The wer-im slammed into a large oak.*

*Icarus spun, splaying blood across the ground from his sliced palm as he waited for Tarn to come at him again. He felt the urge to pounce while his opponent was down but Icarus quashed it. The larger wer-im struggled to draw air from where he lay on his back in the dirt. Finally, breath wheezed into his lungs.*

*"Kn—knocked the breath out of me," Tarn gasped. "We'll give it another go later." He rose, still sneering, but there was a calculating edge to the look now.*

*Icarus backed out of his crouch, confused. "Anytime," he said to Tarn's retreating back.*

*Silas laid his hand on the trunk of an ancient oak as he traced the outline of the dormant dryad dwelling inside. "You see her form mixed with the tree's lifeblood?" The oak's dark zoi aima swirled within the bark in answer to the wer-im's touch.*

*Icarus gazed in wonder at the thin creature inside the giant oak.*

*He raised a hand, curious to see if he could feel the dryad, if he could sense her thoughts as he would any other mythic.*

*Silas caught his hand. "She looks peaceful, docile, delicate even, but never underestimate her, my young Icarus. Beneath the surface, she's the heart of the world, as resilient as the oak, as connected as an aspen, and as determined as a weed. Be aware of what you're doing when you touch a dryad." He released Icarus' hand.*

*With greater caution, Icarus laid his palms to the tree's bark. The massive presence of the oak pressed in on his questing touch. It was a mind like none he'd ever encountered.*

Na'rina shuddered when the next memory flowed.

*Icarus circled with Silas, claws bared, low snarls vibrating in the air.*

*"You're thinking too much," Silas said.*

*"It's what I do," Icarus returned.*

*"You hesitate because of it," Silas replied, launching himself at Icarus.*

Na'rina whimpered, trying to back away from seeing the two fight again like they had during the Kadivas.

"Sorry," Icarus said.

*The tussle blurred until there came a clear moment when Silas*

Jennifer M. Zeiger

*stumbled. Pouncing, Icarus caught his ankles, piercing the delicate skin next to the older wer-im's Achilles. Chill realization hit Icarus a second before he hamstrung his mentor. His claws retracted and he shoved away.*

*Silas snarled. He rolled, surprising Icarus and planting him on his face in the dirt. Icarus felt searing pain across his back as Silas raked a single claw through his skin from side to spine.*

*"You hesitated," Silas accused.*

*"I would have crippled you!"*

*"You can't pause to consider the personal consequences during a fight!" Silas shouted. "You must act—even if it's painful."*

*"I won't cripple you, Silas!"*

*Silas scoffed and pushed away. As he stood, he growled, "You pause again and I'll leave more than one scar in your hide."*

*Icarus lay still until there was no sound of Silas' retreating steps. Pain lanced down his back as he pushed himself to sit up. He paused to catch his breath and blood began to drip down his skin.*

*"He worries for you."*

*Icarus looked up to find Tarn watching. The older wer-im approached and knelt to inspect Icarus' back.*

*"Why?"*

*Tarn shrugged. "Perhaps he's lost too much already and has grown more attached than he should. Or maybe he just knows the ridicule that comes with being mixed blood. Seems to me, you pause precisely because of your non-wer-im side. You were taught to be certain of your actions. Wer-im rarely allow the time for introspection." Tarn shrugged*

440

*again. "Perhaps he's trying to counter your early upbringing."*

As the memories faded, Na'rina found herself gripping handfuls of Icarus' shirt. He circled her waist with his arms.

"Sedessans are only dangerous to those they don't want to share with, Na'rina."

She bowed her head. Some of his memories, particularly the last one, tied her stomach in knots. She agreed with the young Icarus' desire to not hurt his mentor, but Silas obviously did not.

Clearing her throat, she focused on one of the less painful memories, at least to her. "The Sedessan girl, she brought the message about the Chattanooga meeting to my mother." Although Icarus' memory was of a young girl, Na'rina would know that beautifully alien face anywhere.

"*Sa*," Icarus said.

"The Sedessans…" How could she voice it aloud? It was brutal. It broke her heart to think—

"I was shunned," he confirmed as she struggled for words. "My mother is high-ranking among them. Since I was the result of an affair with a wer-im and there was no way to hide my mixed blood, I was a symbol of her shame." His voice turned hard. "So she threw me out."

"You were a child!"

"True, but both Sedessan children and wer-im are self-sufficient at a young age. That's not to excuse her actions, it just explains why I survived until Silas found me."

"Silas."

"*Sa.*" His sigh played through her hair. "He adopted me. He's not always kind, but he's the reason I'm not hunting rabbits in the forest while wearing a loincloth."

A shocked chuckle escaped her. "I doubt you'd be so primitive." Na'rina paused. "My mother said the Sedessan messenger would protect your identity with her life." That fact had disturbed her mother.

"She's like that." There was a smile in his voice now. "I learned loyalty from her. She's my half-sister."

"*Oh.*" Na'rina could see the similarity between the two, especially in the color of their eyes. *Loyalty.* He said that it was one of the things he respected about her. *No wonder.*

"I'll leave you alone now." Icarus breathed a kiss against her hair and pulled away. Watching him disappear into the forest, an ache settled into Na'rina's bones. It felt like the craving for sunlight she experienced after several days of cloud cover. Na'rina hugged herself, yearning for the warmth of his embrace.

Her Rina chuckled.

*Quiet you.*

*He's good for you, my Na'rina, and I feel the doubt building in your mind. You did not throw your upbringing to the wind because you love a wer-im you barely know.*

Na'rina sighed and leaned against the nearest aspen to let the Rina pull her in. She closed her eyes and sank into an uneasy sleep.

*My Na'rina!* Her grove sobbed, dragging Na'rina from sleep with intensity born of desperation. At first all she felt were small bites, tiny in comparison to the hundreds of trees in her Rina, but then those painful nips became a guillotine slice as the first aspen cracked, sawn through and toppled to the ground. Na'rina screamed. The gut-wrenching cry reverberated through the grove, making trunks quake and leaves flutter to the ground.

*They're killing me!*

*Where?* Sensations tumbled in, one on top of another, too fast to make sense of the attacks hitting at several locations. The images wavered with her Rina's cries, but Na'rina stilled as she exerted enough control to see what was happening. To the east, two groups of men sawed through several trees before the wer-im and, surprisingly, Afre, halted the attack. Na'rina watched them fighting and while it was too early to tell which side would win, the sawing had been stopped for now.

To the west, two groups were still attacking the grove.

The men worked quickly, as if they knew their attack would not go unanswered. Even as Na'rina was taking this in, Felis and Icarus bowled into the southernmost group, followed by a frightened but determined Rebecca Simms, holding what looked like a tranquilizer gun. Na'rina shuddered but she knew the wer-im and doctor would protect that portion of the grove.

Na'rina shifted her focus to the fourth area of attack, the one to the northeast. *Take me there.* Her Rina carried her in a reckless rush through the grove's roots. The zoi aima of the trees, a step cooler than her own, smoldered with a tinge of red that signaled outright anger. She'd experienced the effect in herself, but never before had her Rina swayed first toward such a heated response.

*There are more coming up the road!*

Na'rina heard the crunch of dirt under vehicle wheels as they sped toward the men at the northeast location.

*Move me faster. I need to get there before them!*

All color blurred as the Rina shoved her out of the grove. Head spinning, Na'rina landed on one of the men sawing through an aspen trunk. He screamed, and the saw flew from his hands as he fell backward. Fearful he'd overpower her, Na'rina shot zoi aima into his chest and rolled away. A gasp came from the man, and then silence.

Na'rina's vision swam.

*Two more rushing toward you!*

Trusting her Rina, she rolled again just as a heavy body landed where she'd lain. On impulse, she rolled back, slapped her hands onto a blurry face and pulsed zoi aima out her palms. The man went slack and her vision stilled, imprinting his stunned expression on her like a shock of lightning. His slicked-back blond hair resembled a shell and Na'rina recognized his familiar suit and athletic build.

She gagged at what she'd done, but the crunch of a boot drew her eyes away from him.

*One more, and then two cars coming up the road.*

Na'rina leapt to her feet to face the last man. He froze and swallowed. It was then she appreciated what she must look like as she stood with her hands outstretched. To her psychic eye, her zoi aima seethed from her curled fingertips, drawing not only from herself but from the entire grove. To him, a purely physical being, she must resemble a wer-im with claws drawn. She stepped toward him, and he stumbled backward. The faint rumble of engines broke the stillness and the man spun toward the nearby road.

Growling, Na'rina slashed at him although she was too far away. Her Rina responded, lashing out a long, whip-like limb that smacked across the back of his head with a loud crack. He froze mid-step, and then crumpled to the ground.

Na'rina's breath rasped through her teeth in a moment of crystal stillness before a red jeep and a dull blue truck sped into view. Hyperaware, she took in the breathing of the three unconscious men, the zoi aima eddying through everything, and the sap weeping from the trunks of five murdered aspens. Even she could not heal a tree once it was severed from its roots. Her Rina whimpered, but beneath her pain boiled a fury that nurtured Na'rina's own writhing zoi aima.

*This is my home!*

Na'rina reached for her roots. Though she didn't have to motion with her hands to lift the ground, she thrilled as those roots shed their earthy cover and crawled into the undercarriage of the jeep. The Rina lifted, and Na'rina welcomed the corresponding ache in her shoulders. She grinned in determination when she heaved and the red deathtrap flipped, landing with a satisfying glass-shattering crunch as the reek of gasoline filled the air.

In mid-turn, Na'rina's zoi aima rushed from her like she was being sucked dry. *I know this agony!* Tears streamed down her face as her knees thumped into the dirt and she turned stricken eyes toward the blue truck.

Dr. Hector leaned against the front fender, studying her. By his side stood a heavyset, older man. Na'rina recognized him as the one Icarus almost preyed upon at the clearing long ago. At the moment she wished she hadn't stopped him.

All she could do was gasp for air and stare at the small gray box in his blunt fingers as the doctor pushed off the truck to amble toward her.

"Magnificent," he said.

"They'll be happy to know you were right," the heavy man acknowledged. "They won't fire you if you bring it back alive and keep it contained this time." His words carried an implicit threat the doctor didn't seem to hear.

"Imagine what we can achieve." Dr. Hector lifted Na'rina's chin to force her to meet his gaze. "You will show me how to cure the world's ills." Those bespectacled eyes crinkled as he turned the dial up another notch.

Zoi aima flooded from Na'rina, pulling from the grove's and her own store. This wasn't like the experiment at the Four Corners. The doctor was using a perfected version of the device that almost killed her in Tennessee. Her Rina shrieked as the aspens closest to her started to wilt. Leaves fluttered off their branches in a rain of green.

"What setting keeps the creature docile and what setting will kill it?" the heavyset man asked, leaning through the truck window to pull a notebook from his leather briefcase in the front seat.

Dr. Hector shrugged. "Still working on that."

The heavyset man shot him a disgusted look and dropped the notebook back into its case unopened. "Details, Doctor. I need details for my report."

*We're dying!* her Rina sobbed, drowning out the men's

voices.

The aspens closest to Na'rina now bore no leaves and their bark was cracked, seeping sap over blackening wounds, but farther out, Na'rina felt the massive healthy zoi aima of her grove. *That box hasn't touched most of the grove. You are not close to death yet,* she scolded her Rina. Then a thought hit Na'rina. Usually the Rina cut off the lifeblood to a dying tree—a healthy and accepted cycle as some aspens died and new suckers continued the life of the grove—but they didn't have to cut off that zoi aima. *This is our home. We don't have to give up.*

Forgetting her paralyzed body, Na'rina sank her consciousness deep into the ground, reaching for the massive root system connecting her trees. Below her, those roots shuddered in agony, but Na'rina reached farther until she flowed into the vast zoi aima of her Rina.

"What are you doing?" She heard Dr. Hector ask, pausing his argument with the older man to tap her cheek with his index finger but the pokes barely registered.

"What causes her eyes to go totally green?" the other man asked.

*Watch and learn,* Na'rina thought. Zoi aima rushed toward her, suffusing the deadening roots with seething lifeblood. It burned like fire on a frosted limb. In a radius around her, the trunks of the grove shuddered and swayed as in a heavy wind.

"Doctor?"

Dr. Hector turned to look around.

*Now!*

At Na'rina's command, the grove heaved, sending clods of dirt flying. The doctor threw up his hands to shield his face. Without her even directing it, the roots slapped Dr. Hector and the gray box sailed out of his hand and into the trees. He lunged past Na'rina after the device, but several roots snaked around his ankles and, with a resounding *thump*, they submerged him underground up to his neck. A gasping wheeze emanated from him as he watched a thick root lash out and smash the little gray box.

All at once the drain on Na'rina ceased. Zoi aima— seething, angry zoi aima—flushed through her limbs and up into her face, raising her heart rate to a heavy thud. Needing an outlet, she turned to the heavyset man, who bolted for the truck's driver-side door. Roots wrapped around the base of the truck, up through the open door, and out the front passenger window. With a yank, they tightened and the truck lurched and folded in like a tin can. The man cried out, stepping toward the crumpled mass of metal as though it still offered him a way to escape.

"I wouldn't—unless you want to be next," Na'rina warned.

He whimpered and sat down on the ground without

turning away from the road, raising shaking hands into the air. Living shackles sprouted to circle his legs and biceps until Na'rina was sure the man couldn't break free.

Her zoi aima seethed, but as she turned back to the doctor imprisoned in the dirt, the red tinge dissipated and a cold certainty replaced it. Trembling from the Rina still spoke of pain, but no new injuries shuddered in from across the grove. Time was now on Na'rina's side.

She knelt in front of Dr. Hector's exposed head and lifted his chin as he'd done to her. In the tussle, he'd lost his thin glasses and she noticed his intelligent eyes were brown. "It's my turn to get answers from you," she said.

His nostrils flared as his lips thinned. "I've got nothing to say."

"Oh, I very much doubt that," Icarus interjected as he appeared from amidst the trees.

Na'rina felt lightheaded with relief at his arrival. He took in the three men prone on the ground, the shackled older man by the two crumpled and overturned vehicles, and then his eyes came to rest on Dr. Hector, up to his neck in dirt.

Na'rina shot a startled look at Icarus when the rev of an engine carried down the road.

"It's just Felis and the woman," he reassured her. To Dr. Hector, he grinned, displaying his long canines. "Bit off more than you could chew."

The man snorted and looked away. His eyes settled on the motorcycle as it arrived.

"Dr. Simms!" he shouted.

The woman paused with her leg halfway off the back seat of the bike. Felis nudged her and she moved clear for him to dismount.

"After Tennessee, this shouldn't surprise me, Drydanda," Felis called, waving at the mess, "but it still does. How could something so small cause such chaos?"

"You fight with claws," Na'rina muttered, flushing, "I fight with—other things."

"Your restraint could prove helpful," Icarus commented. His eyes were still on the buried doctor.

"Restraint?" Felis exclaimed. "You call this restraint?"

"They're still alive," Icarus retorted. "Are any of yours?"

The wer-im ducked his head.

"How did they find us?" Na'rina asked, not wanting to think about the deaths in her grove.

Dr. Hector lifted his chin in defiance, but Rebecca spoke up before he could say anything. "I think I know."

She approached Icarus and reached a hand toward his head, then hesitated. "May I?" He nodded and she began combing through his hair. "Ah-ha." With a tug, she pulled out a dark hair. When she held up the inch-long strand, it stood straight as a pin. Pinching the thread when Rebecca offered it,

Na'rina felt a miniscule sting of electricity running through it.

"What is it?"

"A tracking device," Rebecca answered. "I'm sorry. I should have thought of it, but when we left the Four Corners this was still in testing. I never thought they'd put a prototype into use. I guess Dr. Hector feared you'd feel something planted on you." She pointed at Na'rina. "So he gambled that, if you escaped, you and the Kadis would stay together. Considering the electricity used during the experiment at the Four Corners, he probably activated the tracker remotely after you escaped. Otherwise, the electricity would have destroyed it."

Na'rina eyed the woman doctor, a little surprised she used Icarus' title, but then Felis asked, "Is it still on?"

"Yeah. It's still sending a signal."

Wrinkling her nose, Na'rina streamed zoi aima into the strand and with a *pop* the tiny sting of electricity died. She held it out between thumb and forefinger, offering it to Felis, who took it, wrapped it in a bit of cloth, and pocketed it.

"Now," Icarus addressed Dr. Hector as he knelt in front of his exposed head, "we have questions Dr. Simms can't answer. Dryads are your specialty, you said. Who told you about them in the first place?"

Even encased in dirt, the man sniggered. "Dryads? Are we in mythology class now?"

"Hector, you know what they mean," Rebecca scolded.

"Energy minds. Who told you about energy minds?"

He glared up at the plump woman until Icarus placed his index finger under his chin and forced him to look away. The claw on that finger drew a small drop of blood. "There's a lot you don't know about us," he said. After a moment of studying the doctor, Icarus dropped his hand. "But I don't want to waste my time breaking you." Standing back up, he stepped over the doctor to approach the heavyset man shackled in roots. Icarus sat to face the man, which allowed him to keep Dr. Hector in his sight even though he'd shifted his focus.

Through the roots, Na'rina felt the man trying to lean away as Icarus fingered the lapel of his black suit jacket. "Not a doctor, obviously. What do you do for Intela Corp?" The man tried to glance back at Dr. Hector, but had to settle for lifting his heavy chin and tightening his mouth in defiance.

"You don't need to say a word," Icarus sneered, laying his palms against the man's temples.

*"No, no, no!"* The man thrashed his head back and forth until Icarus extended his claws to hold him. Then he went still with a grimace as blood trickled down his heavy cheeks, dripped off his face, and disappeared into the black of his suit.

Rebecca touched Felis' elbow. "What's he doing?"

Felis leaned against a large blue spruce and shrugged. "The Kadis isn't all cat. It gives him some—er—other abilities. I've never asked what exactly he is."

"Richard McCormick," Icarus announced, "is an evaluator. He reviews each doctor's work and reports to the board to decide if an employee is meeting his obligations."

"Guess I could have told you that," Rebecca said. "Mr. McCormick and Mr. Martin," she pointed over at the prostrate man with the shellacked blond hair, "are nightmares for everyone."

Na'rina hushed her. "Let the Kadis work." Although she wasn't a part of what Icarus was doing, she suspected digging into a person's mind was draining. Even in contacting trees, she'd been taught to start small and build to more complex things. What Icarus was doing made sweat trickle down the lines on his temples. She shuddered. Mr. McCormick did not welcome Icarus, which would make doing this trickier.

In front of her, Dr. Hector had turned his head as far as he could go to watch. "Parlor tricks," he sneered.

Icarus pulled his hands away and rolled his shoulders. All color had drained from McCormick's face. A choking sound hiccupped from him, relief perhaps, as Icarus released him.

"He's not as informed about the experiments on the dryads," Icarus said, "but he's been studying up to evaluate Dr. Hector. There's more." He leaned forward to continue.

"No, please!" McCormick begged. "I'll tell you everything. Just don't do that again."

"McCormick!" Dr. Hector exploded. "You can't give

them what they want!"

"He's in my head!" McCormick wheezed. "He's rifling through memories. I just watched my granddaughter's birthday party from last weekend."

"Intela Corp will kill you."

"Didn't you hear me? He knows about my granddaughter, my family, even my address. I can't keep anything from him even if I tried."

"Coward!" Dr. Hector spit in disgust.

Na'rina, still sitting beside the doctor's head, cupped his chin and ran a thin layer of zoi aima across her fingertips. His head jerked at the sting of what probably felt like a small electrical shock, but instead of quieting him, he spit at her as well, hitting her knee with saliva. "I know just how fragile you are," he mocked. "You can't hold me forever."

"I can," she answered, holding a calm façade despite her fear. This man always seemed to see inside her, as if he could learn everything he wanted just by watching her.

"If you're here, the older one must be as well," he said with a grin. "What I could do with both of you! I'll know everything there is to know about energy minds when I'm done. The director might actually be right. I'll cure the world's energy problems by harnessing clean energy or…" His eyes lost their focus as he spoke. Na'rina felt the same horrified shock she read on Felis and Rebecca's faces. The man was buried neck deep in the ground and yet he spoke as if he still held the upper hand. "…no more fossil fuels. Global warming could be reversed. The Nobel Peace Prize will be mine. Stuff that in everyone's faces! 'Never amount to anything,' they said, but…"

A low snarl nearly lost under the doctor's rambling was the only warning before a flash of tawny hair hurtled past Na'rina. She rolled, tumbling back over her shoulder and onto her feet.

She heard a now familiar gurgle and then silence.

Silas launched over the now dead Dr. Hector toward McCormick, but smacked instead into Icarus, who jumped over the man to intercept his attack.

"Silas!" The command brought absolute stillness.

Silas loomed over Icarus with nostrils flared, his breath a hiss through his barred teeth. "He experimented on her."

"And now he's dead," Icarus responded. "Is Mona'rina safe? Is she healing?"

Na'rina swayed. *Is she safe?* she asked her Rina.

*Sa. This attack was on you, not her—although she's being a bit vague when I talk to her.*

Na'rina's relief washed through her but it was tinged with wariness as Silas took a step back from the Wer-Kadis and turned brilliant eyes on the rest of them.

"Calm down," the Kadis ordered. "Mona'rina needs you."

Silas grimaced. "I made the hard choice. I did what I had to do for her." He spun and stalked away.

Once Silas disappeared, Na'rina turned to see Dr. Hector's dead face again. She gagged at the coppery smell of the doctor's blood. His gaping mouth and shocked eyes, staring over a slit throat, would haunt her. She'd wanted to kill him—she had even tried to do it—but seeing him dead? It should have brought relief. Instead, a cold hand clutched at her. This was wrong, and if she'd been the one to kill him, she would have hated herself for it. Silas couldn't be right. Mona'rina would never have wanted him to kill like this.

"Wha—" she swallowed and tried again. "What do we do with him?"

"I could use the cars and make it look like an accident," Felis suggested.

"Make it happen," Icarus ordered.

The older wer-im bowed his head. He knelt beside the exposed head and looked at Na'rina.

*Bring him up.* The Rina obeyed and Felis carried Dr. Hector into the trees. Felis wasn't the most sensitive person, but perhaps Rebecca's and her own shock led him to remove the body before going to find help with the "accident" he needed to set up.

Icarus, as usual the calmest one involved, waited for Felis to leave and then returned to sit in front of a terrified

Richard McCormick. Sweat plastered his white hair to his scalp and he tried to wipe it away with the handkerchief from his pocket. With his upper arms held by roots, his motion was stunted but he managed to get most of his forehead by passing the white cloth between shaking hands. "If you don't want me inside your head again, tell me what I need to know."

"In the truck," McCormick awkwardly pointed at the crumpled vehicle, the white handkerchief waving like a truce flag. "Large binder, inside my briefcase…My secretary printed everything on the energy minds for me—It's all there."

Rebecca crawled in through the shattered windshield of the truck, carefully avoiding chunks of glass, and came back with the briefcase.

Na'rina grimaced as she took a good look at the woman. Evidently, she had not left the woods since the Four Corners center. Instead of high heels, she wore tennis shoes, jeans, and a t-shirt clearly meant for a man. They draped around her plump frame with space to spare, but she put the baggy pockets to good use. A notebook peeked out from one pocket and Na'rina picked up the faint clink of glass bottles from another. It appeared the Doc enjoyed working with Felis on the tranquilizer issue. Even now, through the dirt smudging her face, her eyes glowed with curiosity as she joined Icarus on the ground to flip open the briefcase. From it she pulled a heavy, three-inch binder.

Na'rina moved to sit with them, glad to put her back to

the blood, to Dr. Hector's death.

"Intela Corp started in the late 1700s in Europe as an organization to study the natural sciences," Rebecca read aloud, clearly summarizing as she skimmed. "Looks like it didn't make much progress until it moved from Europe to the U.S. in the 1800s. It became a corporation and gained a new CEO. He actually hired a woman as one of his department directors. Looks like it caused a huge scandal! But she was a force to be reckoned with, because the scandal didn't stop her. She's the one who encouraged expansion west and created the special projects department—"

"We call them the Zeta projects now," McCormick interrupted, pointing at the binder and motioning for them to flip forward. "About page two hundred. Keep going. There."

Rebecca stopped on a black and white photo, labeled with a date in the late 1840s, of a group standing in front of a brick building much like what they'd seen at each Intela Corp center. Na'rina's eyes were drawn to a large woman standing in the back row and she went cold.

"She'd been with Intela Corp for a couple decades by the time that was taken, but even when she started to work there, the director knew about energy minds and others," McCormick stated. "She told the corporation where to find you." The man gestured at Icarus and the surrounding forests. "At first, she wanted to know if energy minds could produce harnessable energy, stop eruptions or help mitigate earthquakes, that sort of thing."

"*We throw our elements at each other.*" As Na'rina gazed at Rosharu staring off the page, she accepted the truth in what McCormick was saying. Rosharu had used Intela Corp to fight the oceanids. "*Their storms erode our mountains in bits and pieces. We, in turn, push up new islands or erupt and add land to our bases.*" When she told Na'rina about the feud between oread and oceanid, she'd known Rosharu left something out, but this was beyond anything she expected. Why would Rosharu use other mythics in her fight? She'd offered to help Na'rina. *Was that just a mask?*

"Wouldn't a mass mind be more useful for such experiments?" Rebecca asked, unaware of Na'rina's inner turmoil. Icarus, however, watched her face, reading her expressions.

"She would never allow you to experiment on one," Icarus said at the same time McCormick stated, "Intela Corp's never caught a mass mind."

Both humans turned surprised eyes on Icarus. With his index finger, Icarus tapped the black and white picture. "She's a mass mind."

"Is it who I think it is?"

They all spun around. Silas was leaning against a rock partially hidden by a blue spruce. Rebecca whimpered and clutched the binder close like a shield.

"*Sa*," Icarus answered.

"And you've never captured a mass mind? You're sure of that?" Silas asked McCormick.

Sweat trickled down the man's temples as he stared into Silas' eyes, frozen like a mouse.

"*You're sure?*" Silas bellowed and McCormick jerked.

"Yes!" he squeaked.

Rubbing the back of his neck, Silas bared his teeth in a grimace. "Centuries of watching the company and I never thought to look at photographs. Mona'rina needs to know this."

They watched him disappear among the trees.

*Is he actually gone?* Na'rina asked her grove.

*He's running for the mother grove.*

"He's gone," Na'rina said.

Rebecca slumped in relief and McCormick mopped at his face with a shaky hand.

"Is there a picture of the current director?" Icarus asked, tapping the binder sitting in Rebecca's lap.

McCormick flinched. He shook himself and then waved a weak finger for Rebecca to flip through the pages again. "Toward the back. You don't think the current director has anything to do with this? It's been two hundred years."

Na'rina shared a look with Icarus.

Rebecca stopped on a color picture that took up half the page. The smiling, curly-haired woman was unmistakably

Rosharu. Rebecca tore the page from the binder and flipped back to the black and white photo, setting the two side-by-side. "Look at that," she whispered. "The hair and clothes all look different, but that face and those eyes—"

McCormick grunted and mopped his forehead with his handkerchief again.

Icarus ran a hand over his face. "I'd hoped Silas jumped to the wrong conclusion."

"You suspected?" Na'rina asked.

"Your bloody shirt from the Kadivas. When I asked around, someone remembered Rosharu carrying it after they picked you back up."

As Na'rina stared into his hazel eyes, she knew that detail was the last leaf on the tree for him. Many other things— things only he seemed to see and understand—made Icarus suspect Rosharu but this confirmed it.

"But what does she have against dryads?" he asked.

"We're useful," Na'rina guessed. "Add our abilities to an oread's and she's got a lot to use against the oceanids."

"*Na,*" Icarus said. He took the binder from Rebecca and flipped through it, glancing over each experiment until he found what he wanted. "She's attacking both oceanids *and* dryads. It's personal on both fronts." He stopped on a page and passed the binder to Na'rina.

It wasn't a skill she used often, but her mother had

taught her to read. Na'rina fumbled through the synopsis of the experiment, stopping with her finger on the date associated with it, swallowing as her hand began to shake. "It says 1820. Did this cause the banishment?" She lifted searching eyes to Icarus, begging for the confirmation he could probably provide, but might hesitate to because of his promises to Silas.

He rested a warm hand against her cheek, his violet zoi aima swirling against her senses. "It was a disease, Na'rina, aimed at the connection between dryads and their trees, making it impossible for them to connect again. Silas and I speculated it was an attempt to make it possible for any dryad to travel away from her tree, but in use, it killed both tree and dryad. And if that wasn't bad enough, the disease transferred by touch, so as each nymph realized something was wrong and she couldn't enter her tree to heal, she panicked and sought the help of the nearest dryad, spreading the disease. It ran faster than wildfire.

"Mona'rina and Silas heard through their Rina what was happening. As you know, the old Council's slow to make decisions. If they waited for proof or argued on a course of action, hundreds would die. The dryad population's small to begin with, so they made their own decision without the Council. Silas gathered as many wer-im as he could convince, and they burned the diseased forest and the already dying dryads. Brutal, but it stopped the disease.

"Mona'rina and Silas learned about Intela Corp and they

knew another attack might be coming. Mona'rina had to remain the ruling Drydanda to protect against any future attacks.

"The Council knew nothing about the reasons behind the wer-im's attack or the connection between Mona'rina and Silas, so Mona'rina acted like she knew nothing as well and banished the wer-im from the forests to 'protect' the dryads. It cost them, but it worked. Since then, Silas has put everything into researching Intela Corp and protecting Mona'rina, but he's not had contact with his grove since 1820."

A horrified shudder ran through Na'rina. Her mother had described the silent half of her Rina as the result of rash actions. *What an understatement.*

"Is this what he meant by making the hard choice in a fight even when the personal consequences are great?" Na'rina asked.

Icarus grimaced. "I believe so."

Na'rina withdrew into herself, seeking the Collective Wisdom to guide her. As she dug into the shared memories of the banishment all she received were images of burning aspens and the sharp smell of sap bubbling down the trunks. The clarity of the memories—Silas' memories, she realized—was gut-wrenching, but nothing in Icarus' explanation layered the Wisdom. To keep their actions from the Council, Silas and Mona'rina must have hidden *everything*. She'd never considered that a Drydanda could and would withhold memories from the genetic history. *But why did Mamma keep me in the dark, too?*

"There's nothing in the Collective Wisdom about this," she whispered.

"I know," Icarus said.

"Why is it so personal?" Na'rina couldn't figure that out. "Why would Rosharu use us like this?"

"If Silas knows, he never told me. And he didn't know about her involvement until now."

Na'rina sighed. "If Silas and my mother are unwilling to tell us anything, there's another we can ask." She grimaced. "If we can figure out her answers."

"Are—um—you done with me?" Richard McCormick interjected. "I would love not to die today, and I don't have anything else I can tell you." He looked at Icarus, trembling. "You can rifle through my memories. Can you make some of them just—disappear? I won't remember any of this. I'll quit my job, I'll retire, anything, just please don't kill me or my family."

Rebecca coughed a laugh. "You don't know much about these people, do you?"

"Dr. Hector's very dead!"

"These two aren't like that."

Icarus eyed them both. "You're still willing to help Felis with the tranquilizers?" he asked the woman.

She nodded with a grin. "Absolutely. We're super close to coming up with a counter to the Enhanced Ketamine."

McCormick slapped his hands over his ears. "I know nothing. I know nothing. I know nothing."

With a finger, Icarus raised the man's eyes to look into his own. Hesitantly, Richard lowered his hands from his ears. "Your job within Intela Corp could be useful."

Richard's eyes flickered.

"I will not kill you. And I would never kill a man's family because of his mistakes. If I take away your memory, it won't be clean. Parts of your recent experiences—your granddaughter's birthday—will be lost. If you want to forget, I'll make it happen. As an alternative, I'm willing to leave your memory intact, stage you in the car with Dr. Hector for Intela Corp to find, so you can return to your work, no one the wiser. In return you will pass along information about the experiments you review."

"A spy?" Surprise etched Richard's heavy face. "I don't know if I'd be any good at that. Look how I collapsed here. Intela Corp *would* kill my family and me if I'm caught."

"True," Icarus agreed and Richard winced. "All I ask is that you don't deliberately tell them. If they catch you, tell them you were coerced. They'll believe it because it's what they would do."

Richard licked his lips. "I can do that."

As Na'rina released him from his living shackles and stood back for Icarus to take over, she swayed in exhaustion.

Her head felt packed with pieces of information all fighting for prominence: the banishment, the holes in the Collective Wisdom, Silas and Mona'rina, Intela Corp's experiments, *Rosharu*. She stared at the ground, running over the details again and again.

A hand touched her shoulder and Na'rina's head swung up to meet Icarus' eyes.

"Who else can tell us about Rosharu?"

"My grandmother."

He cupped her face and brushed her cheekbones with his thumbs. She hadn't noticed she'd been crying. "You've got this," he encouraged, confidence seeping into his words like gold filigree. "I'll meet you at Ver'rina's tree after I take care of things here."

Na'rina inhaled deeply, longing to embody the strength he believed she had.

*All right, Grandmother,* she thought as she headed toward Ver'rina's seed tree, *it's time to bandy words.*

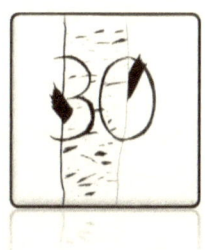

The aspen pulsed with deep green zoi aima that flowed as steady as a calm river. The faint vibration in Ver'rina's seed tree, particularly noticeable in the roots, resembled a person snoring and Na'rina hesitated in waking the fat seed tree.

Finally, she lowered herself to sit facing the tree on the aspen's roots, but before she could place her palms against the black spotted trunk, a muffled thud from behind stopped her. She swiveled her head and all the air rushed from her lungs. Na'rina didn't inhale again until the mountain lion blinked his lazy golden eyes.

He arched in a languid stretch before strolling closer to smell her hair. Warm breath fanned across her forehead.

*This isn't Silas.*

In addition to his golden rather than green eyes, he was too big to be Silas. His paws splayed next to her knees, creating a print larger than her hand. Butting his temple against hers, he ran his body along her shoulder as he passed by, then curled up to lay against her back, tucking his head around to rest beside her right hip. Warmth that she now associated with the wer-im seeped into her lower back.

*Grandfather Levi.* Na'rina chuckled and clapped a hand over her mouth. He'd been here all along. A wer-im right under everyone's noses. "The Council must not know."

"The Council knows water and sunshine but hates the clouds that fill their cup."

"Grandmother." Na'rina looked back at the seed tree, where Ver'rina's bony face protruded, bulging from the aspen's white bark. Her skin stayed white, not turning green-skinned like a dryad who could separate from her tree, but displaying the stage halfway between old-age dormancy and the melding that the Circle dryads had achieved. Although dark smudges under her eyes attested to recent slumber, her eyes flashed with awareness.

"Granddaughter wants the fruit of knowledge."

Na'rina couldn't deny it. "There's much I don't understand."

A rumble vibrated against Na'rina's back.

"He insists I not withhold knowledge out of spite."

It was the most straightforward thing she'd ever heard from Ver'rina. Na'rina shot a glance back at the lion. Perhaps his presence helped her grandmother. "Spite?"

"You only visit when hungry."

A protest died on Na'rina's lips. There had been too many lies for her to start adding to them. "I could say I thought you wanted peace, but I'd be lying," she admitted. "I fear you, Grandmother, fear what you've become."

Ver'rina's face split with a grin. "Truth, sweeter than the honeyed words of the in-between."

Na'rina leaned forward to caress her grandmother's face. A hum came from the old dryad. "I'm afraid," Na'rina said. "I'm finding holes in the Collective Wisdom and those holes are exposing the dryads to enemies we can't see coming."

"The world quakes," Ver'rina agreed, and the lion rumbled, a vibration against Na'rina's spine. "I offer feast of fruit for one thing. Keep my mind on the outside."

Na'rina hesitated. She wasn't even sure how the Circle had succeeded in changing into the last dryadic phase instead of going dormant within their trees like La'meliai had almost done, but it must have required a lot of time. "Can you speak plain?"

The seed tree shuddered with Ver'rina's sigh. "I'll try."

She couldn't expect better. "Deal."

"Ask."

"Rosharu the Oreadanda, do you know her?"

Ver'rina blinked, surprise raising her eyebrows high on her face. Sappy tears began dripping down her cheeks, leaving trails in the powdery bark.

"Old. Very old..." she trailed off even though her lips

continued moving. "Friend," she finally managed, wincing.

"Friend?" Na'rina's mind stuttered. No friend would do what Rosharu had done—would she? "Please explain."

"Oreadanda was old when my roots were young." Strain pulled at Ver'rina's face as she struggled. "No Drydanda for decades until my seed. I learn sky and earth, water and sun in trickles, alone, until Oreadanda came east to find me."

"Came east? She found you and taught you?"

A shallow nod pulled Ver'rina's face farther out of the tree with a grating almost like the creak of old floorboards.

*Old friend, indeed.* Na'rina considered what to ask next. The plethora of questions revolving around Rosharu made her head ache. Rosharu's story regarding the oceanids must have some truth, but there were parts that didn't line up. Perhaps that was the best place to start.

The lion rumbled a warning just before Icarus lowered himself to sit on Na'rina's left. His knee rested against hers, but he only tilted his chin in greeting, silently urging her to continue. If he had questions when she was done, he no doubt would ask them.

"Why does Rosharu hate the oceanids?"

Her grandmother's vibrant eyes studied Icarus for a moment, her lips parting as a small smile pulled her cheeks into tiny bulges in the trunk. Then Na'rina's question hit her and she breathed a keening cry. "*Tragic.* Oreadanda loved the roll of the

472

waves at the toes of Mount Athos, but neither waves nor rock allowed her love."

"She told me a story in which an oread and oceanid loved each other," Na'rina said, thrilled she understood her grandmother's words. "Her mountain must be on the West Coast, against the ocean. She said both died."

Ver'rina tisked. "Twisted limbs. Gnarled, twisted limbs."

"They didn't die?"

"Ocean and Mountain handfasted in secret," Ver'rina answered, "but ocean cannot live without waves and mountain cannot breathe liquid salt. Whirl of wind, breeze in the leaves," the older dryad popped a hand out of her tree to snap. "Breathe and...and...*Gah!*" she snapped again. "Speak plain! Speak plain!"

"A sylph?" Icarus guessed.

"Sylph!" Ver'rina exclaimed.

"An air nymph?" Na'rina asked. "I don't understand."

"A sylph could hold a thin layer of salt water against the oceanid's skin to keep him alive," Icarus answered for Ver'rina and the lion rumbled confirmation "He could wander land as long as the sylph was near enough to maintain the layer."

"*Oh,*" Na'rina breathed, "he must not have been Oceadanda." Another area Rosharu misled her.

"But—but," Ver'rina grabbed her chin with bony fingers, "tiny ears tell and intentions turn to mud beneath their feet."

Na'rina stiffened at the gush of words. She closed her eyes, as if to see them across the back of her lids, but try as she might, she couldn't wrap her mind around her grandmother's meaning. "Mud beneath their feet?"

Ver'rina tilted her head forward to stretch the muscles in her neck. With a pop her shoulders materialized out of the tree. "Speak plain, speak plain," she chanted again. "Waves, salty water fell far inland. Mud beneath feet, mud in the air, mud—" Ver'rina shuddered and several leaves dropped from her branches. "Oceanid in mud, sylph in mud."

"*Oh, no.*" Na'rina gasped in understanding. "If the sylph were caught in a mudslide, she would be cut off from her element. Not dead, but anything she'd caused to happen would be cut off as well. The oceanid would be caught away from the sea without the protective layer."

"Liam…gone." Ver'rina slumped, exhausted.

"Liam was the oceanid and Rosharu was the oread girl," Na'rina confirmed.

A sad nod was her answer.

"No wonder she hates the oceanids. They killed their own," Icarus said.

"Mountain gathered love's body, hid it away from oceanids in Mount Athos," Ver'rina added.

"The oceanids want Liam's body," Icarus said.

Ver'rina's lips rolled in. "Mountain couldn't return him

474

even if she turned soft to the wave's pleas."

"Why?"

"Cave gone beneath the weight of quake and time. Oreadanda helped Levi and me and lost love's grave. Never seen in rock or on rock again… Until now."

A cold like premature frost clutched at Na'rina. Needing warm contact against the ice that settled in her belly, Na'rina grasped Icarus' hand and held it to her stomach. A moment later, Ver'rina's bony fingers covered both their hands. Her fingers were even cooler than Na'rina's, but her grip stayed strong.

"Tell us what happened?" Na'rina begged, yet afraid to hear.

"Handfasted outside the acceptable," Ver'rina answered and her brilliant eyes swung to the giant mountain lion. Joy, pain, love—a deep, unflinching connection like nothing Na'rina had ever seen—passed between them. "Mountain feared for us. Advised secrecy. We did not follow the Mountain's trail until our seeds gave root. Even when small sprouts, mixed blood was filled with claws. Then followed Mountain's trail. Levi protected older Drydanda," Ver'rina moved her hand to her face, "Silas was 'brought' in to protect baby Drydanda. Connection between sprouts never told."

Na'rina leaned forward, eager to understand this vital part of her history. No wonder the Council never knew about

Silas. Even as a baby, he'd only been introduced to them as Mona'rina's protector. And, with her grandfather Levi now a mountain lion, the Council would have assumed he left with the banishment as well. Instead, he'd always been around, right in front of them. The enormity of it boggled her mind. *Alaya was right about how much I don't know about my own family.* She reclaimed Ver'rina's hand, squeezing it in encouragement.

"Confident of rain and sunshine, we did not see the lightning coming. Together, our sprouts were powerful. More than wer-im, more than dryad, more than any other. At that moon, the old Wer-Kadis craved control. Craved what Silas accomplished later—to hold all wer-im to will." A gusty sigh from her grandmother that smelled of aspen sap washed over Na'rina's face. "Someway, somehow, he learned connection of sprouts, and came for them."

"I've heard of that Kadis," Icarus commented. "He lived before my time, but even the wer-im considered him especially violent."

Ver'rina shuddered and then, with a sharp crack, her second hand emerged from the aspen. The bark around that hand cracked and wept sap.

"Grandmother, you're hurting yourself!" Na'rina laid her hands along the split and fed zoi aima into it. As the aspen healed, her back opened and closed in mimicry of the bark beneath her palms.

"Want wind in hair," Ver'rina protested like a child denied her favorite toy.

"Slowly, Grandmother, or you won't have a body worth living in." How did the Circle retain their consciousness without dormancy? La'meliai's dormancy had been brief and even she suffered from trying to be active again. Leaning back after the healing, Na'rina pulled her shirt away from her back to break away the blood she'd sympathetically bled. "The Wer-Kadis came for Silas and Mona'rina, wanting to use them," she said, encouraging her grandmother to continue.

"Mountain offered cave for sprouts to hide," Ver'rina picked up her story. "Crafty Wer-Kadis sniff them out anyway. In fight, sprouts collapsed cave, buried Wer-Kadis." Faster than her wooden limbs usually moved, Ver'rina seized Na'rina's face. The bones of her fingers, more twigs than flesh, pressed hard against her jaw. "Mountain's love, bones she holds dear as her roots, buried as well." Ver'rina sniffed, tears forming. "My sprouts return home, safe from old, crafty cat, but they returned alone. Mountain disappeared. Old friend—never seen since."

Apart from the cry of a hawk, silence surrounded them. Na'rina leaned forward to wipe her grandmother's tears away with her thumb and trailed a comforting mist of zoi aima. Ver'rina sighed deeply. A moment later, Ver'rina's deep green zoi aima washed back as she remembered how to share through the flesh she hadn't inhabited in decades. The lifeblood tasted mossy but it was richly green compared to Mona'rina's due to her unnatural dormancy. Wrinkles fanned out from the corners of Ver'rina's eyes as she smiled.

"Rosharu blames Mona'rina and Silas for the earthquake that buried Liam's bones," Icarus summed up.

The lion grumbled in agreement. Na'rina stroked behind Levi's ear and he rolled his head into her palm as they all absorbed what they'd learned.

The details of the truth were nothing like the story Rosharu told Na'rina, but the loss was the same. It now made sense why Rosharu's story had felt wrong, but why did she choose lava to describe the way her love died when in reality he'd been buried in mud?

"She loves the forest and leaves!" Ver'rina's protest made them all jump, but it was Levi's soft rumbling that calmed the older dryad.

"It was Rosharu in the Theta site wall in Tennessee," Na'rina said aloud as she connected parts of the story. "She was the one who flipped the switch that made me explode. As an Oreadanda, being inside the brick of the building would be no different than moving through earth."

All of the complexes they'd visited were made with brick. Na'rina wanted to be sick. Rosharu encouraged her, fought for her even. Then Na'rina thought about when they'd fought together in the alley. Rosharu hadn't disappeared into the ground because she hadn't wanted to, not because the broken concrete prevented it. *She wanted me to be alone and vulnerable, trusting only her. What would have happened if the wer-im hadn't shown up?* Would it have been like what happened in Tennessee? She recalled the zoi aima of the creature within the Theta Site wall. Such malice seethed in that lifeblood.

"She's not well," Na'rina declared aloud.

Ver'rina cupped her chin, making Na'rina meet her eyes. The seriousness within those green depths sent a warning thrill into Na'rina's stomach. "Sure as sun above?"

Na'rina gulped. "Her zoi aima's not healthy. She controls it somewhat. I sensed nothing when she first greeted me properly, but when I felt her within the wall in Tennessee—" She shuddered.

Ver'rina sighed again. "Ask ground dwellers about her roots."

Icarus leaned forward to touch the side of her grandmother's face. "Why?"

"They'll know if foundation is dying. Oreadanda darken the skies and kill the world." Ver'rina slumped and shrugged off Icarus' touch to retreat into her tree. Exhaustion breathed through the roots beneath their legs.

"I'll do all I can to keep your mind on the outside," Na'rina whispered and her grandmother's gratitude flushed through the zoi aima within the tree.

"Foundation's dying?" Icarus asked.

Na'rina hid her face against his shoulder. "Volcanic." *Darken the skies.* "She might be volcanic."

He wrapped an arm around her, holding her against his side as he mused aloud, "The Rockies dwarves were captured." Of course he would see a connection there. His next words confirmed her thought. "If she wanted to hide Mount Athos' illness, the closest dwarves who would pick up on it would be the Rockies, since the Cascade line died out."

"Mount Athos is in Washington?" Na'rina asked, figuring he'd know since he'd called Rosharu to the Chattanooga meeting.

"*Sa.*"

She shuddered. "I didn't even know my grandfather until now," the lion rumbled against her back, "and now an old family friend might blow up and destroy the world."

When she tilted her head to look at the giant mountain lion, his golden eyes seemed like they could read her heart. She'd missed out on growing up with his influence. But he was wer-im. The dryads would never have allowed him near her after the banishment and now she knew that nothing she believed turned out correct about the wer-im or the banishment. Another thought hit her.

"Grandmother?"

The green eyes appeared, bright against the white trunk.

"Can things be hidden from the Collective Wisdom? Can it be manipulated?"

The eyes squeezed shut in pain. "Difficult. Part of dryad's blood, but Drydanda control zoi aima. I—buried—truth of my sprouts in joy of my daughter. Why not—nudge—the memory to see only some light?"

*Why not nudge it to see only fire?* Those memories were filled with angry smoke and bubbling sap. Na'rina suspected it hadn't been as hard as Ver'rina thought for Silas and Mona'rina to cover everything else beneath them.

The gray of night would soon descend, but after the attack and her grandmother's revelations Na'rina didn't want to move, to leave this spot where she'd found a dryad finally willing to be honest with her.

Leaning against Icarus, she flattened her palms against the earth on either side of her to feel the life swirling beneath them. The ebb and flow washed across her nerves. At the core, this was dryadic. Glorying in the forest's life and at peace with the world. But being Drydanda required more. Being Danda of any sort meant stewardship, care of the bigger picture.

*We've lost sight of who we are.*

With sadness, Na'rina sank deeper into the life beneath the ground, reconnecting for the night with her home.

A twig cracked under someone's heel. Na'rina straightened, disoriented as she saw the gray of dawn. Icarus and the mountain lion—*Grandfather Levi*—were nowhere in sight. *That might be a blessing,* she thought as she caught sight of the woman approaching. *Don't want to scare the wits out of her.*

Rebecca cringed. "I'm a hippo among ballet dancers." She fluttered a hand at her flushed face. "Sorry to disturb you. I just wanted to see if you're okay. You've been sitting there for so long."

"Okay?" Na'rina stretched her arms upward, popping her back, then waved for Rebecca to join her.

The woman sat down with a grimace. "Felis explained about the energy min—I mean the dryad you freed from the Four Corners. And a lot of other things. We've made a mess of your life, haven't we?"

A hiccupping laugh escaped Na'rina. "We've made just as big a mess. Not long ago I wouldn't have believed how many lies and secrets surround me."

"Ditto," Rebecca agreed. "I'm glad to help fix some of the mess." She pulled a small pouch from her pocket. "Felis and I've been trying to develop a sample of the Enhanced Ketamine so we can counteract it. We finally succeeded last night." A huge grin lit her face. "These are the samples we have thus far. We can make more, but we have to find more supplies."

Rebecca handed over a leather pouch. Tucked inside, held by straps like a sheath, sat two darts. "The red one is the Ketamine," she explained. "It won't harm anyone, but if you need to, you can knock someone out for a long time. The blue dart will counteract the Ketamine if you get shot."

"You did it!" Na'rina hugged Rebecca. "What'd you do, test it on Felis?"

Rebecca ducked her head. "We thou—"

*Na'rina!*

She shuddered as her Rina demanded her attention in the same way a Sedessan would grab her by the temples.

*Rosharu came for your mother during the attack.*

*What?*

*Mona'rina went with her willingly. Apparently, Rosharu spent time in the cell next to your mother at the Four Corners center. Mona'rina thinks they were captives together and was surprised Rosharu was alive. She thought Intela Corp killed her.*

*Rosharu told Mona'rina that she stole some machines from Intela Corp. She says they can help control a small explosion in the side of Mount*

*Athos to return Liam's bones to the ocean.*

Na'rina gaped.

*Silas' connection with the mother grove is still strained. It took him until now to convince the grove to tell him where Mona'rina went because your mother swore her to secrecy, knowing Silas would argue against helping Rosharu while Mona'rina is still weak. She didn't want to argue with him.*

*Where is Silas now?*

*He took off after them as soon as he found out. He'll kill Rosharu.* The Rina gasped as she finished getting the story out.

Na'rina shuddered. *How'd you find out?*

*The mother grove.*

*Tell Icar—*

"They're gone!" Afre shouted, his call breaking the chill morning like the cry of a bird. Na'rina blinked as a squirrel chittered.

Beside her, Rebecca held her arm and Na'rina realized she'd slumped forward when her Rina shouted.

Afre's knees hit the dirt as he stopped in front of Na'rina.

"I know," Na'rina said, holding his arms while he fought to draw in a full breath. The faun must have run to warn her.

Afre fought for air. *"You know?* Of course, you know. The Wer-Kadis wants to go after them. If Silas gets ahold of

Rosharu, he'll kill her for sure."

Goose bumps flushed Na'rina's skin as Silas' killing of Dr. Hector flashed through her mind. "I have to go." Hesitating, she looked at Rebecca, who watched in confusion.

"I'm fine," Rebecca reassured, as if reading her thoughts. "Afre can explain everything and help me find my way back."

Hugging them both, Na'rina took off for her seed tree.

"Wow, can she move!" she heard Rebecca exclaim, but she felt she couldn't run fast enough. Rosharu had Mona'rina, and Silas was hunting them.

*Darken the skies.* A mountain nymph's violent death, if she was already volcanic, would inevitably set off the mountain's eruption. And such an eruption could be catastrophic.

Skidding into the small clearing around her seed tree, Na'rina stopped and swayed, taking in the gathered wer-im. It took her a moment to spot Icarus where he spoke with the broad-nosed wer-im she recognized from Chattanooga. As she moved to join Icarus, the other wer-im melted back into the trees.

Icarus greeted her with a nod and pointed to where Felis waited with the car. "We need to find Obek-Ak-Lea up in Washington."

"Obek?" Na'rina asked, matching his long strides. "He's in Washington?"

"Last we spotted him, yes. He'll know how to find

Rosharu and he'll have a gauge on whether she plans to do what she told your mother—or if she's going to destroy the Western Hemisphere." He gestured at the broad-nosed wer-im. "Mason went to the local library last night to look up news on earthquakes in Washington. There's definitely activity around Mount Athos."

Preoccupied, Na'rina didn't hesitate when Icarus opened the car door for her to slide into the back seat. She waited for him to get in the front seat before reaching out to touch his shoulder. "Why did Mamma leave without saying something?"

"Your mother knows nothing about Rosharu's connection to Intela Corp, but with their history, she probably wants to help her."

"She's too weak. This could kill her."

"If she's anything like you, she won't care about the personal cost." Icarus put his hand over hers still resting on his shoulder and squeezed. Na'rina breathed in his warm zoi aima, letting it flow into her core and ease the knot in her stomach.

Finally, she slid back into the seat and buckled the belt across her torso. They settled into silence as the car rumbled down the road. Na'rina heard the rumble of a motorcycle following them. Glancing through the back window, she caught the rider's shock of orange hair. When they reached the highway, he passed the car and left them behind. *Icarus must have given him a task. Does the Wer-Kadis ever sleep?* It was a rueful thought, but her levity faded as mist in sunshine.

Na'rina ignored the rattling of the car and rested her head against the seat. She stared at her reflection which overlaid the mountain peaks through the window. Picturing Mona'rina and Silas along with her own image, it was too easy now to see the similarities between her mother and the wer-im—and herself. The one was so familiar and the other so foreign, yet the arch of their brows and noses, the bow of their lips, and the color of their brilliant eyes reflected each other. It turned her stomach to think she'd missed it.

*I'm blind.* Being a direct descendent—True Born—meant she had the same mix of blood as her mother because there was no father to change it. *Half-dryad, half-wer-im.* Since she was female, her characteristics displayed as dryad, just like her mother. If she'd been a boy her features would have taken more from her grandfather, Levi, like Silas. She snorted. That would have made life interesting.

And Silas—Na'rina gulped, admitting that the wer-im was family—*Uncle Silas.* The name felt odd, but he *was* her mother's twin brother. The truth of it rolled within her like the dark makings of a thunderstorm. Her bright green, gemstone eyes stared back at her from her reflection and there was no denying the connection. *So blind.*

"Malon spotted Owasha off the West Coast," Felis said to Icarus. Na'rina hadn't caught when they started speaking again, but now she listened, wanting to hear the update. "She's whipping up the ocean more than usual but they're still able to keep track of her. Alaya hasn't been seen since the Circle."

"She'll be there," Na'rina said. "She balances Owasha."

Felis shuddered. "I'd hate to see her unbalanced. Anyway, the weather's nuts."

"Could the oceanids be worsening Rosharu's mental state if they're washing away parts of her mountain?" Icarus asked over his shoulder.

Na'rina considered the question. When a storm tore her trees apart, the pain lasted for days while the grove recovered. Trees, however, healed much faster than a mountain. If Owasha's storm damaged Mount Athos, Rosharu's agony would sit inside her like broken bones that hadn't been set right. "Possibly. When we get to the coast, I'll speak with Alaya. Maybe she can temper her sister."

"We'll do that after contacting Obek," Icarus agreed.

She recalled the Appalachian dwarf prince from the Chattanooga meeting. Washington was rather far from home for him but then, if his father, the Ak-Lea, sent him to find the Rockies dwarves, his search would have led him west. Remembering his gruff attitude toward the wer-im, Na'rina asked, "You think he'll agree to help us?"

"We'll have to convince him, but I think his sense of honor will work in our favor."

"Great," Na'rina muttered and sat back. A multitude of details swirled around her like leaves blowing in the wind. They needed to be at Rosharu's mountain yesterday.

In the silence, Felis flipped on the radio and flashed her a teasing smile. She half-bowed a sassy thank you. The bearded wer-im snorted a laugh. Taking in the music, Na'rina closed her eyes and ignored the passing landscape for most of the twenty-some-odd hours it took to get to the coast of Washington.

At one point they stopped. The darkness told her nothing about where they were, but the wind wafting into the car's stale air as Icarus opened the door carried the musky flavor of damp earth and rain. Na'rina caught his hand, her question in her eyes.

"We're just south of Washington. Need to fuel the car," he explained. "I'll find you some food." He held her hand to his lips and then left.

Na'rina glanced out at the reddish glare of the rest stop sign, and then leaned back and closed her eyes again. When Icarus returned, he nudged her knee and held out a plastic bag. It contained two buns wrapped in plastic wrappers labeled: "Honeyrolls."

"Not as good as fresh bread and honey," he shrugged with a wry smile, his reflective eyes sparkling under the edge of his black beanie, "but I said I'd find you food."

Na'rina tore open the plastic and pulled off a sticky bite

between her thumb and forefinger. The bun did not, in fact, taste like bread or honey, but as it dissolved on her tongue, she gave the wer-im a hum. "These'll do," she said regally.

His eyes flashed and she swore he chuckled as he turned to face forward in the car.

"Hold tight!"

The car careened sideways, fishtailing left and right before hitting something and flipping. It rolled once and thudded to a stop upside down against a massive spruce. Na'rina touched the mossy bark through her shattered window.

*Drydanda! That was a spectacle!* The spruce exclaimed. *Think I lost some moss.* He sounded like he'd want to see them roll again just for the fun of watching. Relief filled her, though, that he was fine after having a metal car fly into his side.

"Tree's fine," she announced, staring at her hand as she noticed it shaking.

"Are you?" Icarus asked.

Na'rina looked for him, but he wasn't hanging from his seatbelt like her. He appeared outside her window with blood covering his face from a gash on his left temple. Na'rina touched the cut but she needn't have worried. The flesh already puckered beneath the blood, knitting itself back together.

"Do I look as bad?" she asked.

He chuckled, the relief on his face telling her she was fine, and wrapped an arm around her before releasing her seatbelt. Maneuvering her out the window and around the tree, he set her on the ground.

"Cold!" Na'rina pushed to stand up and hugged the spruce to keep from sliding off her feet.

*Cold?* The spruce asked. *I wondered why my bark feels brittle.* Na'rina didn't respond as she studied the ground, trying to figure out why it glistened with a sheet of ice like on a frozen river. Wind pelted her skin with leaves and other debris.

"The oceanid's storm must have caused a huge drop in temperature," Icarus shouted over the wind. "Looks like Obek hosed the driveway down to ice it over."

"Where's here?" Na'rina accepted Icarus' offered hand and let go of the tree. On the far side of the upside-down car, Felis leaned against the vehicle.

"You slept through Seattle. We're northwest at a cabin the dwarves own. We've gotten reports that Obek's staying here while looking for his Rockies kin," Icarus explained.

"See," she said, pointing at the car. "Deathtrap-on-wheels."

"*Aw!*" Felis threw up his hands, then caught himself against the car when he started to slide. "Give Loretta a break. You can barely walk, yet you expect her to do better?"

Na'rina glared.

"Still consorting with the wer-im, Drydanda?" Obek's deep, gravelly voice carried just loud enough to hear over the wind.

Na'rina turned to greet him and her feet flew from under her. She landed with a heavy *oof* and slid several feet. Obek looked startled.

"I'll answer your questions," she wheezed, "as soon as I'm not sitting on ice."

"My apologies." Obek shuffled forward to assist her. Before helping her to stand, he fitted small shoe-like contraptions with bits of rock sticking out the bottoms over her feet.

"Right this way," he told her, tucking her hand into the crook of his arm. He stood a full head shorter than her as he led her forward, and Na'rina mused that his wider stance and rough shoes allowed for a steadier footing on the ice. When the wer-im fell in behind them, Obek scowled but focused on the driveway and just grumbled while they walked.

The grumbling, as far as Na'rina could tell, was aimed at the wer-im, but Obek allowed them to follow—perhaps on her account—so she let it be. He led them to a squat log cabin with smoke spiraling from the chimney. A wall of heat flushed her skin upon entering but she accepted the steaming mug of tea Obek handed her, taking a seat beside Icarus at the heavy wooden table that dominated the main room. The tea smelled of honey and lemon, and she breathed in the aroma while the others settled around her.

"Why do you bring the wer-im here, Drydanda?" Obek rumbled, getting straight to the point. "We dwarves do not wish to get caught between you and your enemies."

Na'rina steepled her fingers around the mug, soaking in its warmth to help calm her still shaking hands, and explained all she knew about Intela Corp and Rosharu, even hinting at the banishment and the disease, although she kept the specifics regarding her family to herself. Perhaps she followed her mother's mistakes too closely, but she couldn't condemn her family in front of another.

Obek's lips rolled inward into his beard while she spoke. He huffed through his nose when she finished and asked, "You're sure this Intela Corp's responsible?"

She nodded.

"I'll tear them apart!" He slammed a fist on the table, making the mugs jump.

Na'rina pulled her hands away from the clay fast enough to miss the splash of hot liquid.

Felis hissed. He shook his right hand. "Dwar—"

"Your kin?" Na'rina interrupted. "Have you found them?"

Obek's heavy brows lowered and he shook his head.

"My apologies, Wer-im," he said to Felis almost as an aside. Shock raised Felis' brows but Na'rina knew that as the son of the ruling family, courtesy dictated Obek apologize, despite his anger.

"We have not found our Pyrgos kin," Obek admitted. From his low tone, Na'rina knew how much the admission clawed at him. "We fear they are dead. Their tunnels are empty and cold. We've even dodged people in their tunnels, probably people from this Intela Corp. Thus the—" he motioned in the direction of the icy driveway. "We moved west because the trail led us here but now it has..." he muttered and then snorted, "melted. The ground trembles and any trail we could have found has crumbled." He clenched his hands. "You are right about the oread and her mountain. It won't be long now before she loses control."

"How big of an eruption are we talking?" Na'rina asked.

Obek downed his tea and grimaced. "Need something stronger." He moved to rise but Icarus placed a hand over his mug.

"We need you sober."

"Ever out-drink a dwarf?" Obek retorted, but he sat back down. "It'll darken a good portion of the Western Hemisphere," he answered Na'rina, "which doesn't make sense. It's too big for her mountain."

"Why haven't you warned anyone?" Felis asked,

incredulous.

Obek bared his heavy teeth. "Even if we hid the mythics in our caves, Wer-im, there aren't enough supplies for all the mythics to survive. And what of the dryads? It's not like we can store sunshine to feed them. None of us can stop the eruption."

"But what if there *is* a way to stop it?" Na'rina spoke up before Felis could respond.

Obek's face had turned deep red. He went to drink, remembered his mug was empty, and thumped it back on the table. "A way to stop it?"

"*Sa*, but we need help finding Rosharu."

"Why me?" he looked imploringly upward. "If you have a plan, I am honor-bound to lead you into the oread's caves, but you'll have to convince me you've got something solid before I'll go traipsing into that mountain." Obek stood, giving Icarus a defiant look, and went to pour himself more tea. On top of the dollop of honey he added, he gave a generous pour from a bottle he pulled from the cabinet, and flashed Icarus a defiant grin.

The burning odor of alcohol reached Na'rina's nose. She rose from the table and moved into the kitchen with Obek. He froze, watching her rummage through the cabinets until she found what she wanted. With a clang, she set the metal travel mug in front of him. "First," she said, "I need to speak with her." She pointed out the window where wind and rain pelted the glass, but below she heard the roar of waves pounding the nearby sand. Na'rina also heard the scrape of branches against the cabin from an ash, who kept speaking to her about how hollow the ground felt beneath its roots.

"Her?" Obek asked, confused.

"Alaya," Na'rina clarified, extracting the clay mug from his fingers and pouring the contents into the travel container. Holding her breath long enough to screw the lid on, she handed the tea back to Obek. "I need her help."

"But Alaya hates the oread."

"The ash outside that window," she pointed, ignoring his comment, "tells me there are hollow spots beneath this cabin. Makes me think you've got a tunnel to the beach."

Obek took a gulp from his mug. "You remind me of your mother. Except she never asked to use the tunnels. She'd just show up and let herself in."

Pleasure and concern clashed inside Na'rina. Mona'rina was good at dealing with others, but she'd also made a mess of things.

"Follow me." Obek walked to the back of the cabin and opened a door to a staircase lit by a bluish glow. They followed him down the stairs to a landing where the walls turned rough and dirt crunched underfoot. Tunnels shot off in all directions, but Obek chose one unerringly and soon the smell of salt water told Na'rina they were approaching an opening by the ocean.

Icarus stalled her with a hand on her arm and they lagged behind the others far enough for them to speak without being overheard.

"You're not your mother," he whispered.

"I act like her." Na'rina tried to keep walking but he held her.

"You're good with people, like her, but she would never approach Obek and now Alaya, for help."

Na'rina frowned, but squeezed his hand. "Let's hope it'll make a difference."

Icarus bent his forehead to hers. The brief contact flushed warmth through her and she clung to it as they hurried to catch up with Obek. She'd need every bit of strength for what she was about to do. The dwarf leaned against the wall about twenty paces from the end of the tunnel. He waved with his mug at the rain pelting in through the mouth of the tunnel.

"There's the beach."

"Not going out?" Felis teased.

Obek grunted. "I live underground, Wer-im, with roaring fires and hot drinks."

"Stay here," Na'rina told them.

Icarus grimaced but didn't follow. The second she left the shelter of the rock, icy rain beat at her skin and drenched her, plastering her long hair to her head. She pushed forward with head bowed to reach the water. Waves crashed against the shore, threatening to wash Na'rina into the chaos. She knelt in the sand.

"Alaya!" Her shout was a whisper in the roar of the wind. Na'rina couldn't stream zoi aima into the ocean without chancing calling forth Owasha instead, but perhaps she could enhance her voice. Gritty grains stuck to her palms as she pressed them deep into the sand. At first her search met little, but then she found seaweed and salt covered her tongue. She searched farther and found coral.

*Sing for me.*

Na'rina streamed zoi aima through the coral, enhancing it with sound like she'd never done before. *Alaya!* Her call pulsed from the seaweed into the rioting waves. The salt coating her tongue grew stronger. Na'rina spit. This was her chance to contact Alaya and convince Obek she could balance Rosharu, but Na'rina hesitated. There was no sun to heighten her zoi aima, and pulling more to call Alaya would kill the plants she was using. But zoi aima was so similar to energy, she could manipulate them in the same way, and the storm swirling around her spoke of an endless supply. *I can absorb other energy, why not this?*

Bracing herself, she reached for the storm. Chaos struck her. It was like harnessing an avalanche as the air around her deadened in a bubble of calm. Inside, however, the world rioted and her heart beat against her ribs.

*Alaya!* The release trembled from her head down into her toes as the storm closed in, beating at her from the outside again as she lost control. The whiplash from it felt like she'd bounced her brain against her skull.

Na'rina shuddered. Stilling herself, she braced to try again. The storm seethed into her and the bubble of calm washed outward in a small radius from where she knelt. Although the bubble of calm returned, her hair stood on end and her heart beat even harder, making her ribs ache.

"Hold it."

Na'rina's eyes flew open. Alaya stood before her. Her silvery hair whipped about her shoulders as the chaos of the storm—something Na'rina now knew was no small thing to hold—rolled inside the Oceadanda's eyes.

"What?" Na'rina asked.

"Breathe the storm in and out of your lungs like it feeds your body." Alaya's voice beat at Na'rina like the waves pounding the sand. "If you can contain the power in the storm, perhaps you can contain Rosharu's mountain."

"You know?"

"She returned home," Alaya confirmed. "I knew the instant I joined Owasha that the heart of the mountain now feeds its fury."

"Why would you join Owasha? It's driving Rosharu mad!"

Alaya scoffed, and the wind carried the sound, toying with it. "*Na*. The oread set herself up for madness long ago when she stole our brother's body and kept it within her mountain."

"She loved him." Na'rina's heart ached from thudding against her chest, but somehow the thought of Rosharu made it hurt even more. "How can you blame her still?"

The oceanid clicked her tongue. "You do not yet understand, Drydanda. We are not driving her mad. He is. Without returning his body to the water, Liam cannot rest. We're trying to wash him back to the sea, but we can't reach him. His torment is hers so long as his body remains inside Mount Athos."

Cold understanding hit Na'rina. "Even if she wanted to return him, she can't. His grave was buried years ago."

"Rosharu is Oreadanda. She can move through any earth. If she wanted to, she could find his bones."

Na'rina shook her head. "Find and retrieve are two different things. Please don't torment her even more. She's losing it fast enough already."

"I'm sorry, Drydanda. When she explodes, the storm will help dampen the damage." Alaya backed away and disappeared in the next wave. It crashed across Na'rina where she knelt and her bubble shattered like delicate glass.

Struggling to her feet, Na'rina turned to rejoin the

others back at the cave, but the wind shoved her along. Icarus'
zoi aima acted as her beacon in the storm, keeping her headed
in the right direction. Obek needed to see her controlling the
storm if he was going to agree to guide them into Rosharu's
mountain. *Obek needs to believe the impossible.* Exhaustion
threatened to defeat her control.

*You can do this.*

Na'rina couldn't tell if Icarus spoke or if her mind
provided the confidence to bolster her flagging strength, but the
words flooded her with a new will. Closing her eyes, she opened
herself to the fury raging off the ocean. As Alaya instructed,
Na'rina breathed the wind and the waves in and out. The green
in her skin rolled with the storm and a bubble of calm expanded
one foot, then two from where she stood. *Breathe deeper.* As she
inhaled more of the storm with each breath, her heart thudded
against her ribs but the calm swept outward again and again
until it reached the cave just as Na'rina felt the riot of wind and
rain threaten to engulf her.

*Only have to hold it a moment longer.*

In a haze, she saw the wer-im and dwarf rise from where
they waited at the cave entrance. Sure of their attention, she
walked toward them even though the chaos burned in her veins.
The centered part of her noticed Obek left his mug on the
ground when he stood. He stroked his beard. Felis grinned but
his eyes were huge as a startled cat's. But it was Icarus behind

him who she focused on, drawing strength from the familiar, pleased look on his face.

"All forces have a counter," she addressed Obek in a voice that rolled like Alaya's with the waves. "The fury of the wind and waves, the tremor of the earth, the life on its surface. We are made to balance each other."

The dwarf scooped his mug off the floor. "And I'm caught in the middle." He pivoted and stalked up the tunnel.

Felis went after him, close on his heels. His words filtered behind him. "See her eyes? So crazy. Wonder..." the sound faded. *Always curious.*

Na'rina came close to smiling but even that tiny movement would break the glass cage of her control. Icarus rushed to her the minute the others turned the corner. She released the storm's energy through the soles of her feet and behind her with a deafening clap that shoved her against Icarus' chest. She listened to his heart while her body recovered.

Sappy tears still streaming down her face, she thanked her stars the water dripping from her hair had hidden them from Obek. Between her tears and her gasping to catch her breath, she explained to Icarus Alaya's revelation about Rosharu and Liam.

"Ver'rina said his body was lost," Icarus said.

Na'rina shuddered a sigh. "Alaya says Rosharu should be able to find his bones."

"Maybe she *is* trying to control the explosion to get his bones back to the ocean?"

"If Obek's right, she's not controlling it, she's feeding it." Na'rina shook her head. "I'm scared, Icarus. The machines my Rina talked about, if they're like the devices Dr. Hector experimented with, they'll sap everything from my mother and feed the explosion into something Rosharu can't manage." She pushed back on his chest to look up at him. "She'll kill everyone and use my mother to do it. If I can reach my mother, I can explain and maybe get her to stop helping Rosharu."

Tension pulled the lines at his temples tight. Na'rina traced the lowest scar on his cheek while he stared out at the storm raging behind her.

"We have to hurry," Icarus said. "Even without Mona'rina's help, Rosharu could destroy the West Coast. We might have to convince Rosharu to do what she told Mona'rina she was doing, but if Silas reaches her first—"

"A violent death would make Mount Athos explode uncontrollably just as surely as if Rosharu ordered it."

"Silas has been away from Mona'rina and his grove for so long trying to protect them. He won't forgive Rosharu for using his sister—especially when it puts her in danger," he said, shaking his head.

Na'rina growled. *It all comes back to the inability to forgive.*

"How stupid are we?" Na'rina raged. "The oceanids

refuse to forgive Rosharu for loving their brother. They killed him for that love, for sky's sake! Then Rosharu takes her love's body and won't forgive the oceanids in turn. She loses his remains and blames the dryads. Now we're going after her because we blame her for our losses. We've learned nothing from our past!"

"Na'rina."

She pulled away to head down the tunnel. "If I've learned nothing else from you, it's that none of us is 'peaceful' by nature. At least wer-im don't hide it. And now we're headed to find Rosharu, which puts us in the way of Silas and my mother while they're…"

They passed Felis at the bottom of the stairs to the cabin. "What's she on about?"

Na'rina glowered at him but shut up before they entered the cabin. Obek eyed her like she might be hiding the storm inside herself, ready to unleash it at will. She flashed a smile and headed toward the kitchen for a glass of water. Salt stuck her tongue to the top of her mouth. When she came back, the dwarf handed her a headlamp and a towel.

"You dripped on my floor," he grumbled.

Na'rina dried her hair while he explained that while the tunnels would take them most of the way to Rosharu's mountain not all of them were rigged with lights.

"One other thing," he said before leading them back

down the stairs. "Mountain nymphs don't welcome dwarves into their homes. I'll be leaving you after getting you inside Rosharu's mountain. I won't have a crazy Oreadanda focused on me."

"Where are the other dwarves?" Felis' question echoed in the stairwell.

"Out searching," Obek answered.

"Have you checked the Intela Corp center here?"

The dwarf paused on the landing. "Didn't know about it until you explained your story."

Silence fell as they left behind the lighted area and clicked on their headlamps. The spotlights danced along the dark tunnel walls, and Na'rina resisted a shudder. She listened to the pad of the wer-im's feet and Obek's heavy breathing instead of staring at the earth pressing in all around them. *It's no different than traveling into a plant's roots.* The thought, however, didn't change the dust constricting her throat, making her aware she was not within a plant, where the air was clean and tinted by the plant's unique flavor.

"Just a little farther." Obek's voice grated against the walls but Na'rina welcomed the information. It gave her enough to forge ahead and soon they were facing a heavy, locked door. Obek produced a key and its clank echoed into the darkness as he unlocked the bolt.

"You won't be able to hear me once we're out in that

mess," he said, "so listen up. We're headed north up the beach about three hundred yards. Keep the water to your left if you lose sight of me and keep moving. Rosharu's mountain has an offshoot ridge that meets the ocean. When we reach it, we'll follow it inland to a cave there."

Obek repositioned his headlamp over his ears and with a groan, tried to shove the door open against the wind. It barely budged. Icarus lent his shoulder and rain drenched them as the door creaked outward. Holding it open, Obek looked back at Na'rina. She shook her head. There was no way she could hold back the storm with a bubble of calm for three hundred yards.

"She needs to save her strength," Icarus shouted.

Obek huffed, but barreled forward into the storm. Felis followed him out, but Na'rina hesitated, bracing herself to reenter the chaos. Icarus gripped her hand and they left the protection of the tunnel together.

Cold bit into her already shivering body. She clung to the warmth in Icarus' touch and tightened her grip when their fingers grew slick. His claws pricked at her, revealing how hard he had to hold on to keep the wind from tearing them apart. With her shoulder turned against the gale, she kept moving.

Icarus' warm grasp faded as she lost feeling in her fingers. She slowed to a stop, realizing she'd lost his hand and couldn't hear the waves, which should have been to her left. A form appeared ahead and she stepped forward but stumbled.

Icarus caught her, pulling her tight against his side and guiding her forward.

Only when they reached the offshoot of Rosharu's mountain did they find a small reprieve among the rock that sheltered them from the ocean storm blowing from the north. They followed the ridge until hands appeared and hauled them into a cave.

"Horrible weather." Obek released Icarus' collar and lowered his headlamp to keep from blinding the wer-im.

"Look on the bright side," Felis said, "it'll get warmer from here."

Obek scowled. "Positively boiling," he grumbled as he turned to lead them into the mountain.

"Have you been here before?" Felis asked.

"*Na.*" Obek stopped at a fork in the tunnel. Pulling a small mallet from his pocket, he tapped on the rock.

"Then how do you know the way?"

"Hush!" Obek tapped again and tilted his head with his eyes closed. "That way." He pointed with the mallet at the left fork.

"Does the rock talk to him?" Felis asked his Kadis.

Obek shot them a withering look.

Icarus shrugged.

Glad the two wer-im were keeping Obek occupied, Na'rina breathed in the gritty air and grimaced as her body began to thaw. The other's blood returned heat to their bodies but a dryad's usually required sunlight to warm up. Thankfully, the tunnel's air carried plenty of heat. It just took her longer to absorb it. By slow degrees, her body began to tingle with renewed sensation.

Na'rina's desire for warmth faded the deeper they walked into the mountain. The heat turned stifling and each breath burned in Na'rina's nose. She braced a hand against the tunnel wall but pulled back when her palm burned at the touch.

"How much time do you think we have, Obek?"

Obek paused to reply, but the ground jolted, throwing everyone off balance. Na'rina's foot caught on something and she hit her knees.

"We have to keep moving," Obek ordered, stalking ahead, but his impatience under the bravado hid an edge of fear.

Icarus gave Na'rina a hand up and they hurried to catch up with the dwarf.

"With volcanoes," Obek grumbled, tapping the wall occasionally with his mallet, "you never have enough time."

"Cheery fellow," Felis tried to tease but he squeaked when the ground shook again.

"Horrible... Unnatural... Writhing..." Obek uttered a litany of complaints about the mountain and its crazy oread until they reached another fork in the tunnel. He paused to listen when he gave the wall another tap of his hammer. No sound came to Na'rina's ears but the dwarf pointed to the left. "You'll find the oread at the bottom of that tunnel."

"You're sure?" Felis asked, gazing into the darkness with open apprehension.

Obek bared his teeth. "I can hear her moving through the rock." He turned to Na'rina. "And this is where I leave you, Drydanda."

Na'rina caught the dwarf's shoulder before he could brush past her. His cheeks were pale under his dark complexion but he stood still at her touch. "Thank you, Obek-Ak-Lea," she said. "You've proven once again the Ak-Leas hold to their honor."

Obek flushed and bowed but when he looked back up, his expression was sober. "This is a suicide mission, Drydanda. You succeed and the Ak-Leas will always support you."

Na'rina hugged him. It was impulsive, a gesture of the young dryad she'd been before meeting the wer-im, but it felt right.

"You're crazy, Drydanda, but good luck." Obek patted her back.

Na'rina watched Obek shuffle away, sipping from a flask he pulled from inside his vest, until his heavy shoulders disappeared into the darkness beyond their headlamps.

Obek had led them honestly, but they soon understood he left as early as he could justify it. No side tunnels appeared to lead them astray along the long path to the cavern they sought, but with each step, they drew closer to the mountain's rioting core.

Na'rina reached with her zoi aima to gauge the writhing energy below. Tingles grew along her skin until they became a fire rolling through her body, raising a sheen of sappy sweat. Finally, when they turned a corner, Na'rina stutter-stepped at the sight of the reddish glow that confirmed they were close to Rosharu's hiding place.

Hot and cold energy swirled ahead of them, brushing Na'rina's senses with rioting heat, the bitter taste of beetles, and the sweet tang of fresh leaves mixed with moss. She staggered and halted.

"My mother's using the machines."

"Wer-Kadis."

Felis jumped and spun into a low crouch. Behind him Na'rina caught a flash of orange hair.

"*Sa?*" Icarus asked.

The orange-haired wer-im flashed a grin at Felis before answering. "Silas entered the mountain by way of a cave on the north side. He's almost reached the cavern ahead."

Icarus nodded. "Stay on Silas. Keep him away from the

Jennifer M. Zeiger

oread."

The wer-im bowed and disappeared back up the tunnel at a ground-eating lope.

"Creeps me out," Felis admitted as they watched him go.

"Why?" Na'rina asked.

Icarus edged forward to peer into the cavern beyond while Felis scowled at the darkness where the orange-haired wer-im disappeared.

"He's a tracker. Cat can find anything," Felis admitted, "and sneaks up on everyone. He looks like a flippin' tabby and wham! He jumps out of nowhere. It's deceiving."

Na'rina chuckled, giddy from the taste of energy she'd absorbed from the mountain. "What's his name?"

"Name?" Felis pulled at his beard, frowning, and then shrugged. "Doesn't have one, as far as I recall."

Icarus came back from the cavern entrance. "Mona'rina's down there all right," he confirmed. "Air's practically buzzing with her zoi aima."

Na'rina's heart ached for her mother, but she had to ask. "Did you see Rosharu?"

"She's sitting on an island of rock but she's surrounded by bubbling magma. I couldn't see if there's a way to reach her without exposing myself."

Closing her eyes, Na'rina reached out again to feel the machines' energy, which was mixed with the tangy, sweet taste of her mother's zoi aima. It was hard not to focus on her mother's overflowing lifeblood but as she separated the zoi aima and the sting of electricity, a mental picture of the cavern took shape.

"My mother's to the right. Once we're inside, I'll head for her. Felis, just beyond her sits the first machine, destroy it and the others beyond it. Icarus, Rosharu's island is closest to the wall and the cavern floor on the far side. If you head left, I think you can jump the gap to reach her." Na'rina opened her eyes to find both wer-im watching her. "Rosharu will retaliate as soon as she sees us. We should run in, but as you do, be careful. The cavern floor's narrow beyond this entrance and it drops off into the magma within about three yards."

They nodded before turning to run for the red glow at the end of the tunnel. Icarus passed into the cavern first. The ground shook and Na'rina fell in the tunnel entrance. Fist-sized rocks dropped around her.

"Move!" Icarus yelled.

Na'rina rolled to get out of Felis' way but he jumped to avoid her anyway. When he landed, he slid on the dust and debris of the quaking cavern floor. Icarus' hand flashed out, grabbing his shirt and stalling his forward plunge before he sailed out over the magma pool. A wall of heat slapped against them as Na'rina rushed to help haul Felis back from the edge.

"Eesh!" Felis tried to hug them both but Icarus pushed

him toward the first machine while the ground continued to tremble beneath them.

"Later," he ordered. "Go!"

Felis bolted.

Na'rina blinked as sappy tears ran down her cheeks from the heat blurring her vision. Felis reached the first glowing egg-shaped machine a second later. *Not a gray box.* Relief washed through her at that.

"You're too late." Rosharu's voice rumbled from where she perched on her island. The oread watched Icarus sauntering along the left-hand wall of the cavern. He displayed a complete lack of urgency but Na'rina could see his writhing zoi aima. Determination swirled through him, a deluge just waiting to break free its dam. For now, he kept Rosharu's eyes away from the Mother Drydanda and Felis.

Na'rina searched for her mother. From her zoi aima, she knew the other dryad stood to her right, but it took her a moment to distinguish her mother's green-brown mottled skin from the cavern wall. Tears poured from Mona'rina's eyes as she streamed zoi aima into the six egg-like machines placed around the cavern. The machines transferred that energy into heat and fed it into the rock below. Her mother's mottled coloring rolled in her skin, a mute testament to the energy undulating through her.

Mona'rina's shorn head swung around and she locked eyes with Na'rina. "You should have stayed away."

"*Na*, Mother," Na'rina said, approaching her. "This eruption will destroy our groves and everything in between."

Mona'rina shook her head. "Rocks you've overturned without a clue what you're looking at beneath. We owe our lives to Rosharu."

"Do you know what's under the rocks? You know about Rosharu and Liam. Do you know the torment he and Rosharu share unless his bones are returned to the ocean?"

A thin line formed between her mother's brows but the zoi aima streaming from her did not slacken.

"You know about Intela Corp. Do you know Rosharu's their Zeta projects director? You know, the director of the experiments they perform on mythics like us?" Na'rina stopped when they stood face-to-face.

"You're misinform—" Mona'rina started, but at that moment Felis reached the first machine. Being connected to it, she felt his touch on the device. She pointed and Na'rina's skin crawled with the energy her mother streamed to the machine.

"Felis!" Na'rina shouted.

Electricity zapped out of the egg into Felis' chest. His high-pitched scream echoed throughout the cavern. He hit the ground like a sack of bones, the device bouncing until it came to rest a few feet away from him.

"You're trying to distract me, Na'rina."

"Mother!" Na'rina growled. "Intela Corp attacked my Rina at the exact time Rosharu came to you for help. How do you think the humans knew which grove to attack? How did they know when they attacked you earlier where my grove ended and yours began? They just happened to pick the perfect spot to start cutting?"

"A mythic's obviously involved, but that doesn't mean it's Rosharu. She herself was captured. I'm sane only because of the hours she spent talking to me through the wall between our cells."

While they spoke, Felis pushed to his feet. With three running steps, he kicked the first machine into the bubbling magma. Mona'rina screamed as the dull metal device dissolved, taking a part of her zoi aima with it.

Na'rina gripped her mother's shoulders. Pain, exhaustion, and confusion washed through the contact. "We questioned one of the men after the attack, Mamma. Rosharu's been working with Intela Corp for a couple of centuries. She—" Na'rina paused when the mottled coloring affecting her mother's skin rolled through her eyes. *I'm going about this all wrong.*

Jennifer M. Zeiger

"Mamma, we spoke to Obek-Ak-Lea. He says this eruption will darken most of the Western Hemisphere."

The zoi aima streaming from her mother wavered. "Obek assured you of this?"

"*Sa.*"

"Mona'rina?" Rosharu's question rumbled through the cavern.

Na'rina risked a glance over her shoulder. Rosharu stood on her island, watching them. Behind her Icarus slid along the narrow ledge of rock against the wall. "Silas heard our interrogation of the Intela Corp man," Na'rina added. "He's after Rosharu."

Mona'rina paled. "He's here? Why did you let him come?"

Na'rina threw up her hands. "I can't control him, Mamma. We have to do something."

Mona'rina whimpered and stumbled backward. Na'rina swung around in time to see Felis hurl another machine, trailing green and blue zoi aima like a comet, into the magma. The machine pulled at Mona'rina's lifeblood still, despite her mother no longer streaming to it.

"*Na!*" Rosharu bellowed as Felis headed for the third machine. She tracked him with a snarl on her lips. Vibrations trembled through the ground and a wall of rock shot up from the floor. Through the soles of her feet, Na'rina sucked the energy from those vibrations into her body. The wall juddered to a stop. Felis jumped, braced his hands on the stone, and vaulted over the wall.

Rosharu's knees hit the ground. She sank her hands into the earth as she lifted the next machine into the air on a rock pedestal. Na'rina countered again, sucking the energy out of the vibrations and shuddering at the heat that came with it. The pedestal stopped, but well above Felis' stalky reach.

The wer-im stooped, picked up a rock, and jumped at the opposing wall instead. Hitting with his feet planted, he launched higher, and at that moment pitched the rock. It hit the machine on its rock pedestal with a dull clang. The egg teetered, then tumbled to the floor, where Felis kicked it into the surging liquid below.

Mona'rina whimpered again, but she grasped Na'rina's shoulder to draw her attention.

"We can't stop the eruption," she panted through gritted teeth, accepting Obek's assessment of the eruption with the swiftness that had made her such a good leader for the dryads, "but if we convince Rosharu to help, we can weaken it." Mona'rina swayed and Na'rina caught her and lowered her to sit on the cavern floor.

"*How?*" Na'rina asked, relieved to be working with her mother now and not against. "She wants us to suffer."

Her mother cupped her face in chilled hands. "Liam.

He's more important to her than anything else." She pushed Na'rina away, encouraging her toward Rosharu.

The heat in the cavern already burned Na'rina's skin, but as she approached the magma pool, it seared the air in her throat as well. Across the pool, Rosharu snarled, still watching Felis. The cavern rumbled in response to her.

"Rosharu!" Na'rina voice rang out clear and strong despite the scorching air drying her mouth.

"Go away, Na'rina. You chose the wer-im."

"And you chose Liam. Would he have wanted you to destroy yourself?" Na'rina stopped at the edge of the rock with the magma bubbling below. Tears streamed down her face as heat pulled sap to her pores. Soon she wouldn't have enough moisture for her body to protect itself.

Rosharu's dark head swung around and she stared at Na'rina. Her eyes flickered to Mona'rina where she sat against the wall. "He'll be at rest when I'm done."

"Will he?" Na'rina held her hands out pointedly. "There's no control on this eruption. It will hurt the oceanids, sure. It'll kill Silas, my mother, and me, absolutely. It'll kill you, too—but there's no guarantee Liam will make it to the ocean. You'll leave him in endless torment, alone."

"He'll make it," Rosharu insisted.

"We can guarantee he makes it to the ocean with the three of us working together," Na'rina insisted. "He'll be at peace."

Rosharu scowled, eyeing Na'rina and her mother. Her expression turned icy as Felis pitched another egg into the magma and Mona'rina did nothing to prevent it.

Behind her, something moved. Na'rina spotted the orange-haired wer-im, the tracker, pointing frantically while blood dripped from his hand. Na'rina followed his gesture to catch a streak of tawny fur flying toward Rosharu.

"Watch out!"

Rosharu spun and roared at the lion descending on her, making streams of dust fall from the ceiling. In a mass of fur and limbs, they hit the ground with a thud that reverberated through the cavern. Giving up on stealth, Icarus raced for the ledge.

*I have to help him.* Na'rina's heart beat against her ribs as she pulled energy from the roiling magma. The energy burned through her veins, pulling sticky sap from her pores. She gasped. Like the bubble of calm she'd created in the storm, the magma in front of her hardened into a steaming, gray mass.

Desperate to help Icarus, she streamed energy into him until she hit that perfect resonance. Between one step and the next, smooth as honey, Icarus shifted into the lynx. He leapt off the ledge, and Na'rina breathed in the dry heat assaulting him and felt the tension in his leg muscles as if they were her own. The cavern rumbled and debris rained on her head but she swayed in place and kept her eyes fastened on Icarus.

"Na'rina!"

Na'rina's attention split. She clung to the sensations of the lynx as she turned to find her mother standing behind her. Her mottled coloring now resembled the rough bark of an aspen.

"Mamma, what's wrong?" Na'rina clasped her mother's fingers and the skin crackled.

"When Silas changes, I shift toward a more tree-like form. Usually it's fine but I'm too weak now to shift properly." Mona'rina shuddered and her skin cracked from elbow to wrist with a tearing sound. Instead of weeping sap, the wound darkened into an old gouge like on aspen bark. She hugged her arm against her stomach. "If I can shift back to my dryad self, Silas will be forced to shift back, too. It's the way of twins. But I'm too weak. I need you to heal me as you would a tree."

"Is that even possible?" Na'rina pulled her mother into an embrace, shocked at the frailty in the other dryad's body. The cavern shook. Nearby, a geyser of steam blew out the flooring, making way for a flowing river of molten rock to bubble forth.

Mona'rina trembled. "*Sa.*"

Na'rina steeled herself. Such healing would be exhausting and she already doubted whether they'd be able to control the eruption enough to make a difference, but if Silas killed Rosharu, it would all be for naught anyway.

Before connecting with her mother, she isolated the stream of zoi aima she fed to Icarus. In no way did she want to cut that stream off and leave him writhing on the floor for Silas to kill.

Something cracked behind her. She risked a glance and saw Rosharu's island wobbling side to side with its three occupants circling one another.

"Hurry, Na'rina," Mona'rina urged.

With a shuddering breath, Na'rina tilted her forehead against her mother's temple. For the first time in Na'rina's life, Mona'rina didn't filter the connection. The Mother Drydanda ached for her brother, physically experiencing slivers of pain through her chest. As a counterpoint, a knot thickened in her throat over Rosharu's betrayal. Anger simmered as that truth solidified. Under it all a dark cloud swirled, weaving weakening tendrils of pain and exhaustion through Mona'rina's resolve. Na'rina recognized the feel of it and almost reached to see if there was a kudzu nearby to help them.

Pushing all that aside, Na'rina turned to her mother's hardened skin. She shuddered. Dryads existed as half-ethereal beings. Zoi aima mixed with their physical bodies like water through sand, but what she felt in her mother showed too much sand and almost no water.

*Start at the top,* she coached herself, layering her healthy zoi aima through her mother's cheeks, forehead, stubbled scalp, and neck. As the healing took hold, Na'rina's left cheek split open, wept blood, and then closed. Just that one portion of healing left her shaking.

Just as she braced to continue, pain seared through her left calf and she flinched—but it wasn't her wound. Silas clawed at Icarus' leg and she felt the phantom blood dripping down her ankle. Na'rina groaned. She isolated Icarus' sensations like she had the zoi aima she streamed to him, and then refocused on healing her mother, feeling like a river with too many tributaries.

She moved to Mona'rina's back and a large fissure opened across Na'rina's shoulders. Na'rina cried out and Mona'rina held her tight, sharing the pain. She felt Icarus hesitate, feeling her wounds just as she experienced his. The fissure bled for the moment it took to heal, soaking her shirt with sticky blood.

*Don't worry about me,* Na'rina insisted even as the healing left her gasping. *Keep Silas away from Rosharu.* Icarus growled, but lunged at Silas as the other wer-im circled toward Rosharu again. Na'rina returned to healing her mother.

Layering zoi aima from Mona'rina's hips all the way down to the soles of her feet, Na'rina flushed her healthy lifeblood through her mother's hardened skin.

"That's too much at once," Mona'rina objected, trying to draw away a little.

"We don't have time." Na'rina held tight and kept the

zoi aima moving between them. Fissures cracked open along her calves and one opened over her right foot. As the healing took, they watched Na'rina's blood trickle from the wound, through Na'rina's toes, then congeal on the floor from the heat. Finally, the wound pulled together. They sighed in relief as they lifted their heads.

"You did it," Mona'rina said with a mix of pain and pride. Then she winced as a roar reverberated through the cavern, echoing until it ended in a yowl akin to when Na'rina had woken Silas on the ship.

Something cracked and they looked to see Rosharu's island break at the base and tilt into the far wall with a crash. The three occupants rolled onto the ledge of the main floor.

Rosharu fled to the right, passing Felis on his way to help his Kadis. She headed for the nearest tunnel and skidded to a halt at the sight of the orange-haired wer-im lying on the ground. Stumbling and favoring one side, she continued around the cavern for a different exit.

Silas, fully wer-im again, shook his head to clear it. Before he recovered, Na'rina cut the stream of zoi aima to Icarus, feeling a slight relief as her lifeblood came to rest. Icarus became wer-im again as he scrambled to get between Silas and the fleeing Rosharu. Felis joined him but Icarus shoved him toward the slumped form of the orange-haired wer-im.

"Na'rina." Her mother pulled her attention back. She

pointed. There, on the far side of the river of molten magma, Rosharu knelt with her head bowed and shoulders heaving. Russet blood trickled down her arms into the earth as she pushed to stand up. She stepped once before stumbling and clutching at a wound on her hip. "We need her if we're to control the explosion."

"What if she sinks into the mountain?" Na'rina asked. It's the first thing she'd do if pursued and close to her grove.

"And become part of the magma?" Mona'rina shook her head with a shudder. "We can reach her before she's desperate enough for that."

Mona'rina stepped forward and stumbled. Na'rina caught her mother's shoulder as she swayed with exhaustion. Without speaking, she moved in front of her mother to handle the magma between them and the mountain nymph.

Rosharu raised her head to stare at them through the steam from the magma as they approached. She tried to rise again but the mountain heaved and she hit her knees again. "Stay away from me!" Rosharu shouted, wiping at the dust and blood on her face.

Na'rina studied the slow, inexorable river of magma between them while biting her lip. *Breathe the storm in and out of your lungs like it feeds your body.* Alaya's words echoed in her mind, but she hesitated. The storm had been cold. This would be hot on a level that might burn her from the inside out. She was already drained from healing her mother, but with Mona'rina teetering on the edge of dormancy Na'rina was the only one capable now of deadening that river to reach Rosharu. She breathed in the heat. Her zoi aima roiled as it fed off the magma between them and her skin darkened as the new energy licked at her lifeblood with tongues of flame.

"It'll kill you," Rosharu said as her brows drew together.

*Does she care?* Na'rina couldn't tell as she breathed deeper and the magma river hardened to a steaming ridged mass. Na'rina jumped it with Mona'rina close behind. Although it roiled in her veins, Na'rina clung to the energy. She'd need every bit soon enough.

Rosharu cringed and tried to crab crawl backwards as they dropped to their knees in front of her. Mona'rina grabbed her ankle before she got too far and Na'rina scuttled forward to seize her arm.

Rosharu panicked, searching the cavern for help. The egg machines were gone. Felis was nowhere in sight, but Na'rina guessed he'd taken the tracker out of the mountain. Icarus faced off with Silas, distracting him instead of engaging him in an all-out fight. No help presented itself.

"Rosharu, we ha—"

"*Na!*" The nymph's eyes glazed and both dryads felt her awareness sink into the mountain without her body. They still held onto her ankle and arm but her mind grew more distant the longer they stared in surprise. With the physical touch, however, they hadn't lost her completely.

"Follow her!" Mona'rina cried.

Na'rina shared a look with her mother that held both resolve and distaste. Neither liked forcibly connecting with another being but with everything falling apart for Rosharu, there was only one place she'd retreat to—and that place held the key to getting her to help them.

"Liam," they said at the same time.

They clasped hands and followed the zoi aima that spoke of Rosharu's awareness within the mountain.

A deluge of sensations surged through Na'rina as she became vulnerable to the world around her. Just like with her Rina, the connection opened her to Athos' agony at the pressure building within him. Beside his enormous presence, Mona'rina's anger and Rosharu's bitterness were tiny wounds.

*My Rosharu clutches her festering bitterness close.* Athos shoved out all other sensations as he narrowed in on Na'rina. His attention brought with it an immense weight. *You feel her bitterness and have seen her actions,* he rumbled. *Let me show you her torment.*

*Now?* Na'rina asked, bewildered, as the mountain heaved again and Rosharu's, and now Mona'rina's, awareness grew more distant.

*Now. If you succeed, I can heal her body, but not her heart or mind. Perhaps with you, a friend, who knows it all and still cares, she will find hope.*

An image flooded her mind. It was of an oceanid with silvery skin and hair. His broad shoulders and height rivaled Rosharu's but his powerful presence was softened by love when he smiled at the young Oreadanda. She smiled back with joy filling her face with sunshine. Rain splattered their shoulders. The love on the oceanid's face melted into terror as water and earth washed over him and he clawed to stay above the mudslide. Chest-tightening agony hit Na'rina when the earth entombed him. Rosharu fought to reach him, shoving globs of mud away in heaps that bloodied her hands, but she still hadn't found him by the time the rain subsided. Hours later she discovered his body, long dead, in a deep washout near the beach. The torment started again, and Na'rina shuddered.

*I understand,* she said.

*He relives dying hundreds of times a day,* Athos moaned, *and we live it with him.* Na'rina had never met an element—rock, river, or tree—that felt weary, but as Athos spoke, he seemed to slump and his bones crackled as though brittle.

*Peace,* she encouraged as she distanced herself from his massive presence enough to feel Rosharu's and her mother's zoi aima again. He let her draw away. Within Rosharu's lifeblood, she now picked up on the silvery sheen of Liam, the small bit of him that could not rest without the waves.

*Help me reach them,* Na'rina begged Athos.

The stomach-dropping sensation reminded Na'rina of when her Rina carried her through other root systems. The world blurred and Na'rina whooshed past the other nymph's zoi aima until Athos hauled her to a stop within a massive tunnel on the western side of his slopes.

Again, as with her Rina, he projected her into the tunnel ahead of the streaming zoi aima of the other two.

*Catch them,* the mountain instructed.

Rosharu's lifeblood rushed toward her with the deep russet color of her actual blood, its presence carrying that same majestic aura as when they first met.

Na'rina opened her ethereal arms and stepped in front of it. The impact of catching Rosharu's awareness threw her backwards and the oread's projection appeared, holding her down as they landed on the tunnel floor.

"Leave me be!" she shouted.

Na'rina clutched at her, trying to copy what she'd seen La'meliai and Alaya do when she called the Council. There was no doubt, however, that Rosharu had more experience in this form. The mountain nymph slid from her grasp, turning to continue down the tunnel.

*Stay put!* Athos commanded, freezing Rosharu just as Mona'rina's awareness reached them. Her ethereal form materialized as the mountain continued. *At least consider the Drydandas' offer to help Liam. I do not want to die knowing we'll leave him in torment.*

"He'll make it," Rosharu said aloud.

*Not likely.* Between them appeared a projection of the mountain. *Left alone, the magma will vent here and here.* Athos directed their attention to two large tunnels, one facing east, the other southeast, away from the ocean. It was clear an eruption through those tunnels would level most of the mountain but would leave a wall nearest the ocean on the west side. *I've caved in several sections of these tunnels, but the patches are thin.*

Rosharu grimaced but then looked to Na'rina. "If I work with you, do you swear you'll get his bones to the ocean?"

"I swear."

The mountain nymph tilted her chin, accepting Na'rina's emphatic response, and turned to Mona'rina. "And you?"

"You tortured us. Now you require *our* promises?" Rage colored Mona'rina's cheeks olive even in her ethereal state.

At the mention of torture, the Collective Wisdom crashed into Na'rina and, through their connection, into Rosharu as well. Na'rina hadn't known her mother's torture had already been added to the genetic history, but her own experiences whirled with her mother's and it stole her breath. Rosharu recoiled as if someone socked her in the stomach.

Na'rina gasped and shoved the images away. "Enough! We've no time." As though to emphasize her words, Athos heaved and a large chunk of the ceiling crashed into the floor of the tunnel. "*Please,* Mother."

Mona'rina raised a brow and Na'rina, as always, felt the implied censure, but she held the stare until Mona'rina turned back to Rosharu. "I will help to free Liam and mitigate the eruption."

Rosharu sighed, shuddering. Within her expression lurked something haunted.

"How do we do this?" Na'rina asked.

"This way." Rosharu motioned for them to follow her down the tunnel. As she moved, a peeling sensation prickled along Na'rina's skin.

*It's the storm washing away layers from my shoulders,* the mountain explained.

Na'rina shuddered, realizing this was part of the oceanid's incessant attack on Rosharu.

"Here." Rosharu threw her arms wide as they entered a massive cavern.

"Wow." Na'rina gawked at the enormity, but dark dread seeped through the connection from her mother.

Rosharu led them farther in and the roof vanished into darkness. The space echoed with vastness.

Mona'rina groaned. "It's Liam's cavern."

"*Sa,*" Rosharu agreed, "and as you probably suspect, here's the problem." Her zoi aima streamed through the cavern, bringing a reddish light to their awareness. Understanding dawned on Na'rina as she saw the far side of the cavern. It ended in a wall of rubble, as if it'd been blow apart. The magnitude of what Silas and Mona'rina had done—caving in this cavern—washed over Na'rina. It'd be like chopping down a quarter of her grove.

"That half is as thick as this side is spacious," Rosharu said bitterly. "Liam's bones and the tunnel to the surface are buried under all that. I can cave in more of the other two tunnels but one of you will need to hold pressure on the newly caved rocks to keep them from popping like a cork."

"I will do that," Mona'rina offered. The longer they remained in Liam's cavern, the more haunted she appeared.

"If you fail," Rosharu said with a hint of her previous cutting edge returning, "the eruption to the southeast will destroy your groves."

"She knows," Na'rina interjected before her mother could explode. "While she does that, what will we be doing?"

"I will press the magma to the western tunnel. It must have enough force behind it to blow out the far side of the cavern. You, Na'rina, must shore up the tunnel to carry the magma or it'll vent out every other available crevice. Then, you must fulfill your promise." She pointed toward the rubble. "Liam's there. Make sure his bones reach the ocean."

"You want her zoi aima in the magma?" Mona'rina asked, incredulous.

At that moment, Athos heaved and something cracked. The nymphs snapped back to their bodies with a slap to their mental awarenesses. They tumbled apart as the mountain convulsed and fought the rolling of the floor to reach one another and reestablish contact.

"Hurry!" Rosharu shouted, scrambling through the debris with terror on her face.

But Na'rina could only stare in horror at the far side of the cavern. Magma poured out the wall, cascading down into the pool below, and chunks of the ceiling now cluttered the floor, obscuring any sign of Icarus.

*"Icarus!"* Na'rina searched for him. Athos' rumbling drowned out her voice but her zoi aima flowed over the rocks, searching everything it touched for that familiar violet zoi aima.

Silas crawled free of a pile of rubble. Na'rina's questing lifeblood brushed against him and she recoiled. Although they'd forced him into his wer-im form, his blood still ran hot and the mind behind it roiled with little thought except that he *had* to act. Even across the cave, his blood-shot eyes told of the cliff over which he teetered as he zeroed in on the three nymphs.

Behind him, a dark head appeared over a boulder. Na'rina breathed in Icarus' reassuring spicy scent.

Rosharu grabbed her hand and she flinched. "Na'rina, we have to hurry."

She was about to turn when Silas spun to face Icarus, bringing what looked like a hollow reed to his lips. Na'rina couldn't hear the dull *tha-ump* as Silas exhaled but she watched the dart shoot out of the end of the reed.

*"Na!"*

With her zoi aima still touching Icarus, the prick of the dart phantomed into her shoulder. They both stumbled but Icarus actually crumpled to his knees.

It was a mark of Silas' single-minded anger that instead of turning toward Rosharu, he headed for Icarus, who wavered, fighting the tranquilizer. He'd plucked the dart from his skin but Na'rina felt the wash of wooziness flushing through him.

"Na'rina!" Rosharu tugged on her hand.

Na'rina pulled away. "Silas will kill you the minute he's done with Icarus."

"She's right," Mona'rina said from where she sat on the floor with her head hanging between her knees. Gasping, she struggled to speak. "We won't succeed if Silas kills you first. I can't—I can't reach Silas." The last word came out a sob.

Na'rina wanted to weep with her. There was so little time. Athos groaned and heaved as she scrambled to find a way to stop Silas.

Felis bolted into the rolling cave from a side tunnel. He stopped between Icarus and Silas, trying to keep his feet while he took in the situation.

An idea hit Na'rina. She fumbled in her pocket for the dart pouch Rebecca had given her, wincing as the fabric scraped against her tender skin. Her fingers closed around the leather bag. Pulling it free, Na'rina sucked energy from the cave without pausing to consider the pain it'd cause.

"You're burning!"

She barely heard Rosharu but a small part of her thanked the other nymph for smothering the flames licking at the skin on her shoulders.

Na'rina enveloped the tiny dart pouch in a bubble of zoi aima and energy. It was what she planned to do with Liam's bones, but she'd never actually moved an object with straight zoi aima. Relief hit her as the pouch floated in the air when she dropped her hand.

"Felis!" she shouted.

His shaggy head spun toward her and she shoved the pouch at him across the cave. It sailed through the air, over Silas' head as he jumped for it, and smacked into Felis' chest. He clutched it, shock and amazement covering his face.

"Give him the antidote!" she yelled, pointing at Icarus.

Seeing Icarus, understanding drained Felis' face to a waxy color and he moved just in time to dodge Silas' pounce. Felis had never claimed to hold his own against Silas but he was quick and if he could manage to give Icarus the antidote, he wouldn't have to fight the huge wer-im alone.

Na'rina finally turned back to the other two nymphs. Her mother gave her an approving nod.

"The magma's energy is burning you." Rosharu held up Na'rina's hand for her to see the darkening in her skin. The green on her palm looked almost black. "Try to funnel the heat back into the energy you send out and keep it away from your body. It might keep you alive."

Na'rina gulped as they rejoined Mona'rina. She already felt brittle and, where she'd burned on her shoulders, her body bled over the charred skin unable to completely heal itself. Her mother was in no better condition, but it didn't matter. They had to act anyway.

As the three connected again, the deterioration of the mountain rushed to greet them. Rosharu gathered her will to collapse more of the two eastern tunnels. The zoi aima flowed within her, a deep, relentless force that slammed into the rock walls. Athos shook when miles of rock crumbled into the two passageways.

Rosharu screamed. Her head reared back, breaking their connection with a mental snap. Na'rina's eyes swam with black gnats from the mental whiplash. She shook her head to clear it as she and her mother pulled Rosharu back into the connection.

Magma rushed toward the newly caved-in sections and Mona'rina threw out a wall of energy to hold the rocks. With a whoosh of air from her lungs, the magma stopped. *Do something,* she begged Rosharu, trembling under the strain while the pressure in the tunnels grew.

Na'rina gripped her hand and breathed in energy from the cave again. Sap wept from her palms as her body tried to protect itself. It stuck her skin to the other nymphs but the scalding energy roiled through her, turning her blue and green lifeblood a purplish brown. She needed to funnel the heat out of her body—and soon.

*Protect Liam's bones,* Rosharu commanded, holding the magma in place against the growing pressure.

Na'rina sent out her zoi aima toward Liam's cavern, siphoning as much heat into the questing lifeblood as she could manage. Still, her skin split along her arms and fire licked out of the wounds. More sappy blood wept from her to stop it.

*Now, Rosharu!* Mona'rina begged. *Too much more will kill her.*

*Not until she has him.*

Mona'rina whimpered. Her grip within Na'rina's fingers trembled.

Now that she didn't have Athos or Rosharu directing her along, the massive tunnel seemed longer than she remembered. As Na'rina passed through it, she layered zoi aima along the stone to make it stronger for the coming magma. Where the lifeblood touched the walls, they slowly began to melt from the heat she siphoned. At last, her awareness shot into Liam's massive cavern. Streaking across the open space, she dove into the rock beyond.

*Here,* Athos guided.

Bones, porous in texture compared to the rock, met her questing search. She cradled them within a pocket of energy as she had the dart pouch. *I have him!* she shouted.

Rosharu again gathered her will and shoved. Athos screamed and Rosharu lost control of the flooding deluge she'd sparked.

Magma exploded out a vent above Mona'rina's blocked tunnels. She shot out a stream of zoi aima to block it with energy alone, and Na'rina felt her mother's body sag against her shoulder back in the cave where they knelt.

She lost that sensation as the bulk of the magma careened into Liam's tunnel. Fire coursed against her zoi aima where she shored up the walls. It fed back through her lifeblood. *I'm bathing in magma,* she whimpered. Her skin split down her thigh and tongues of flame licked through the gaping wound. It ate at her as embers into wood.

*Hold together, my daughter.* Mona'rina's whisper vanished as another vent spurted forth on her side of the mountain. A stream of zoi aima blocked it but the response came slower, almost watery.

*Mamma?*

*I'm proud of you, Na'rina.*

A third vent cracked open, and the zoi aima her mother streamed to stop it trickled like a mountain stream.

*Don't,* her mother said, catching her intention a moment before Na'rina fragmented her awareness further. *I can't absorb zoi aima from you at this point anyway.*

*Mona'rina?* Rosharu asked as she rejoined their connection.

*Help my daughter.*

Rosharu's aid came just in time. The magma slammed into Liam's cavern. It stalled against the centuries-old cave-in and a scream seethed through Na'rina's teeth as she held the walls against the boiling mass.

*Shore up the walls,* Rosharu warned just before she gave the magma another shove.

Athos' western slope blew. The outer wall of the cavern, the tunnel, the very side of the mountain disintegrated, throwing Na'rina's bubble of energy around Liam miles into the sky along with lava, embers, and stone. While fire dripped down her calf, the lava scorched her protective shell, searing her awareness into a burned husk. She struggled to hold it together but distance severed her stream of energy with a forceful snap that threw her body across the cave floor.

*I promised!* She reached out again, searching, mindless of the pain suffusing her physical body. Something battered at her. The insistent thumping against her leg pulled her back to the crumbling cave where they all sat. Blinking hard, her eyes finally focused on Icarus' intense gaze.

"You were on fire." His glance at her leg brought her eyes down to the charred skin along her thigh and calf.

"I'll—" She swallowed. "I'll heal."

"Na'rina." The sob in Rosharu's voice snapped their attention to where the mountain nymph was cradling Mona'rina's body in her arms. "Not again," she sobbed. "I can feel her dying." Even as she spoke, Rosharu's arms began to turn ethereal. "*Na!*" She struggled to hold the dryad.

"*You killed her!*" Silas attacked Icarus from the side and Na'rina rolled with the force that sent them tumbling. Icarus smacked against a boulder with a *thwack!*

Silas spun and his brilliant eyes sighted in on Na'rina with murderous intent. "You've killed her. We were this close to being a family again and you stopped me from protecting her!" The growl snarling out his lips sent an icy shock through Na'rina.

Her heart beat spiked. "She's alive."

"Don't lie to me! I've always been able to feel her." He roared and kicked Icarus just as he was pushing to his knees to stand. With a whoosh of air, Icarus hit the floor again.

"*Stop!*" Na'rina protested, inching backward toward Rosharu and Mona'rina. Her hand came to rest over a fist-sized rock. Silas stepped toward her, and she pitched it at him. He dodged it with a hiss but he didn't move fast enough to avoid the second rock she threw immediately after the first. It smacked his shoulder and spun him a little sideways. With contempt, he turned back toward her.

"Hardly enough to take me down," he snarled, his eyes

flickering between cat's slits and his normal round irises.

Na'rina's heart stuttered. If Silas changed now, it would surely kill her mother. She shoved to her feet, sucking in energy from the mountain below. Her body protested and she stumbled, fighting not to vomit as color swirled in the darkened skin on her hands and the gritty taste of dust filled her mouth. But the energy gave her the strength to move, so she clung to it.

With a feral grin, Silas launched at her. Na'rina threw up her hands, shooting energy out her palms in a shower of sparks that slammed into his chest. She ducked as his shirt burst into flame. That wasn't her intent but it worked. He sailed past and tucked into a roll. When he hit the floor, he rolled back and forth until the fire died and he could regain his feet.

His jewel eyes narrowed, the irises slitted like a cat's again.

"Silas!" she cried. "You'll kill her for sure if—"

He launched again. Na'rina spun away, stumbling as the cave heaved in the aftershocks of the eruption. Catching her shoulder, Silas' spun her back to face him. His grip on her arms made her skin shriek but she struggled until he sank his claws into her flesh.

She stilled, shocked, and his lips pulled up to show his longer canines in a growl.

Na'rina grabbed his arms and shot energy into his body. Even though she gave it all she had, she may as well have stung him with a bee. He flinched, then grinned.

"Silas, please!" she pleaded.

Something struck him from the side. For a second, Silas held onto her. Na'rina screamed and collapsed the instant his claws pulled free of her arms. Through her tears, she saw Icarus fighting his mentor. She whimpered. The Kadivas had been bloody but this was brutal. Like liquid flames splashing trees, blood splattered the ground as the combatants rolled.

*"Na'rina!"*

Rosharu's desperate cry pulled her away from the terrible fight. The mountain nymph still fought to clutch Mona'rina to her chest, shifting her arms as the Drydanda slipped through her grasp.

Na'rina crawled toward them, dragging her bleeding leg and whimpering as the movement scraped her burned skin. "What's happening?"

"There's not enough of Athos left for me to be physically present." Rosharu urged Na'rina to take her mother, managing to shift her body across the floor a few inches before her hand passed through. "She saved enough of the eastern slope for me to heal, but…" she tried to move Mona'rina again. "Just like Liam… I can feel her fading but there's nothing I can do!"

Na'rina reached her mother's side. The zoi aima within the older dryad flickered around her heart, disappeared, flickered dimmer, and disappeared again.

"Hold on, Mamma." She pulled her mother against her and gasped at the contact with her burned skin. Although she knew Mona'rina was beyond absorbing zoi aima, she streamed some toward her mother's laboring heart anyway. It sank through.

"Silas!" Icarus' roar brought their heads around in time to duck as Silas pounced at Na'rina. His jump went long and he rolled when he hit the floor. Icarus followed, landing between Silas and the nymphs. "What are you doing?" he shouted, confused and frustrated.

Silas spit a hiss and Icarus flinched but he sidestepped Silas' next attack and attempted to wrap his arms around the older wer-im as he had in the Kadivas. Silas threw him and Icarus huffed as he hit the ground. Silas pounced, landing with his hands around Icarus' throat.

*Na!* Na'rina pushed herself toward them, desperately wanting to stop Silas, but Rosharu's ethereal hands clasped her face in an icy grip. They held no substance but the cold shock made Na'rina go still.

"She's dying," Rosharu said again.

In her peripheral, Na'rina saw Icarus buck beneath Silas' hold and roll free.

Na'rina held in a sob, not wanting to draw Silas' attention. "I don't know what to do," she admitted, helplessness making her stomach churn.

"You escaped prison with a stupid vine!" Rosharu exclaimed. "Surely you can do something."

But the vine hadn't kept her alive. A thought struck Na'rina and her heart clenched with a small flicker of hope. Struggling not to pass out, she touched the veins of the aspen leaf beneath her skin and filled it with zoi aima until it glowed golden under her collarbone. She swayed. The leaf floated to the surface to meet her fingertips. She laid it over Mona'rina's heart as Rosharu's faint form leaned in with held breath.

"Please take it in," Na'rina begged. *"Please."*

A cry made Na'rina duck, clutching her mother close. Silas and Icarus skidded to a halt a few yards away and Icarus jumped, caught the larger wer-im between the shoulder blades, and drove him to the ground, preventing him from reaching Na'rina.

As they wrestled, Silas pinned Icarus again. Smashing his head against the ground, he pulled one arm back, claws extended, for a killing blow. The claws came down, but Icarus broke free, spinning around the larger wer-im and grabbing Silas from behind. His hands clasped Silas' head, framing the surprised expression on his face.

Na'rina stared at the cold realization in Silas' gemstone eyes, followed by a haunting relief as his eyes fell to where Mona'rina lay in her lap. Behind him, Icarus' face set in grim determination despite the tears brightening his hazel eyes. A sharp *snap* and Silas' features froze. His head twisted at a terrible angle, and Icarus let his body crumple to the floor.

The torment on Icarus' face twisted Na'rina's insides. "He wouldn't stop," she whispered.

Rosharu inhaled sharply, and Na'rina looked down just as her leaf sank into Mona'rina's chest, turning the spot over her heart a rich gold against mottled green-brown skin. Na'rina waited, unable to breathe. Finally, a slow thud pulsed beneath her fingers and she wept in exhausted relief.

"I can't feel her," Rosharu complained.

"Her heart's beating," Na'rina said, holding her mother close. "My zoi aima's keeping her heart going."

A shuddering sigh escaped Rosharu. "I've done terrible things," she moaned. "Liam would hate me now. There's no forgiveness for any of this."

Na'rina gently set her mother on the floor and leaned over to lay a hand against Rosharu's cheek. The self-loathing hanging in the mountain nymph's lifeblood swirled with a cloying thickness.

"There's always a way to forgive," she said, swaying as she pushed a tiny stream of zoi aima into her palm to warm Rosharu.

Rosharu tried to clasp her hand as tears streamed from her eyes. "Can you forgive me? Please, Na'rina, forgive me."

Athos' awareness leaned in, waiting for her answer. Na'rina could not help but think of her own family's terrible actions. Rosharu just suffered longer with her torment, and had lived alone in it for so long she'd lost all understanding of the consequences.

"We all carry scars. You are not in this alone." Na'rina gave a feeble smile. "*Sa*, I forgive you, Rosharu."

She held the oread's deep brown gaze, conveying her conviction as the words rang true inside her. She did forgive Rosharu. With another sigh that ended in a grateful sob, Rosharu faded as mist into the trembling floor. Na'rina stared at where she vanished. Her mind felt numb and even the shuddering of the cave seemed distant.

A hand touched her shoulder. "Na'rina?"

She raised uncomprehending eyes to Icarus.

At the blank look on her face, he sank to his knees, his own pain vanishing behind a curtain of concern. "You're not healing." He glanced at her leg, where sappy blood oozed over blackened skin.

Na'rina swayed at the thought of the zoi aima required to heal that wound. "I can't—"

He held her hands and his violet zoi aima brushed her palms in a silent offer to help. Na'rina would have wept if her body had the moisture for tears as she accepted his offer. His zoi aima washed through her, cool for once as it soothed the damage from the magma's fire. Finally, the bleeding along her leg stopped. The wound beneath the blackened skin would have to heal on its own, but she'd be strong enough to leave the mountain on her feet.

Icarus started to draw away but Na'rina clung to his hands. She sensed the seething pain of his grief barely concealed behind his concern for her. After Rosharu, she could not leave him alone with that.

"Icarus, I'm sorry."

He shook his head. "It's not your fault. He would've killed you."

"Doesn't make things any easier."

Tears pooled in his eyes. "We succeeded," he said, giving her a smile that did not reach beyond his mouth.

"Yeah," she agreed, hoping it was true. She wasn't sure if Liam's body made it to the ocean, but now was not the time to voice her uncertainty. Instead, she pulled him into an embrace.

Pulling her close, Icarus wept. Shudders shook him and Na'rina held tight, wishing she could absorb his pain while she stroked his back. The scar trailing from his spine out into his ribs raised the skin beneath her fingertips. He bore so many such scars—and the most terrible of them were not visible. Na'rina ached for the fresh scars he now bore, knowing the internal ones would take years to heal. If his life was any indication, he *would* heal, but it would not be quick.

Chancing a rebuff, she connected with his violet zoi aima again and let the grief seething through him wash through her as well. It stole her breath. No words would ever suffice against such anguish and so she let his tears soak her shoulder in silence. When his shaking stilled, she withdrew her connection to allow him to pull himself back together.

"I'll go get Felis," he finally said. "We'll need him to get Silas and your mother out of here."

"Where is he?" Na'rina hadn't seen him since she tossed the dart pouch at him.

Icarus gestured across the still-shuddering cave. "Trapped. Some boulders fell on him. He's fine. I just didn't have time earlier to free him."

Na'rina watched him walk away and then crawled back to her mother, pulling her body into her lap again. Her fingers searched out her mother's weak but reassuring pulse while she waited.

Smoke and ash further darkened the heavily clouded sky over the ocean. A light rain had coated everyone with streaks of black ash, but now even that had calmed, though the air hung thick with the residue of the eruption. It'd be months before that residue faded.

Na'rina sat in the sand, her mother's head resting on her thighs. She watched the occasional rise and fall of her mother's chest, reassuring herself that Mona'rina still lived. To her right lay Silas' body, where Icarus had gently set him after carrying him from the mountain. On her left Icarus sat with his arms across his knees, his eyes fixed on the waves.

"Felis will be back soon," he said, breaking the silence. "You're sure you're all right?"

It was a fair question. She winced when she took in the gouges from Silas' claws on his chest and arms, but his wounds did not hinder him like hers did. She'd barely made it out of the mountain on her burned feet. Beneath the streaks created by ashy rain, her skin resembled the deep shades of a pine and her soles were blistered as if she'd walked on coals. She craved water so badly she wondered if her organs were sticking together. But it was the blackened skin down her thigh and calf to which Icarus referred.

"I'll heal."

He met her eyes, assessing for himself before his eyes invariably shifted to the body on her far side. Finally, he pushed to his feet. "I'll be within earshot if you need anything." She watched him wander up the beach before looking back to her mother to check her breathing.

Reassured, she assessed her leg again. The blackening

would disappear eventually, but Icarus' concern was warranted. She'd bear the ridges left by the burn for the rest of her life.

The ground rumbled and Na'rina looked down the coast toward Mount Athos. The tunnel they exited by dropped them out over a mile south of the mountain, but she could still see the crater that could swallow her grove marring the western side. A small section of the mountain's majestic peak remained in a curved wall on the eastern side but Na'rina couldn't see it now through the cloud of smoke still belching from the mountain.

She sighed. If the wind blew right, ash would fall on her grove hundreds of miles to the west, but the explosion hadn't been the cataclysmic event they'd feared. Nonetheless, doubt shadowed Na'rina's relief. She'd lost the bubble around Liam's bones before they reached the ocean. If the oceanid still tormented Rosharu, Na'rina shuddered to think what she would do once she healed enough to travel the physical world again.

"Drydanda."

Na'rina raised her head to find Alaya standing at the edge of the muddy ocean. Even the oceanid carried ashy streaks in her silvery hair and across her beautiful face.

"I'm sorry," Na'rina said. "I didn't know where else to go with the explosion."

Alaya shook her head. "You did what you had to do, just as we did what we could to dampen the damage. Owasha and the others may never admit it, but they're proud of their part in all this. And our brother can now rest."

"It worked!" Na'rina shifted to lay her mother on the sand before she jumped up. Pain shot through her soles, but she stumbled over to throw her aching arms around Alaya.

The oceanid laughed, returning the embrace. "Liam would have liked you. He loved unguarded affection."

Na'rina retreated a step, blushing, but Alaya smiled as she helped her back to her spot on the sand. The oceanid paused to gaze at Silas and Mona'rina and then shook her head.

"Your cost in this has been greater than most." She kissed her fingers and laid them against Na'rina's cheek where they left drops of water on her skin. "Farewell, Sister." Then she disappeared back into the murky water.

Not long after, Na'rina heard the rumble of a car behind her. Felis and the orange-haired wer-im appeared to carry Silas's body, and then Mona'rina, to the new car Felis had acquired. Na'rina didn't want to know where he found it. When they returned, Felis helped her to her feet, his expression unusually solemn.

"Ready for another car ride?" he asked.

Na'rina cringed. "As long as I can sleep the whole way."

"You might need the rest, Drydanda," he said with an irrepressible hint of mischief. "You're looking positively green."

"Well, that's not natural." Na'rina slapped his shoulder before accepting the other wer-im's arm for him to help her to the car.

"You're not natural," Felis shot back, turning toward the beach to get Icarus.

"Too true."

Na'rina hobbled toward the road and the idling blue car. With each step, she leaned on the orange-haired wer-im's shoulder. "Think I'll call you Dante," she told him.

He grinned.

"Can't name the strays, Drydanda. They'll never leave if you do," Felis called over his shoulder.

"I've got a name now. I can't be a stray," Dante said, still grinning.

Na'rina shared his smile and then glanced back toward the beach where Icarus tossed a stone into the waves with an angry heave.

"He'll land feet first," Dante said.

Na'rina snorted, caught off guard by the image of Icarus as a lynx spinning to land on his paws. But the wer-im was right. Icarus would be all right.

Epilogue

Ver'rina's eyes opened when Na'rina touched her bark. Her face did not leave the trunk as it had when she'd sought answers from her grandmother; instead, those lively eyes remained inside the bark, a part of the tree just as her smiling lips were a ridge in the trunk.

She smiled back. "You're slowly changing, Grandmother."

"Tell me of the wind and rain." Ver'rina started every conversation now with those words.

Na'rina sat down beside Ver'rina's face. A hand appeared from the bark to stroke her hair. Although Ver'rina wanted the changes happening in her body, she clung to the ability to touch with actual fingers.

"There's no improvement in my mother." Na'rina leaned back against Ver'rina's bark. "Her Rina says she's getting better, but it's imperceptible."

"Although you returned her twin's body to the seed tree,

she still feels the hole. In time, sunshine will be attractive again."

Na'rina bowed her head. Ver'rina held the unwavering belief her daughter would heal. She insisted Mona'rina's dormancy stemmed from grief more than from injury. *Perhaps she knows something I don't.*

Ver'rina moved on. "And the wer-im?" She asked this every visit. Her grandmother liked Icarus, but Na'rina suspected the question was a way to honor Silas' memory. She'd expected Ver'rina to grieve for her son, but her philosophical acceptance had surprised Na'rina. "I lost sprout centuries ago," she'd said. "He rests now instead of always fighting."

"Icarus is working to take Intela Corp apart," Na'rina answered her grandmother's question. "Obek-Ak-Lea is helping." She paused. "He seems to be healing, treating this as a way to continue Silas' fight."

Ver'rina's fingers paused in her hair. "How are you, Granddaughter?"

"Healing, too. I think my feet will always be darker." She lifted a foot to show Ver'rina the pine color of her sole.

Ver'rina smacked the back of her head. "I was not asking about your roots."

Na'rina rubbed her head and gave her grandmother a reproving look before continuing. "The Circle officially made me the lead Drydanda yesterday. My Council stays. Ser'ored tried to convince the Circle that we haven't addressed the current threat sufficiently since Intela Corp's still operating, but they decided how we handled Rosharu's immediate threat was a promising start and they hold confidence we'll succeed in the future. With that, they supported my pardon of the wer-im."

"It's time for this season," Ver'rina agreed. She laid her fingers against Na'rina's collarbone, tracing the vein-like ridges of the leaf beneath her skin. When Mona'rina sank back into her grove, the leaf had remained outside the seed tree. According to Ver'rina, only Mona'rina could have willed that and her grandmother viewed it as Mona'rina passing her blessing onto her daughter.

Na'rina touched the ridges of the leaf. As far as she could tell, her mother was beyond consciousness, but again, maybe her grandmother knew something she did not.

Ver'rina paused in stroking her hair as the sound of approaching steps reached them. Na'rina picked out Icarus' dark hair through the trees but she didn't recognize the noisy footfalls.

Ver'rina's eyes closed and her hand disappeared.

"I wouldn't have come, Kadis, I promise. I know you prefer me to keep my distance with Intela Corp still watching me, but he insisted."

Na'rina hid a smile as Icarus stepped out of the way for Rebecca Simms. She sported hiking boots instead of heels but sweat drenched her shirt.

"I'm so not made for traipsing around the woods," she complained, but with a grin.

"Then why are you?" Na'rina asked, softening the words with an answering smile.

Rebecca gulped water from a purple bottle and plopped down beside Na'rina. Icarus disappeared into the trees, though the warm feel of his zoi aima placed him within hearing distance.

Rebecca pulled something from her pocket. "The director tracked me down."

Chills ran up Na'rina's spine. Everyone assured her it would take decades for Rosharu and her mountain to recover enough for the oread to move about the earth again. "Did you see her?"

"No. She sent one of her lawyers to my house, which was weird enough." Rebecca shook her head. "He gave me this." She handed Na'rina a black rectangular device. "And then he grabbed my head and spoke some strange words. I asked him to repeat himself, but he just told me to get this to you and left."

"Sedessan," Icarus said.

Rebecca jumped with a cry as he reappeared from the trees.

"Why would Rosharu send a Sedessan to Rebecca's house instead of here?" Na'rina asked.

"Only one way to find out." Icarus knelt in front of Rebecca with his hands held out, asking for permission. She eyed him cautiously. Considering all she'd witnessed of Icarus, she had good reason to remain hesitant about him touching her.

"He won't hurt you," Na'rina reassured her.

"Have you seen the claws on these things?" She didn't resist, however, when Icarus laid his palms against her temples. Within seconds her eyes glazed and she began muttering under her breath. Then a deep voice rolled from her lips.

*"Na'rina Drydanda,"* the voice rumbled like a boulder tumbling down a hillside, *"I tried to send someone you'd trust. Perhaps it's a wasted gesture but I know you've no reason to believe anything I say.*

*"When Liam died, his pain became my own. I thought I could endure it and keep him close, but then I lost his body in the cave-in that Mona'rina and Silas caused to defeat the old Wer-Kadis. Everything changed then because I could not relieve his agony without destroying myself in the process. His agony became everything and I destroyed myself anyway.*

*"Things spiraled. By the time Intela Corp began capturing any mythic they could find, I no longer cared. I believed whatever they discovered would be destroyed when I died. You found a better way, but now my mistakes live on to haunt us. The flash drive I send you contains a virus. In my saner moments, I realized the human's discoveries were dangerous and I had this safeguard made. Plug it into the Zeta site mainframe in the Four Corners location and it will destroy the entire network.*

*"This is the best I can do to help you. I can't take back what the humans know without a Sedessan attack that would endanger more than*

*help. Thankfully, human lives are brief, and if the mythics can stay out of human hands long enough, we'll fade into legend once again.*

*"Thank you, Na'rina Drydanda. I'm humbled—broken—but you've restored my faith in the forgiveness and peace the dryads so treasure. You've made me believe in an existence worth healing for.*

*Yours always, Rosharu Oreadanda."*

Rebecca slumped against Icarus with a heavy shiver. She mumbled something against his shoulder.

"What?" He pushed her upright.

She cradled her head in her hands. "My head's pounding. Was I even intelligible? You said he wouldn't hurt me."

"The longer the message, the harder it is on the messenger." Icarus held a hand out to help her rise. "I'll take you back to your car."

Rebecca groaned and eyed that helping hand. "Can the other guy take me?"

"Afre went home," Na'rina said, studying the flash drive Rebecca handed her during the message. She touched the leaf beneath her collarbone with her other hand. How she missed the faun! Afre had touched the leaf in parting and promised to return. And she trusted his word.

"Not the hooved fellow," Rebecca said. "Felis. He's less…" she trailed off, reconsidering whatever she was about to call Icarus.

Never far from his Kadis, Felis appeared out of the trees, a mischievous glint in his yellow eyes. With a teasing bow, he helped Rebecca to her feet. Na'rina thanked her before they headed toward the road.

After they left, Icarus sat on the spot Rebecca vacated, resting his thigh against Na'rina's.

"Tarn's not returning?" she asked.

"The humans are still operating. I told him to stay with La'meliai and I think he was pleased with the order."

"That doesn't bother you?"

He twined his fingers with hers. "Can't blame him. And Felis loves his position." He stared at their hands before admitting, "It's good in some ways. It's one step removed from Silas' influence. Lets me figure out me instead of always being the tool he created."

Na'rina scoffed. "You weren't a tool to him. He just believed Mona'rina was dead and lashed out. If he'd known the truth things would have been different." Icarus knew all this—they'd discussed it before—but he didn't relax at her words. "Think about it," she pressed. "Who else did he tell about his connection to my mother? No one. He trusted no one else but you with his most closely-held secrets."

When he finally sighed in agreement, Na'rina pulled the flash drive from her pocket. "Sounds like we have a new goal."

"*Sa.*" His face lifted in that pleased look she loved. "It'll go a long way in taking Intela Corp apart."

She tucked the flash drive back into her pocket and leaned against his shoulder. They fell quiet and Ver'rina's roots hummed beneath their legs, though the aged dryad did not reappear from her trunk. Silence breathed around them until Icarus tapped the root protruding beside his hip. Still without appearing, Ver'rina withdrew the root to one side to reveal a small hollow beneath.

"Your grandmother's a wonderful confidant," Icarus said, withdrawing a bottle from the hollow. The hum in the seed tree glowed with pleasure.

Na'rina gaped. Afre's honeyed wine. She couldn't remember the last time she'd seen the bottle or her backpack, but its liquid contents shimmered in the sunlight.

"Shall we?"

Na'rina smiled as her Rina marveled. *Seems like a good way to celebrate "an existence worth healing for."*

She agreed. Maybe the world had finally turned right-side up again.

## Glossary of Mythical Creatures

**Dwarves**: A mythical race of short, stocky humanlike creatures who are generally skilled in mining and metalworking and who interact with both the mythic and human worlds. There are three races in the North Western Hemisphere: The Omichlodis or Appalachian line, the Pyrgos or Rockies line, and the now extinct Vathies Rizes or Cascade line.

    **Ak-Lea**—One of the leading families of the dwarves.

**Fauns:** In Greek mythology, this creature looks like a man with a goat's horns, ears, legs, and tail. Here fauns are lovers of truth and are friendly to those they choose deserve their loyalty.

    **Oba-Afren**—Title for the king of the fauns.

**Nymphs**: A mythological spirit of nature imagined as a beautiful maiden inhabiting rivers, woods, or other natural locations. Here, not all nymphs are female.

    **Auloniads**—In Greek mythology, these are nymphs said to inhabit wheat.

    **Dryads**—In Greek mythology, these are nymphs said to inhabit trees or forests.

        **Drydanda**—Title for a queen of the dryads. This dryad typically has more mystical capabilities than the rest of her kind. For example, a Drydanda can travel any distance from his or her tree whereas most dryads are

563

constrained to about a fifty-mile radius of their tree.

**Ored**—Formal name for a pine or spruce tree. If the tree has a nymph, the nymph's name carries this as a suffix, for example: Ser'ored.

**Meliai**—Formal name for an ash tree. If the tree has a dryad, the nymph's name carries this as a suffix, for example: La'meliai.

**Rina**—The name for an aspen grove. Aspens are usually more than one tree connected by their roots belowground. An entire grove bears the name Rina as a single entity. Any dryad attached to the grove bears Rina as a suffix, for example: Na'rina.

**Dry**—Formal name for an oak tree. If the tree has a nymph, the nymph's name carries this as a suffix, for example: Ana'dry.

**Ptelea**—Formal name for an elm tree. If the tree has a nymph, the nymph's name carried this as a suffix, for example: El'ptelea.

**Naiads**—In Greek mythology, these are nymphs said to inhabit rivers, springs, or waterfalls.

**Oceanids**—In Greek mythology, these are nymphs said to inhabit the sea or ocean.

**Oceadanda**—Title for a queen of the oceanids.

> This oceanid typically has more mystical capabilities than the rest of her kind. For example, an Oceadanda can travel out of the ocean whereas other oceanids cannot.

**Oreads**—In Greek mythology, these are nymphs said to inhabit mountains.

> **Oreadanda**—Title for a queen of the oreads. This oread typically has more mystical capabilities than the rest of her kind. For example, an Oreadanda can travel any distance from her mountain whereas most oreads cannot travel beyond a specific range.

**Sylphs**—In Greek mythology, these are nymphs said to inhabit the air.

**Sedessan:** A humanoid species who can pass messages psychically and alter memories through touch. Sedessans interact with humans on a regular basis, although humans are not aware they are "other." They are often hired as messengers if the mythic parties involved don't trust each other. Sedessans carry the stigma of being devious.

**Wer-im:** A humanoid species, with claws that retract into their hands and feet, who bears resemblances to specific cats. Humans have sometimes called them were-cats but they are not always shape-changers. They can often pass as human but must disguise tufted ears, stripes, and other catlike features.

**Wer-Kadis or Kadis**—Title for the leader of the wer-im. This wer-im holds his position by combat.

## Glossary of Terms

**The Circle**: A group of ancient dryads, now totally part of their trees, who have succeeded in staying alive for the last phase of a dryad's life. During times when the Drydanda and her Council cannot make decisions, the Circle steps in to vote for the "forest" or dryad nation.

**Collective Wisdom:** A genetic history of the dryads that is accessed as actual memories and is used most often by the Drydandas to help them in ruling.

**Council:** A group of five who help the Drydanda rule.

**Kadivas:** The official name for the leadership challenge, or fight, of the wer-im, used to determine the Wer-Kadis.

**Mythic**: Any creature humans view as mythical (nymphs, dwarves, elves, wer-im, Sedessans, fauns, etc.).

**Omichlodis Mountains:** Traditional mythic name for the Appalachian Mountains. This name is often still used by the dwarves to indicate their race.

**Pyrgos Mountains:** Traditional mythic name for the Rocky Mountains. This name is often still used by the dwarves to indicate their race.

**True Born:** Usually a dryad is born from the mating of a dryad with another dryad or mythic, and a tree takes seed with the dryad's conception. Rarely, however, the tree seeds first in response to some kind of trauma. When this happens, the resulting dryad looks almost identical to his or her parent and has the same abilities, except stronger.

**Vathies Rizes:** Traditional mythic name for the Cascade Mountains. This name is often used by the dwarves to indicate their race, however this race of the dwarves is also believed to be extinct.

**Zoi aima:** The energy, also referred to as lifeblood, within any living thing.

## Acknowledgments

You know the credits at the end of a movie? They go on and on and on and on… There's a reason for that. A beautifully made movie takes oodles of people to create.

A book is just like that. The finished product doesn't seem that huge. It's a stack of paper covered in words, but if those words contain the magic to draw you into a different world, then you can be sure there are oodles of people behind that magic.

Here are my oodles of people. Thank you, Lord, for each of them.

My family. Hours have been poured into encouragement, beta reading, voice recording and dancing, trailer making, and more. I can't even express how much they mean to me.

Speaking of beta reading. Nate, Curry, Molly, Leslie, Nick, Mom and Dad, and Myles. Thank you, thank you, thank you…

People who can draw always amaze me. This is not a skill I was blessed with. My niece, Esther, however, is blessed with this skill. I couldn't be happier with how the chapter headings turned out. Thank you, Esther.

Next comes Felicia Chernesky. Your editing skills polished this novel to something I could only have hoped for when I started. Thank you for your patience and guidance.

Right along with Felicia is Justin Allen who took my vague idea for a cover and turned it into an amazing reality. I couldn't be happier with how it turned out.

And last, but most important to me, thank you to my husband, Nate. You're always there, encouraging me to pursue my dreams and never letting me settle when things seem impossibly difficult. I love you beyond words.

## Note from Jennifer:

Hello Dear Reader. I see you've finished reading *Quaking Soul*. I hope you enjoyed it. Thank you for giving of your valuable time. I am blessed to have such a fulfilling job, but I only have that job because of people like you. People kind enough to spend their hard-earned money and give my books a chance. For that I am eternally grateful.

If you enjoyed this book and would like to help, please consider leaving a review on Amazon, Goodreads, or anywhere else where readers visit. The most important part of how well a book sells is how many positive reviews it has, so if you leave one, then you are helping me continue on this journey as a full-time writer. Thanks in advance to anyone who does. It means the world to me.

Feel free to contact me (all details can be found at www.jenniferzeiger.com), as I would love to hear from you.

Jennifer M. Zeiger

**Other Books by Jennifer M. Zeiger:**

The Adventure includes three different multi-ending Adventure stories for young readers, giving them 26 possible endings to find.

**Moonrise Mountain:** Legend tells of the wild horses that live atop Moonrise Mountain. Now you're out to discover if legend is true, but first, you have to reach the top of the mountain, and each choice you make will bring unforeseen dangers.

**Temple of Night and Wind:** Many have entered the Howling Maw in search of its treasures. None have returned. But now your village is starving and the Maw's treasures are your last resort. So down into the Maw you venture…

**The Tournament:** To free your uncle from life in the King's mines, you enter the Tournament. However, this is no typical contest, and its lack of rules makes success all the more difficult, and defeat all the more deadly.

Pick wisely, Dear Reader, for success or failure depends on your choices.

Jennifer M. Zeiger

**Jennifer M Zeiger** grew up in the Rocky Mountains of Colorado and she now lives in South Carolina with her husband, Nate.

In 2017, Jennifer kickstarted her writing carrier, literally, by publishing her first book, *The Adventure*, after running a successful Kickstarter. *The Adventure* is a multi-ending Adventure book for young readers that contains three stories with eight to ten endings each.

With *Quaking Soul*, Jennifer has now realized her dream of publishing a novel. She plans to continue producing adventure books and novels in the future.

Visit her online at jenniferzeiger.com.

Jennifer M. Zeiger

www.ingramcontent.com/pod-product-compliance
Lightning Source LLC
Chambersburg PA
CBHW051548100726
47898CB00001B/20